A DCI F
YORKSHIRE CRIM
BO

CRUCIFIX KNOT
REMEMBER NOT OUR SINS

ELY NORTH

RED HANDED PRINT

Copyright © 2025 by Ely North All rights reserved.
This book or parts thereof may not be reproduced in any form, distributed, stored in any retrieval system, or transmitted in any form by any means—electronic, mechanical, photocopy, recording, or otherwise—without prior written permission of the author, except in the case of brief quotations embodied in critical reviews and certain other non-commercial uses permitted by copyright law.

Website: https://elynorthcrimefiction.com
To contact ely@elynorthcrimefiction.com
https://www.facebook.com/elynorthcrimefictionUK

Cover design by Cherie Chapman/Chapman & Wilder

Cover images © rebius (corn) / merydolla (cross) / Ronks (sky) – Adobe Stock Photos

Disclaimer: This is a work of fiction. Names, characters, businesses, places, events, locales, and incidents are either the products of the author's imagination or used in a fictitious manner. Any resemblance to actual persons, living or dead, or actual events is purely coincidental.

Published by Red Handed Print
First Edition
Kindle e-book ISBN-13: 978-1-7638413-2-1
Paperback ISBN-13: 978-1-7638413-8-3

Contact Ely North

ely@elynorthcrimefiction.com
Website: https://elynorthcrimefiction.com
Facebook https://facebook.com/elynorthcrimefictionUK
Sign up to my newsletter.
QR below

Previously... in Wicker Girl

The Past Never Stays Buried
4th June 1989. Twenty-two-year-old Iona Jacobs is struck in a hit-and-run near Ravensbane Wood, Ashenby. Her unborn child survives, raised in Scotland by her grandmother. The case is never solved. Two men are linked to Iona's last hours: Reverend Nicholas Hartley and gamekeeper Malachi Abbott.

Present Day—Fire in the Woods
On Beltane night, Malachi Abbott witnesses an orgy and a Pagan ritual in Ravensbane Wood—something placed inside a wicker effigy and burned. Next morning, walkers find a severed foot in the ashes. DCI Frank Finnegan assigns DI Kumar and DS Stoker to the investigation. Ashenby closes ranks. Hooded figures stalk the woods. Strange symbols appear.

Death and Dark Deeds
Lord Hampton vanishes, later found barely alive after escaping a mineshaft. Malachi Abbott dies when his car plunges into the river—brake lines cut, £20,000 hidden in

his wardrobe. Reverend Hartley hangs from the church bell rope—suicide, accident, or murder?

A Pattern Emerges

Each death echoes an old Ashenby legend: three witches executed centuries ago—drowned, buried alive, hanged. Their killers: a lord, a gamekeeper, a vicar.

History repeating?

They Have Their Man

Evidence piles up against Lord Hampton: the blackmail money, old grudges, links to both victims. He's arrested for murder.

But a cold-case reveal shocks the police—the daughter of Iona Jacobs, Morrigan Penhallow, has been living quietly with her grandmother, in Ashenby. Because of a rare condition, Morrigan appears twelve years old.

She calls herself... The Wicker Girl.

The Wrong Man?

Have Hampton and the police been played? With doubts mounting, police release him without charge. Can truth survive in a village built on secrets? And in Ashenby... is someone still watching?

Still waiting?

Still hunting?

Can you catch the killer before the police do?

1

Saturday 21st June 3:30 am – North Yorkshire

Twelve minutes before the summer solstice.

The warm night air is pungent with the intoxicating perfume of drying hay and the sweet drift of gorse blossom.

Two hundred yards from the edge of Ravensbane Woods, a hill rises like a recently buried skull—round, grass-patched, its summit offering a perfect vantage point across the Dales to the east. The sky, moments ago a deep navy, is shifting from slate blue to indigo. A million stars pinprick the stratosphere.

In the hush, an owl hoots twice. Distant sheep murmur from unseen paddocks. A lazy zephyr transports woodsmoke in sporadic gasps.

Edwin Featherstone lies on his stomach at the treeline, elbows braced in the grass, binoculars pressed tight to his eyes. His shirt clings to his back with sweat. He's been out here an hour and still nothing—none of the wild rutting Malachi Abbott claimed he saw during the Beltane Festival. Just firelight, chanting, and cloaks. Edwin shifts, annoyed. Half turned-on, half bored.

He tugs a hip flask from his jacket and takes a sharp nip. The whisky bites—it's the cheap stuff—but tonight's not about comfort. It's about curiosity. And maybe, if Malachi, God rest his soul, wasn't full of shite, something more—much more.

He checks his watch—3:35.

Not long to go before the solstice sunrise.

He squints at the fire on the hill.

Not a bonfire, not a party. A proper structure. Tightly built, the flames kept low, controlled. Shapes move around it—thirty, maybe forty, all dressed in dark cloaks or long skirts, figures indistinct but rhythmic. Chanting—not song, not speech, but something low and continuous, like Gregorian monks warming up for a requiem. From somewhere unseen, a massive drum casts out a slow, dull thud—each note a deep-bellied echo that shudders through Edwin's chest and coils in his gut.

He adjusts the focus. Zooms in on the spindly frame of Birch, a regular in his pub. Unmistakable even in silhouette with that mess of blond hair. Next to him is Oak, taller, meatier, broader, beard like a bird's nest. The Ashcroft sisters are here too, Lunara and Prudence, hand in hand.

How sweet.

Edwin is a little surprised to see the postmistress, Lilac Penhallow, in attendance.

'Daft old cow. She's too bloody long in the tooth for this caper. And I certainly don't want to see *her* getting her kit off,' he murmurs.

But the woman next to Lilac — well, he'd pay good money to see her in the buff.

Violet Fox stands still and central, watching. All of them. The whole bloody Wicca commune and many from the village.

He lowers the binoculars, wipes a bead of sweat from his brow, then raises them again. No one's naked. No writhing. No Pagan sex. Just smoke, muted recital like at a church service, and casual movement, as if they're waiting for a bus.

The gathering parts as a small figure approaches, leading a ram that limps forward—a great, black-shouldered beast with curling horns and a matted coat.

Edwin's heart sinks

'That's Morrigan,' he whispers.

Morrigan Penhallow, the *Wicker Girl*.

Except she's no girl.

She arrived with her grandmother a decade ago and hasn't aged a day since.

A body trapped in time.

It's a moot point amongst the villagers. No one asks anymore what's wrong with her. A "condition," her grandmother used to say before shutting down the subject.

People keep their distance, not because of her unfortunate affliction, but because… well, she's just weird.

Watching, mysterious, appears from nowhere, silent for the most part, and of course, the rumours.

Veiled whispers she has the second sight, especially of those who are about to die.

Edwin feels the twitch of anticipation again, though it quickly sours in his gut.

Violet steps forward. Her hands rise. The chanting ceases. She speaks. Not loud—almost too quiet to catch—but measured. Words with no context. The sort of language that makes your skin itch, even when you don't understand a word.

Morrigan moves into the firelight. She's wearing the headdress of a raven—feathers, beak, glinting eyes stitched or painted, it's hard to tell. A staff in her right hand, taller than she is. She lifts it high and screams.

A piercing, rapid, warbling screech, like a banshee.

The sound tears through the hush. It bounces around the hills and fells, folds into the shape of the land and returns softer but more terrible, as though it's woken the dead.

Edwin blinks.

He doesn't know why he's watching anymore. This isn't the orgy he was expecting.

The golden yellow hue of the sun begins to rise, banishing darkness, raining forth light.

Slowly, inexorably, it grows.

Gasps from the worshippers tickle past Edwin's ears.

All but Violet and Morrigan drop to their knees to witness and pay homage to the summer solstice.

Morrigan raises the staff and takes the dagger from Violet's hand. She draws it quick and hard across the ram's throat.

The animal jerks. Blood pours.

It stumbles, lowers to its knees as if exhausted. Then rests, slumping gently to its side. The blood gurgles into a vessel—a broad, shallow bowl held steady by Birch.

Violet takes the bowl. Dips her fingers. Walks slowly, daubing each forehead of the kneeling with a smear of blood.

Edwin wriggles back. The grass rasps under him. His stomach knots.

'Sod this for a game of bow and arrows,' he mutters, throat dry. 'Bloody Malachi. Lied through his back teeth.'

He hears a crack—small, but sharp.

A twig.

Behind him.

He freezes.

Turns his head slowly.

A young woman standing in the gloom. Pale face. A gash on her head. Blood on her cheek.

Edwin's mouth dries.

'No, it can't be,' he murmurs, dread surging.

He blinks. Rubs his eyes. Looks again.

Gone. Like she was never there.

Edwin's voyeuristic ardour is departing rapidly.

On the hill, Morrigan turns. Though she cannot possibly see into the woods, she raises her staff once more.

Then—another scream.

This one is different. Sharper. A harrowing, mournful cry, like an eagle gliding across a deep valley. It echoes through the trees as Edwin's fear punches through the surface.

He fumbles for his flask, stuffs it into his pocket, binoculars dangling from his neck. He doesn't run exactly, but he moves fast, hunched. Keeps low.

The woods seem thicker than before, the trees less forgiving.

He doesn't look back.

Can't look back.

Too terrified of what he might see.

2

Tuesday 24th June 10:00 am

Farmer Amos Baker kicks off his boots outside the front door and enters the kitchen, the smell of a cooked breakfast tantalising his taste buds.

'Polly!' he calls out.

His wife's voice returns fire from upstairs. 'It's keeping warm in the oven.'

Amos pads into the kitchen and retrieves the breakfast plate and sits at the table. It's 10 am, and he's ravenous. He's been on the go for five hours, nearly a day's work for some folk. But not for a farmer, not at this time of year. Farming is hard work at the best of times, but a mixed farm is even harder. With sheep and cattle to tend, and crops to water and spray, it's all go from dawn until dusk. With the early start to spring and the constant warm weather, everything is a few weeks ahead of schedule. And late June is prime haymaking season.

He licks his lips as he squirts a dollop of brown sauce on the edge of the plate. Bacon, eggs, mushrooms, tomatoes, sausage and fried bread. He tucks in, sighing contentedly as Polly enters the room and flicks the kettle on.

'How's your morning been?' she asks, leaving a drift of fruity perfume in her wake.

'Aye, not bad. Good progress. I've cut two of the four hay meadows. Will be drying nicely.'

He shoots her a quick glance.

Dressed head-to-toe in black, she's a far cry from her usual frumpy farmer's-wife look.

'It's still not too late,' she says, hoping. 'A quick wash and throw your suit on, you could still make it.' She pours water into the teapot and gives it a stir.

Amos sighs, a mixture of irritation and guilt. 'I can't afford to take the rest of the day off at this time of year. The forecast is for rain on Friday. That means I have to get all the paddocks slashed today, then turn the grass tomorrow and get it bailed by Thursday otherwise it could be ruined. It's a good harvest, Polly, and if this warm weather keeps up, we're going to need it by late autumn.'

Polly places a cup of tea on the table. 'The service will only be an hour long.'

'Plus all the chitchat afterwards. Then the wake at the hall, and no doubt many will move onto the pub.'

'You can shoot off straight after the service. You don't have to hang around.'

His cutlery clatters onto the plate. 'For God's sake, woman! Can't you let it go? I've too much to do, and why would I want to attend the funeral of Reverend Hartley?'

Polly glares at him. 'You used to be good friends with Nicholas once upon a time.'

He grizzles. 'Aye, a lifetime ago. A lot of things have changed since then.'

'Yes. You being one of them.'

He sighs but doesn't rise to the bait.

'Right, well I'll be off. I'm picking up Mrs Selkirk on the way. Not sure what time I'll be back. There's a meat and potato pie in the bottom of the fridge. If I'm not home by four, put it in the oven on medium.' She kisses him on the back of the head and walks to the entrance.

Racked with guilt, he spins around. 'Polly?' he asks softly.

She stops and turns. 'Yes?'

He offers her a resigned smile. 'Nowt. I'll see you later. Thanks for the grub, love.'

She nods and disappears out of the door.

Replete, the sun warm on his face, Amos stands at the kitchen threshold, tea in hand, surveying his modest kingdom.

Undulating hills roll outward, scattered with his flock like tufts of lint on a blanket. In the foreground, golden fields lie freshly cut, their stubbled lines a promise of winter feed. And further off, at the edge of his land, the tall green husks of maize sway gently—slow-dancing in the breeze that drifts through Gallows Meadow, teasing the leaves. More fodder for his small herd of cattle in the winter months.

He loves this time of year. Not so much the winters—not anymore.

His old bones don't cope well with the cold.

The arthritis. Old injuries. And his hands are always cold, even now.

He and Polly are nearing retirement age, but Amos has no intention of stopping.

Not yet.

He's a practical man, a realist.

He once hoped the farm might stay in the family.

But his son, Martin, a middle-manager at an oil company in Aberdeen, has no interest in farming. Neither his daughter, Hazel, who's a triage nurse in London. They visit separately twice a year, sometimes three, for long weekends. Out of duty more than desire, he suspects.

The grandkids love it, of course. Running wild. Climbing hay bales. Disappearing into the woods.

But they're too young. He can't leave the farm to them.

He figures he's got another five years at most before it all has to change.

Eventually, he'll have to sell—his life's work, and his father's, and his grandfather's before him.

Hexley Farm will be swallowed up, not by a neighbouring farmer, but by some faceless conglomerate. A team of accountants, land surveyors, and strategic planners.

Then what?

He and Polly will move somewhere smaller. Maybe a retirement village by the sea. Not down south, though—never that.

A bungalow with a view, perhaps. Whitby, Scarborough, or somewhere quieter—Runswick Bay, Staithes.

And he's realistic about other things too.

He probably hasn't got a long life ahead. All those years working with farm chemicals.

They said it was safe back then, but the truth's out now.

Not good.

He half expects to wake one morning with a lump. Or to find himself suddenly drained of energy or develop some hideous skin disease that disfigures him.

That's why he avoids doctors. All their poking and prodding, questions, tests, blood samples, sign this, sign that.

What do they really care?

Truth is, he's afraid of what they'll find.

And once your mind knows—well, that's the end—isn't it?

Better to live in ignorance.

Yes, another five years on the land, at a push. Then ten slow, quiet years in a chair by the window. That'll take him into his eighties.

That'll do.

Everyone dies eventually. Some sooner than others.

It's a lottery.

Finishing his cup of tea, he pulls the door shut on the farmhouse and heads off towards the barn and his old, faithful tractor.

He has no idea that soon, *today,* his existential turmoil will end.

Peace beckons for farmer Amos Baker.

Well... after a brief, terrifying and excruciating death.

But there's no gain without pain—is there?

3
Tuesday 10:25 am

The turquoise 1968 Ford Anglia parks discreetly at the back of the church alongside an old green single-decker Bedford bus. Frank removes the keys and taps the steering wheel affectionately.

'Well done, Beatrice. You're a pleasure to drive, you little beauty.'

Prisha and Zac, wedged into the back seats without seatbelts—standard for a 1968 Anglia—share a look of mutual relief.

Zac leans over, fumbling for the mechanism to tilt the passenger seat forward, eager to escape the coffin on wheels.

'You know, my lads are always nagging me to take them to Alton Towers or Disney World. But I'll tell them there's no need. They can go for a ride with Uncle Frank in his classic car. If it's an adrenaline rush they're after, then nothing beats a ride in the Ford Anglia. Base jumping from the Eiffel Tower has nothing on this.'

'Your problem is you don't appreciate timeless elegance,' Frank replies.

Zac finally finds the latch for the seat and throws the passenger door open, clambering out ungainly as Prisha follows him.

'You had the right idea, Prisha, getting picked up in Pickering. You've only had to suffer half the journey.'

'Long enough.'

Frank alights and manually locks the car with the keys. He runs a hand over the bonnet as though caressing a child on the head.

'Good lass,' he mutters.

'It's called objectophilia,' Zac states.

'What is?' Frank enquires, adjusting his tie.

'When people form emotional, romantic, or sometimes sexual attachments to inanimate objects such as cars. In some cases, they even believe the object reciprocates their feelings or has a personality or soul.'

Frank eyeballs him. 'Does everything have to come down to sex with you?'

He shrugs. 'Not everything. Anyway, it's not me who has a fetish for a car that's nearly sixty years old.'

'This, sunshine, is a work of art.'

'It's a mobile death trap and shouldn't be allowed on the roads.'

'Oh, stop your squawking.' He eyes the Bedford bus, clearly less cherished than his Ford Anglia. 'Don't see many of these about now. Mid 50s, I think. I went to school in one of these.'

'Were you the driver?' Zac asks as Prisha snorts with laughter.

'Oh, very funny.' He squints at the grille, where a cluster of twigs has been bound into a pentagram. Beads, feathers, and talismans dangle behind the windscreen. Above them, the old destination blind still reads: **127 RIPON**.

'It belongs to the Wicca commune,' Zac says.

'Does it indeed.' His gaze drifts back to Zac. 'Come here,' he says as he attempts to fasten the top button on Zac's shirt. 'Make yourself presentable. You're attending a funeral.'

'Ouch! You pinched my neck-skin.'

'Stop blathering and keep still.' Having fastened the top button, he slides the knot up on Zac's tie and pats him on the shoulders. 'There. That's better. Now you look the part.'

Prisha grins. 'You scrub up quite well, Zac. I can't remember seeing you in a full suit before.'

He gives her the once-over. 'Aye, you're not looking too bad yourself,' he replies, admiring the crisp, white blouse, smart lightweight jacket, and figure-hugging black skirt.

They both cast a sideways glance at Frank in his rumpled, old-fashioned suit, which was probably bought in a closing-down sale back in Dick's day.

He sticks his thumbs under his belt and pulls the waistband over his paunch.

'Right, Reverend Hartley's funeral. We're here for two reasons: one, to show a dignified police presence, a sign of respect; and secondly, to observe and listen. Now, most of the villagers of Ashenby will know your faces, but they don't know mine. At the church, we'll be last in and sit at the back. Just before the service ends, we'll quietly exit. You two stand near the gate so that everyone walks past you. I'll mingle.'

Zac frowns. 'It's not a bloody cocktail party, Frank.'

'No, but unobserved, I may pick up some tittle-tattle. All three of us are singing from the same hymn book, pardon the pun. We don't believe for one minute Reverend Hartley took his own life. The coroner recorded an open verdict, which means it's our job to find out which bugger put the bell rope around Hartley's neck and pushed him towards the hatch. Finding his killer may point us towards the killer of Malachi Abbott. I don't want this case going cold.'

He checks his watch. 'Eh, up. Look lively. Service is about to kick off in five.'

Inside the church, the organist coaxes a dirge from the pipes. It lacks any discernible structure—its dissonant progressions and unresolved cadences create a jarring, aimless drift. A modulating jump in key brings little relief, only further tonal confusion, and more pain—for the mourners.

Frank grimaces and throws a glance at Zac, then Prisha, who's wedged between them.

'Organist is having an off day,' he whispers.

Zac's pained expression conveys his agreement. 'Aye. He's either been on the syrup or they roped in a passing chimpanzee to do the honours.'

'Shush,' Prisha hisses. 'Show some respect.'

It's fairing up to be a hot day outside, the thermometer already nudging twenty-eight degrees. But inside, it's cool, dim, sombre.

The turnout is strong, as one might expect for a seemingly well-liked parish priest. Zac and Prisha scan the pews, recognising more than a few familiar faces.

The schoolteacher, Prudence Ashcroft, and her sister Lunara, the librarian. Lilac Penhallow, the postmistress. Various members of the Wicca commune, including Violet Fox and the big lad known as Oak. Up front sit Lord and Lady Hampton, heads down, silent. On opposite pews are the local publican, Edwin Featherstone, and Peggy Thornton, the cleaner who first discovered the body of Reverend Hartley. Prisha also spots the old lady, Mrs Selkirk, seated in a wheelchair studying the Order of Service booklet, alongside Mrs Baker, the farmer's wife from Hexley Farm. No Mr Baker, she notes.

Frank leans across again. 'The bishop's noticeable by his absence,' he murmurs.

Zac shrugs, unmoved. 'So?'

'It means there's trouble at mill. Hartley served the church faithfully for nearly forty years. I'd have thought they'd have wheeled out one of the big guns.'

'You think they're distancing themselves?'

'Possibly.'

They both receive another scowl from Prisha.

'Shut up, both of you. You can talk in the car on the way home.'

'Pardon me for breathing,' Frank mutters as he picks up the Order of Service. It's a plain cream booklet, with Reverend Nicholas Hartley's name printed on the front above a happy smiling face of a man much younger than the one who recently died a violent death.

Eventually, the organ falls silent, much to Frank's relief. The final chord hangs like smoke, unresolved. Into the hush walks the new vicar—Reverend Mavis Crowther—her cassock flaring slightly with each step. She's short, round, and steady, with an explosion of grey curls and spectacles so large they distort the size of her eyes. There's a faint clink of her silver cross as she moves to the lectern.

She clears her throat once, gently. No microphone needed. Her voice, when it comes, is brittle, like a dried leaf.

'We gather today to remember and commit to God our brother in Christ, Reverend Nicholas Hartley, who served this parish twice in his long tenure with the church. We come in sorrow, in love, and in belief of the resurrection.'

There's a rustle of hymn sheets. A few coughs. A sniffle near the front.

'Let us sing together the words of the first hymn—The Day Thou Gavest, Lord, Is Ended—number one-one-two in your Order of Service.'

The organist strikes up again, more confident now, as the congregation rises stiffly.

The hymn is sung with thin voices, barely lifting above the stone walls. Prisha mouths the words without sound. Zac doesn't even bother. Frank, more accustomed to the ancient rituals of the church, thanks to his wife's faith, belts it out with gusto—an enthusiastic baritone with all the subtlety of a foghorn and none of the pitch.

There's an odd detachment in the air, a restraint that goes beyond grief. No one has quite decided how they're supposed to feel.

When the hymn ends, Reverend Crowther steps aside. A brief reading from Corinthians is offered by Peggy Thornton. She's understandably nervous, tripping over the words, gripping the lectern to hide her trembling fingers.

Next up, the eulogy.

There's a slight shift, a palpable tightening of spines, as Lord Hampton rises from his pew. He walks slowly to the front, his cane tapping on the stone flags, a soft clink with each step. His dark suit is immaculate, collar crisp, movements slow but measured.

'What's with the bloody cane? Is he playing the sympathy card?' Zac mutters under his breath.

Prisha kicks him in the shin and glares as Frank lifts a pen from his jacket pocket and finds a blank space in the Order of Service.

'What are you doing?' Prisha hisses.

'Taking notes.'

'Give me strength.'

Hampton takes the lectern with deliberate solemnity. He places a sheet of paper before him and lifts his head, eyes sweeping the congregation like a man accustomed to having his words heard.

'Nicholas and I went back a long time—right back to 1985, when he first arrived in Ashenby as a young vicar, full of conviction, full of fire. In those early days, we were close. Friends, not just in faith but in life. We were of a similar age, with a similar outlook—idealists, I suppose. Naïve enough to believe good intentions were all you needed to put the world to rights.'

He pauses, lets out a deep sigh.

'But life has a way of turning such faith into something quieter. Something more cautious. And as time passed, our paths... diverged. Not in one great moment, but in small, imperceptible ways. Until one day you look across and realise the man who once stood beside you is now standing very far away.'

He glances down, steadying himself. It's perfectly pitched—just enough emotion to suggest grief, not quite enough to betray something deeper.

'We weren't always in agreement, especially in recent years. But I never lost my respect for Nicholas. His gentleness. His dedication. His refusal to give up on those others had already given up on. He was in the truest sense a shepherd.'

He shifts slightly, voice quieter now.

'But even shepherds can lose their way. Those who lead can carry burdens they cannot share. As it says in Psalms: "For when I kept silent, my bones wasted away."'

The quote lingers. Some in the congregation nod, recognising the verse. Others are puzzled. A few glance at one another, including Frank and Zac.

'There's a cost to silence,' Hampton continues, eyes scanning the front pews. 'And sometimes, in trying to protect others, we lose a part of ourselves.'

He draws a breath, steadying himself.

'Whatever Nicholas carried—whatever burdens he bore—may they now be laid to rest with him. His secrets die in sacred soil, and I pray his soul has found the peace that eluded him in life. Remember not our sins.'

He steps down in silence, the mourners still, wary.

Reverend Crowther resumes the service as if nothing is amiss, her tone unchanged. But among some in the congregation, there are surreptitious glances, flickers of unease—averted eyes, a nervous twitch here and there.

There's an edge in the air. Something unsettled.

It's not lost on the three officers at the back of the nave.

'I'd just like to say that everyone is welcome to join me at the village hall for tea and biscuits after the service. After that, Lord Hampton has generously put money behind the bar at The Crown if anyone cares for something a little stronger. Reverend Hartley wasn't immune to a wee tipple now and again,' she says with a wistful smile. 'Now, let us stand to sing our final hymn—*Rock of Ages*, number one-eight-two in your Order of Service.'

The organist offers a passable introduction, a touch steadier than before, as the congregation rises. Then, as if grateful for something familiar, they launch into a rousing rendition—voices stronger now, though whether from conviction or relief, it's hard to tell.

"Rock of Ages, cleft for me, let me hide myself in Thee..."

The hymn speaks of refuge, of sins washed away.

Amongst the rows of solemn faces and hooded eyes, no one seems quite sure who is hiding from what—or even what sins they're hoping to leave behind.

4

Amos stares at the red Massey Ferguson tractor with a mixture of weary affection—the sort reserved for an old sheepdog that's seen its best days and is now waiting for the vet to arrive, or more likely, the farmer with his shotgun.

The tractor's been a good servant, no denying it, but it's reached the stage where he's forever tinkering with it himself or ringing the mobile fitter from Crawley's Dealership.

This time it's the three-point linkage at the back—the hydraulics are playing up again. Sometimes they lift smoothly and without fuss; other times, they jam solid or refuse to go higher than a foot or two. Today's one of those days. He's managed to hitch the big rectangular slasher easily enough, but when it comes to lifting it upright to get at the blades for sharpening, the hydraulics won't have it.

He's phoned Dave—the mechanic—but he won't be out until early afternoon.

As ever, Amos makes do. True, the paddocks won't be the cleanest cut he's ever done, but it will be good enough, at least until next time.

He yanks open the cab door and hauls himself up, boots scraping the metal step. Before he settles in, his eyes land on a small object lying on the seat. He picks it up, turning it over in his fingers.

'Where the bloody hell's that come from? It wasn't here earlier, unless I was sitting on it,' he ponders, staring at the fine braided fawn disc. On one side is an incomplete circle in red; on the other, a representation of a crucifix.

He wonders for a moment if Polly left it for him. She's into her arts and crafts, but he immediately discounts the idea as preposterous. Not giving it any more thought, he tosses it onto the dashboard, gets comfortable in the seat, and starts the engine.

It's a bumpy ride back and forth across the fields, but Amos is in his element. The tractor's running smooth, the slasher's doing its job, the sun is out, and at last, Radio 2 is playing music from the sixties. There's a sense of peace in being alone in the wide expanse of the Dales. No inane chatter, no boss—only time, and even that seems to stretch out in these long summer months.

He turns the wheel in a tight arc as he nears the fence line. There's movement from behind a hedge in the adjoining field. His eyes narrow for a moment, but he assumes it's a sheep that's strayed from the main flock up on the hill. Lining up the wheels, he begins the return pass up the paddock.

A flash of light catches his eye—and before he registers what it is, the front wheels are already over it.

Slamming the brakes, he reaches instinctively for the lever to shut off the drive powering the slasher blades, but it's too late. The metallic clanking and high-pitched whine from the housing tell him everything he needs to know.

He's driven over fencing wire. It's become coiled around the shaft.

'Damn and blast!' he growls.

He's a tidy farmer, unlike some. Never leaves old gear or discarded wire lying about. Everything is taken back to the barn and properly binned. But fencing wire's one of those insidious buggers—half-buried for years, forgotten, until one day a loose end pops up like a snare.

It'll be a pain to remove if the hydraulics are still playing up.

He glances out the rear window.

'Bugger it,' he mutters.

Killing the engine, he grabs a pair of wire cutters from the backpack behind the seat and lowers himself gingerly to the ground.

He vibrates his lips like a bored horse as he eyes the slasher—three feet off the turf. Ten years ago, even five, he'd have shimmied under there without a second thought. But Father Time crept up on him when he wasn't looking, and now anything more strenuous than walking sets every joint groaning.

'There's nowt for it,' he mumbles, as the 11 o'clock news crackles from the cab.

Maybe I should've gone to the funeral, he thinks, but it's a fleeting thought.

He drops to his knees and rolls onto his back with a painful grunt.

'Christ,' he hisses, as pain shoots through joints he didn't know he had.

He catches his breath, then wriggles, headfirst, under the slasher, cutters in hand.

The wire isn't as bad as it could've been—maybe six feet of it, looped around the shaft above the blade carrier. Could've wrapped tighter. Could've bent something. Still, it's tight enough.

He grabs the end and begins unwinding it slowly, awkwardly. After a few turns, he sets the jaws of the cutter and squeezes hard. He used to have a grip like a vice. Now, the arthritis in his hands makes even this a test of endurance.

Grimacing and groaning, he channels everything into one solid bite.

Clink.

A section of wire drops into the grass.

He rests, breath ragged, as the soft tones of *Magic Moments* by Perry Como drift from the cab. For a moment, he's cast back forty-five years—to their wedding reception. He and Polly, dancing to this very song.

It was a good day.

She's been a good wife.

He—not such a good husband.

Grouchy. Short-tempered. Doesn't show her the attention she deserves.

The funeral will be well underway by now.

Reverend Nicholas Hartley.

It's true—they'd been friends—close friends once. But all that changed.

One summer's day.

After that, it was never the same. He sold his soul to the devil. Well, not quite the devil. He sold his soul for five acres of land.

Devil, land—what's the difference?

He grips the wire, unspooling the last of it, muttering curses.

A dull thunk like a boot on the cab step.

Freezes. Listens.

A faint tremble through the chassis of the tractor.

Another vibration.

'Hello?' he calls out.

Nothing.

The final coil comes loose. He exhales.

The cough of the diesel engine.

Adrenaline explodes through his bloodstream.

'What the bloody hell? Stop!'

His cries are muffled beneath the slasher's thick metal housing.

Writhes frantically sideways.

Stops.

A whirr.

Blades slowly spin, but within a second pick up speed.

The hydraulics, now working perfectly, lower the rotary cutter.

One scream, short and sharp, echoes under the machine.

Followed by a dull, squelchy splat.

The blades, a rotating blur.

Designed to shear through long grass.

But just as efficient at slicing through flesh and bone.

5

Prisha and Zac have taken up positions near the gate as the mourners file from the church. Frank is loitering with intent near the graveyard trying to look inconspicuous.

Zac grins. 'Old Frank's probably helped solve thousands of crimes in his long career.'

Prisha tracks his gaze. 'And?'

'He may be a good copper, but he'd never have cut the mustard as a secret agent. Look at him, trying to act invisible. He looks like a flasher waiting for his next victim.'

Prisha resists a smile as Mrs Baker, pushing Mrs Selkirk along in a wheelchair, approaches.

'Ladies. How are you?' she asks.

Mrs Baker smiles faintly. 'Fine. It was a lovely service, don't you think?'

'Yes, it was. Very fitting. And how are you getting along Mrs Selkirk?'

The nonagenarian stares at her for a moment until her memory kicks in.

'Oh, you're that young lass, Inspector Kumar,' she says with a chuckle. 'Yes, I'm ticking along nicely.' Her face drops. 'Rum do all round if you ask me. I've lived in Ashenby all my life, and nothing like this has ever happened before. Malachi murdered. The vicar dangling from a rope. Lord Hampton abducted. This apple has a rotten core. The last time we had a kerfuffle like this was when the young lass was killed in that hit-and-run thirty-odd years ago.' She sighs wistfully. 'Bonny lass. Heart of gold.'

'Now, now, don't go getting yourself all bothered,' Mrs Baxter says, rubbing a hand over Mrs Selkirk's shoulder.

'Never found the bugger who did that, either,' Mrs Selkirk continues, seemingly lost in the past. 'That was another rum do.'

Zac shuffles. 'I take it you're talking about Iona Jacobs?'

'Aye, that's right.'

'Did you know her personally?' Prisha probes.

'Oh, aye. Back in those days, I used to grow lavender in my front garden. Iona often came past on her bike and picked a few sprigs to put in a vase in her bedroom. Said it helped her sleep. The most beautiful eyes you ever saw. And spirited,' she adds with a chuckle. She snaps out of her reverie. 'Now, the offer's still open, inspector—if you're ever passing, feel free to pop in for a cuppa and a slice of cake.'

'Yes, I will. Thanks. Are you heading to the village hall?'

'Yes, I'm fair parched. Could murder a cup of tea.'

Zac opens the gate as Mrs Baker navigates the wheelchair past the old stone piers, then hangs a left to take the path towards the village.

'People have long memories,' Zac notes.

Prisha nods as she casts her gaze back towards the church.

The vicar shakes hands with various members of the community and engages in soft platitudes of thanks. Peggy Thornton, appearing shell-shocked, and accompanied by her brother, is the next to saunter towards the gate.

Prisha offers her a commiserative smile. 'How are you doing, Peggy?'

The elderly woman hesitates before gazing at her. 'Oh, I'm getting by. It's all been a bit of a shock.'

Her brother puts an arm around her shoulder and gives her a gentle hug.

'To be expected,' Prisha replies.

'I'm not sure if that image will ever leave me. He was such a kind man.'

Prisha nods. 'Yes. Testified by the turnout. I reckon most of the village were here today.'

Peggy's distant gaze changes to one of concern. 'Have you... do you... know what actually happened to him yet? Did he take... well, you know. Did he do that to himself, or do you suspect someone else was involved?'

Prisha throws Zac a glance before replying. 'Ahem, we're still investigating. The coroner recorded an open verdict. We know the medical cause of death—asphyxiation due to hanging. However, there is insufficient evidence at the moment to determine Reverend Hartley's intent or the precise circumstances under which the death occurred.'

The brother removes his arm from her shoulder and nudges her in the ribs. 'Go on, Pegs,' he whispers.

Peggy's eyes widen in horror as she shakes her head.

It's not lost on Prisha. 'Is there something you'd like to say, Peggy?'

'What? No. Just that, well, I knew Reverend Hartley a long time and there's no way he'd have done...' She breaks off, caught in her own private hell. Her voice lowers as if embarrassed to utter the word. '... well, there's no way he'd have done that. Knowing I was cleaning that day. That I'd find him. Always put everyone else first. He wouldn't have put me through that.'

Her brother looks annoyed and sighs. 'Come on, Pegs. Let's head to the village hall for a cuppa and then home. You look exhausted.'

As they shuffle by, the brother glances over his shoulder. 'You know where we live, inspector.'

Prisha smiles but is slightly puzzled by the parting shot and doesn't respond.

Zac grimaces as they disappear out of the gate. 'What was all that about?'

Prisha's eyes narrow. 'Not sure.'

'Eh up,' Zac says. 'Here they come. The Wicca lot. Now, Prisha, best behaviour.'

Prisha's eyes wander onto Violet Fox, and the Ashcroft sisters, Lunara and Prudence as they saunter forwards. Oak, the giant bear of a man, lumbers behind.

Smiling benignly, Prisha tilts her head in recognition.

The three women blank her, staring dead ahead. Oak shrugs then nods in respect.

The obvious snub on such a solemn occasion, when petty grievances should be put aside, infuriates Prisha.

'Ms Fox!' she calls out.

Zac drops his gaze to the ground and shakes his head. 'Here we go,' he murmurs.

Violet halts as if hitting a brick wall and turns. 'Yes?'

'We're still investigating the deaths of Malachi Abbott and Reverend Hartley.'

The silence hangs for a second as the entourage sends daggers through the air.

'Good for you. After all, that is your job. Isn't it?'

'Yes, it is. We'll be paying you and your little clique a visit in the next few days. Just routine. A catch up.'

Violet does not alter her demeanour of cool indifference one iota. Here stands a woman who is not cowed by authority, or veiled threats. A strong woman. A calm woman.

'Whatever.'

She turns on her heels, and followed by her group, exits the gate.

Zac heaves. 'What is your problem with that woman?'

Prisha looks at him. 'She's the schoolyard bitch, and it pisses me off.'

'Oh, great. If I got a bee in my bonnet every time someone pissed me off, I'd never get out of bed.'

They both fall silent as they watch Lord and Lady Hampton make whispered small talk with the new vicar. After a few nods, and the obligatory handshakes, they head down the narrow path.

Lord Hampton keeps his head down, but Lady Hampton is breathing fire.

'Ah, Inspector Kumar. I'm surprised you had the gall to make an appearance today.'

'Just showing my respect.'

She huffs. 'Ha! Respect. You arrested my husband on suspicion of the murder of Malachi Abbott, then released him without charge. Do you realise the damage you've done to our reputation? I've had several speaking engagements cancelled. My husband has been asked to stand down from various charitable organisations he was involved with. And my "so-called friends" have been very noticeable by their absence. When you accuse someone of a crime, it doesn't matter if they're vindicated—the stink lingers.'

'Let it go, Abigail,' Lord Hampton whispers, grey and tired.

'No. I will not let it go. Who do these people think they are?'

Prisha takes a deep breath. 'I'm not sure we used the word—*vindicated*, Lady Hampton. I can't control how people react. I'm just doing my job.'

Lady Hampton's nostrils flare. 'If you knew how to do your job correctly, then you wouldn't arrest the wrong man. And while we're on the matter, how are you progressing with finding the abductors of my husband, or has that been conveniently brushed under the carpet?'

'We're still investigating.'

Lady Hampton's lips turn downward. 'The catch-all phrase—*we're still investigating*. Meaning, you have no idea who abducted Noah, who killed Malachi Abbott, and how or why Reverend Hartley was found hanging in this very church. If I were your superior, I'd have put you out to pasture, inspector. You're not fit for purpose.' She half turns to leave, but not before firing one last salvo. 'I suppose you became an inspector not on merit but to meet quotas. A young coloured woman to keep the woke brigade happy.'

Prisha flushes and is about to retaliate when Zac jabs her in the ribs with his elbow.

'Rise above it, Prisha. Sticks and stones,' he mutters.

The church gate squeaks shut as the Hamptons depart.

'Christ, I'm like public enemy number one around here. You'd think it was me who'd bumped off two people.' She offers Zac a fierce gaze. 'You know what this is, don't you?'

Zac rubs his beard. 'A funeral?'

'No, it's a cabal. The village closing ranks. Those in charge calling the shots and blaming outsiders, hoping to divert attention.'

Zac is about to placate her when Frank arrives, mobile phone pressed to his ear.

'Okay, thanks. I'll send two of my officers over there right away. As you say, probably a freak accident, but with recent past events, it's worth taking a closer look.'

He ends the call and stares at his officers.

'What?' Zac asks, concern etched across his features.

'There's been an accident at Hexley Farm.'

'That's the Baker's place,' Prisha states. 'What sort of accident?'

'A fatality. Not sure how, why or even who yet.'

'Mrs Baker left for the village hall a moment ago, and I haven't seen Mr Baker. You don't think…'

Frank cuts her off. 'Let's get some hard facts before making assumptions. I want the two of you to check it out. Let me know what's happened and I'll accompany Mrs Baker back to the farm.'

Zac frowns. 'In case it escaped your attention, Frank, we don't have any bloody transport.'

Frank fishes the car keys from his pocket and reluctantly hands them over.

'Take Beatrice. And be gentle with her. She's an old girl, not a burlesque dancer.'

6

Prisha and Zac step out of the Ford Anglia, much to the bemusement of the uniformed officer, PC Malone.

'Budget cuts, sarge?' Malone asks with a smirk as they stride forward.

'Very funny,' Zac replies. 'We were actually attending a funeral in Ashenby, and DCI Finnegan, for reasons best known to himself, decided to take Chitty Chitty Bang Bang for a spin.'

Prisha takes in the scene at Hexley Farm before facing Malone. 'So, what have we got?'

Malone's grin slips as he nods at the patrol car where PC Carter sits in the driver's seat, with a youngish man in the back.

He pulls out his notebook. 'Not good, ma'am. Looks like a farm accident. In the back of the patrol is Dave Charney. He's a mobile-farm mechanic. Works for Crawley's tractor dealership in Ripon. He received a call from a Mr Amos Baker just after eight this morning. Mr Baker said the hydraulics were playing up on his tractor.' He nods towards a field and the red tractor, some distance away, and one ambulance and two figures in hi-vis jackets.

'Dave Charney arrived just after eleven thirty, earlier than he anticipated. Knocked on the door, no answer. Then he saw the tractor in the field. He drove his vehicle in there and spotted the legs and torso—of what he thought was Mr Baker—poking out from underneath the grass cutter. Assumed he was having a go at fixing it himself. No engine running. He called out, no reply. Tapped Mr Baker's boots with his foot. Still no response. Then spotted a wet patch on the ground near the slasher. Stooped. Had a closer look, noticed it was red. Alarmed, he jumped into the cab, raised the slasher and pulled the tractor forward a few feet.' He pauses, wincing, a grey sheen spreading over his face. 'Then... he took another look. It's not pretty, ma'am. I've seen some bad stuff in my time, but I hope to God I never have to see anything like this again.'

'Has Mrs Baker been informed?'

'No. We're still trying to locate her. We got her mobile number from the mechanic, but it's diverting to voicemail. She's not in the house. Door was open. We checked.'

Zac sighs. 'She was attending the funeral. Probably switched her mobile off before going into church and forgot to switch it back on again. They're holding a wake at Ashenby Village Hall, followed by drinks at the pub. Get onto Control and tell them to send a car out there to collect her and DCI Finnegan.'

'Righto, sarge.'

'What about forensics and the undertaker?'

'On their way, sarge.'

'Good. Nice work, Malone.'

Prisha and Zac head on foot across the field towards the two paramedics in attendance.

'Shit the bed,' Zac curses. 'I don't believe it.'

'What?'

'Blair Kilpatrick.'

'The super-sleuth paramedic?'

'Aye. What are the chances? Haven't bumped into the bugger for eighteen months and now twice in the space of six weeks. North Yorkshire's answer to Columbo.'

'Ah, Sergeant Stoker, and...' he studies Prisha with a roving, lecherous eye as he bites into a Cornish pasty. '...Inspector Kumar.'

She blanks him and stares at the tarp covering the body.

Blair nods across to his partner, thirty feet away, who is on his haunches sucking in air.

'You met my mate Bob last time, didn't you?'

'Aye,' Zac replies.

'Ashenby Church. The vicar who topped himself.' He half-smiles and takes another bite of his food, then lowers his voice. 'Bob's not cut out for the job. If you can't stand blood, guts, shit, and piss, then find another profession—that's my mantra. Care to take a look?' he says, gaze drifting onto the tarp.

Prisha nods. 'Yes.'

Holding his food aloft, as if it might become contaminated, he crouches and yanks the cover back.

Zac swallows hard and averts his gaze.

Prisha remains unmoved as Bob, in the distance, dry retches.

From the chest down to the feet—the body is in perfect condition. Just like a man lying on his back in the sun. However, the only part remaining of his head is about one-fifth of the back of the skull. The rest lies around him. Skin, blood, bones, brain matter, clumps of hair. The neck is a bloodied stump with a huge flap of skin hanging over the top of his chest, part of his shirt ripped away.

Blair finishes the pasty with a certain amount of satisfaction and rubs the flakes from his fingers.

'Obvious what happened,' he says nonchalantly as Prisha bends and replaces the tarp back over the deceased. 'I had a quick word with the mechanic, who raised the alarm. Hydraulics had been playing up. I reckon the old farmer was busily cutting grass and something jams. Gets out of the cab. Leaves the engine running. Squeezes underneath the slasher to see what the problem is and... bang, the blades start up again. Seen similar things over the years. Farmers... they cut corners. "Get the job done" is their philosophy.'

Zac gazes at Blair. 'According to the mechanic, the tractor wasn't running when he arrived.'

Blair shrugs. 'Obviously ran out of fuel.'

Prisha throws him a cold stare and heads to the tractor. She jumps into the cab and checks the fuel gauge—half-full, keys still in the ignition. She turns them. Engine instantly fires. She turns it off and drops to the ground.

'And there goes that theory,' Zac adds. 'Right, thanks for your efforts, Blair. We'll take it from here. Forensics and the undertaker are on their way.'

'No probs. Come on, Bob. Time to go.'

As the ambulance trundles over the field towards the farmhouse, Prisha inspects the cab of the tractor again.

Zac stares up at her. 'It does look like an unfortunate accident. It's an old tractor, and it's possible with faulty hydraulics, the blades began spinning once Mr Baker was underneath it.'

'Hmm...' is her only reply as she scans the interior.

'And, as much as I'm loath to say it, Blair does have a point; farmers take risks no sane person ever would. They're always fighting three things: time, the weather, and the bank manager.'

Prisha is about to descend when she notices something wedged between the dash and the windscreen.

She reaches out and picks it up.

'Hell,' she whispers.

'What?'

She holds it aloft. 'The same coin as found in Malachi Abbott's car. A braided crucifix.'

Leaping from the cab with a supple dexterity the late farmer would have envied, she frowns.

'I'm beginning to believe in Finnegan's motto,' she states.

'Which one? He has so bloody many.'

'There's no such thing as *coincidence*.'

7

As Prisha takes photos on her phone, a piercing wail reverberates around the countryside.

Zac glances towards the farmhouse as muted voices carry on the air.

He winces. 'Mrs Baker, I presume.'

Prisha nods. 'Yes. You stay here and wait for the undertaker and forensics. I'll try to console her and get a timeline of events.'

'Rather you than me.'

She saunters up to Frank, who is hovering on the doorstep, face grim, lips hardened.

He takes Prisha by the elbow and steers her away from the entrance.

'Is it him, Mr Baker?' he whispers.

'We assume so. Unfortunately, there's nothing left of his head. He went under the slasher, probably to fix it, and it must have started up again whilst he was underneath.'

Frank rubs a hand over his chin. 'Holy shite. I checked with Mrs Baker to see if they employed a farmhand. She said they do occasionally, but not today. Old Amos Baker has been busy slashing grass for hay. That's why he wasn't at the funeral today. Is the rest of the body intact?'

'From the neck down, yes.'

'Hmm, still, we'll need a formal ID. Was he wearing a wedding ring?'

'Yes. I have photos on my phone.'

'Good, but it's only circumstantial. We'll still need dental records.'

'How is she?' Prisha asks, her gaze fixing on the front door decorated with hawthorn branches.

Frank shakes his head. 'Not good. Wants to see him.'

'She can't. It's horrific.'

'No, not yet, but we still have a duty of care to the next of kin. If she insists, then maybe from a safe distance with something covering his head. A chance to say goodbye. Hopefully, the family liaison officer will be able to dissuade her.' He takes a deep breath and releases it in a whoosh. 'Anything suspicious?'

'Not on first appearances. However, I found this in the cab.'

She hands him the crucifix coin sealed in an evidence bag.

Frank grimaces. 'Same one as found in Malachi Abbott's vehicle, and similar in style to the one Morrigan Penhallow gifted to Zac.'

'Also, the mechanic said the tractor was switched off when he arrived. It still has plenty of fuel left. Which begs the question, how did the slasher start up on its own?'

'Fair point. I want you to find out who makes these bloody things,' he grizzles, brandishing the braided disc. 'And secondly, we'll need to call in a forensic vehicle examiner to see if it *is* possible the blades started up by themselves, then take it from there.' He pauses. 'Treat it as suspicious at the moment but keep it quiet. We just buried one bugger under dubious circumstances. The last thing we need is for the villagers to think there's been another murder. They're edgy and distrustful as it is.'

'Okay, Frank.'

'Right. I'm heading back to the village.'

Prisha is bemused. 'What for?'

He checks his watch. 'I reckon most of the mourners will have tired of tea and biscuits by now and will be heading to the pub. And alcohol has a way of loosening tongues. I'll take Beatrice. You and Zac grab a lift back to Whitby with patrol. And softly, softly, with Mrs Baker.'

As she watches the vintage car trundle away, she throws a glance back at the farmhouse. She knows her strengths, but also her weaknesses. And dealing with the next of kin is not her strong point.

The kitchen is predictably neat and tidy, with a lingering aroma of home cooking. Mrs Baker is sitting on a sofa, nursing a cup of tea, flicking through an old-fashioned family photo album.

Prisha sidles up to Police Constable Julie Markham, the uniformed FLO, who is busy at the sink.

A woman in her early fifties with a dyed-blonde bob, dazzling blue eyes, and a curvy frame that she carries with confidence. A smattering of makeup and a hint of perfume suggest pride in her appearance. She exudes a calming aura of someone who's seen everything and doesn't rattle easily. Julie's the kind of officer families remember long after the dust has settled.

'Any other close family members?' Prisha asks in a hushed tone.

She nods. 'A son in Aberdeen. Works in the oil and gas industry. And a daughter, a nurse in London. Both have been informed and are making arrangements. Still, I can't see either arriving for at least another five to six hours.'

Prisha glances at Mrs Baker. 'Is she still insistent on seeing the body… sorry, her husband?'

'Yes. I tried tactfully to explain that it's initially treated as a crime scene, and no one is allowed near until forensics have finished, but I don't think it sank in.'

'What's her first name?'

'Polly. Husband Amos. Son and daughter, Martin and Hazel.'

'Did you give any details about the injuries?'

Julie frowns. 'No, but only because I haven't been given any specifics yet.'

Prisha bites her lip. 'Okay. I'll fill you in when I leave.'

She wanders over to the sofa. 'Mrs Baker, Polly?' she says softly.

Mrs Baker pulls her face away from the old photographs.

'Oh, Inspector Kumar. Sorry, I didn't hear you arrive.'

'Can I?' she says, pointing at the couch.

'Yes. Of course.'

Prisha takes a seat and pulls out her notepad. 'I know this isn't a good time, but it is important that I fill out some missing details to do with the timeline of events.'

She nods her acquiescence. 'I understand. When can I see him?' Tears well in her eyes.

'As Constable Markham, Julie, explained, even though it appears to be an accident, initially, every fatality is treated as a potential crime scene. Forensics will be arriving shortly. Once they've left, then it may be possible for you to see your husband... from a distance.'

'But I want to hold his hand and tell him all the things I should have told him years ago.'

Prisha squirms, feeling hot. 'We can't stop you, but I'd advise against it.'

'Why? What's he like? All I've been told is that there was some sort of accident involving the tractor.'

She squirms a little more and shuffles her bottom against the cushion.

'Ahem, it appears your husband, Amos, was fixing something under the slasher. We believe the blades may have started whilst he was below them.'

She closes her eyes and performs the sign of the cross over her chest.

'Sweet Lord. His face... is it...'

Prisha cuts her off. 'I'm afraid so. The rest of his body is unscathed.'

Mrs Baker puffs out air, deflated.

'Polly, when was the last time you saw your husband?'

'This morning. He came in for his breakfast about ten. I left for the funeral a few minutes later and went to collect Mrs Selkirk.'

'And any other contact in between?'

'No. I switched my phone off before entering the church. He wouldn't have called me, anyway. He's flat out this time of year,' she pauses and sniffles. 'He's always flat out. He said we'd give it another five years on the farm then sell up and buy a bungalow by the sea. That damn tractor,' she hisses, anger flaring for a moment. 'It was always playing up. I don't know why he didn't buy a new one. We have the money.'

Her attention returns to the faded photographs. 'This was us on our wedding day,' she says, gently rolling a finger over the image.

Prisha glances at it. 'He was a handsome young man.'

'Yes. A real catch.' She flicks through the pages, smiling wistfully. Hovering over one photo, she chuckles. 'This is the four of them together. They were all great pals back then. They earned the nickname the Odd Bunch from some in the village. If only he'd come to the funeral, then this wouldn't have happened. I asked him repeatedly, but once he'd made up his mind about something, or someone, then there was no turning back. He was a stubborn old mule.'

Prisha's gaze flits to the photo.

Four young men dressed in eighties gear, standing around a brazier, cans of beer in hands, smiling for the camera.

Humouring her, she asks, 'Why were they called the Odd Bunch?'

'Their professions.'

'Sorry?'

'Amos the farmer. Malachi the gamekeeper. Nicholas, the man-of-the-cloth, and Noah—Lord Hampton. A motley crew if ever I saw one.'

Prisha blinks hard and swallows. Her mind buzzes and crackles with electrical impulses. With a gargantuan effort, she tries to restrain herself from diving in too deep, too soon. Now's not the time.

But still, dipping a line in the water couldn't do much harm.

'And Amos was good friends with all of them?'

'Yes. They got up to some mischief together.' She catches herself. 'Oh, I don't mean anything illegal, just silly men's stuff. You know, making homemade wine and beer, shooting in the woods, long treks, and camping out. I didn't mind. It was a good break for Amos, a chance to let his hair down, unwind. He was always in a far better frame of mind the next day having spent time with his friends. Men, they never really grow up, do they?'

'No. I suppose they don't. When was the photo taken?'

'In the mid-eighties.'

'Did they remain friends over the years?'

Polly turns the page to a set of baby photos. 'No. They drifted apart. It was sad, really. I always felt that once the friendship group had broken up, Amos was never quite the same. Less fun, more serious, grumpy. He'd stay out in the fields all day. But that's friendships for you. They come and go throughout life. It's not like family, is it?'

'No, it's not. And when would you say they drifted apart?'

'Late eighties. I was pregnant with my son, Martin. At first, I thought that was the reason their friendships waned. You know, becoming a father, but Amos insisted it wasn't.'

'And when was Martin born?'

'December 1989.'

Sensitive to the situation, Prisha has enough to be going on with, but one final thing.

Rising from the sofa, she pulls the evidence bag from her pocket and holds it between her thumb and forefinger.

'Polly, I found this in the tractor cab. Do you know what it is?'

She pulls her eyes away from the memories on the page and stares at the object.

Her mouth drops open.

Brow creases.

Pain weeps from her eyes.

Tries to form words but appears catatonic.

PC Markham steps forward, concerned. 'Polly?'

Polly lifts a trembling finger and points at the coin.

'It's... it's...' she stammers.

PC Markham gives Prisha a discreet nod, the intention clear—time for Prisha to leave.

Prisha drops the coin into her pocket and turns on her heels.

'It's the death knot,' Polly blurts out.

As Prisha pulls the kitchen door shut behind her, she spots Zac closing the farm gate as two forensic vehicles bump and rattle across the field towards the tractor.

'In safe hands now,' he explains. 'Charlene Marsden is leading the team. I saw Frank leaving in the coffin on wheels. Where's he buggered off to?'

'Headed to the pub in Ashenby to eavesdrop, hoping someone might let something slip.'

'It won't take long before the bar is abuzz with the news of Mr Baker. And how's the old lass holding up?' he asks, nodding towards the farmhouse.

'She was doing okay until I showed her the coin. It was like I'd hit her around the head with a kipper.'

His jaw tightens. 'Why?'

'Didn't get to the bottom of it. She almost went into shock. Became hysterical. Pointed and called it the death knot.'

'Meaning?'

Prisha shrugs. 'Like I said, I didn't get any further before she had a meltdown. But I did glean some very interesting intel.'

'Oh, aye?'

'Amos Baker used to be...'

Zac holds a hand up as a patrol car rolls into the farmyard. 'Tell me in the car. Our carriage back to Whitby has arrived. PC Jacko Jackson was in the area.'

The car performs a rapid three-point-turn.

'I'll call you tonight to discuss it,' Prisha explains as they amble towards the car.

'Why?'

'This could be critical information, and I want it kept under tight wraps.'

Zac wrinkles his nose. 'It's Jacko. He's as straight as a die.'

'It doesn't matter. People can let things slip without even noticing. For the moment, this new information is only for me, you and Frank.'

8

Prisha points at the farm track. 'Just pull up over there on the left, Jacko. I'll get out here.'

'You're not going to walk up that bloody lane, are you?' Zac asks. 'It must be over a mile long, and it's stinking hot.'

'Two miles, actually. Anyway, it's a beautiful day and it will give me a chance to unwind,' she replies as Jacko pulls the vehicle up alongside a sign that reads—Clegg Farm.

'I don't mind taking you all the way to the front door, ma'am,' Jacko says.

'No, really. I want to walk.'

'You staying at Adam's tonight or heading home?' Zac enquires.

'Heading back to Whitby. I'll just collect my car and overnight bag and set off. Adam will be in the fields until dusk. Farmers, eh?' she says with an ironic smile.

'All right. Speak later.'

She waits until the patrol car rounds a bend, then removes her jacket and slings it over her shoulder. Closing her eyes, she breathes in the sweet perfume of grass and wildflowers in bloom. Buzzing insects, the chirrup of birds, and bleating sheep the only sounds. A warm breeze tickles her face.

She's in her happy place. Peace and serenity. Away from the horrors of the real world.

Looking down at her shoes, she grimaces.

'Hmm... maybe I should have got a lift to the door.'

As she nears the top of the hill, Prisha bitterly regrets her decision to walk the two-mile gravel track.

Fit, disciplined, a daily runner with a good diet and strong legs, she's completely underestimated the conditions. Even in her usual gear—moisture-wicking leggings and high-tech trainers—the uphill slog in this heat would be punishing. But today she's dressed for a funeral: a tight skirt restricting her stride, a tailored blouse clinging to her back, a fitted jacket trapping heat, and shoes with modest heels but cruelly pointed toes. To make matters worse, every hundred yards or so, a small piece of grit lodges in her shoe and stabs at her hardened feet.

She pauses again, one hand holding onto the drystone wall for balance as she removes a shoe and shakes out the offending stone.

Halfway up, she'd untied her ponytail, which was beginning to pinch at her scalp. At first, she felt a sense of relief, but as she nears the brow of the hill, the wind picks up and swirls her hair around, adding to her agitation.

Eventually, she enters through the farm gate and pauses to catch her breath. Dehydrated, sweaty, mascara running, hair—now a bird's nest, she surveys the farmyard, panting hard.

Adam's tractor is parked outside the barn. The two sheepdogs are lolling in the shade at the side of their respective kennels. Both notice her but don't rise, merely offer a faint wag of their tails in recognition.

Her eyes once again refocus on the tractor.

Adam said he was cutting grass all day. Why's his tractor parked up? Hmm... maybe come back for a snack. No. He takes all his food and drink with him for the day. Probably a mechanical issue. Unless he's noticed a broken fence wire and has taken the quad bike out to fix it. No, he usually takes the dogs with him when that's the case.

She notices the wheels of another vehicle from underneath the chassis of the tractor. Taking a sideways step, she cranes her neck.

'Oh, no. Not the bloody vet again. He must spend half of his income on vet bills. He's in the wrong game. It's the vets who make all the money, not the farmer.'

She teeters uncomfortably towards the front door, removes her shoes, and places them on the mat.

Entering the house, she pauses to appreciate the cool air inside. High ceilings, fans, shades, and Venetian blinds make the rooms an oasis in a desert.

Padding into the kitchen, she runs the cold tap, fills a glass with water, and thirstily gulps it down, then repeats.

She catches her reflection in the glass-fronted oven door.

'Christ, what a picture,' she murmurs to herself. Placing her handbag on the kitchen counter, she ambles down the corridor towards the master bedroom to collect her overnight bag.

Pushing open the door, she gawps, unable to comprehend the sight.

Stunned, shocked, frozen.

The two naked bodies stop their animalistic gyrations and stare at her in wide-eyed horror.

Red-hot pokers penetrate Prisha's brain from either side of her skull as her senses abruptly comprehend the situation.

'You bastard!' she screams, turning on her heels and rushing away from the scene. Grabbing her handbag from the kitchen, she exits the house and marches across the farmyard towards her car.

A voice calls out.

'Wait, Prisha, I can explain.'

Adam.

Prisha's confusion, sorrow, hurt, and humiliation are rudely elbowed out of the way by a new emotion—anger.

She wheels around. 'What fucking planet are you living on? You can explain—really?'

Adam is still fastening his jeans, his naked torso glistening with sweat. 'Just give me a moment.'

'No, don't explain. I get it. The pretty little vet wanted to see our bedroom decor. As you were showing her around, a sudden gust of wind exploded through the open window and blew all your clothes off. In a state of shock, you both fell naked onto *our* bed. Your penis just happened to be in the upright position, and unfortunately for all concerned, you entered her. Yes, I understand. It could happen to anyone.'

The horrified vet appears in the doorway, hurriedly adjusting her dishevelled garments before scurrying like a rat across the yard towards her car.

'That's right, bitch! Keep running. Because if I get hold of you, I'll pull your fucking tits off!'

Adam approaches cautiously. 'Prisha, calm down. It was a one-off. It wasn't supposed to happen.'

Prisha appears calm, but it's merely part of the cycle, like when a wave crashes onto the beach, then ebbs away, before rebuilding energy to attack the shore once more.

An engine roars, tyres screech, and the vet tears off like a Formula One driver. A plume of dust kicks up behind her.

Adam takes another tentative step forward, hands raised in front of him.

'Prisha,' he begins softly, 'honestly, it just sort of happened. I didn't see it coming.'

Prisha nods her head. 'Is that right? Tell me, did you see this coming?'

'What?' he asks, puzzled.

Her left arm whips around, fist like a lump hammer, and smashes into his nose with a brutal, satisfying crack.

Adam staggers back and drops to his haunches, hands clutching his nose as crimson drips through splayed fingers.

'Fud... I dink you've broden my node.'

Prisha sneers. 'Oh, cry me a fucking river, big boy. Count yourself lucky I don't have a knife to hand, otherwise I'd be feeding your cock and balls to the dogs. Smallest bloody meal they'd ever get.'

She jumps in her car, fires the engine, and takes off at a similar speed to the pretty young vet. Glancing in the rear-view mirror, her last sight is of Adam falling onto his backside, still clutching his face, red rivulets carving a path down his chest.

'Bastard!'

9

Wednesday 25th June 10:15 am

Frank parks outside reception at the Whitby Holiday Park situated above Saltwick Bay and alights. He gazes out over the sea, sunshine skipping along gentle breakers, a soft breeze tousling his hair.

A woman's voice calls out. 'Eh up, Frank.'

He spins around and smiles. 'Now then, Sue. You look younger every time I see you.'

'Get away with you. Smooth talker,' she says, grinning as she pulls at the reception door. 'What brings you out here? Don't tell me... Meera's finally kicked you out, and you want to rent a caravan?'

Frank chuckles. 'No. But who could blame her if she did.'

'So why are you here?'

'I fancied a walk on the beach. It's been a while since I've been out this way.'

Sue grimaces. 'Ooh, yes. Not since that poor sod was lashed to Black Nab. Did you ever find out who did it? It all went very hush-hush.'

Frank throws another look across the bay towards the huge rock. It rises like a brooding sentinel from Saltwick Bay, its dark silhouette etched against the silver-grey tide and turquoise horizon.

'Can't say too much, Sue. But if it's any comfort, one of the buggers ended up dead, and the other…' His voice tails off.

'The other?' Sue prompts.

'Let's just say they're at large, presumed dead.'

'Good riddance.'

He sticks his hands deep into his overcoat. 'Okay if I leave my car here for a while? I'll only be half an hour or so?'

Sue smiles. 'Aye, of course it is, Frank. I tell you what, why don't you pop in on your way back and I'll make us a cuppa? I have homemade sausage rolls for my morning snack. I dare say I can spare one.'

Frank nods. 'Sounds like a plan, Sue. See you soon.'

He meanders to the top of the steps and studies the beach far below. A disconsolate figure is lethargically throwing stones into the water.

'There she is,' he murmurs to himself.

The steps down to the beach are not for the faint-hearted. Some are half-washed away, while others have large drops between each riser. It's hard on the knees, especially for a large man.

'Jeepers bloody creepers,' he curses, navigating the arduous descent.

Prisha doesn't lift her head as he approaches; she merely bends, picks up another pebble and casts it into the sea without enthusiasm.

'How'd you know where to find me?' she mumbles as Frank sidles alongside.

'Zac. He said it's one of your hidey-holes when you need a bit of time-out.'

'Yeah. It's quiet, peaceful. Those steps prevent the old, the infirm and the lazy from coming down here.'

Frank chuckles. 'I managed it.'

She finally peers at him, resisting a smile. 'You're not infirm.'

He raises his eyebrows. 'Thanks. Meaning I'm old and lazy?'

She kicks at the sand. 'I suppose Zac told you about Adam?'

Frank rolls his shoulders. 'Aye. A rum do.'

'I suppose all the station knows now. All sniggering, making jokes.'

He turns to her. 'No. They're not like that, Prisha. They're a good bunch. You're highly regarded.'

Finally, anger bursts through. 'I can't believe it, Frank. I caught him bollock naked shagging the bloody vet.'

'Aye, Zac said. One question I forgot to ask though—'

She looks at him. 'What?'

'The vet—man or woman?'

A faint smile passes her lips, brief, transient. 'A woman. A very pretty woman.'

He scratches at the stubble on his chin. 'Not as bonny as you though, I'll wager.'

She gazes out over Black Nab, the waves lapping around its base.

'Apart from the pain I feel in my heart, do you know what other emotion is even stronger?'

'No.'

'Humiliation, Frank. Bloody *humiliation*. I'm a copper, for God's sake. I should have twigged ages ago. He was always checking his phone and running off at odd times. Late at night, Sunday mornings. Always with a plausible excuse. Cattle out on the road. A broken fence. An irrigation pump on the blink. Off he'd trot. And muggins here believed him.'

'Why wouldn't you? They're all valid reasons for a farmer.'

She picks up another pebble but doesn't toss it into the water, merely stares at it, tears staining her cheeks.

'I feel broken and empty. Like I'm worthless.' She turns to him as the waterworks increase. 'What am I going to do, Frank?'

Frank encircles his powerful arms around her and pulls her head into his chest and sighs as she sobs uncontrollably.

'Come here, lass. What you're going to do is feel sorry for yourself for a day or two. Mope around and lick your wounds. Eat a lot of chocolate and cake. Then you're going to pick yourself up off the floor, dust yourself down, and get back on the bloody horse.'

Sobs mingle with laughter. 'Christ, Frank, could you fit any more clichés into one sentence?'

The laughter doesn't last long before the tears return with a vengeance.

'That's it, girl, let it all out,' he whispers. 'It'll get worse before it gets better. And for what it's worth, that lad is a bloody fool, and he'll realise it one day. If I were in his shoes and courting you, I'd never have looked at another woman for the rest of my days. I'd have pinched myself every morning to make sure I wasn't dreaming. A beautiful, smart, intelligent woman with a wicked sense of humour—what more does a man need? And you can cook.'

'You're not helping,' she sobs.

He chuckles. 'No, 'appen not. I'm bloody useless at this sort of thing.' He pulls a clean handkerchief from his pocket and hands it to her. 'Here, use this. You're getting snot all over my coat.'

She pulls away slightly. 'Sorry,' she says, blowing her nose.

He places his large hands on her slender shoulders. 'Right, listen to me, lass. Take as much time off as you need. Although knowing you, you'll be climbing the walls after a couple of days. Do you hear me?'

She nods and dabs at her eyes. 'What about the investigation?'

'The investigation will continue just fine without you. Zac can hold the fort until you're back. He can team up with Dinkel. That'll make his day.'

Laughter comes again. 'He'll end up killing him.'

Placing a finger under her chin, he gently lifts her head. 'Prisha, this is life. Shit happens. We deal with it. Humans are resilient. And you're the most resilient person I've ever known. You'll bounce back bigger, better, and stronger—do you hear me?'

Her eyelashes flutter. 'Yes. I hear you, although I'm not sure I believe you.'

'Right, are you coming or do you want your own space?'

'I'll stay here for a while. Try to get it all out. Think things through.'

He smiles and gives her one last hug. 'Right, call me any time of day or night if you need a chat or just a shoulder to cry on. Like I said, I'm bloody useless at this caper, but I know how to listen. God knows I've been married long enough.' He turns and stares at the formidable steps. 'I'm not looking forward to tackling those buggers,' he mumbles. 'I'll see you when I see you.' He wanders off across the sand. 'And if I stumble across Adam, I'll wring his *bloody* neck.'

Prisha watches him go with a warm heart. 'Frank,' she calls after him.

He stops and glances over his shoulder. 'What?'

'You're not useless. Thanks.'

He offers her a reassuring smile. 'Aye, whatever,' he mutters, then tramps across the beach. 'Hellfire, I've got sand in my shoes now. That's all I bloody need.'

10

Dinkel is seated at his desk in the corner, headphones on, gazing out of the window as Frank stands in front of Zac, who is sitting side on to his laptop.

Frank's just broken the news.

Zac stares up at him. 'Dinkel. Dinkel. Dinkel,' he stammers.

Frank frowns. 'Aye, that's what I said. Are you having some sort of brain malfunction?'

Zac slumps back in his seat. 'Aw, come off it, Frank. Not Dinkel. Why me?'

'Because I *bloody* said so, that's why. It'll do him good to ride shotgun with you until Prisha's back on deck.' He glances at the door as Superintendent Bank bustles through into the incident room. 'Eh up, Laughing Gravy's landed. I wasn't expecting her in here today.'

She strides directly over to him. 'Ah, Frank, can't stay long. I had a meeting in Durham with the Strategic Oversight and Governance Committee. Thought I'd call in on my way back to Northallerton. How's the investigation going?'

'Which one, Anne? We do have multiple investigations running concurrently.'

Her eyes narrow. 'Operation Raven. I'd have thought that was obvious. It's been just over six weeks since you released Lord Hampton without charge, the main suspect in the death of Malachi Abbott. Surely you must have made some progress?'

Frank massages his chin. 'Ah, right. Yes, no new developments to write home about, but we're throwing everything at it with our limited resources.'

'I see. And what about the cold case Dinkel is working on?'

'Iona Jacobs. Again, not much progress, Anne.'

'Right, well you've had long enough. I know you didn't want to inform the next of kin we'd reopened the case until you had something solid to go on, but it's time you informed the mother. What's her name?'

'The postmistress in Ashenby—Lilac Penhallow.'

'That's right. You need to visit her, Frank, and let her know. The last thing we need is for her to find out second-hand from someone. That would be a public relations nightmare.'

'Anne, don't you think we should wait a little longer?'

'No, I don't. I want you to pay her a visit personally and explain what's happening. Do I make myself clear?'

'Yes, ma'am.'

'And what was that I heard on the grapevine about an incident on the outskirts of Ashenby, yesterday?'

'Yes, appears to be an accident,' he mutters, tapping Zac on the shin with the toe of his shoe. 'The tractor is with vehicle forensics now, giving it a thorough examination.'

Banks narrows her gaze. 'No links to our investigation then?'

Frank puffs out a sigh. 'Probably not, but until we have all the forensic analysis to hand, we're keeping an open mind.'

Banks is an expert at decoding shilly-shallying and obfuscation, being an expert in the dark art herself.

'Hmm...' She scans the room, her eyes drifting to Dinkel, then to Zac and back onto Frank.

'Where's Prisha?'

'She's taking some time off.'

She frowns. 'You've let her take holidays during a high-profile murder investigation?'

'No. Not holidays.'

'Is she ill? What's wrong with her?'

Frank shifts his weight. 'She needs a break. For her mental health.'

'I don't follow?'

'She's broken up with her boyfriend. It wasn't a mutual decision, if you know what I mean.'

Banks shakes her head aggressively. 'No, I don't know what you mean. Prisha is a professional senior police officer. She's not a love-struck teenager. She knows the score. We leave personal problems outside the station door.' She pulls her phone out. 'I'll call her now. Get her back on duty. We're short-staffed as it is.'

Frank reaches out and lays his hand on top of her wrist.

'No. You won't,' he advises firmly.

Banks glares at him. 'I beg your pardon!' she snaps.

Frank sighs. 'She needs rest, Anne.'

'Poppycock. What she needs is to be leading this investigation.'

Frank's head reddens and swells in size. 'For God's sake, woman!' he bellows. 'Do you always have to be such a hard-nosed bitch? The lass is heartbroken. She'll be of no use to man nor beast at the moment. She's *my* officer, and I've given her time off.'

'She's not *your* officer; she's *our* officer.'

'And I'm her immediate supervisor. She answers to me!'

She throws Zac a glance, who averts his eyes to the carpet as she takes a step towards Frank.

'And I'm *your* immediate supervisor, Frank, and *you* answer to *me*,' she states, voice unnervingly robotic.

Frank sucks in air, his barrel chest expanding.

'Have you no heart, Anne? Don't fight me on this one; I'm begging you. There'll be no winners. A few days, a week at most.'

Taking one last look around the room, she turns on her heels and stomps towards the door.

Frank gazes down at Zac. 'What are you bloody gawping at, sergeant? Haven't you got work to do?' he shouts.

'Yes, boss,' he replies as Frank storms to his office, slamming the door behind him.

Dinkel removes his earphones and looks over at Zac.

'It's very quiet in here today. Where is everyone?'

II

Prisha emerges from the bathroom in her dressing gown, a towel wrapped around her head, sporting a face mask as the door buzzer beeps. She stares at the monitor and spots Zac standing outside the entrance at the bottom of the flats.

She presses a button. 'It's open. Come on up,' she says, unlatching the door.

In the kitchen, she flicks the kettle on and pulls two cups from a cupboard.

'Hello!'

'I'm in here,' she shouts, dropping two teabags into the cups.

Zac saunters in and stares at her. 'Christ, you look like a panda bear.'

She smiles. 'My eyes were all puffed up.'

'Ah, I see.'

'Tea?'

'Please.' He leans against the wall. 'I was just passing. I'm on my way to collect Sammy from football.'

The kettle clicks off. She lifts it and pours the water.

'I thought football season had finished?'

'It has. He plays five-a-side on West Beach two nights a week. Him and a few mates.'

'How's the investigation going?' she asks, dunking the teabags.

He sighs heavily. 'Slow. That's another reason I called by.' He hesitates, wondering if now is a good time to talk shop. 'But only if you're up for it. I wasn't going to ask about your insights last night when you called. You were too upset.'

He takes a seat at the table as Prisha places the cup in front of him and sits down opposite.

'Yeah, sorry about that. My emotions were... a little raw.'

'Don't apologise.'

A warm smile briefly visits. 'Thanks for listening.'

'Anytime.'

She takes a sip of tea. 'Okay, when I was in the farmhouse, Mrs Baker was flicking through a photo album, you know, the old-fashioned ones that only people from a certain generation still have.'

'Yes, I know the type. The mother-in-law has a whole box of them.'

'There was a photo of Amos Baker, Malachi Abbott, Reverend Hartley, and Lord Hampton. They were standing around a fire in an oil drum, clutching beers, all smiling.'

'How long ago?'

'Mid-eighties.'

'So, forty-odd years back?'

'Yes. They're all of a similar age, so I'm guessing they'd have been in their mid to late twenties. Mrs Baker looked fondly at the photo and said some of the villagers had a nickname for the four of them—the Odd Bunch—because of their diverse professions.'

'Is being a lord a profession?'

She shrugs. 'Not sure. Anyway, the fact they were all mates rang alarm bells. Three of the four are now dead in potentially suspicious circumstances, and one was abducted and left to die in a mineshaft, if we're to believe Lord Hampton's version of events.'

'You still don't buy his account?'

She purses her lips. 'Let's just say there are major discrepancies in his story, and I'm keeping an open mind.'

'Okay, what else?'

'According to Mrs Baker, the group drifted apart. She was pregnant with her first child. He was born in December 1989. She initially thought Amos had distanced himself from the friends because he was about to become a father.'

'Time to put away childish things and knuckle down to the serious duty of raising a bairn?'

'Something like that. But Amos denied that was the reason. She didn't elaborate. Anyway, here's my theory. All four men lived in or around Ashenby in 1989. Iona Jacobs hit-and-run happened in June 1989. The friendship group was fading by the end of the year, or earlier. Question is—why?'

'You think one of them could have been the driver in the hit-and-run, possibly with one or more of the others in the vehicle?'

Prisha taps a fingernail against the edge of her cup. 'It's a possibility, don't you think?'

'Aye, possible. All keep quiet. Thick as thieves. Then after a while, the guilt begins to eat away at them. The blame game begins, recriminations. All of them would be implicated if they were aware of a serious offence being committed and not reporting it. That's perverting the course of justice and assisting an offender. The former carries a maximum of life imprisonment.'

'I've witnessed friendships crash and burn over a lot less.'

'True. Your theory's got legs, but proving it is another thing, especially with three of them now dead. And we're investigating the deaths of Malachi Abbott and Reverend Hartley. Iona Jacobs is a cold case and a separate enquiry being led by the intrepid DC Dinkel. We're stretched thin. Cherry-picking elements from different investigations is a good way to tie yourself up in knots in my experience.'

Prisha gazes out of the kitchen window. 'Only if you become focussed on the minutiae. If you zoom out and take a wider approach, the events of June 1989 could be the conduit, the thread through time, that links the recent deaths.'

Zac rubs a hand through his beard, less than convinced. 'I don't know, Prisha. If we take that approach, all I see is a tangle of fishing line never to be unravelled.'

She leans towards him, animated. 'Think about it for a moment. The mother of Iona Jacobs is Lilac Penhallow. The surviving child of Iona is Morrigan Penhallow. Both living in Ashenby.'

Zac becomes flustered. 'Neither Lilac nor Morrigan Penhallow would have been capable of tampering with the brakes on Malachi's car, let alone luring Reverend Hartley into the bell tower, overpowering him, and slipping a rope around his neck. And as for the death of Mr Baker, we both saw Lilac at the funeral yesterday. She couldn't have been in two places at once.'

'We didn't see Morrigan though, did we?'

He grimaces. 'Oh, come on, Prisha. Morrigan's not built for murder. She's four-foot nothing.'

Prisha taps on the table as her mind spins.

'Lord Hampton is the sole survivor,' she murmurs.

'And he was also at the funeral at the same time Baker died. So he's in the clear. Anyway, you're getting ahead of yourself. We don't even know if Baker's death is suspicious. Let's wait and see what vehicle forensics has to say. We have three deaths and only one is officially murder. I think you're assigning importance to the fact they all used to be mates. But that was forty years ago. I hear what you're saying, but the facts are tenuous at best.'

'You're forgetting about the braided coin. Found at two crime scenes.'

He huffs and relents, knowing that when Prisha gets the bit between her teeth, she won't let go.

'Okay, we'll play it your way. What do you want me to do in your absence?'

She smiles, eyelashes fluttering. 'First, convince Frank the Iona Jacobs cold case and Operation Raven may be inextricably linked. We run them concurrently, cross-referencing facts, dates, and information. Second, we need to know if that slasher blade could have started up on its own. If it couldn't, then we have another murder on our hands, and it strengthens my theory about the links between the four men. And lastly, find out who made the crucifix coin, and what it signifies.'

He raises an eyebrow. 'Okay, that will take care of tomorrow morning. What do you want me to do the rest of the day?'

'Very funny. It's good to keep busy.'

Silence settles. Prisha's thoughts, a moment ago sharp and searching, are hijacked again by emotion—shock and disbelief first, then the deeper wounds of rage, betrayal, and grief.

She tries to snap out of it.

'And how's Dinkel?'

Zac turns his mouth up. 'Tits on a bull. And talking of tits—he's getting on mine.'

'Don't be mean. He's not that bad.'

Zac raises an eyebrow. 'He's a dick. Today we were in town, following up on a break-and-entry that happened overnight. It was near lunchtime, so I sent him to the bakery. I told him to get me a sausage roll. He asked, what if they don't have any left? I replied, get me something else. Do you know what he came back with?'

'What?'

'A chocolate eclair. Numbskull. Faulty wiring. God plugged the yellow wire into the slot where the red was meant to go.'

Prisha chuckles. 'He's different, I'll give him that.'

There's a momentary lull in the conversation.

'Superintendent Banks dropped by today.'

'Oh, yes. And?'

'Wanted to know where you were. Frank said you were taking time off for your mental health. Banks wasn't happy. Got her phone out and was about to call you, but Frank stopped her. They had an argument, but he stood his ground. He shouted at her and called her a hard-nosed bitch.'

Prisha clasps a hand to her mouth. 'He didn't?'

'Gospel. She stomped off, and Frank stormed into his office and closed the blinds. I didn't see him for the rest of the day.' He tugs at his short-cropped beard. 'So, any idea when you'll be back?'

Her gaze is distant. 'Not sure.'

'How are you feeling?'

'Like crap.'

'Understandable. You still having those nightmares about the ravens in the field?'

She nods. 'Occasionally.'

'Has Adam...' He backtracks. 'Any contact?'

She shakes her head. 'No. I've blocked him on everything.'

'Good idea.'

Pushing back in her chair, she sighs. 'I'll have to go to the farm at some point. I've stuff there, clothes and what-not.'

'Leave them. It will be a painful reminder of what he's lost. Serve the *bastard* right.'

'No chance. There's a pair of Nike trainers that cost me three hundred quid, and a pair of Armani jeans worth a small fortune and fit me like a glove. And...' she pauses and nods at the windowsill. 'I want to return that.'

Zac stares at the engagement ring. 'Don't be daft. Get it on eBay. Silver and diamonds—could pay for an exotic holiday abroad.'

'No. I want to get my belongings, and hand the ring back. Draw a line in the sand. Otherwise, he has an excuse for getting in touch with me. Once that's done, I can close the book. Done and dusted.'

Zac checks his watch and makes a move.

'Got to go so soon?' Prisha asks, her face mask cracking slightly.

He winces. 'Afraid so,' he says, taking another slurp of tea. He rises slowly. 'Don't get up. I'll see myself out.' He pulls at the kitchen door, then stops and gazes at her. 'Prisha, I just want you to know...' His voice falters.

'Yes?'

'That... well... I'll be glad when you're back at work. See you soon.'

As the front door closes, the nausea returns, heavy, hollow, and tangled with tortured thoughts.

12

Thursday 26th June

Frank's jowls undulate like a bulldog chewing a toffee.

'Is that what she said?'

Zac is standing in front of Frank's desk. Outside, early morning sunlight skitters along the River Esk.

'Aye.'

'When did you speak to her?'

'Called round at her place last night on my way to pick up Sammy from five-a-side.'

'Hmm...' As he leans back in his long-suffering chair, it groans and creaks like it's ready to throw the towel in. 'I don't like it when investigations intersect. It all goes to pot.'

'That's my sentiment.'

'I understand Prisha's theory about them being friends a long time ago. But that's all it is—a theory.'

He swivels his chair to stare out of the window while he taps a pen on the desk.

'Having said that, her success rate is a lot higher than her failure rate. But on the other hand, if she thinks one of those four men were involved in the hit-and-run on Iona Jacobs, and that's why they're being bumped off, well... there's only one of the buggers left—Lord Hampton. And if he wasn't involved in Iona's death, then it's going to be nigh impossible to prove who the perpetrator was. Which means a lot of shoe leather and paperwork all to no avail, when we could have been focussing on the recent suspicious deaths.'

He rocks back and forth, pushing the chair's structural integrity to breaking point.

'What to do? Take a gamble and start from ground zero with Iona Jacobs, or stick with our hand, and keep the investigations separate?'

'Was that a rhetorical question, Frank?'

'Yes. But feel free to have your tuppence worth; every other bugger does.'

'I agree with you about becoming distracted, limited manpower, ongoing cases to contend with. It's like spinning plates. Eventually, no matter how good a plate-spinner you are, you'll end up with too many plates in the air. And something has to crash to the ground.'

'I can feel a gear shift into reverse coming.'

'We live and breathe this job every day, year in, year out. Despite our best intentions, we can become immune to the human cost. I got to thinking about Iona Jacobs. A young lass. Only twenty-two. Her life cut short because someone ran into her. It's a miracle her unborn baby survived. We know Iona's mother and daughter are living in Ashenby. That can't be easy for them—never finding the answer to what happened. I put myself in Lilac Penhallow's shoes for a moment, as a parent. How would I feel if something happened to one of my lads, and I never found out the how and why? It would eat away at me like a cancer.'

Zac abruptly stops as he recalls Frank's own never-ending nightmare—his daughter who went missing thirty years ago, never to be seen again.

Embarrassed and ashamed of his thoughtlessness, he reddens.

'Sorry, Frank. I wasn't thinking,' he mutters. 'I'm an idiot.'

Frank stares at him. Blinks. Sighs. 'I won't challenge you on your last sentence, but it's not your burden to carry, lad. That's mine and Meera's lot in life.' He brightens slightly. 'How is Prisha, by the way?'

'You know Prisha. She's built from armour plating... but...'

'What?'

'She's hurting.'

'Aye. Bones mend, wounds heal, but a broken heart is a lot more complex.'

He rises from his seat and puffs out his chest.

'No, you're right, Zac, sometimes we can lose sight of what our purpose is. We'll run both investigations side by side, with equal focus and man-hours devoted to both. That young lass deserves justice, as do her mother and child. If we can find out who knocked Iona off her bike, then maybe—and it's a big maybe—it could give us the clue to unravelling this whole sorry mess. By the way, when will you have the vehicle forensics report on the tractor and slasher?'

'I'm calling round there tomorrow afternoon.'

'Good. I assume the consensus amongst the villagers is that it was a freak accident, which might just curb the rumour mill.'

'It may turn out to be true.'

'Aye. And it may not. Right, you can bring Dinkel up to speed on everything on the way to Ashenby.'

'Ashenby?'

Grabbing his jacket from the hatstand, he slips it on.

'Yes, no time like the present. Round Dinkel up. I want some background on Iona Jacobs. We'll have a quick recap, then you, me, and Dinkel will take a drive out to the scene of the crime. Get a feel for it.'

He hesitates and battles with an unwelcome thought.

'Afterwards, I better pay a visit to Lilac Penhallow and inform her we've reopened the case. Not looking forward to that. I might also drop in on Lord Hampton while I'm out that way.'

'What for?' Zac asks, puzzled.

'I made notes of his eulogy at the funeral. Want to quiz him about a few things he said. Okay, look lively. We can't sit around here all day with our thumbs up our backsides.'

Zac grins. 'Righto, Frank. Now you're talking.'

Dinkel populates the interactive whiteboard like a geek on amphetamine, clearly excited.

'He's good, isn't he?' Frank says with a chuckle.

Zac stretches out in his chair and begrudgingly nods. 'With tech stuff.'

Dinkel taps the faded colour photograph on the board with a ruler. It shows an attractive young woman with strawberry blonde curls and a playful smile, her face fresh with the kind of glow that hasn't yet savoured disappointment. She wears a stonewashed denim jacket over a baggy white T-shirt, a slogan—CHOOSE LIFE—emblazoned across the chest. Matching stonewashed denim jeans ride above white socks scrunched around her ankles and scuffed trainers that hint at long walks and longer nights. Her jacket collar is turned up just so, and a pair of medium-sized silver hoop earrings catch the light—simple, yet bold. She radiates an aura of carefree charm and the vitality of youth, yet tinged with just enough rebellion to worry a mother.

'Bonny looking lass,' Frank says, sighing.

Dinkel frowns. 'Not sure what the slogan means. Maybe she was an anti-abortionist.'

'Wham!' Frank states.

'Sorry, sir?'

'It was a pop duo from the eighties. George Michael and Andrew... somebody. The T-shirt represented an attitude. Pro-peace, anti-suicide, youthful optimism.'

Dinkel remains stubbornly confused.

'You must have heard the song, *Wake Me Up Before You Go-Go*?'

'Can't say I have, sir.'

Zac grimaces. 'For Dinkel, anything before the millennium's a blank book in a forgotten library.'

Dinkel rises to the bait. 'That's not true! I...'

'Get on with it,' Zac growls. 'I can feel myself ageing.'

Dinkel shuffles. 'Right, Iona Jacobs was born in 1967. Only child of Mrs Lilac Jacobs. Mr Jacobs passed away when Iona was ten. In 1994, Mrs Jacobs reverted to her maiden name, Penhallow. Iona was raised, interestingly enough, on the tiny island of Iona in the Inner Hebrides, off the southwest coast of Scotland.

'According to Lilac's statements, Iona left home aged nineteen. Apparently, she was a good singer and intended to move to London to find fame and fortune. Her mother said she had a rebellious streak.'

'I take it she never made it to London?' Frank queries.

'No. She worked on reception at the Grand Hotel in Scarborough for eighteen months before moving to Ashenby.'

Zac shakes his head. 'You couldn't get two more polar opposite places than London and Ashenby.'

Dinkel swipes the board with two fingers, and a row of postcards fills the screen.

'Here we have postcards from Scarborough, Whitby, Staithes, Robin Hood's Bay, and some of Wensleydale, all sent from Iona to her mother. Nothing untoward in them. In fact, they're quite cheery and optimistic.'

Frank shifts his weight. 'Do we know why she moved to Ashenby?'

'Yes, according to Lilac, she was offered a job at Ravensbane Castle as a maid. The money was a little better and the cost of accommodation a lot cheaper. She lasted about six months at the castle before working as a barmaid and assistant cook at The Crown, where she also lodged. The landlord at the time was one Colin Featherstone.'

Zac raises his eyebrows. 'Interesting. Current landlord is Edwin Featherstone. Possibly related.'

'And the scene of the crash?' Frank asks.

Dinkel nods. 'Ashenby Lane which runs south to north. She was about two miles from the village. Cycling in a northerly direction, according to witness testimony.'

'Okay, move on,' Frank commands.

A new screen flashes up, full of neatly typed bullet points.

'Sunday, 4th June 1989. Iona finished her shift at the pub at 2 pm. At 2:15 pm she cycled the short distance from the pub to St Mary's Church at the other end of the village. There she chatted with Reverend Nicholas Hartley for about twenty minutes, according to him.'

Zac pulls out his notepad. 'And this chat with Hartley, what was it about?'

'Nothing of any note. Idle gossip about some of the villagers. The unusually warm weather. According to Hartley, he said Iona was heading back to the pub by the scenic route, Ashenby Lane. The only slightly incongruous fact is that Iona had recently started attending church, which is C of E. But Iona's mother, Lilac, said Iona wasn't into organised religion at all. She was more in tune with the "old ways", as she put it.'

'Interesting,' Frank mutters.

'Iona left the church at approximately 2:45 pm.'

'Any witnesses apart from Hartley?'

'Only one, sir. Carl Lawrence, aged nineteen at the time. He drove a red Mini Cooper and said he saw—what he assumed was Iona—heading off down Ashenby Lane round about the same time. Apparently, she went everywhere on her bike, so the locals were used to seeing her come and go.'

'And is this Carl Lawrence still alive?'

Dinkel reddens. 'I haven't got around to checking if the witnesses are still alive yet, sir.'

'That's okay. Carry on.'

'That was the last sighting of Iona until a 999 call was made reporting an accident on Ashenby Lane. Details are scant, only that it involved a young woman on a bicycle. The caller was Malachi Abbott.'

'Time?'

'About 4 pm.'

Frank turns to Zac. 'You and Prisha have spent quite a bit of time in that neck of the woods recently. How long is Ashenby Lane?'

Zac sucks in air. 'Maybe three miles, four at a push. Narrow single road. It's flanked on one side by Ravensbane Woods, and on the other by wheat fields. Quiet, isolated, low-traffic use.'

Frank squints at the board. 'Any forensics, Dinkel?'

'The only thing documented was a few flakes of white paint near the crash site. Potentially, they came from the vehicle.'

'Did they run lab tests on the paint to determine what make and model it came from?'

Dinkel taps the board, and a scanned image pops onto the screen.

'They did, but as you can see, the scan is illegible.'

'Damn it,' Zac curses. 'You'll need to find the original document. And this is a major unsolved crime, so the paint flakes should still exist—somewhere.'

Dinkel winces. 'In theory... yes. But so far my attempts at locating the physical evidence have been fruitless.'

Frank huffs, rising to his feet. 'Right, we're going for a little day trip to Ashenby, the site of the hit-and-run. Zac, afterwards, you and Dinkel have a chat with the landlord, Edwin Featherstone. See if he has a contact for the landlord from '89. And Dinkel, when you get back to the station, identify every person who gave a witness statement and find out if they're still living, and compos mentis. Then we'll pay them a visit. Oh, who was the lead investigating officer?'

'DS Raymond Strickland.'

'Was he indeed?' Frank says with an element of surprise. 'Old X-Ray. Well, well.'

'You know him, sir?'

'Indeed I do. He's a good ten years older than me, but our paths did cross on occasion.'

'Why did you call him X-Ray?'

'Because he was as blind as a bat without his glasses.'

'Is he still alive?'

'Very much so. I see him occasionally on the golf course. I don't think he recognises me, but I never forget a face.'

Dinkel's eyebrows twitch. 'I didn't realise you played golf, sir?'

Zac grins. 'He doesn't. The beer garden at the back of the White House pub backs onto the golf course.'

Frank throws him a disparaging glance. 'X-Ray's a member of the Whitby Golf Club. I'll make a mental note to catch up with him.'

Zac rises and walks towards the board. 'Dinkel, you said Iona left the pub at 2:15 pm. How do we know that?'

Dinkel taps the board, and two handwritten witness statements materialise.

'Howard Price and Mark Hardaker. Aged eighteen in 1989. They left the pub at the same time as Iona. They were driving a Ford Fiesta, and tooted to Iona as they left. She waved. They confirmed the time.'

'And do we know the colour of their Ford Fiesta?'

Dinkel hurries to his desk, sends an empty mug clattering to the floor, and grabs a manila file with both hands, flipping through it like he's lost something vital.

'I haven't managed to get everything onto the whiteboard yet. It's a work in progress.'

'That's all right,' Zac replies, checking his watch and tapping his foot against the grubby carpet.

'There was a note somewhere about it.'

'No rush, Dinkel. I've got nothing better to do.'

He brandishes a sheet of paper as though holding Excalibur. 'Aha! Here it is.'

Zac is unimpressed. 'Top work. The colour of the Ford Fiesta belonging to the lads?' he reiterates, the annoyance in his inflection evident.

Dinkel speed-reads the document, then gawps at Zac.

'Well?' Zac bellows.

'The car... the car was white.'

'Well, what a surprise.'

13

Sunlight sneaks through the tangled canopy of birch and oak trees, painting the bitumen in fleeting streamers of watery gold. In the opposite field, young wheat canoodles with an amorous breeze, teasing a bumper harvest.

Insects hum.

Birds trill sweet melodies.

Peace and tranquillity take brief refuge beneath the English summer sun.

It could almost be 1989, when Iona Jacobs pedalled this very lane, at this same time of year.

The three officers exit the cars, Dinkel madly flicking through his folder.

Pulling a photograph out, he hands it to Frank.

'I think this is the spot, sir. No coordinates, but if you look at the photograph, this is where there's a sharp bend in the road. The stone wall demarcating the edge of the woods looks exactly the same. And even this tree here looks familiar, although obviously a lot larger.'

Frank pauses, reflective. 'Hang on, constable. Let's catch our breath. We're near the site of where a lovely young woman lost her life—not instantly, but this was her battlefield where she fell. Let's take a moment to remember her.'

All three fall silent, absorbing not just the smells and sounds of the place, but something deeper, something intangible. As if the spirit of Iona Jacobs lingers here still, watching, waiting for someone—*anyone*—to care enough to untangle the knot.

The silence stretches.

Frank closes his eyes as a sense of melancholy floods him until he almost drowns in the sad, sweet emotion. He mutters something the other two don't catch.

He breaks the painful daydream with a sharp intake of breath and a shake of the head. Lowering the photo, he scans the bend in the road, the wall, the stretch of tarmac where a young woman's destiny was snatched from her.

'Aye, I think we're in the right spot, Dinkel.'

Zac peers over Frank's shoulder then performs a slow three-sixty of the area.

'And look, Frank, the ditch where Iona was found is still here,' he says, edging to the side of the road.

Frank and Dinkel follow him.

'You're right. A man-made culvert to allow water to run-off on the corner. Crude but effective if designed correctly.' He peers at the photograph again, then looks up.

'And I reckon, straight ahead, maybe a few feet away is where the photographer would have been standing when he took this shot.'

Zac takes a few steps back. 'So the bike was lying about here,' he states, pointing at a spot in the road before spinning sideways. 'And Iona would have been in the ditch about...' another step to his left, '...here.'

Frank nods. 'Okay, Dinkel, what does the crash scene report say?'

Dinkel shuffles as if embarrassed. 'Erm, it's... how can I put it without sounding offensive?'

'You're with friends now, lad. No one's going to take offence. What does it say?'

'Not a lot, sir. Bike found on the road. Young female found unresponsive in nearby ditch. Suspected hit-and-run by a motor vehicle.'

'Tyre marks?'

'No mention, sir.'

'What direction did they assume the vehicle was travelling from—behind or in front of Iona?'

He winces. 'It doesn't specify.'

Zac frowns. 'Christ, Frank, you were around in the eighties. Were you always so thorough?'

Frank throws him a steely gaze. 'The force was in a state of flux, moving from the old ways to the new ways. Some officers were reluctant to leave the tried and trusted methods behind. Crime scenes weren't as forensically challenged as they are today. And remember, we had none of the modern technology. But I agree. If Dinkel has the full report, then it's shoddy at best, negligent at worst. But at least we still have some photos to go on. If we put our collective noggins together, maybe we can figure out which way the vehicle was heading when it hit Iona.'

He deliberates over the narrow single-lane road again.

'From where we're standing, the road runs south to north. We're approximately two miles from Ashenby to our south. Another two miles north, up the road, and there's a T-junction. Bearing left takes you towards Ravensbane Castle, Lord Hampton's abode. Turning right, takes you in a long three-mile arc back to Ashenby and the pub. So, whoever was driving the vehicle either came from Ashenby, north or south, or came from the Ravensbane Castle end. Agreed?'

Zac nods his admiration. 'Nice deduction. Glad to see you're not ready for liquid food just yet.'

Frank harrumphs. 'Dinkel, hand the rest of the photos around. Let's see if there are any clues as to which way the vehicle was travelling.'

All three study the photos.

The crumpled bicycle and broken wicker basket. The shots of the road, north and south. The adjoining wood, and opposite, the wheat field.

Frank grunts. 'That's an old-fashioned bike she was riding. No gears,' he notes.

Zac scratches his head. 'Here, Frank, take a look,' he says, pointing at an image.

'What?'

'You see the small marks on the road, like little marbles? They're scattered all around.'

Frank adjusts his spectacles.

'Aye, and they appear to be reddish in colour, but the photos are too bloody grainy and out of focus see what they are.'

'Could they be berries from the trees?' Dinkel suggests.

Frank stares up at the overhanging foliage. 'No. Oak trees drop acorns, but not early June. Birch trees don't bear fruit or nuts—just flowers, called catkins. They look a bit like miniature corn-on-the-cob.'

Zac squints closer at the photo. 'So what are they?'

Frank strokes his chin and ponders. 'Early June is too early for blackberries or raspberries,' he murmurs. Becoming distracted, he tilts his head back and sniffs the air. 'That aroma. Smell it?'

Zac and Dinkel inhale in short, rapid breaths.

'I can smell woodland, sir.'

'No, not that. Something far more alluring.'

Zac checks his watch. 'It has just gone eleven, Frank. The pubs will be open. You sure it's not the whiff of beer drifting your way?'

'Most amusing, sergeant.'

His eye catches something in the grassy undergrowth. He edges forward and crouches.

'Well, I'll be buggered,' he chuckles.

'What?'

Rising, he offers the fruit to Zac. 'She stopped to pick wild strawberries.'

'Here's to you, Iona,' Zac states, popping the fruit into his mouth. 'Hell, that's the sweetest strawberry I've ever tasted.'

Frank's gaze returns to the photo. 'Iona was riding south to north according to witness testimony. The strawberries are scattered behind the bike, which means...'

Dinkel jumps in. 'The vehicle was travelling from the north,' he says, pointing up the road. 'It hit the bike, and the force of the impact sent the strawberries behind, back southwards, towards Ashenby.'

'Precisely,' Frank says, bearing a modest grin. 'Now we're getting somewhere, even if it is thirty-six years overdue. Right, I best go see Lilac Penhallow and inform her we've reopened the case into her daughter's death.'

Zac stares back down the road. 'Hey, Frank, guess who lived less than a mile from here, on the same road? In fact, Iona would have cycled right past his place.'

'Who?'

'Malachi Abbott.'

14

Zac parks up outside The Crown.

'Why are we here again?' Dinkel asks.

'I want another chat with the landlord, Edwin Featherstone.'

They step out of the vehicle and take a moment to enjoy the warmth of the sun.

'And you, Dinkel, my little badger baiter, are going on a bike ride.'

'I am?'

'Yes. You are.'

'Where to?'

Zac wonders if Dinkel will ever get with the programme.

'You'll set off from here and cycle to St Mary's Church. From there, take Ashenby Lane and ride to the spot where Iona was found. Now, remember she was riding an old-fashioned bike without gears. So don't go tearing along like you're wearing the yellow jersey in the Tour de France. A nice sedate speed. Time each section, then I'll meet you at the village green in about an hour.'

Dinkel ruminates. 'Right. One slight problem.'

'What?'

'I don't have a bike?'

Zac saunters towards the pub. 'Initiative, Dinks, initiative. Beg, borrow or steal. I'm sure you'll find a way. Then again...' he adds under his breath as he enters the subdued lighting of the pub.

He looks around.

A couple of hikers are ensconced in a corner nursing half-pints and a packet of crisps. Last of the big spenders.

An elderly man is in a nook, nose inside the Racing Guide.

A young man from the Wicca quickly finishes his pint, and nods at Zac as he leaves.

'It's all go in here,' Zac murmurs as he approaches the bar.

The landlord, Edwin Featherstone, appears, sporting a blank expression.

'Back again, sergeant?'

'Looks like it.'

'Coffee?'

'Nah. Give me a pint of bitter shandy.'

'Coming right up.'

He pulls a pint glass from the shelf, half fills it with lemonade, then lines it up under the beer pump.

'Was that Birch from the Wicca commune?' Zac asks as he watches the tall spindly man stride rapidly up the street towards the heart of the village, head down, hands stuffed into pockets.

'Aye.'

'A regular, is he?'

'Semi-regular.' The landlord emits a deep sigh. 'It's a shock about Amos Baker. Any news?'

'Still investigating.'

'A terrible accident. He was always grizzling about his tractor playing up. Don't know why he didn't bite the bullet and buy a new one. He had the brass.'

'So, how long have you been a landlord?'

'Too bloody long.'

'The excitement too much for you?'

'Very funny. If it weren't for the passing tourist trade, I'd have shut up shop years ago.'

'I thought the local pub was the nerve-centre of a village.'

'It was, in the good old days. The locals were your bread and butter. Day-trippers—icing on the cake. I remember when this place was heaving every night. Now, half the houses in the village are second homes for city slickers. The young 'uns from the village move out as soon as they can. No one wants to go into farming these days. And the older generation, well, there's this thing called death that keeps paying a visit.'

'Aye, the Grim Reaper has been putting in a bit of overtime round these parts lately.'

Featherstone places the pint on the bar. 'That's four pounds, please.'

Zac hands over a fiver and pockets the change. He takes a long, steady draught of shandy, then smacks his lips together with quiet satisfaction.

'Very refreshing. So, Colin Featherstone—any relation of yours?'

The landlord's eyes narrow. 'Maybe. Why you ask?'

'A cold case we're reviewing. Colin was the landlord in 1989.'

'He's my dad.'

'Still alive?'

'No, he passed on ten years back.'

'Sorry to hear that.'

'What's this cold case?' he asks, rubbing the counter down with a grubby tea towel.

'A hit-and-run on Ashenby Lane. Young lass called Iona Jacobs was left in a coma. They eventually switched off her life support. Remember her?'

Featherstone's demeanour shifts to that of a man who's been informed he needs a root canal—without anaesthetic.

'I do. Vividly. I was only about fourteen at the time, but she lodged in one of the upstairs rooms. Worked behind the bar and helped in the kitchen.'

'What do you recall?' Zac asks, pulling out his notebook.

Featherstone puffs out his cheeks and then releases the air in a slow hiss.

'Traumatic is the word that comes to mind. Iona was a special girl... woman. My mam and dad thought she was smashing. She wasn't with us long. Maybe a few months, but she fitted right in. Same sense of humour. Hard worker. Didn't mind mucking in when asked. I got to know her especially well. Her bedroom was across the hallway from mine.' He averts his eyes slightly embarrassed. 'I wasn't doing very well at school at the time. You know, getting bullied. Well, Iona was like a big sister to me. She taught me how to stick up for myself, not just with my fists, but with witty comebacks. Said the pen is mightier than the sword, and that bruises fade but words live on forever. I didn't really understand what she meant at the time, but now I do.'

He almost tears up.

'You formed a close bond,' Zac notes gently.

'Aye, that we did.' He sniffs and straightens. 'So, this cold case, any breakthroughs?'

Zac takes another gulp from his pint and shakes his head.

'Early days. Just acquainting myself with the facts.'

His reply is economical with the truth.

'I doubt you'll catch the bugger responsible now. Probably long dead.'

'I know you were only young at the time, but there must have been plenty of theories swirling around the village?'

Featherstone tilts his head. 'At first, everyone was in a right tizz. Casting aspersions. There were a couple of lads in the village who were boy racers. You know, knackered old cars held together with Hammerite and fibreglass. Go-faster stripes down the side. They used to whizz up dale and down dale. The finger was pointed at them... at first.'

'You recall their names and the cars they drove?'

'Yeah, Howard Price owned a Ford Fiesta, and Carl Lawrence drove a red Mini Cooper. But they had watertight alibis.'

'So, with them cleared of any involvement, I assume the village gossip would have moved onto someone else?'

'Yes, a few locals began inferring—no, *insisting*—it was an outsider, a day-tripper, a tourist. They became quite vocal and had a bit of status around here. Eventually, it became like an acknowledged truth. You know, like if something's repeated enough times by enough people, it becomes a fact.'

Zac finishes the rest of his pint. 'Aye. Today it's called social media. And who were these locals?'

Featherstone gazes around the near-empty pub, leans forward, and lowers his voice.

'Uncanny, really. Three of the buggers are recently dead. And the other one lives in a bloody great big castle up the road.'

15

Zac is loitering by the village green, takeaway coffee in hand, enjoying the rare treat of Yorkshire sunshine—until a sudden shouting match across the road spoils the relaxed ambience.

At first, he tries to ignore it, his eyes fixed on the bakery's window and its many enticements. As the voices rise, so does his curiosity.

He crosses the road, drawn by the escalating racket.

Dinkel is shrinking under a full-volume bollocking from a woman in her early thirties—stout, packed into skin-tight activewear that does her no favours, tattoos etched up her forearms, and a stud twinkling in one nostril like a warning light. Next to her, a young lad props up a small BMX bike, looking like he wishes he had a different mother.

'You should know bloody better at your age!' the woman shrieks in Dinkel's face.

'But I've explained. I'm a police officer.'

'I don't care if you're the Lord *fucking* Mayor of Leeds. You had no right.'

'But I paid him.'

'Like bloody hell you did.' She turns aggressively to her son. 'Jamie, did the man pay you?'

The boy shakes his head.

The woman fumes. 'See? That bike cost my hubby and me a small fortune.'

'I haven't damaged it,' Dinkel replies, apologetic, embarrassed, and sweating profusely.

Zac slips his smirk away and marches into battle.

'Is there a problem here, madam?' he demands in his deep Scottish brogue, projecting authority.

The woman stops haranguing Dinkel and stares up at Zac.

'Yes, there's a problem here! This half-witted numpty stole my lad's bike and went on a joyride.'

Dinkel pleads his case. 'That's not true! I entered into a contractual agreement with the boy. I paid him ten pounds.'

The woman takes a step forward, sizing Zac up.

'Anyway, what business is it of yours?'

Zac pulls out his warrant card.

'Detective Sergeant Stoker. North Yorkshire Police. Power to arrest *and* charge.'

The woman visibly shrinks. 'You need to arrest this man.'

'That's not going to happen, love. You see, he's one of mine.'

'That's police corruption.'

Zac smiles. 'Aye, quite possibly. We all have our tribes though, don't we? But I'm a reasonable man. So let me work this out so we can all walk away from this situation with everyone happy.'

He focuses on the lad.

'Jamie, did my colleague pay you ten pounds?'

The boy shakes his head and mumbles, 'No.'

Voice hardens. 'Empty your pockets. *Now!*'

The boy, taking as much time as he can, pulls the linings out of his trouser pockets, and scrunches a fist around something.

'Open your hand,' Zac demands.

The lad's fingers slowly uncurl to reveal a ten-pound note.

The mother's face reddens as she contains her anger. 'Oh, you little...'

'See?' Dinkel yells.

The previously mute boy becomes suddenly vocal and animated.

'You said you wanted the bike for half an hour, tops. It's nearly an hour you've had it. That's why I rang me mam. I thought you'd nicked it.'

Zac instantly deduces the truth of the situation.

'I see. I'd say that was a breach of the commercial agreement you entered into, wouldn't you, Jamie?'

The boy and mother nod enthusiastically.

'Yep. Defo,' Jamie replies.

Zac turns to Dinkel. 'Okay, constable. Ten pounds for thirty minutes—pro rata—twenty pounds for an hour. Wallet out, sunshine.'

'But—'

'Shut it.'

Dinkel reluctantly peels off a crisp tenner from his wallet and hands it to the lad, but the mother is quicker, and like a cobra's strike, she snatches the note from Dinkel's hand.

Zac, pleased with his work, ends the situation.

'Right, everyone happy?'

'I suppose so,' the mother says, swiftly magicking away the money into one of her many tight pockets. 'Come on, Jamie, you lying little shit.'

She gives the lad a clip around the top of the head for good measure—not hard, but enough to feel it.

Zac scowls. 'If you hit your child like that in Scotland or Wales, you could be charged under the equal protection law. There's no such thing as reasonable chastisement anymore—it's classified as assault.'

The woman turns. 'Good job I don't live in *fucking* Scotland or Wales then, isn't it?'

As she storms away, Jamie jumps on his BMX, throws a parting glance over his shoulder, and shouts at Dinkel.

'Loser! You ride like my gran—and she's dead. Nonce, paedo, wanker!'

The officers allow themselves a few seconds contemplation, not unaccustomed to the slurs.

Zac winces. 'Hmm... usual shite. One day, maybe, they'll come up with a new insult. Then again, they're not known for their sparkling repartee.'

Dinkel takes a deep breath. 'Thank God that nightmare's over.'

'I think you got away lightly there, Dinks, my old chestnut peeler.' He drags his gaze away from the retreating mother and son, and back onto Dinkel. 'Why are you so sweaty?'

'Why do *you* bloody think?' Dinkel retorts angrily. 'I rode a child's bike three miles there and three miles back. My knees were just about touching my ears. It's nudging thirty degrees. And then I get accosted by a chav and her lying, conniving sprog. Oh, and I'm twenty quid out of pocket.'

He pulls a hanky out and dabs at his face. 'How do you do it?'

Zac frowns. 'Do what?'

'Deal with the public... the flotsam and jetsam of life. They're just so... repulsive, argumentative, nasty.'

Zac sighs. 'First thing is, the majority of the public are law-abiding citizens. It's only the ten per cent that spoils the barrel. Secondly, Frank taught me a long time ago, never to be cowed by anyone, or any situation. And his most important lesson—let them know who's boss. That woman there—she's on benefits. Knows every trick in the book. And so do I—and she knows that. Fuck with me, I fuck with her. I can pull her into the interview room and get all her details—name, address, the lot. And I'll let her know I'll be passing it on to the benefits office, and maybe making an unexpected visit to her home, anytime of day or night. No doubt she has a loser boyfriend or husband who's into the smack or meth. Result for her... a world of pain. If they wanna throw a bucket of shit over me, then I let them know I'm gonna throw a bucket of shit right back over them. And my bucket is way bigger than theirs.'

'How do you know she's on benefits?'

'I can smell it.'

'You mean lit...'

'No, not literally,' he snaps, before reflecting. 'Although yes, sometimes.'

'But a lot of people on benefits are in genuine need.'

'Very true. And I have no axe to grind with them. But there are those who milk the system. Those who think it's a game to beat. You need to read your history, Dinks, and learn how the welfare system was created. It was intended as a temporary safety net to stop people falling into poverty. It was never meant to be a lifestyle option.'

'Maybe she's just fallen through the cracks.'

'More likely on crack,' he notes. 'But if you go down that route, then you take free will out of the equation.'

'What do you mean?'

'People *know* right from wrong. They decide which path to follow—that's called free will. Me, I don't give a shite about the bad eggs. I'm here to defend the good eggs. That way you make a better omelette.'

Dinkel ponders for a moment. 'And the omelette is... society?'

'Correct.'

Dinkel's unsettled. 'I'm not sure I'm cut out for…'

'Of course you are. You're just in your apprenticeship. Any more questions?'

'No.'

Zac can't help but smirk. 'I have one—how long did it take you to cycle to the site of the hit-and-run?'

Dinkel heaves a sigh of weary relief. 'Eighteen minutes.'

'Good. Then a job well done. Today, we've made progress. It's called detective work, Dinks, and don't you forget it.'

'No, I don't think I ever will.'

16

Lady Abigail Hampton is less than enamoured to see Frank standing on the doorstep.

'Chief Inspector Finnegan,' she says wearily, her face registering disapproval. 'What can I do for you?'

'I was in the vicinity and thought I'd have a quick word with your husband, if he's home.'

She's not immaculately dressed for once: a baggy jumper, well-worn jeans, and slip-on worker's boots replace her usual polish.

His appraisal doesn't go unnoticed.

'You'll have to excuse my attire, inspector. I'm in the middle of gardening.'

She opens the door wider and glances down the extravagant hallway.

'He's in his study,' she says, closing the door and marching briskly ahead, leading the way. 'What is it this time? Haven't you hounded him enough?'

Frank needs to walk a tight line. 'Lady Hampton, you may call it hounding, but we are merely performing our duties.

If you haven't noticed, there has been a spate of suspicious deaths recently.'

She peers over her shoulder.

'Malachi Abbott and Reverend Hartley—yes, I'm aware. I saw you at Hartley's funeral on Tuesday.'

Sharp as ever, it takes her only a moment to reassess Frank's angle.

'Wait... the local farmer—Mr Baker—you don't think that was suspicious?'

He trots out the well-worn line that's both shield and sword, depending on who's asking.

'All deaths are treated as suspicious until proved otherwise.'

'I heard it was a tragic farming accident.'

'And it probably was. Still, Ashenby is a quiet village. The last suspicious death around here was back in 1989. A young woman by the name of Iona Jacobs. Knocked off her bicycle in a hit-and-run. Never recovered consciousness.'

His bait doesn't get a bite.

'Long before my time.'

'You've never heard of her?' Frank presses, struggling to keep pace with Lady Hampton's brisk stride.

'Should I have?' she replies curtly, turning left past a row of ancient oil paintings featuring grumpy old men in long wigs and ermine-trimmed robes, clutching swords or ceremonial sceptres.

Frank averts disaster as he sidesteps a huge Grecian vase.

'She was employed here at Ravensbane for a while. As a maid. But as you said, long before your time.'

Pushing open the study door, she holds her arm out, gesturing him inside.

'Tea, inspector, or is this a flying visit?'

Frank licks his lips. 'Actually, I could murder a nice cuppa. White, one sugar.'

She raises one eyebrow at his turn of phrase. 'Biscuits or cake?'

'That's very kind of you, Lady Hampton. Whatever suits.'

Lady Hampton presses the intercom button on the wall.

'Magdalena, are you there?'

'Yes, madame,' replies a female voice with a soft Eastern European accent.

Lady Hampton tuts and shakes her head. 'It's ma'am, not madame. How many times must I tell you? I'm a baroness—not the maître d' of a brothel.'

'My apologies, Lady Hampton. How can I help?'

'Tea and cake for two. And bring a fresh bottle of spring water and a clean glass for his Lordship.'

'Cake?' replies the bewildered voice.

'Yes cake! Ciasto.'

'Ah, ciasto.'

She purses her lips as she points Frank towards the fireplace.

'Just can't get the staff these days, inspector. The country's gone to rack and ruin.'

'Yes, it must be galling for you,' Frank replies so drily it floats over Abigail Hampton's head.

He takes a seat on the couch adjacent to Lord Hampton, who is resting in his favourite armchair next to the hearth with a blanket around him despite the warmth of the day.

Lord Hampton barely looks up.

'My husband has been unwell of late, inspector, so please don't outstay your welcome.'

Frank leans forward, studying him. 'Oh, I'm sorry to hear that. What ails you, Lord Hampton?'

Hampton finally shifts his bleary gaze onto Frank.

'Not sure. And neither are the damned quacks. Useless, the bloody lot of them.'

'Noah,' his wife scolds. 'Doctor Julian Brant is the finest physician in the North of England.'

'It doesn't say a lot for the rest of the buggers, does it? Overpriced charlatans. They pretend to know what they're doing, hiding behind a smokescreen of science. But when it comes down to it, they're no better than the old shamans and charmers from Pagan times, peddling their leeches.'

'What are your symptoms?' Frank enquires.

Hampton glares at him. 'Why—are you a bloody doctor now as well as a detective?'

Frank chuckles. 'No. I'm not.'

Hampton sighs and leans back in his chair. 'Always got a damned thirst, but only for water. The thought of anything else makes me dry retch. And as for food... forget it. I have a tingling in my fingers, and my lips feel numb. And I'm continually exhausted.'

Frank notices the blue hue of the lips and shoots a concerned glance at Lady Hampton.

'They've done all the blood tests, inspector. And of course, my husband, being the stubborn old goat that he is, refuses to go to hospital.'

'If they don't know what's wrong with me here, then being in hospital's not going to make any difference,' he grizzles.

'They've no idea?' Frank quizzes.

Lady Hampton sighs. 'Not really. They're leaning towards a heart condition. He has low blood pressure, chest pains, dizziness, and stomach cramps.'

'I know what it is,' Lord Hampton declares. 'It's the big C. Terminal. My time is up. We all have a sell-by date.'

'Oh, stop being melodramatic, Noah.'

A knock on the door interrupts their bickering.

'Enter.'

Magdalena bustles in carrying a tray and places it on a small coffee table in front of the fireplace. She picks up the bottled water to fill the glass but is sharply rebuked.

'That's all, Magdalena.'

'Very good, ma'am,' she replies meekly with a half-hearted attempt at a curtsy.

Lady Hampton stares at the offerings on the tray and clicks her fingers twice—a crisp, imperious snap meant to summon obedience.

'Wait! What is that?' she demands, pointing at the plate of food.

Magdalena takes a step forward. 'Ciasto. Cake, madame.'

'It looks more like quiche.'

'Yes, quiche, ciasto. It is sausage, cabbage, and onion in a pastry.'

'For the love of blood and money,' she mutters under her breath. 'Go on, get out, just go.' She shoos the maid away in an agitated manner.

'Madame.'

Frank leans forward and picks up a slice and takes a bite, pastry crumbs dropping to the floor. He savours the food like a connoisseur.

'It's good, very good indeed.'

Lord Hampton awkwardly adjusts himself in his seat. 'You're too harsh with the staff, Abigail. You need to treat them like children. A little patience, understanding, and, dare I say, kindness, goes a long way.'

Lady Hampton quickly pours herself a cup of tea then picks up a pair of gardening gloves from the shelf.

'Balderdash. They're paid staff. They do as they're told; otherwise, they know where the door is.' She glances at Frank. 'I'll let you pour your own tea, inspector. I'm in the middle of tending my greenhouse. It's my only sanctuary away from this madhouse.'

'Very good.'

Striding towards the French windows and terrace, she fires off one last barb.

'And remember what I said—not too long. I don't want my husband overdoing it in his condition.'

'Ten minutes max, Lady Hampton.'

There's a brief pause as Frank fills his teacup from the pot, adds milk and sugar, then takes a genteel sip, his thick finger struggling to slip through the handle.

'She's always been hard work,' Lord Hampton chunters, with a weary sigh. 'Highly strung. I think if we'd had children, it may have softened her.' He turns to Frank. 'So, inspector, why the visit? I'm sure you're not here solely for the tea and Polish cuisine.'

Frank places the teacup on the tray and clears his throat.

'Ahem, no, I'm not. I'm glad your wife's gone. Makes it easier to talk openly.'

'Well then, you best start talking.'

'It's come to my attention that many moons ago, yourself, Amos Baker, Reverend Hartley, and your gamekeeper, Malachi Abbott were all good friends. *Very* good friends.'

'It's not a secret. What of it?'

'But those friendships didn't last, did they?'

Hampton heaves and licks his lips as if in pain. 'We were friends in our twenties. Long time ago, inspector. We drifted apart. There's no smoking gun, no hidden mystery. Are you still friends with acquaintances from your twenties?'

Frank nods and puckers his lips. 'No. Fair point. But it can't have passed you by that three out of the four are now dead.'

'So what? We're old men. People die.'

'You're hardly ancient, Lord Hampton. What are you—sixty-seven?'

Hampton chuckles. 'I'm well into the death zone.'

'Sorry?'

'The death zone, inspector. Surely you've heard of it? Once men pass the age of sixty, their chances of death rise exponentially, year on year. There's been many studies highlighting the fact.'

'No, I wasn't aware of the term. That's cheered me right up. I turned sixty last year. '

'My condolences, inspector. My sage advice would be to put your affairs in order sooner rather than later.'

Frank frowns and finishes the remaining Polish pastry. 'Anyway, my point is...'

'I know what your point is. You think because I used to be good friends with the three deceased, then I'm next on the list. As far as I'm aware, Malachi's death is the only one that's suspicious. Hartley took his own life, and Amos Baker's was a farming mishap.'

Frank stares at him askance. 'Lord Hampton, it's barely six weeks ago since you were abducted and imprisoned in a disused mineshaft. You may have been the first of the four men targeted.'

Hampton omits a throaty laugh that obviously pains him. 'The Glorious Twelfth, inspector.'

'What?'

'We breed red grouse on the estate. Come the twelfth of August, the grouse shooting season begins. It's a big money-earner for the estate. Animal rights activists have made many attempts over the years to sabotage our business. This year they assumed that a little fright might make me reconsider our endeavours.'

Frank's scepticism is obvious. 'Hang on, you've never mentioned any of this before. Are you saying you've had death threats in the past?'

'No, I haven't. But sabotage, yes. This year they went a step further.'

'You think the people who abducted you were part of some animal rights mob?'

'Yes. It makes perfect sense now. They never intended to kill me. It was a warning shot across the bows. What other reason would they have for leaving me in a mineshaft with two bottles of water? It was obviously meant to frighten and intimidate me. Leave me there for a few days to reflect on the error of my ways. I assume they'd have returned at the weekend to release me. There's no other explanation for it. However, I'm not a man who is ever intimidated or cowed by threats, however extreme.'

'And why only mention this now?'

'Because of my illness, I've spent a lot of time thinking. Not much else I can do. And it's the only logical reason. And if you missed my earlier comment—I *do* believe I'm dying. Damn what my wife or the doctor thinks. My time is up. No one's fault, and I'm going to make sure I die here at Ravensbane Castle, my ancestral home, not in some soulless, noisy, dysfunctional hospital.'

Frank sips his tea and changes tack. 'The eulogy you gave the other day was very touching.'

'Thank you.'

'If a little cryptic.'

'It wasn't meant to be.'

'Wasn't it?'

'No. What part are you referring to specifically?'

Frank retrieves the notes he made at the funeral, scribbled on the back of the Order of Service.

'On the surface you were paying tribute to an old friend, acknowledging a past closeness, a gradual drift apart, but ultimately showing measured respect. However, I took the liberty of taking a few notes of your more obtuse comments.' He fumbles his spectacles onto his nose and squints at the hastily written scribbles, wishing he had better penmanship.

'I'm all ears, inspector.'

'Okay, I'll begin. Even shepherds can lose their way. Those who lead carry burdens they cannot share. There's a cost to silence. In trying to protect others, we lose a part of ourselves.

And finally, you ended with, and I quote, "Whatever Nicholas carried—whatever burdens he bore—may they now be laid to rest with him. His secrets die in sacred soil, and I pray his soul has found the peace that eluded him in life. *Remember not our sins*." You also quoted from Psalm 32—*for when I kept silent, my bones wasted away*.'

Frank removes his glasses, folds the pamphlet, and slips it into his jacket pocket.

'Mere words, inspector. They can be interpreted in any way the listener so wishes.'

'No, I don't think so. I'd say your words were deliberately chosen.'

Frank clasps his hands and inches forward on the couch.

'I'm not a religious man. I have no time for gods or the Holy Trinity. However, for better or worse, my wife is deeply religious. A true Christian. When it comes to scripture and theology, she's a bit of a know-it-all. I asked her to give me a synopsis of Psalm 32, which she willingly did. I then asked her to put it into layman's terms so even an idiot like myself could understand it.'

'And what did your wife say?'

'In a nutshell, Psalm 32 refers to the spiritual and physical torment of unconfessed sin. My question is—whose unconfessed sin? When you were standing at the lectern, were you speaking about Reverend Hartley, or... about yourself?'

Hampton guffaws then breaks into a sudden coughing fit. Frank pours a glass of water and hands it to him.

'Here, drink this.'

Shakily, Hampton takes a few sips from the glass before collapsing back into the folds of the armchair, exhausted by the attack.

'Hartley was a complex man whom I once knew. He changed over the years and became part of the woke brigade. He was more bothered about trans rights than the righteous path. I'm old school, inspector. Not quite fire and brimstone, but the New Testament and parts of the Old have been a template for my life.'

'You mean you cherry-pick what suits you at a particular time?'

Hampton puffs out air. 'I'm in no fit state to sit here arguing with you about theology. Now, if you don't mind, it's time for my nap.'

'Of course,' Frank replies graciously as he rises and makes his way to the door. He pauses and turns around. 'If you genuinely believe you're dying, then doesn't your faith encourage confessing one's sins before meeting your maker?'

'I'm Church of England, not bloody Catholic. Protestants believe faith in the Saviour gets you into heaven, regardless. Catholics think you need the Church, the sacraments—*and a pocket full of silver*. And when I do confess my sins, it'll be privately, to *my* God—not to a man in a frock, nor a bloody woman, and certainly not to a Detective Chief Inspector. Good day, Mr Finnegan.'

'Good day, Lord Hampton. I hope your condition improves. Oh, and tell Magdalena the ciasto was scrumptious. I must get the recipe from her when I next visit.'

Frank is sitting patiently in the car, phone to ear, as mind-numbing muzak plays through the speaker. He taps idly at the steering wheel, admiring the shimmering lake and peacocks strutting around.

A click.

'Doctor Julian Brant, how can I help you?'

'Ah, Doctor Brant—DCI Finnegan here. We briefly met at Lord Hampton's place a while back. Can I have a little chat?'

17

Dinkel is beavering away on the interactive whiteboard as Zac and Frank pull up chairs and wearily sit down in front of it.

Frank checks his watch. 'A productive day all up.'

'Aye, a few things are starting to fall into place,' Zac concurs. 'How'd you go with Lilac Penhallow?'

'Okay, I suppose. She took me into the back, and we had a cuppa. Told her we'd reopened the case on Iona.'

'What was her reaction?'

'Hard to say. I told her that nothing might come of it. She just nodded and nursed her cup of tea, then said thanks with a sad, wistful look. I don't like getting people's hopes up, Zac. If we could have waited a little longer until we had something concrete, it would have been better. Anyway, she knows now.'

'Was Morrigan there?'

'No.' Frank's attention returns to the whiteboard. 'Dinkel, let the dog see the rabbit.'

'Sir.'

Dinkel taps the board, bringing up a map of Ashenby Village and the surrounding countryside. A web of red lines overlays the screen. Dinkel points to the first line, which denotes the route from the pub to St Mary's Church.

'Okay, this what we know from the witness statements from 1989. Iona leaves The Crown at 2:15 pm. It takes seven minutes to cycle to the church on the outskirts of the village, which takes us to 2:22 pm,' he explains, tracing the line with a ruler.

'Once there, she chats with Reverend Hartley for approximately twenty minutes. She leaves the church at 2:45 pm and sets off in a northerly direction along Ashenby Lane,' he continues, his ruler indicating the route.

'The time of 2:45 was confirmed independently by Hartley and by Carl Lawrence, driver of the red Mini Cooper. I think we can take it to be pretty accurate. It took me eighteen minutes to cycle from the church to the crash scene, which brings us to approximately 3:03 pm.'

'And the alarm was raised at 4 pm by Malachi Abbott,' Frank states.

'Correct. He lived about a mile south of the accident site. He said he left home at 3:40 pm.'

Zac squints at the board. 'One mile in a car—let's say three to four minutes, max. Meaning, he would have arrived at the crash site no later than 3:44.'

'That's in the ballpark. He assessed the situation, assumed Iona was dead, then returned home to call emergency services.'

Frank scowls. 'Did he not render assistance at the scene?'

'No.'

'Why not?'

Dinkel shrugs. 'If that question was ever posed then it never made it into the report.'

'That's bloody queer,' Frank reflects. 'Okay, let's back up a bit. Malachi arrives on the scene at 3:44. Let's say he spends about four minutes assessing the situation. He then jumps into his car and drives back home, probably a damn sight quicker. Add another three minutes. Meaning he returned home around about 3:51 and called a nines at 4 pm.'

Dinkel nods. 'A nine-minute gap but well within the range of discrepancy, I'd say. Add a minute or two to each action and we're nearly at 4 pm.'

Frank and Zac both nod in agreement.

'However,' Dinkel continues, 'we're not certain what time Iona reached the crash site. The earliest possible time is 3:03 pm, but as we deduced earlier, sir, she stopped to pick wild strawberries before she was hit. How long for—we don't know. Which means there's forty minutes unaccounted for between 3:03 and 3:44 pm when Malachi encountered the accident.'

Frank steeples his fingers together. 'What bothers me is Malachi's behaviour. He didn't check to see if the girl even had a pulse. Wouldn't that be everyone's first reaction?'

'It is odd,' Zac says. 'He was a gamekeeper, so not squeamish. What's the transcript of the nines say, Dinkel?'

'Not a lot. He asked for ambulance and police. Said a young woman had been knocked off her bike. Gave the location, Ashenby Lane. Said he'd wait at the site for their arrival. The operator asked what the woman's condition was, and he replied—*I think she's dead.*'

'Why would he assume she was dead?' Frank murmurs.

Zac points at the map. 'Which service was first on the scene?'

'Ambulance arrived from Ripon, ten miles away, at 4:22 pm.'

'So Malachi was sitting around for twenty minutes waiting for the ambulance to arrive, and in all that time he didn't once check for vital signs?'

'Something doesn't add up,' Frank notes. 'Okay, one to ponder. What else have we learned today?'

Zac shuffles in his chair. 'My chat with Edwin Featherstone. His late father, Colin, was the landlord of The Crown in 1989. Iona was well liked by everyone. At the time, fingers were pointed at two young local lads. In particular—Howard Price, owner of the white Fiesta, and Carl Lawrence, owner of the red Mini Cooper. They both had a reputation for driving like young men do, i.e.

recklessly. However, the gossip soon stopped when they provided alibis.'

'What were their alibis, Dinkel?' Frank asks.

Two scanned handwritten sheets appear on the screen.

'Howard Price and Mark Hardaker were the two friends who witnessed Iona outside the pub getting on her bike at 2:15 pm. They both went back to Howard Price's parents' house afterwards. They listened to music and had a few more beers. Price's father confirmed the lads arrived there just before 2:30 pm, and that Hardaker left about 5 pm.'

'And Carl Lawrence?'

'He went to his girlfriend's place, just outside Ashenby. Arrived just before 3 pm, stayed until 6 pm. Girlfriend confirmed this, as did her parents.'

Zac cracks his neck, releasing tension. 'Which brings me to my last point, Frank. Once alibis were provided by the lads, a small clique of locals began hawking the idea around that it must have been an *outsider*, a tourist out for a drive in the country. This particular, influential clique comprised the following—Reverend Hartley, Malachi Abbott, Amos Baker, and Lord Hampton—the Four Amigos. Apparently, they banged on about the *outsider* theory so much it took on a life of its own. What was mere speculation soon became an accepted truth.'

Frank grunts. 'Hmm... Malachi's name keeps cropping up over and over again. And one more thing, whoever was driving the vehicle must have passed Malachi Abbott and

Mrs Selkirk's places on Ashenby Lane. Any mention of that in either of their statements, Dinkel?'

'No, sir. According to Abbott, he was decorating his kitchen.'

'And Mrs Selkirk?'

'She was gardening.'

'If she were out in her garden, then she must have seen a vehicle pass.'

'People do stop for calls of nature, sir.'

'I suppose. Right, for what it's worth, I visited Lord Hampton earlier. Quizzed him about his peculiar eulogy, and all the references to confessions and sins.'

'And?' Zac asks.

'Gave nothing away. But the bugger's hiding something. And he's now come to the conclusion he was abducted by animal rights activists as a warning to curtail his grouse shooting business.'

'Why has he only just brought that up?'

'That's exactly what I asked. He's not well, to be honest. Had a lot of time to stew in his own thoughts.'

'Faking it?'

Frank frowns. 'No, I don't think so. He looks like death warmed up. Says he's convinced he's dying of cancer. I rang his doctor after I left.'

'About?'

'Just wanted to make sure it wasn't all an act. It's not. They suspect his heart, but Hampton's refusing to go to hospital.

Anyway, it got me thinking—about Malachi Abbott, and the small traces of aconite they found in his system. Mild aconite poisoning can mimic heart trouble—sweating, weakness, dizziness, irregular heartbeat.'

'You think he's been poisoned?'

'It's a possibility.'

'And what did the doc say?'

'Said they hadn't tested for anything exotic, but they will now. Results should be back in about a week.' He checks his watch again. 'Right, time to slake my thirst. Who's up for a pint or two at the White House?'

'I'll be right with you, Frank,' Zac replies, leaping from his chair. 'Give me a moment to shut down my laptop.'

'Dinkel?'

'Not tonight, sir. I want to spend another hour or two here. I need to confirm which witnesses are still alive.'

'Impressive, lad. But don't overdo it. Everyone needs downtime. And good work today to both of you.'

As the officers amble down the stairs, Frank shoots Zac a knowing glance.

'Are we singing from the same hymn book, sergeant?'

'Aye. One of the Four Amigos was responsible for hitting Iona Jacobs. They all close ranks and start the rumour mill, creating a smokescreen about an outsider.'

'Spot on. Could explain why they drifted apart as friends. The death of a young lass is a heavy burden to carry.'

Frank pushes open the glass door onto the rear car park, and they both step out into a warm summer evening.

Zac hesitates. 'It's a strong theory. But why wait thirty-six years?'

'Maybe there's someone out there like us.'

'I don't understand?'

'Someone who's been playing detective and has recently come to the same conclusion—one of the Four Amigos is responsible for Iona's death.'

18

Zac ambles through the beer garden at the rear of the White House pub and places two pints of Guinness on the weathered bench. He takes a seat opposite Frank, who is gazing at an elderly golfer sauntering along the fairway towards the green.

Frank massages condensation from the glass and casts a gaze over the becalmed North Sea.

'You were right, Zac.'

'About?' he replies, lifting the pint to his mouth.

'How we get so caught up in the day to day we forget about the human tragedy.'

'Ah, today on Ashenby Lane... Iona?' He takes a large gulp, splitting the G of the Guinness logo, then wipes the creamy suds from his top lip.

'Aye. It was uncanny. I felt something. Like she was there, a few feet away from me in the middle of the road, imploring me to help, to find the solution, to set her free.' He finally takes a giant swig of stout, bypassing the G on the glass by a good two inches. 'Thirty-six years she's been dead and buried, and how long was the case active?'

'Ten weeks then put aside. But as you know, any unsolved major crime is always active.'

Frank snorts. 'My blue arse. You know as well as I do that's management speak for the benefit of the family, public, and media.' He takes another draught. 'Ten bloody weeks, and by the looks of it, only a couple of officers assigned to the case.'

'This one's got to you, hasn't it, Frank?'

'Aye, it has. Not sure why? I think it's her age, and the fact she was treated like roadkill. Like she didn't matter. I tell you what, if it had been Lord or Lady Hampton found brain dead in that ditch, or any high-profile person, the kitchen sink would have been thrown at it. No expense spared. Unlimited resources.'

Zac sighs and leans back. 'Same old system, Frank. Power and money—an invincible force. We come across it all the time, the way they get away with murder, sometimes quite literally.'

The cheeks on Frank's face harden as he glares back.

'Aye, well not this time. I'm going to find out who knocked Iona off her bike if it's the last thing I do.'

Zac frowns. 'Remember emotion, Frank. One of the first things you taught me when I joined you. Don't let emotion cloud your judgement.'

'Sage advice for a young officer starting out. Do as I say, Zac, not as I do. You've a long career ahead of you, but I'm about spent. Only a few years left, at most. So, bugger that adage.'

'Christ, don't say that, Frank. I'm not sure I could handle this job without your happy, cheery face greeting me every day.'

Frank hides a smile. 'Very funny.' His eyes drift to the golfer, now on the green. 'Well, I'll be buggered,' he mutters.

'What?' Zac says, twisting around.

'Talk of the devil! That's X-Ray Strickland lining up for a putt.'

As the diminutive, aged golfer carefully swings the putter, Frank shouts out.

'Oi, X-Ray!'

The man jerks and strikes the ball with too much venom, sending it careering way past the hole, skidding across slick grass and into a deep bunker.

'Fuck it.' Ray Strickland spins around, angry as hell. 'Daft bugger!' he yells, shaking his fist.

Frank smiles and waves. 'Ray, it's me, Frank.'

Ray squints and meanders forward. His demeanour changes from a man on a rampage to one of a more sanguine nature as he recognises the cause of his downfall.

'Eh up. Frank bloody Finnegan. How yer going, lad?'

Frank sticks his arm over the fence, offering his hand. 'Better than your golf game. Yerself?'

'Oh, can't complain... apart from silly buggers yelling out as I'm taking a putt. Got a comp tomorrow. Thought I'd have a quick solo round to sharpen my game. Been a bloody disaster! That's golf for you. You need competition, otherwise it's just a walk in the park.' He pauses and eyeballs Zac.

Frank lowers his voice.

'You're just the man I want to see. We're investigating a cold case you worked on back in 1989. Fancy a pint and a chat?' He turns and points. 'Meet my sergeant, DS Zac Stoker. It's his shout.'

Ray casts a desultory glance back at the green, the bunker, then at the pub, and finally at the half-empty Guinness glasses on the table.

Licks his lips.

Contemplates.

For about two seconds.

'Aye, why not. I'll hop over the fence. Mine's a pint of Theakstons Best.'

Frank smiles. 'Zac, do the honours.'

He grits his teeth. 'I bought the last bloody round!'

'Oh, shut up, you tight Scottish sod, and get the drinks in. It all works out in the end.'

'Aye, your bloody end,' Zac grizzles as he knocks back the remaining Guinness.

Ray Strickland takes a generous quaff of beer and smacks his lips together as he contemplates Frank's question.

'That's a nice drop. Always tastes better when it's free,' he says, winking at Zac. He becomes serious. 'Iona Jacobs?' he mulls.

'Young lass, aged twenty-two. Hit-and-run. Sunday, June 4th, 1989. She was on a bike. Just outside Ashenby, near Ravensbane Estate.'

Ray's eyes light up. 'Ah, yes. I remember now.' His face darkens. 'Sad business. She was on life support for a month or so. Pregnant as well. They ended up performing a C-section and then pulled the plug on the young lass.'

'That's right,' Frank says. 'What can you tell us about it?'

Ray grimaces and stares into his pint. 'Not much you won't have already learned from the case notes.'

Frank bites his lip, realising it could be a lost cause.

'Malachi Abbott, gamekeeper for Ravensbane Estate. He was the first on the scene. Called a nines. What can you tell me about him?'

'Yes, Malachi. He was our prime suspect initially but came up clean.'

'How do you mean?' Zac enquires.

'We breath tested him. Clear. And we also found a few flakes of paint on the road and on the bike.'

'That's right. White flakes.'

'Yes. Malachi's car at the time was a dark green Land Rover Discovery. No match, and no damage.'

Frank taps the table absentmindedly. 'What about the local vicar, Reverend Hartley? Apparently, he was the last person to speak with Iona.'

Ray looks heavenward searching his distant memories.

'That's right. He was pretty shook up if I remember rightly. Very upset.'

'And what about the Hamptons, owners of Ravensbane Estate?'

'I do recall going to see them, as I remember the suits of armour in the huge hallway. Lord and Lady Hampton would've been in their early sixties at the time. They had a son.'

'Noah Hampton, the current lord,' Frank says, helping out.

'Aye, that's right. Again, nothing of any note.'

Zac can feel Frank's impatience. 'What about a local farmer from Hexley Farm called Amos Baker?'

Ray's face is a blank. 'No. That name doesn't ring any bells.'

Zac persists. 'There were two young lads who saw Iona set off from the pub on her bike—Howard Price and Mark Hardaker. Price drove a white Ford Fiesta. Were they ever under suspicion?'

Ray's face creases with the mental effort. 'We had a look at them, but they both had alibis, so we never took it any further.'

'Did you inspect the Fiesta for damage?'

'I can't recall, but we would have done. If they had been involved, we'd have known about it. It was a thorough investigation. Door knocked every house in the village and surrounding farms. Checked all the cars—nothing. Every lead we had turned into a dead end. We held a sneaking suspicion it was an outsider, possibly a day-tripper. It was a lovely spell of warm weather at the time. We figured that maybe some mates had driven out into the countryside, had one too many pints at a country pub, then hit Iona and decided to leg it while they could. Only a theory, mind.'

Frank expels air. 'I've got to say, Ray, the case was mothballed pretty quickly.'

Ray Strickland takes umbrage at the inference.

'Have you forgotten what 1989 was like, Frank? It was a bloody nightmare. You think Iona got short shrift? Let me remind you of what we were up against that year. New Year's Day, two bodies turn up at Catterick Garrison. Double murder. Chief Constable Burke had just taken the reins—hell of a welcome.

'Then, April—three murders in one day. Mother and daughter found dead, and a lad stabbed at a Scarborough campsite. All within hours.

'Come August, a pensioner in Ingleton was beaten to death. The killer flees to Scotland, murders a widow there, and tops himself before trial.

'Seven murders that year, Frank. Resources stretched thin, officers working around the clock. Iona's case didn't lack importance—it was a victim of circumstance.'

Frank vaguely remembers the calamitous year. 'Fair enough. No offence intended.'

Ray mellows. 'None taken.'

Frank tries one last shot. 'Anything else? A niggle, a suspicion that was never fully explained? A dodgy alibi? Anyone acting suspiciously?'

Ray takes another gulp from his pint. 'Sorry, Frank, it's a long time ago. I have trouble remembering what I had for breakfast this morning.'

Frank nods. 'Aye, understood.'

The conversation turns to more mundane matters as the three men slowly drain their glasses. Family, children, grandchildren, holidays abroad, investment opportunities, recurring ailments, and the parlous state of the National Health System.

Eventually, Ray places his empty pint down and rises.

'Well, it's been a nice catch up, Frank. We must do this again sometime. Don't mix much with the crew from the old days. Mind you, most of the buggers are dead. Can't believe you haven't opted for early retirement. You must have a screw loose.'

Frank chortles. 'And what would I do in retirement—play golf?'

'Worse ways to spend your days. Right, I best be off. Told the missus I'd be home by six. All the best, and thanks for the pint, Zac.'

'The pleasure was all yours.'

They watch on as Ray ungainly straddles the wooden fence then plods across the green to retrieve his golf buggy.

'Worth a stab in the dark,' Frank says, clearly disappointed.

Zac twirls the empty glass around in his hand. 'This thing isn't going to fill itself, boss.'

Frank stands and grabs the glasses. 'You've got hollow legs. One for the road, then I'm ready for my tea. I wonder what Meera's got on the menu tonight? Probably rabbit food considering the weather.'

'Oh, Frank!' Ray calls out.

Frank takes a step towards the fence as Ray hurriedly approaches, pulling the buggy behind him.

'What?'

'There was something.'

'Go on.'

'Malachi Abbott. He lived not far from where Iona was found. Semi-detached workers cottages.'

'That's right.'

'He had next door neighbours. Can't recall their names now.'

'The Selkirks?' Zac prompts.

'Aye, that name rings a bell. Anyway, the woman next door said something a little contradictory. There was a time discrepancy between when Malachi *said* he left to go to Ravensbane Castle and when *she* said he left. It should be in the case notes.'

'Did you get to the bottom of it?' Frank asks.

Ray shrugs. 'You know what it's like, Frank. People's recollections vary enormously. One person sees black; the other, white. It was a small anomaly. Not sure why I even remembered it. Righto, all the best.'

Frank ponders a while. 'The subconscious is a mystery, Zac. It has a way of clinging onto clues the conscious mind has long ago discounted.'

'Well, here's a conscious clue for you: Guinness—pint—bar.'

19

Friday 27th June 10 am

Zac has barely finished rapping on the door when it cracks open a fraction.

The old woman stares up at him through spectacles balanced on the bridge of her nose.

'Oh, it's you again,' Mrs Selkirk says in her brittle, flinty voice.

Zac and Dinkel smile warmly.

'Yes, DS Stoker and my colleague, DC Dinkel.'

'Where's the pretty one?'

'I thought I was the pretty one?' Zac says with wry smile.

The old lady grins as the door opens further.

'Aye, you're not a bad looker. If I were fifty years younger, I'd keep you on your toes.'

Zac raises his eyebrows in surprise. 'Fifty years younger? No, surely you mean five?'

Mrs Selkirk chuckles. 'I should coco.'

'Do you mind if we come in, Mrs Selkirk? Just some routine questions.'

She doesn't reply, but the door swings back as she grapples with her Zimmer frame and shuffles towards the couch as they follow her inside.

'I'd offer you a cup of tea and a slice of cake, but I'm not too sharp on my pins today.'

'Not a problem. We can do the honours if you like?' Zac offers.

'Aye, that'd be champion. Mine's white, two sugars,' she replies in a laboured breath as she collapses onto a cushion. 'Ginger cake's in the biscuit tin on the side. I'll have a slice.'

'Dinkel. Tea for three and a slice of cake for Mrs Selkirk,' Zac says, taking a seat opposite Mrs Selkirk.

'Coming right up.'

Mrs Selkirk sighs. 'Which one is it about today?'

Zac frowns. 'Sorry?'

'Malachi, Reverend Hartley, or Amos Baker? That's obviously why you're here.'

Zac retrieves his notepad and smiles. 'None of the above, actually.'

'Oh?'

'It's about a historical investigation we've reopened. A cold case.'

'Go on then. Get on with it.'

'It's about a young woman, Iona Jacobs, who was knocked off her bicycle a few miles down the lane from here back in 1989. You mentioned her after Reverend Hartley's funeral.'

The old woman's hands tremble. 'Oh, tragic. Truly tragic. Her memory has lived with me for a long time. She was a smashing lass. And bonny, too.'

Zac reads from a list of bullet points on his notepad.

'We've reviewed all the witness statements from the time and there are a few questions you may be able to help out with. I appreciate it's a long time ago, but...'

'My body may be failing me, sergeant, but my mind is as sharp as a tack. I remember it as if it were yesterday. A Sunday, June fourth. Lovely summer day. Not a breath of wind. I was gardening. My husband had gone fishing with his mates to Whitby. And my girls were both off at friends' houses. Teenagers at the time. Didn't get much peace and quiet to myself in those days, so when it did come along, I relished it. And I enjoyed nothing better than pottering in the garden. Jasmine, lavender, roses, pansies. Right out here on the front. Now look at it—just a patch of grass and weeds.'

'Ahem, yes. Well, getting back on track. We came across a slight anomaly in the timings of the events.'

There's a clatter and crash from the kitchen as a cup shatters on the flagstone floor.

'Don't worry, I'll sort it. Nothing major. Just a cup,' Dinkel cries.

Zac throws him a disparaging glare before refocusing.

'According to your neighbour, Malachi Abbott, gamekeeper for Lord Hampton at the time, he said he set off for Ravensbane Estate at around 3:40 pm. He came across Iona's body a few minutes after setting off, then drove back home to ring for the ambulance and police.'

The woman nods, as if digesting the information, but appears vague.

Zac fears the worst. 'According to your statement, *you* said Malachi left for the estate a lot earlier. Just after 3 pm. But you did agree he returned about 4 pm, give or take.'

'Yes, that's right. I was questioned about it at the time.'

Dinkel interrupts the flow again as he places the teas down on a small coffee table.

'Here you are, Mrs Selkirk, a nice cuppa for you. I'll get you that slice of cake now.'

'Thank you.'

Zac shakes his head and grits his teeth.

'Just to recap, Mrs Selkirk. Malachi said he left home at 3:40 pm. You said he left closer to 3 pm. But you're both agreed on what time he arrived back to call the services. Correct?'

'Aye, get on with it, lad. You're certainly going a long way round the houses.'

Zac clears his throat, sensing he's onto a loser.

'Can you explain the time discrepancy?'

'Malachi was wrong. Simple as that. I think it comes down to our professions.'

'Sorry?'

'Well, he was a gamekeeper, so timekeeping wasn't as important to him. What's thirty, forty minutes when you're out and about in the woods. Whereas with me, timekeeping was essential.'

'What was it you did?'

'I was a staff nurse at York District Hospital, as it was called then. Working night shifts at the time of the accident.'

A tingle shoots down Zac's spine as Dinkel places the cake down in front of Mrs Selkirk, accidentally kicking the table and slopping the drinks.

'Don't worry. I'll get a cloth.'

Mrs Selkirk leans towards Zac. 'Clumsy young bugger, isn't he?' she whispers.

'Nightmare,' Zac replies, hiding his annoyance... badly. 'So, you were a nurse?'

'Yes, that's what I meant by timekeeping. Had to be on my toes. Taking vitals, observation, turning patients, dispensing medications every two hours on the dot. I wore a little fob watch pinned to my tunic.'

Zac rubs a hand through his beard, recalling the witness statements.

'There's nothing in the statements about you attending to Iona at the crash scene.'

'No. Because I didn't.'

His eyes narrow. 'I don't get it. Malachi discovers the body of Iona after being involved in a hit-and-run. He came back here to raise the alarm, but he never mentioned it to you? Didn't ask for your assistance knowing you're a nurse?'

'That's right. I was in the kitchen making a brew when I saw him pull up at about four o'clock. He was in a right palaver. Disappeared inside for a moment, then took off again like a bat out of hell. It wasn't until later—oh, maybe four-thirty or thereabouts that he returned and explained what happened.'

'Did you ask him why he didn't ask for your help?'

'Aye, I bloody did. Said he was panicked and not thinking straight. Said there was nowt to be done for the lass, anyway. Said she was dead. But she wasn't. Severe head trauma. In a coma for weeks. The bairn she was carrying was still alive, but after a while it began to deteriorate. The doctors had declared Iona brain dead. They were only keeping her alive because of the baby. They came to the decision that they needed to perform a Caesarean to save the child. Once it was out safely, they turned off life support.'

Zac exhales, feeling exhausted yet mildly exhilarated at the same time.

Mrs Selkirk makes light work of the cake and then washes it down with a few gentle sips of tea.

'She wasn't though,' she adds as an afterthought as another clatter emanates from the kitchen.

'She wasn't what?' Zac questions.

'Brain dead. Well, she was, technically. But if there was no life in her, then why did she say his name?'

Zac is becoming ever more baffled and wishes he had Prisha's incisive mind on hand.

'I'm sorry, Mrs Selkirk, I don't quite follow.'

The old woman sighs as if dealing with a rather thick child.

'I said I was on night shift. I worked in the ICU, where Iona was. I took special care of her. One night I was giving her a bed bath, and her eyes briefly flickered open. Her mouth parted, and she muttered his name.'

'Who's name?'

'Nicholas.'

20

Zac has called a momentary time-out as he puts a flea in Dinkel's ear.

'Can you *please* stop clattering about and breaking things like a geriatric Clydesdale with myopia? This investigation is at a critical juncture, and I want silence, not constant interruptions. You're ruining the flow,' he hisses in a strained whisper.

'I'm sorry. I couldn't help it. What do you want me to do?'

'Nothing. Unless you can come up with some relevant questions, then just keep quiet... please.'

Zac resumes his seat and updates his notebook before focussing on Mrs Selkirk.

'And she definitely said Nicholas?'

'Yes. As true as I'm sitting here.'

'Did you mention this to the police at the time?'

'No. Why would I? It was weeks after the accident and had no relevance to the case as far as I could see. Anyway...' she pauses and fidgets. 'I didn't want to add any more fuel to the fire.'

'What fire?'

'The rumour mill. Gossip mongering. There's nothing folk like better than tittle-tattle, especially if there's sex involved.'

At the risk of repeating himself, Zac repeats himself.

'I don't understand?'

She rubs her hands together and stares wistfully into thin air.

'Doesn't matter now, I suppose. There were rumours that something was going on between Reverend Hartley and Iona. Idle gossip. When it became common knowledge Iona was carrying, well, folks put two and two together and came up with five. I always had a soft spot for the Reverend. There's no way he'd have been up to no good with Iona. I think they were just friends. He was a broken man for quite a while after the accident. He lasted another twelve, eighteen months in the parish before he moved on. I was surprised when he returned a few years back to finish out his tenure here. Thought this place might have held too many painful memories for him. Or perhaps that's why he did return. You know, slay the demons.'

'And why did you assume that when Iona uttered the name Nicholas, she was referring to Nicholas Hartley?'

She shrugs. 'There were no other men with that first name in the village at the time. And with her being... friendly with him, it seemed obvious.'

'Did Iona ever regain consciousness again?'

'No.'

'What happened to the baby after it was born?'

'It was premature. Twenty-eight weeks, I think. It was in an incubator for a long time. Poor wee mite. I didn't have much involvement, but the grandmother gained full custody. I believe she lived in Scotland.'

'Pssst.'

Zac ignores Dinkel's attempt at attention grabbing.

'It's funny,' Mrs Selkirk continues, 'but all these years without anyone showing any interest in the fate of Iona, and then all of a sudden there's a flurry of interest.'

'A flurry—who else has been asking about her?'

'It was about a year ago, maybe longer. I'm good with dates from forty, fifty years ago but not with recent ones. Odd that, isn't it?'

Zac forces a smile to humour her. 'Yes. The mind is a mysterious beast. You were saying—a flurry of interest?'

'Oh, that's right. Well, a slight exaggeration, just one other person.'

'*Who?*' There's an unintended bite to his voice.

'That flighty woman from the commune, you know, the hippies.'

'Yes, I'm aware of the Wicca on Ravensbane Estate. The woman?'

'Violet. Can't recall her last name.'

'Violet Fox?'

'That's the one. She was interviewing all the older locals about a year ago. Doing research for some history book she was working on, about tales and legends associated with the area. Said she was a history professor. Not sure whether I believed her. She was here for a good three hours. Somehow we got onto the tale of Iona Jacobs. She was very interested.'

'Psst!'

Zac raises a weary eye and gazes over at Dinkel, who is standing behind Mrs Selkirk making hand signals.

'Excuse me a moment, Mrs Selkirk.'

He ambles around the back of the couch as Dinkel twitches his head towards a photo on the wall.

'What?' Zac hisses.

'The photo,' he whispers. 'Take a look.'

It's faded with time, the colour a washed out hue. It's some sort of village gathering. In the centre is a middle-aged Mrs Selkirk, flanked by two teenage girls, all happily smiling. Behind them are a small circus tent, a couple of clowns and a crowd of people.

Zac studies it intently for a moment. 'What am I supposed to be looking at?'

Dinkel points to the left side of the image. 'These four, in the distance. Ring any bells?'

Zac takes a step forward, lowers his head and squints at the group of men who were accidentally caught in the shot.

'It looks like a young Reverend Hartley with a few mates. What of it?'

'The date in the bottom corner—April 2nd, 1989.'

Zac looks at the faded ink and shrugs. 'Yeah, and?'

'Two months before the fatal hit-and-run.'

Zac is losing patience fast. 'Dinkel, if you have something to say, then bloody well say it.'

He taps the images of the men. 'Take a closer look. Yes, definitely, Reverend Hartley. A strong, handsome fellow. But the other three. One bears an uncanny resemblance to Lord Hampton. And this one, side on, holding a beer, could be Malachi Abbott, and the other, walking out of shot... well, a passing resemblance to Amos Baker, don't you think?'

Zac scrutinises the photograph in more detail. 'Yeah, possibly. But so what? Some sort of village fete; it's not unexpected they'd be there.'

Dinkel raises a finger, not in revelation but in quiet correction.

'Behind them, wandering off, back to camera—this young woman. Denim jacket, jeans with turn-ups, white trainers, blonde curly hair...'

'Oh, I see. Iona Jacobs, possibly.'

'Exactly.'

Zac takes a deep breath. 'Ten out of ten for your eyesight, Dinkel. It's sharper than mine, but unless you have any illuminating deductions you can propose, then I don't see what your point is.'

Dinkel grins. 'You haven't spotted it yet, have you?'

He's in imminent danger of getting a thump.

Zac lowers his voice. 'Get to the point, Dinkel, otherwise you'll be sucking hospital food through a straw for your evening meal.'

As proud as punch, Dinkel's forefinger taps at the glass.

'Here, way off in the background. A car. And by the shape of it, quite unique—a Citroen 2CV. And... it's white.'

A smile slowly spreads across Zac's face. 'Bugger me backwards. You're right. In the case notes, do we have a list of all the cars the police inspected at the time?'

'Yes.'

'Was a white Citroen 2 CV listed?'

'Definitely not.'

Zac turns around. 'Mrs Selkirk, this photo on the wall, from April 1989, some sort of village fair—can you tell me about it?'

Surprised, she shuffles around, then smiles. 'Oh, yes. The Easter Pageant. On the village green at Ashenby. That's me with my two daughters. It was nice and sunny when that was taken, but a few moments later, it absolutely bucketed it down. We got drenched.'

'And these four men to the left. That looks like Reverend Hartley and *possibly* Lord Hampton?'

'That's right. The Odd Bunch we called them at the time. Only in jest. There's also Amos Baker and Malachi Abbott. Inseparable in those days. Of course, they weren't supposed to be in the damned photograph, but my husband wasn't the best with a camera in his hand.'

He carefully lifts the frame from the wall and hands it to her.

'And this car here, right in the background, nearly out of shot—I don't suppose you recall who the owner was?'

'Yes, of course I do. Didn't get many of that type around these parts. Odd-looking car.'

'And who did it belong to?'

'Reverend Hartley.'

21

Prisha slams the door behind her, breathless, exhausted after pounding the coastal trail to Sandsend and back.

Even a long, hot shower can't shake the black dog of anxiety and despair that stalks her every moment.

Her emotions are like a spicy goulash simmering in a slow-cooker.

Fear and fury. Hurt and humiliation. Loss, longing... loneliness.

Shame.

It baffles her, the sharp dagger of shame, like this is all her fault.

It wasn't she who shattered the crystal bracelet of trust.

Such a delicate trinket.

No chance of ever gluing those pieces together again.

She's in a battle, maybe the biggest battle of her life.

Negative thoughts are unwelcome and uninvited visitors.

Let them in, and they *will* outstay their welcome.

Maybe lodge indefinitely, like squatters.

But if she's anything, then it's practical.

A healthy breakfast of avocado on sourdough toast, with two poached eggs, and a glass of freshly squeezed orange juice, lifts her spirit.

After cleaning away and tidying her flat, she peruses the bookcase, knowing the best thing in a crisis is to keep actively busy—one of her grandmother's many mantras.

Confuse the mind with the banality of the every day.

Don't let the guard down, otherwise the malevolent brood of dark thoughtlings will slither and slide under the door, a black inky ooze, pooling in the hollow where her heart was ripped out.

Focuses.

Nothing in her book collection whets her appetite.

Gazes around the room.

Catches his voice.

Imagines his boyish smile.

His laugh.

Swallows hard, refusing to slip into melancholy reflection.

She's always loved her little top-floor flat in Whitby. A perfect location not far from Whalebone Arch. A brisk ten-minute walk to the harbour front. Thirty minutes to the Abbey.

Always loved.

Past tense.

It's smaller now than it was a few days ago. Claustrophobic. Like she's hoarding memories that devour the space, inch by inch.

'Stop it!'

Her eyes drift to the shelf under the coffee table. She reaches for the book.

The Three Crones by Reverend Hartley.

It seems a lifetime ago, but barely six weeks have passed, and she's totally forgotten about Hartley's publication on local legend and folklore.

Out of sight, out of mind.

She remembers flicking through the book in the office at St Mary's the day Reverend Hartley was found at the end of a rope in the bell tower.

At the time, she skim-read the foreword, which was the equivalent of a film-trailer. That's where she'd learned about the witch trials of 1643, the crones of Ravensbane Wood, the gruesome executions of three women, subsequently followed by the harrowing deaths of the main male persecutors.

One drowned, another hanged, the last one—buried alive.

Two of the deaths match Malachi Abbott and Hartley's demise—drowning and hanging, respectively. Lord Hampton had somehow miraculously escaped his deadly imprisonment in an ancient mineshaft—or so he said.

It deserved more than the cursory skim she'd given it. Today, she intends to read it properly.

Confuse the mind with the banality of the every day, she repeats.

She hasn't yet had her morning caffeine hit, and Whitby is awash with cafes and good coffee.

Slips the book into her backpack and heads to the door.

Stares at the scarf still hanging on the hook.

She can't help herself.

Presses it to her nose and breathes in Adam's scent.

Exhaling in jittery spasms, she places the scarf around her neck.

Locks the door, skips down the steps.

Outside, she drops the scarf into the wheelie bin.

'*Fuck* you,' she whispers.

The coffee is strong, black, and offers an instant kick. Prisha relaxes at an outside table of a busy cafe adjacent to the Old Town Hall, in Market Place. Taking a delicate bite of the moist lemon drizzle cake, she cherry-picks her way through the book, starting with subjects that pique her curiosity.

Unlike the cake, the writing is rather dry. The author, Reverend Hartley, was definitely old school. Facts, figures, references, footnotes, old maps, sketches, grainy photographs. Not a flicker of the writer's soul seeps through—just cold data lined up like fence posts.

This is going to be hard work, she thinks.

A rather laborious thirty minutes elapses as she indulges in another brew, occasionally breaking off to watch the increasing visitor numbers who drift aimlessly by. Like meandering wildebeest on a perpetual migration, she wonders if they have an ultimate destination? Or are they all simply following the herd, thereby creating a self-fulfilling momentum, mistaking movement for meaning?

She sips again, the bitterness of the coffee grounding her as much as the thought. Maybe that's all any of them are doing—wandering in loops, hoping the next turn leads somewhere different, somewhere better.

Clearing her head, she zones in on the words on the page, stifling a yawn as sunshine bathes her in warmth.

The clock ticks—slowly.

Turns yet another page. Eyelids flutter.

Maybe her inability to concentrate is the setting. Too much hustle and bustle.

Should I go to the library?

Instantly, she dismisses the idea. It's only a stone's throw from the police station, and the last thing she wants is to bump into anyone from work.

She couldn't bear to endure their sympathetic looks, as if she were an old pet making its final trip to the vets.

Turns the page. A new chapter.

She reads suddenly enthralled.

Her heart skips a beat, and not because of the caffeine.

Devouring the text, she re-reads it again to absorb the importance. *Chapter XIV – Of Knots and Judgement*

In the spring of 1643, during the height of the English Civil War — when Cavalier faced Roundhead — under a waning moon, with a fever still smouldering from the writings of King James, 1st of England: the Great Witch Purge began.

Three village women were charged with calling blight upon the fields and barrenness upon the once fertile wives of the parish. The trials were swift, their names lost to formal record, though locals remember them as the Crones of Ravensbane Wood, or just simply, The Three Crones.

They were wise women, by some accounts — herbkeepers, midwives, and lonely widows who spoke more to trees than to men. But in those days, such traits meant one thing only: witch.

Their sentences were brutal and symbolic.

One was hanged from the ancient oak at Gallows Meadow, on the outskirts of Ashenby. Another was bound in heavy chains and drowned in Ravensbane Lake, her lungs filled with peat-dark water. The third met a crueller fate still — sealed alive in a disused mineshaft beneath the wood. Her name, presumed to be Maggie, survives only in the site's grim moniker: Maggie's Tomb.

Affixed to each of the condemned was a crude sigil — a braided disc woven from hemp and gut, daubed in soot and pinned to their garments with iron nails. It became known as the Crucifix Knot. Its design was sanctioned by Lord Richard Hampton, 7th Baron of Ravensbane Castle and local magistrate, as a symbol of holy justice.

The same knot would later appear in sermons and printed decrees, intended as a warning; that sin, once committed, must be purged.

Yet not all ends as the righteous intend. The three chief accusers — Lord Hampton, his sergeant-at-arms—Tobias Crompton, and Reverend Ezekiel Harrow of St Mary's in Ashenby—each met peculiar and grisly deaths.

Reverend Ezekiel Harrow was found hanging in the low woods, his body suspended by a poacher's snare around his neck from the bough of an ash tree. His hands were nailed together in prayer around a blood-soaked Bible. A Crucifix Knot, carved deep into his bare chest, had been packed with ash and wax. His tongue was missing; his eyes plucked out. Scattered around the base of the tree were slivers of his broken crucifix, arranged in a near-perfect circle.

Tobias Crompton was found face-down in Ravensbane Lake, knees bent as if he'd been forced to kneel. His hands were tied behind his back with twisted bramble, and a sack of stones hung from his neck by a rope. A Crucifix Knot had been nailed into his spine through his severed tongue. When they pulled him out, waterweed coiled around his throat like a noose.

And Lord Richard Hampton, the great persecutor, was found days after failing to return from a solitary ride through the woods. His horse was discovered grazing at the edge of Gallows Meadow, blood on its flank, the saddle empty. Hampton's body was unearthed in a shallow grave beneath the very oak where one of the witches was hanged. His throat had been slit, his tongue cut out and nailed to his forehead, and his eyes replaced with crow stones. A Crucifix Knot had been carved into the flesh of his chest and stitched closed with horsehair. His magistrate's seal was rammed down his throat. It is said he was still alive when buried. Some believe the earth had rejected him — spat him back out like a bad seed.

Whether these tales are true is open to conjecture. As with all such 'good stories', it's entirely possible they were born in reality but, over the centuries, have been exaggerated and embellished for the entertainment of the locals. It is true, however, that the three men responsible for the deaths of the women met unfortunate — some say mysterious and grisly — ends. But are such tales merely Pagan fancy? Whatever the truth, the Crucifix Knot remains a mark of order. A sign that the law must be obeyed, or ruin will follow. Though whose law it speaks of... remains open to debate."Epitaph

"One more name deserves mention, though it rarely survives the retelling — that of Osric Penhalion, a prosperous landowner whose fields bordered Ravensbane Wood. It was whispered that Penhalion knew the three women to be no witches but merely healers and hedge-practitioners, women who read runes, treated fevers, and helped barren wives conceive. He'd even engaged their services himself in the past, to heal sick animals. He might have spoken in their defence,

but silence suited his position, and fortune, better. He let them perish rather than risk being branded himself.

One wild autumn night, during a storm that shook slates from the roofs, Penhalion was tending to a spooked horse in his barn. He was found hours later by a farmhand, his body slumped in straw, and blood. A large scythe, fixed to a beam overhead, had wrenched itself free and cleaved his skull clean in two—each half still attached by sinew to the neck. Some say a Crucifix Knot was carved into his ample belly, and his tongue was nailed to the barn door. As with the other deaths, whether this is truth or tavern-talk has been lost in the mists of time. Murder or accident? If the former, no man was ever brought to justice."

'What the actual hell?' Prisha murmurs. 'Folklore or not—someone has used this as a blueprint for murder.'

She turns the page and almost drops the book. A fine pencil sketch takes up a full page. It depicts a circular braided disc containing a cross, a replica of the ones found in Malachi's car and Amos Baker's tractor cab.

Below the sketch—the caption:

The Crucifix Knot.

'I don't believe it.'

The shapeless, bickering tide of humanity has vanished from her world. She stares down at the cobbles of the marketplace, her mind sharp, burning, as the words churn inside her.

Distracted by her thoughts, she's oblivious to a figure that silently approaches from the shadows.

22

The aroma of dirty oil and warm rubber permeates the air—a not unpleasant smell, Zac thinks.

He glances around the vehicle forensics bay—all bright strip lighting and half a dozen machines he doesn't recognise, apart from one. The old red Massey Ferguson tractor sits centre stage like a guilty exhibit, the slasher still bolted to the rear.

A noticeably short man at a cluttered desk turns from his laptop. He rises briskly and approaches, blue overalls, faded and threadbare with years of use, the knees stained dark with oil. His glasses are thick-rimmed and smudged, giving him the look of someone who hasn't cleaned them since he was an apprentice mechanic.

'Detective Sergeant Stoker, I presume?' he says in a dry tone.

Zac flashes his ID. 'That's me.'

'Reception rang through. Terry Claymore—Forensic Vehicle Examiner. I've just finished going over the tractor.'

Zac offers a hand. 'Appreciate you making the time.'

Terry pulls a dirty rag from his back pocket, performs a perfunctory wipe of his palm, then shakes hands.

'It's my job, sergeant.' He leans back on the heels of his boots, emitting a leathery squeak. 'Your colleague was here about six weeks ago. A DI Kumar?'

'That's right.'

'The old Land Rover Discovery belonging to Malachi Abbott. Brake fluid lines cut. Tampering. Any progress?'

'We're still investigating.'

His eyes narrow. 'Hmm... that's the difference between humans and machines.'

'What is?'

'With machines, there are no lies, no artifice. What you see is what you get.' His face darkens. 'Unlike humans, who lie, cheat, deceive, steal, betray, and kill.' There's a certain amount of venom in his words.

'Right, yes, well can we...'

'Take my ex-wife, for example. Married for twenty-three years. Two kids. I thought we had the perfect marriage.'

Zac squirms a little. 'I see, well...'

'But it was all a lie. Do you know she had numerous affairs with players from my local cricket club during that time?'

'Ahem, no. I wasn't aware of that.'

Terry stares off into the distance. 'Bastards even had nicknames for the both of us. Apparently, they referred to me as Short-Leg, and my wife as Sticky Wicket.'

'People can be cruel,' Zac murmurs, wondering how the conversation started.

'Not only that, but she'd secretly created a slush fund. Private bank account. Came home from work one day and she'd taken everything.'

'Everything?'

'Yes, lock, stock, and barrel. Had the removal men in while I was at work. Didn't even leave a kettle, a cup, or a solitary teabag. Everything gone.' He hesitates and reflects. 'Well, apart from my collection of novelty egg cups.'

'At least you could still enjoy a boiled egg for breakfast,' Zac replies, trying to lighten the mood.

He fails miserably as Terry squints at him.

'No pan or spoons, sergeant. Have you tried boiling an egg without any implements?'

'Not recently.'

'She'd left a note, which read—*It's over. I can't take it anymore. I won't be back. You'll be hearing from my solicitor.* A machine would never do that to a person.'

'No, I don't suppose it would.' Zac exhales, suddenly feeling like an agony aunt. 'Was this recent?'

Terry shifts uneasily. 'Yes, about ten years ago.'

Zac ponders, searching for something vaguely wise to say. 'Sometimes it's best to move on. You know what they say?'

'What?'

'The sweetest revenge is a life well lived.' He's not entirely convinced of the veracity of his adage. 'Or something like that.'

An awkward silence follows as Zac wonders about the man's sanity.

Terry claps his hands together with a loud crack, making Zac jump.

'Right, let's get down to brass tacks, Sergeant Stoker. I haven't got all day. You may want to take notes, but everything will be in my detailed report, which I should have to you by close of business today.'

They walk amongst us, Zac thinks, following Terry towards the tractor.

'Know much about tractors, sergeant?'

'Noisy, smelly. They plough fields.'

Terry stares back. 'So, a novice?'

'I think the term—clueless—would be more fitting.'

Terry takes a deep breath and sighs. 'Another one. Ah well, never mind. If I say something you don't understand, then you must interject and ask for clarification. Are we reading from the same cricket scorecard?'

'Yep.'

'And by the way, I'm quite certain the reason Mr Baker was beneath the slasher was to extricate a piece of fencing wire that had become entwined around the blade shaft.' He holds up a two-foot length of mangled wire. 'Forensics recovered several more fragments from the scene. It's a habitual problem on a working farm.'

They line up alongside the tractor.

'Right,' Terry begins, 'you've got three systems in operation: the tractor's engine, the hydraulics, and the PTO—the Power Take Off shaft. The PTO draws rotational power directly from the engine when it's running.' He points at the slasher. 'That power is transmitted down the driveline to the rotating shaft of the slasher, which spins the blades, via the gearbox and coupling. With me so far?'

'Aye, I think so.'

'Now, a critical point—so pay attention,' he says as he climbs into the cab and mimics turning the key. 'If the tractor engine is off, there is no power transmitted to the PTO.'

Zac grimaces. 'Hang on, back up a little. Is there a lever or button to transfer power from the engine to the PTO?'

'A lever, yes,' he replies, tugging on a small metal lever beside the driver's seat. 'Mechanical on these older models.'

'So even if the lever was in the *ON* position, if the engine's dead, it still couldn't transmit power?'

Terry stares at him as if he's an imbecile. 'If the engine's not running, where would it get power from?'

'Erm... it can't run off the battery? Electrical power?'

Terry purses his lips. 'No. The PTO is purely mechanical. It cannot run off electrical power.'

'Okay, got you.'

As Terry dismounts, he mutters under his breath. 'This is going to take longer than I expected.'

He crouches at the rear of the tractor and lifts the yellow plastic PTO shaft guard.

'Here—see this? There's a shear-pin between the tractor and the slasher. It acts like a mechanical fuse. If the blades jam, this snaps before anything else gets wrecked.'

Zac raises his eyebrows. 'Meaning?'

'Power's cut instantly. Think of it like an electrical fuse. If the wiring overheats, the fuse blows—same principle. It creates a physical break in the driveline.'

'Right, got you. What about the hydraulics? The mobile mechanic at the farm mentioned Mr Baker had been having trouble with the hitch?'

Terry points to the three-point linkage.

'The hydraulics only raise or lower the slasher. They have no effect on blade rotation. The PTO and the lift arms are separate systems.'

Zac rubs his chin. 'PTO lever off, engine off, hydraulics off... I think I'm following. But could a fault in the wiring or hydraulics override that?'

'Not unless someone bypassed the safety systems or rewired the tractor, and my forensic examination has found nothing untoward.'

Zac looks impressed. 'Okay. What about the slasher gearbox; could it freewheel if it was in neutral?'

'Nope. It's passive unless driven. If the shear-pin's broken, the blades won't spin; there's no connection. And this shear-pin is intact, meaning it could transmit power, but only if the PTO was engaged and the engine was running.'

Zac nods. 'So basically, mechanically, there's no way it started itself.'

'Correct. If the engine's off and the PTO is disengaged, the blades are inert. The only way they move is if someone starts the tractor and re-engages the PTO.'

Zac taps the side of the cab. 'So you're telling me this wasn't a farm accident—it looks like someone started it deliberately?'

'That's the only plausible theory.'

Zac pauses. 'Okay, here's a scenario for you.'

'Go on.'

'Baker runs over a piece of fencing wire, hears it wrap around the shaft. He disengages the PTO via the lever, then uses the hydraulics to raise the slasher for access.'

'Reasonable so far.'

'He jumps down, leaving the tractor running. While he's under the slasher, vibrations cause the PTO lever to slip back into gear and the blades spin. Could that happen?'

Terry removes his glasses, breathes on the lenses, and wipes them with his oily rag, not really achieving much.

'Technically possible. But is it plausible? Extremely unlikely.'

'Farmers do take shortcuts, though. Pushed for time, stubborn by nature.'

'True. But on a Massey of this age, the PTO lever's mechanical. It wouldn't slip unless it's loose, or tampered with. If the spring's gone, or someone's tied it off with baler twine... maybe. But I've dismantled the lever—some wear, yes, but still sound. And according to the scene report, the engine was off when the mechanic arrived. Still had half a tank of fuel. For your scenario to hold true, the tractor should've still been running, or out of fuel.'

'Hmm... okay, Mr Claymore. One final question. If you were giving evidence in court, what would you say when questioned by the prosecution as to the likely sequence of events that led to Mr Baker's death?'

Terry doesn't hesitate. 'Simple. Someone manually re-engaged the PTO and lowered the slasher while Baker was underneath.'

23

The man approaches Prisha.

'Inspector Kumar?'

No response.

'Inspector Kumar?'

This time the voice is louder, more urgent. It breaks through her wall of thought.

Raising her head, she gazes up at an older gentleman, grey hair, slightly balding, attired in clothes typical for his age.

'Sorry?' she murmurs, the kindly face and slight smile stirring a vague memory.

'It's me, Marcus Eldridge,' the man proclaims.

She repeats the name slowly, rising. 'Marcus Eldridge?'

'Yes, Marcus Eldridge. Professor of semiotics? You came to me...' he pauses and looks heavenwards. '... maybe eighteen months ago. You were in the middle of a murder investigation. There was a motif that puzzled you. You asked for my advice. I'm an old friend of Charlene Marsden—remember? We finally deciphered the cryptic emblem, if you recall. An acorn.'

It's like someone turned the light on in a pitch-dark cellar.

'Of course,' Prisha exclaims, remembering the Happy Camp murders. 'Professor Eldridge, how are you doing? Good to see you,' she says, shaking hands.

'I'm doing very well, thank you. And yourself?'

'What... oh, yes. Absolutely fine.'

Professor Eldridge notices the book on the table.

'Ah, *The Three Crones* by Reverend Hartley. I have a copy in my library. Although God knows where.'

'You've read it?'

'Yes. A long time ago. Can't remember too much about it now, but I make a point of purchasing a lot of local authors. There's much knowledge in these small-press books. Need to keep the flame alive, as it were.' A pregnant pause. 'Well, I can see you're busy. I'll keep mov....'

'Can I buy you a coffee or a tea? Piece of cake?'

He smiles benevolently. 'Normally I'd take you up on the offer, but not today. I'm heading to the pub for some liquid refreshment.'

Prisha stifles her amusement. 'I wouldn't have taken you for a midday drinker, professor.'

He chuckles. 'I'm not, really. It's my little treat. One day a week I venture into Whitby and try a different pub and a couple of new brews to excite my palate. Two pints is about my limit.'

'Right, well... good to see you again, Professor Eldridge.'

'Likewise.' He turns then stops. 'Don't suppose you'd care to join me at the pub? We could discuss the merits of Hartley's book if you want? I'm heading to the Abbey Wharf just around the corner, and if we get a move on, we may even snaffle a table on the balcony overlooking the river. Beautiful day for it.' He frowns severely. 'Oh, of course. You're probably on duty, and that's a no-no.'

Prisha smiles. 'I'm actually... off duty, so, yes, I'd love to join you for a drink... and discuss the book.'

As Prisha sips her gin and tonic, and Professor Eldridge nurses his pint of Whitby Whaler, they engage in light conversation on the balcony of the Abbey Wharf.

Sunlight dances on the rippling water of the river, the gentle slosh against the quayside providing a soothing backdrop. For the first time in days, Prisha feels a weight lifting from her shoulders. The weather, the warmth, the relaxed atmosphere, the drinks—it's one of life's simple pleasures.

As their chatter fades, Eldridge shifts the topic.

'Any intriguing cases on your desk, inspector?'

'Call me Prisha. And yes, actually.'

Eldridge's eyebrows arch with interest. 'Anything you can share?'

She trusts him implicitly; after all, he provided the breakthrough in the *Happy Camp* murders.

She offers a sly smile. 'Well, I can only speak in general terms.'

'Understood completely.'

'There has been a spate of suspicious deaths recently, and the nature of the deaths has an uncanny resemblance to a specific event in history.'

'A copycat killing?'

'Yes.'

She retrieves the book from her backpack and flips to the chapter about the Crucifix Knot.

'Take a look. As an expert in symbology, what's your take on this passage and the sketch?'

Eldridge slowly flips the pages, his expression shifting subtly. After a couple of minutes, he sets the book down.

'Hartley was more of a folklore enthusiast than a rigorous researcher. His account is fascinating, though its accuracy is debatable. Gruesome tales nonetheless.'

'Have you encountered the Crucifix Knot before?'

'Yes, but I'm no expert.'

She shows him an image on her phone—the braided medallion bearing the Crucifix Knot.

He chuckles. 'Ah, yes. A replica of the one depicted in the book. The cross is an ancient symbol, predating Christianity. The Egyptians had the ankh—a cross with a loop, like this one—symbolising life. In prehistoric Europe, the sun cross within a circle represented the sun and the cycle of seasons. The Celts merged the Christian cross with the Pagan sun wheel, creating the Celtic cross. Early Christians were hesitant to use the cross openly due to its association with execution. It wasn't until Emperor Constantine's conversion in the 4th century that the cross gained prominence in Christian iconography. The history of the cross is a tapestry woven from various cultures and beliefs.'

Prisha nods, absorbing the history lesson.

'So, the Crucifix Knot might have origins predating the 1643 witch trials?'

'Undoubtedly. Likely Pagan in origin. In Hartley's account of *The Three Crones*, the Crucifix Knot is depicted as an evil talisman. Its original meaning could have been distorted over time.'

'And the incomplete circle on the rear?'

His brow furrows. 'That's more obscure. But perhaps it signifies something unfinished. A circle represents unity and eternity; a broken circle could imply disruption or a threat to an existing belief system.'

'And why the red twine?'

'It could symbolise lineage, heritage... a family thread running through time. Or it could be more primal—sacrifice, martyrdom. The act of spilling blood to seal a vow, a curse, a warning.' He trails off, studying the image on Prisha's phone again. 'Although...' he pauses deep in thought.

'What?'

'The fact that it's twine, different from the braided material forming the rest of the coin, could indicate something.'

'Such as?'

'That someone's bound to it. A ritual thread, perhaps. Possibly a Chosen One.'

'Like a leader?'

'A leader, a warrior, a deity.'

Prisha says nothing for a moment. The ambient hum of the quay fills the silence between them.

'The case you're working on sounds intriguing, if a bit gory.'

She meets his gaze fully, no smile, no charm—just quiet urgency.

'The killer doesn't leave fingerprints. Or DNA. They leave that coin, or medallion, or whatever you want to call it.'

'As if they're marking something. Or someone?' Eldridge suggests.

'Exactly. And whatever it means, I need to work it out, and quickly. Because there's one thing I'm certain of.'

'What's that?'

'They haven't finished their killing spree yet.'

24

Meera is sitting on the settee adjacent to Frank as he attempts to read the local newspaper.

Her mouth is agape as she glares at her husband, condensing the belated news he's just offloaded.

For once, she's lost for words... well, momentarily.

'I don't believe it,' she finally announces.

Frank's eyes don't stray from the newspaper print as he reads about the furore over the temporary Ferris wheel currently being erected on the top of Whitby's West Cliff.

'Aye, well. These things happen.'

Feeling her eyes boring into his soul, he relents and shoots her a glance.

'I thought I could feel a draught. Why's your mouth open? Are you catching flies?'

'And this happened when?' she snaps.

'Tuesday, after the funeral of that vicar in Ashenby. Prisha had left her car at the farm. Got picked up in Pickering, then dropped off at the bottom of the farm track. Walked up to the farm. Caught them at it in the bedroom.'

'It's now Friday.'

'So?'

'You only decide to mention it now, that Prisha caught Adam at it with another woman?'

'It slipped my mind. Had a hell of a week. We're short-staffed at the best of times, but with Prisha away, we've been busier than a bag of ferrets in a chaff sack.'

Meera drops her attitude and softens.

'How is she?'

'I had a chat with her on Wednesday. She was distraught. Zac called around later to see her. And he's been texting. She's wounded, but you know Prisha; she's got bigger gonads than any man I know.'

'Do you think they'll make it up?'

Frank finally relinquishes his paper, realising he won't be allowed to read it in peace.

'I can't see it. She'd be soft in the head if she went back to him. She deserves better—a lot better. Prisha has one of those personalities you don't want to get on the wrong side of. She doesn't strike me as the forgiving type. In fact, she reminds me a lot of you.'

'In what way?'

'You hold a grudge like an alcoholic clinging to a whisky bottle.'

'I do not!'

'Like hell you do. You still bring up the time I put your white knickers in the washing machine with a red towel.'

'You put it on hot!'

'I rest my case.' He pauses. 'Oh, one other thing I should mention,' he adds sheepishly.

'Go on.'

'Had a bit of a run-in with Superintendent Banks earlier in the week.'

Meera rolls her eyes, well accustomed to Frank's frequent tussles with the Super.

'Here we go.'

'I accused her of being a hard-nosed bitch... in front of Zac. Lost it for a moment.'

'You didn't! My God, Frank, your days are numbered. And the upshot?'

'I rang her from my office. Gave her my sincerest apologies and offered my resignation.'

He heaves a sigh heavy with reflection.

'It was unprofessional. I let emotion cloud my judgement. Me and Anne have had many a heated argument over the years, in the privacy of my office, but to say such a thing in front of a junior officer is unforgivable. Shows a lack of respect. I'm ashamed of my actions.'

'You said you called her—what did she say?'

'Silence for a good thirty seconds. Then she laughed. Admitted she could be—in her own words—cold. Then said if I ever did it again, I was for the high-jump.'

'You kissed and made up?'

'Well... not sure about kissed. But let's say the status quo was reinstated.'

Meera exhales, shakes her head. 'You're on thin ice, Frank.'

'I've been on thin ice most of my career.'

'And what caused your outburst?'

'Prisha. I gave her time off. Anne wanted her back in the office. That wasn't going to happen—not whilst I'm still in charge of my officers.'

Meera reflects on her husband's strengths and weaknesses. Silence descends and Frank takes the opportunity to resume reading the local paper.

But not for long.

'You do realise what tomorrow is?'

'Aye.'

'You haven't forgotten?'

'No.'

'I'll be doing the usual.'

'Thought as much.'

'Will you come with me this year? It's been a while.'

Frank huffs and puts the newspaper aside.

'If that's what you want, love. Then of course I will.'

'I've already bought the single white rose.'

Frank swallows hard as his emotions rise to the surface.

'Yes. I saw it in her room.'

'You went in?'

'For your information, I go in every single day. Never miss.'

'You've never said.'

'Aye well, there're times when grief's public, and times when it's private.'

Meera tears up. 'What happened to her, Frank?'

He expels a long, slow breath of air as the lump in his throat threatens to constrict him.

'I don't bloody know, love. No one does. What a copper I am, eh? Can't even find out what happened to my own daughter.'

'It's not your fault.'

'Isn't it? It was me with her on the beach that day. It was me who should have been looking out for her.'

'You went to get ice cream, Frank. Like any good dad would do.'

'Ha, any good dad wouldn't have left their child alone on a crowded beach.'

More subdued silence as each of them wrestles with their inner turmoil of an anniversary that relentlessly comes around, year after year, after endless year.

'A single white rose for your Yorkshire Rose,' Meera whispers. 'That's what you called her—my sweet Yorkshire Rose.'

Frank's face hardens as he attempts to block the tears.

He rises and calls the dog.

'Come on, Foxtrot. Time for your walk.'

The dog looks at him dismissively.

'You may get a treat.'

The dog immediately plants itself down in front of him, staring up expectantly as Frank attaches the lead.

'Go for a couple of pints, Frank. Unwind.'

'Aye, maybe I will.'

'I'll have tea on the table by the time you get back. Steak and chips with onion gravy.'

'Smashing.'

He leads the dog to the door, stops, and gazes back.

'I couldn't have survived all these years without you, Meera. Love you.'

25

Saturday 28th June 11:37 am

It's a perfect Saturday morning in Whitby—clear skies, salt in the air, and just enough breeze to stop the heat from sticking. The sun sits fat and gold above the harbour, bathing West Cliff in light.

Zac plants his foot and flicks the football sideways. Sammy chases it with a burst of energy, laughing as Thomas intercepts and thuds it back with a precision that surprises everyone, including himself.

Behind them, the giant Ferris wheel rises like a skeleton of white steel, half-built, arms still bare. A couple of hi-vis workers mill around the base, dragging cables, calling instructions over the clang of scaffolding.

'When's it open, dad?' Thomas asks, breathless, shielding his eyes to squint up at the structure.

'Not sure, mate. Soon, I think. Next week maybe?'

'It's going to be higher than the Abbey,' Sammy says, gazing at the giant structure.

Zac laughs. 'I reckon so.'

'Can we go on it?'

'Course you can. If you've saved your pocket money.'

'Ha ha, very funny, dad,' Thomas says, kicking the ball, which whacks into Kelly's shins.

'Watch it, you little savages.'

She kicks the ball back, but it skitters past them and rolls down a grassy bank.

The boys chase it down the slope, trainers thudding, cheeks pink.

The jingle of an ice cream van drifts through the air—bright, tinny, irresistible. The boys freeze mid-kick.

'Dad...'

'Oh no,' Kelly groans.

'Come on, mam! Please?'

'It will ruin your lunch!'

Zac raises a hand in surrender and pulls a tenner from his pocket.

'Alright. I'll have a 99 with crushed nuts. Go queue up.'

Kelly rolls her eyes but relents, taking the note and shepherding the boys towards the van. The smell of sugary-sweet churros and fresh donuts wafts on the breeze as they wander off.

Zac strolls to the railings, resting his arms on the warm, chipped paint. Below, West Beach stretches out in a lazy sprawl—stripy deckchairs, toddlers digging holes, gulls wheeling overhead. The beach huts pop with colour—red, turquoise, lemon yellow—like sweet wrappers scattered across the front. A woman with a sunhat lifts her dog over the final step onto the sand. The tide is low, the sea glittering and becalmed as the tide slowly retreats.

He takes a breath and lets it rejuvenate him—salt, a faint smell of diesel from the boats, fried onions from an unseen burger stand. His eyes close for a moment. Not a police radio in sight. No crime scene. No death, no blood, or guts. Just the sea, the sun, and the distant sound of his boys laughing.

His gaze drifts along the beach where he spots the couple—unmistakable.

They're holding hands as they amble towards the sea.

'Hell. I forgot,' he murmurs as Sammy comes running up.

'Here you go, dad. Your 99 with nuts.'

Zac takes the ice cream cone, pulls out the Flake and takes a bite as his focus returns to the beach.

Sammy sucks on a rainbow-coloured ice lolly as he follows his father's gaze.

'Is that Uncle Frank and Aunty Meera down there?'

'Aye.'

'What are they doing?' he asks as Kelly and Thomas join them.

Kelly squints toward the shoreline. Her voice softens.

'I think it's time you told them, Zac. They're old enough now.'

Zac exhales slowly. 'They're placing a single white rose at the water's edge.'

Thomas frowns. 'Why?'

'Because a long, long time ago, they had a daughter.'

Thomas glances at Sammy. 'I've never met their daughter. I've met their niece. Where's the daughter?'

Zac's voice is steady, but low. 'She went missing. On this very day, years ago. Uncle Frank had taken her to the beach—right down there. It was packed. A proper summer's day. He went to buy ice creams. When he came back, she was gone.'

Sammy's brow knits together. 'Did she drown?'

'We don't know. If she did, her body was never found.'

Thomas hesitates. 'Was she taken? Like... by someone bad?'

Zac doesn't answer straight away.

'Maybe. That's the worst part. No one knows. She vanished without a trace.'

Thomas shakes his head. 'But you and Uncle Frank are police. You can find anyone.'

Zac tries to smile but can't quite manage it. 'We like to think so. But sometimes...' He lets the words trail off.

He looks back towards the couple by the sea.

Meera kneels. Frank stands a step behind, one hand on her shoulder. The white rose lies in the surf, nudged gently back and forth by the tide.

'Every year,' Zac continues, 'Meera comes back. Sometimes with Frank, sometimes alone. Just to mark the day. To remember.'

Thomas swallows. 'That's really sad.'

'Aye. It is.'

'What was her name?'

'Rose. Rosy Finnegan.'

Zac turns from the railing, brushing the thoughts away like sand from his hands.

'Right, what are we having for lunch—fish and chips or pizza?'

'Pizza!' both boys yell in unison.

'Pizza it is then.'

The lads scurry off, kicking the football between them, ice lollies clutched in sticky fingers.

Kelly slips her arm through Zac's.

'Christ,' he mutters. 'How do you live with something like that?'

'I don't know,' she says. 'It's one thing to lose a child. But not knowing... that's a life sentence.'

Zac nods, lips pressed thin. 'If anything ever happened to—'

She cuts him off with a finger to his lips. 'Shush. Don't say it. Just be here. With us. Live in the moment.'

He offers a weak smile, then glances one last time towards the sea.

'Aye, come on then. Twenty minutes in the amusement arcades, then grub.'

Far below, on the beach, the water picks up the rose and gently carries it away.

26

Sunday 29th June 10:05 am

The drive from Whitby to Clegg Farm is usually a leisurely forty minutes, thirty if you're in a rush.

Not today.

Prisha has deliberately taken a convoluted route, stomach in knots, her mind in a feverish battle.

She certainly doesn't want to see him—Adam.

And yet—desperately wants to see him at the same time.

Close to walking the forgiveness route, she weighs up the pros and cons.

The war between *logic* and emotion is intense. No prisoners.

He cheated. He'll do it again. No matter what he says, he'll do it again.

Maybe not? A lesson learned, perhaps. A misstep. An aberration. And who am I to cast the first stone? That kiss with Zac. I didn't encourage it. Yet when it unexpectedly arrived out of nowhere, I didn't resist. I should, and could have, but I didn't. In fact, the opposite. Fatal attraction.

Hang on a moment. Big difference between one kiss and having sex. Two different things entirely.

Are they? If we'd been somewhere more appropriate than out in the open, what would that kiss have led to?

Nothing. I'd have stopped way before it went any further.

Would you really?

Yes, of course I bloody would! I'm loyal and have will power. Self-restraint.

You're a hypocrite. And you're not looking at the big picture.

What big picture?

You wanted to be with Adam for the rest of your life. Get married. Resign from the force. Raise a family. Live a quiet existence as the capable farmer's wife. Do the accounts. Get involved with the children's schools and sports activities. Help on the farm. Provide a loving home in an idyllic setting away from the death and scumbags you have to deal with. Are you really going to throw all that away because of one minor hiccup?

One minor hiccup! I caught him naked playing horizontal Olympics with the pretty little vet! That's not a hiccup; it's a sniper shot to the head.

You're overreacting. Emotional. Judgement clouded. You just need a little time, that's all.

Really? You think so? I suppose... maybe you're right. I've talked to him a dozen times about setting up security cameras around the farm. If he did, then I could check in on him by phone throughout the day and night. Keep an eye on the toerag.

Snoop on him? You're crazy! That's not going to create trust. It would be toxic.

Well, what do you suggest?

Simple, a second, and final chance.

And set myself up for more pain in the future. What if he does it again?

And what if he doesn't?

How would I know?

You're a copper. You'd know.

I didn't know last time, did I? Trusted him implicitly. It was only by chance, a pure fluke, I caught him out.

Well then, we're nearly here. What's it to be? I say second chance. You?

I'm... not sure.

Big picture, Prisha. Look at the big picture. Kids running around the farmyard. Long walks in the hills. Cooking the Sunday roast. Making the perfect home for the perfect family.

Yeah... and while I'm slaving away over a hot stove or changing shitty nappies, he could be playing hide the sausage with some random in the hay shed.

Come on, Prisha. One last chance—just one. He deserves that. You deserve it.

Oh, God... I don't know.

Parking the car outside the front door, she grabs a shoulder bag then glances around the farmyard. The tractor's next to the diesel pump, but no sign of Adam.

For the first time since she was a little girl, she's unsure what to do. She doesn't appreciate the feeling. She's always in control, right or wrong; she knows her own mind. But not today.

Indecision about so many things.

Maybe call him?

No, could appear needy.

Should I go inside, and quickly gather my belongings, then scarper?

No, looks weak—avoidance.

Then what?

Her quandary is solved as Adam appears from the barn.

'Oh, Prisha. Thought I heard a car. Just refuelling the tractor. Cutting hay up on the top paddock.'

He says it as if nothing's amiss.

As he saunters towards her, his features become more evident.

He has two black eyes and a small band-aid over his nose.

Guilt and self-loathing swamp her.

Swallows.

'Hi,' she replies meekly. 'How's the nose?'

A grin. 'Not broken. Just badly bruised. Two shiners though.'

'Yes. I can see. Did you go to the hospital?'

'No.'

'I'm... sorry. I shouldn't...'

He cuts her off. 'Don't apologise. You had every right.'

'No, I didn't. You never have the right to physically hurt someone. Or emotionally, for that matter.'

The arrow hits.

'Yes. I know. Sorry.'

He shuffles, hands in pockets, dirt smeared cheeks, but handsome as hell all the same in Prisha's eyes.

'How about a cuppa and we can talk?' he suggests hopefully.

A shake of the head. 'No. I've come to get my things.'

'Really?'

'Yes.'

His facade melts as he suddenly approaches, all haste and concern.

'Prisha, look, I know it was wrong. But you must believe me, it was a stupid one-off.'

'Why?'

He shrugs, seemingly uncertain himself.

'I... I don't know. She was here. We flirted. One thing led to another. I swear on my mother's life it will never happen again.'

'How do I know that?'

'Because it's true. A stupid mistake. I was weak.'

'Yes, you were.'

Nearer still, almost at touching point.

'Please, Prisha, forgive me? I was a dickhead. Please give me, *us*, another chance. I'll make it up to you.'

The words are familiar to Prisha. Having dealt with way too many domestic violence incidents in her uniform days. The battered wife, the contrite tearful husband swearing blind he'd change.

They never did.

Leopards can't change their spots any more than aggressive males can stop using their fists to vent their anger and frustration on a weak target. It's ingrained. In their nature. Words can't mask it.

But still... her heart is pounding. Her feelings for him are so strong she wants to believe, desperate to trust again.

She falters.

'Ahem, I should really collect my things and get going.'

She turns to head into the house.

'Please, Prisha, I'm begging. Life is shit without you. I need you. You need me. We're good together. Don't throw it all away over one stupid, irrelevant mistake. Surely, I deserve another chance?'

She doesn't like the words—*I deserve*—like everything is about him. Nothing about her.

Nevertheless, her barriers are disintegrating at an alarming rate.

She hesitates and pushes the door open.

'I... I need time. Alone. To think things through.'

A backdown, her resolute defiance in retreat.

Adam breathes. 'Yes. Of course. As long as it takes. I'll be waiting. Whatever you decide, I'll agree to. Just please think things through. What we are together. Our life. Our future family. Everything. It's not worth throwing away over nothing.'

She turns and offers him a thin smile, then enters the house.

In the bedroom, she pulls open the wardrobe and gathers a couple of blouses, her precious Armani jeans, and her expensive Nike trainers. She drops them into the bag. Heading back down the hallway—she stops.

'Perfume,' she murmurs, remembering her expensive bottle of Chanel Coco Mademoiselle in the bathroom.

Entering, she spots it straight away. Slips it into her shoulder bag. Turning to leave, she hesitates—then slowly pivots on her heels.

There are two toothbrushes in the holders attached to the wall. A blue and a pink one—his and hers. Adam's little touch, not her idea.

But lying forlornly on the counter is another toothbrush, this one—green. Lifting it up, she inspects it.

She can't drag her eyes away as logic and emotion restart their bickering.

Why is there another toothbrush?

Don't start, Prisha. It's just a toothbrush. Big deal.

But why?

Could be all manner of reasons.

Such as?

Adam's spare, or an old one he never got round to binning. More likely, he uses it to clean gunk from the plughole. Perfect for those hard-to-reach gaps.

Yeah, right. He's a farmer, not a contestant on Queer Eye for the Straight Guy.

Don't do it, Prisha. You're searching for trouble when there's none to be found.

Hmm... am I? He didn't go to hospital.

What?

For his nose. He didn't go to hospital.

So what?

Then how did he know it wasn't broken?

I don't know. Maybe he saw a doctor instead.

Or a vet.

Oh, please. Let it go.

Dropping to her haunches, she pulls open the bathroom cupboard doors and peers inside.

Sees it.

She reaches in, pulls the small box out, and rises.

'Lying bastard,' she hisses.

The balloon of hope inside her doesn't explode—it simply deflates.

In her heart of hearts, she knew.

What have you got to say for yourself now?

Emotion remains uncharacteristically silent.

Cat got your tongue? Come on, out with it. You had plenty to say before.

I... was... wrong. You were right. Happy?

Yes. Thanks.

She surprises herself. Anger is in abeyance.

All she feels is a soft sadness—not intense. More like the moment you reach the end of a good book, or your favourite TV series wraps its final episode. A gentle, disappointed kind of reflection that passes quickly.

She calmly walks back out into the farmyard where Adam stands by the tractor. The click-click-click of the diesel pump ticks away.

A roguish smile.

'Get everything?'

'Yes.'

'Good. We'll be able to work this out, Prisha. In a few months from now, it will be nothing more than a minor blip. All relationships have their ups and downs.'

She drops the bag into the car and takes a step towards him.

'Who does the green toothbrush belong to?'

His eyes flick sideways, then back.

'Green tooth... oh, I was having a clean-out. Must've forgotten to bin it.'

'You've always been a bad liar, Adam. That's why it's so easy to tell when you're telling the truth.'

He holds his hands out.

'Christ, Prisha, what's wrong with you? You're paranoid. It's a bloody old toothbrush.'

'No, it's not. I checked the bristles.'

A cynical laugh. 'You've got to be joking. Is this what it's going to be like now? You—always suspicious, always accusing?'

She pulls the engagement ring from her pocket.

'Catch.'

She flicks it into the air.

Lurching forward, he snatches it one-handed.

'I don't believe you're doing this. You didn't even give us a chance.'

She pulls a small box of tampons from her coat, holds it up to his eye level.

'Tampax,' she says, flat and cold.

He shifts on his feet. 'They're yours because they're certainly not mine.'

A tight smile. 'No, they're not. I've never used Tampax in my life. I use Lil-Lets.'

He shakes his head and lets out a hollow snarl.

'You've been bloody snooping.'

'I'm a detective. I prefer the term *investigating*. And you, you lying, snivelling piece of crap, have been caught out, red-handed again. Twice in one week. That's a top effort.'

She turns, climbs into the car.

The window's already down as she starts the engine.

'Bye, Adam. Take a good look at what you once had. The best thing that ever happened to you. And you blew it. Have a happy life.'

This time she doesn't bother looking in the rear-view mirror.

The dead weight of hurt and betrayal melts away as the car bumps and rattles down the steep track, leaving Clegg Farm, and Adam, far behind.... forever.

27

Monday 30th June 8:33 am

Prisha emerges from her early morning dental appointment with a sore mouth and a significantly lighter bank balance.

'Daylight robbery,' she mutters, pulling her phone from her pocket.

She ambles down Skinner Street, then cuts across Flowergate, flicking through emails, texts, Facebook, and WhatsApp.

Nothing of any note.

She's fooling herself.

And she knows it.

She blocked Adam on everything.

Ghosted him.

It's impossible for him to get in touch—unless he turns up in person.

But who does that these days?

A stalker, maybe?

Still scrolling, she steps off the pavement without looking.

The violent buzz of a motorbike rips through the morning air.

She halts—instincts flaring—as the bike screams past, inches from her.

Feels the heat brush her jacket.

Shock gives way instantly to rage.

'You stupid little dickhead!' she yells after the rider, who's already disappearing into the distance, gearing down, engine snarling as he takes a corner.

An older man across the road stops walking his dog and glares at her.

She notices.

'Can I help you?' she snaps.

'It was your bloody fault, love. So busy with your nose in that phone. You could've got yourself killed.'

'He was speeding, actually. But thanks. If I want your advice, I'll ask for it.'

'Suit yourself, sweetheart. Your life... or death.'

He moves on, muttering under his breath. The dog lingers, nose glued to a lamppost, legs stiffening against the yank of the leash.

Prisha watches them go, then glances back down the road.

The bike is long gone.

She draws in a long, slow breath, realising only now that her hands are trembling slightly.

Not from fear—more the sudden jolt of awareness.

The little twat on the bike believes he's invincible.

He's not.

And for the first time ever—she experiences the same realisation—*neither is she.*

28

Frank parts the Venetian blinds and peers into the office. It's a sorry-looking sight. Only Zac and Dinkel are in today, and they're sitting so far apart from each other they'd need semaphore signals to communicate. Frank doesn't like a quiet office. He relishes the chatter, the excited exchange of information, the occasional cheer as a vital piece of evidence falls into place. A quiet office means one thing in his book—an investigation stalling.

He's not feeling full of vim and vigour himself after yesterday. But taking a deep breath and geeing himself up, he enters the incident room.

His entrance receives only casual glances from both men.

'Gordon Bennett, I know it's Monday morning, but it's dead in here. I've seen more life in a Cornish pasty. Where's the energy, the zest, the excitement of the chase?'

Zac yawns as Dinkel twiddles a pen in and out of his fingers, a recent trick he's learned.

Frank holds his palms up in defence. 'Whoa, calm down, not all at once.'

His attempt at sarcasm falls flat.

Zac eventually speaks. 'Sorry, Frank, it's just a little stagnant in here without Prisha around. Old Noddy in the corner over there won't be hosting his own talk show anytime soon.'

Frank leans against a table and sighs. 'Yes, I feel it too. But let's keep positive. If we cross our fingers, maybe she'll return before the end of the week.'

He straightens and claps his hands together, hoping to create some urgency.

'Right, let's have an update on the Iona Jacob's case. Zac, do the honours.'

The door creaks open as Prisha walks in backwards, balancing a cardboard tray containing four coffees in one hand, and a large paper bag in the other. She places her load on the table.

'Morning,' she declares. 'Coffees and cinnamon donuts for everyone.'

For a moment, the three men are stunned—before erupting into cheers. Frank and Zac each throw their arms around her.

'Great to have you back, Prisha,' Zac says, grinning madly.

'Aye, you're like a breath of fresh air breezing in here,' Frank adds, grinning. 'I was just about to call the paramedics to see if these two buggers still had a pulse.'

Prisha is a little overwhelmed at the rock star welcome.

Frank rests his hand on her shoulder, serious.

'I'll only ask the once, but how are things between you and... you know?'

Prisha feigns an anaemic smile and folds her hands together in dramatic fashion.

'A closed book. All over. Done and dusted. And I was nearly done and dusted twenty minutes ago when a little sod on a motorbike nearly wiped me out. Speeding down Flowergate. I'm not joking, I was an inch away from being hit.'

'Did you get his plate?' Frank asks, concerned.

'No. It happened so fast.'

Zac chuckles. 'Never a copper around when you need one, is there?'

'Very funny. Now, I have to say, I'm itching to get back to work.' She glances at Dinkel. 'Thanks for the nightly email updates on the cases, Dinkel. Doesn't do to fall too far behind with the homework.'

'My pleasure, ma'am. Good to have you back on deck.'

Frank swiftly arranges three chairs in front of the whiteboard.

'Zac was just about to do the brief on the Iona Jacobs case.'

'Excellent,' she replies, taking a seat. 'Okay, maestro, where are we at?'

Zac devours the donut in seconds and washes it down with strong black coffee, clearly energised.

He steps up to the board. 'Friday was a very interesting day. Me and Dinks paid a visit to Mrs Eileen Selkirk. So, I'll begin there.'

Tapping the board, a display of names and timelines appears.

'To the crux of the issue, June 4th, 1989. Malachi said he left home for the Ravensbane Estate at 3:40 pm. Eileen said he left around 3 pm. People can vary a little in the timing of events, but forty minutes is way off.

'At the time, Eileen was a nurse working in the ICU at York. She said timekeeping was imperative in her job, you know, checking on patients and dispensing their meds on the dot. Even had a little watch on her uniform. Malachi was a gamekeeper, probably a job where time moves a little slower. Although Eileen is ninety-five and frail in body, her mind's razor sharp.'

Frank stretches his legs. 'Let's run with Eileen's version for a moment. If Malachi left home at 3 pm, we deduced it takes about three minutes to get to the crash site by car from his place. So, about 3:03 to 3:05, let's say. When Dinkel went on his little cycling expedition the other day, he confirmed Iona would have arrived at the site at 3:03 pm. Now, I'd call that a smoking gun, wouldn't you?'

Zac raises his eyebrows. 'On the face of it, yes. He rounds the sharp bend, maybe going too fast for a narrow country road, clips Iona, and panics. Except—he was heading north, and from the wild strawberries on the road that we spotted on the crash scene photographs, we concluded the car which hit Iona was travelling south, due to the fact the strawberries were behind the bicycle.'

Dinkel raises his hand 'Is it possible he passed Iona, remembered he'd forgotten something, turned around, headed back home, then hit her?'

Prisha glances at him. 'It's possible, but is it plausible? If he'd already passed her, he'd be aware of her presence on the road and would likely drive slower. Plus, another thing; Malachi and Mrs Selkirk are both on the same page as to the time Malachi arrived back—4 pm. If Malachi *did* hit Iona just after 3 pm, what was he doing for the best part of an hour?'

Zac nods in agreement. 'Let's not forget the police checked his Land Rover for damage and there was none, and his car was dark green, whereas the paint flakes at the scene were white. Moving on,' he continues as a copy of the photograph from Mrs Selkirk's wall appears on the screen. He taps on it.

'Thanks to Dinkel's eagle eye, we have this little beauty. A moment captured in time. I used my phone to take a snap of the photo, so I apologise for the poor quality. Front and centre are Mrs Selkirk with her two teenage daughters, April 2nd 1989, a month before Iona was hit. It's at the Ashenby Easter Fair, held on the village green. To the left—four men—unwittingly captured in the frame. Reverend Hartley and Noah Hampton are clearly discernible, and Eileen confirmed the other two men are Amos Baker and Malachi Abbott. Four men in their mid-twenties enjoying a drink and an afternoon out together.'

He leans forward and points at the image of the young woman.

'This we believe is Iona. She has her back to the camera, but her height, hair colour, and, more importantly, the clothes she's wearing match the photograph we have of her on file.'

Prisha nods. 'Yes. The way her jeans are turned up at the bottom, the bunched-up white socks, and she's wearing the same loop earrings.'

'Correct. Now cast your gaze to the back left—a car—or, to be more precise, a white Citroen 2CV. Dinkel cross-checked the initial investigation, which lists every vehicle and their owners that were visited in the area. There's no record of a Citroen 2CV, a very distinctive make and model of car for that neck of the woods. Now get this—according to Eileen, the car belonged to Reverend Hartley.'

'Now we have Hartley in the mix,' Prisha states.

'Yes,' Zac replies. 'All conjecture, I know, but what if the conversation Hartley and Iona had at the church preceding the hit-and-run wasn't as innocuous as Hartley made out in his statement? Maybe they argued, or Iona revealed she was pregnant, and the child was his. There were rumours floating around the village the pair were more than just friends.'

Frank grimaces. 'Okay, let's run with it for a moment. There's possibly a heated argument, or a bombshell dropped, and Iona takes off on her bike, maybe to calm down or think things through. Hartley stews for a few minutes, then in a fit of anger, or remorse, jumps in his car and takes off after her.'

Dinkel interjects. 'But surely he'd have left the village via Ashenby Lane, sir? It runs right past the church. Which brings us back to the same issue—he'd have been driving north, and the vehicle that hit Iona was driving south.'

'Hmm... fair point.'

Zac frowns. 'Or, he knew she was heading back to the pub via the scenic route and was hoping to catch up with her as she re-entered the village from the far end. That way he would have been driving south.'

'We've got a lot of hypotheticals,' Frank comments, puffing his cheeks out. 'Let's say Malachi and Hartley are both suspects, but proving it is another thing. And of course—they could be totally innocent. Anything else on the Iona case we need to be aware of before we move on?'

'Just one thing of minor interest, probably nothing. But when I was talking with Eileen, she mentioned we weren't the only people who had taken a sudden interest in Iona recently.'

'Oh, aye?'

'About a year ago, Violet Fox, unofficial leader of the Wicca commune, spent a few hours with her. She was conducting research for a book she was planning to write about local tales and legends from the area. Not sure how they got onto the topic, but Eileen said Violet seemed very interested in Iona's death.'

'That bloody woman,' Prisha snaps. 'I didn't like the cut of her cloth the first time I clapped eyes on her. Why would she be snooping around into Iona's death after thirty-six years?'

Zac holds his hands up in defence. 'Hang on, Prisha. She did say she was a history professor, and we know the Wicca lot are into their Pagan folklore and rituals, so her doing research for a historical book is entirely plausible.'

'Doesn't explain her fascination with Iona, does it?'

'Eileen never said it was fascination. She said Violet was *interested*. Maybe just idle chatter during her research. Anyway, I have one last bombshell from our visit to Mrs Selkirk. She was working night shift at the time of the hit-and-run, and one of her patients was Iona. As you know, the doctors pronounced Iona brain dead and were keeping her alive until it was safe to deliver the baby. One night, as Eileen was giving her a bed bath, she said Iona briefly opened her eyes and uttered a single word—Nicholas.'

'Do you believe her?' Prisha asks.

'Yes. What possible reason would she have for making it up? She didn't even tell the police at the time as she thought it would only inflame the rumours.'

'So, two scenarios; Iona and Hartley were in a relationship, possibly she loved him, she wakes up and utters his name.'

'Yes.'

'Or she was indicating who was driving the car.'

'That's my take on it.'

Frank takes a sip of his coffee. 'Okay, let's move on to Operation Raven and the three suspicious deaths.'

Zac taps the board, and an officious-looking report populates the screen.

'Okay, the big news. This is the official report from vehicle forensics. I paid a visit to their workshop on Friday afternoon and spoke with their chief examiner, Terry Claymore, a quirky little character. But to give him his due, he knows his shit, and he's obsessively thorough.'

'So what's the big news?' Frank asks.

'There's no way the slasher on the tractor could have accidentally lowered onto Amos Baker. It required human intervention.'

'Was he one hundred per cent certain?'

'Totally. He explained all the mechanics and how everything worked. Pulled things apart to check for wear and tear. No electrical or mechanical faults. And the icing on the cake—if it *had* been a malfunction, the tractor would have either been running when the mechanic arrived, or the tractor would have run out of fuel. Neither was the case.'

'Have you checked the mechanic out?'

'Aye. Local lad. Good reputation. Hard worker. No disputes with anyone. Likeable and easy-going. Glowing report from his employer. If he was involved, there's no clear motive. But gut instinct—he's in the clear.'

'So, we have two murders. Malachi had the brake lines cut on his vehicle, and some bugger deliberately re-started and lowered the slasher onto Amos Baker.'

'Yes.'

'But nothing further on the death of Hartley?'

'No.'

Frank waggles a finger in his ear and turns to Prisha.

'Thoughts, or anything to add?'

'Yes, as it happens. I have some intel on the braided coin found in Malachi's car, and in Baker's cab. It has a name.'

'Which is?'

'The Crucifix Knot.'

29

Prisha finishes her recap about the possible significance of the Crucifix Knot. The book, *The Three Crones,* is passed around as *Chapter XIV – Of Knots and Judgement* is silently read by her colleagues.

Frank doesn't like the way things are going.

'We've got more loose ends than the time Meera tried knitting a tea cosy.'

He rises wearily and fronts his team as Prisha takes a seat.

'Okay, let's take a moment and piece together what we have in a linear fashion. Flipping back and forth between these two cases, which *may* not be linked, is toasting my crust.'

He picks up a marker and begins a list of bullet points on the board.

Iona Jacobs Hit-and-Run 1989
- Accident or intentional?

- Original investigation hampered due to staffing issues/events at the time.

- Missing evidence i.e. the white paint flakes, testing results.

- Contradictory times of Malachi leaving home.

- No record of Hartley's white Citroen ever being assessed.

- Iona pregnant - no knowledge of the father. Hartley or other?

- Iona wakes from coma - says a single word - Nicholas. A call to her lover, or a recollection of the driver?

Operation Raven
- Monday, May 1st - 3 am - Lord Hampton abducted. Imprisoned in disused mineshaft. **Attempted murder?**

- Monday, May 1st - 12:20 pm - Malachi leaves The Crown in Ashenby. Brake lines cut. Car crashes. Drowns in river. Traces of aconite. **Murder.**

- Thursday, May 4th - 9:10 am - Reverend Hartley hanged in St Mary's. **Accident, suicide, murder?**

- Tuesday, June 24th - Amos Baker decapitated under slasher. **Murder.**

Theories
- Possible link between the Three Crones Witch Trials—deaths similar, professions similar, Crucifix Knot on or near victims.

- Crucifix Knot left at the scene of Malachi and Baker's murder, but not at Hartley's nor Hampton's attempted murder.

- Is the Knot a marker of death or something else?

- Possible involvement in Iona's death - Hartley last to see her. Malachi discovers body. Hampton and Baker's involvement—none so far?

- Lord Hampton - undiagnosed illness - relevant or not?

Critical Lines of Enquiry
- Re-interview witnesses still alive from Iona's case.

- Find original lab report on white paint flakes. Make and model.

- Who's making the Crucifix Knot? Similar in appearance to the Wicker Girl medallion, Morrigan Penhallow gave to Zac (refers to herself as The Wicker Girl).

- Aconite - obtained from monkshood / wolfsbane - plants that grow in abundance in the area. Who has herbal knowledge? Wicca commune, or someone else?

He attaches the top to the marker pen.

'Okay, anyone got anything to add?'

Zac shakes his head. 'No, I think you've just about nailed it, Frank.'

Dinkel raises his arm. 'Erm, there is one thing, sir. It may be irrelevant.'

'Go on, lad, let's hear it.'

'You remember when Iona first arrived in Ashenby, she worked as a maid at Ravensbane Castle for about six months?'

'Aye. What about it?'

He pulls his notepad out. 'I've been doing some calculations.'

'Let's hear them.'

Dinkel flicks through his notepad, then taps it with a pencil.

'According to the original investigation, when Iona was admitted to the hospital on June 4th, they discovered she was eighteen weeks pregnant. Well, going back eighteen weeks from June 4th takes us to approximately the end of February, early March.'

'The date she conceived?'

'Yes.'

'And?'

He shuffles in his chair. 'Ahem, well that's it, really.'

Frank stares at him unblinking. 'As you alluded to at the beginning, what's the relevance?'

Dinkel reddens and fidgets with the edge of his notepad. 'Erm, I'm not quite sure, sir.'

Frank scratches his head. 'Okay, lad, well, ten out of ten for due diligence.'

'Wait, Frank,' Zac says, coming to Dinkel's defence for once. 'I think I know what he's getting at.'

'You do? Good. Then educate me.'

'He's asking—was Iona still working at Ravensbane Castle when she fell pregnant? And if she was working there at the time, did her pregnancy have anything to do with Lord Hampton? Let's not forget, she left Ravensbane to go and work at the pub. The question is, why? And Ashenby Lane joins the only road that leads to the castle. What if she wasn't heading directly back to the pub as she told Hartley, but on her way to see Lord Hampton?'

'Is that what you were getting at, constable?' Frank asks, staring at Dinkel.

Dinkel nods. 'Yes, I think so. It was more of an abstract thought than anything concrete.'

'Abstract is for painters and philosophers, lad, not detectives. Turn up with abstract in a murder trial and the defence barrister will be spitting out your pips.'

'Yes, Mr Finnegan.'

Frank muses. 'Hmm... the waters become murkier. Did Hampton get Iona up the plum duff and dismiss her? Did she leave of her own accord, keeping the pregnancy a secret from him? Or is it just another false lead? Dinkel, those postcards Iona sent back to her mother—I want you to study them and see if Iona ever mentions a date when she left working at the castle and started work at the pub. If she did leave in late February—early March, then maybe there was a good reason for it. And by the way, abstract or not, good work.'

Dinkel visibly grows. 'Thank you, sir. I'll get onto the postcards today.'

Frank claps his hands together, pleased with the teamwork and the lateral thinking. His gaze drifts onto Prisha, who has been noticeably silent, preoccupied.

'Are you still with us, Prisha?'

Zero response as she stares out of the window.

'Prisha?'

'The motorbike,' she murmurs, eyes glazed.

Frank wonders if she's returned to work too early.

'A near miss can make us think of what might have been, Prisha. An inch closer. A second earlier. It seems like life and death are nothing more than chance and circumstance. And after all you've been through recently, well, I can unders...'

She rises to her feet, shaking her head.

'No. Not that motorbike,' she whispers, edging towards the board. 'What if we've been focussing on the wrong thing?'

'I don't follow?' Frank says, perturbed by her unusual behaviour.

As if someone's flicked a switch, she becomes animated.

'Vehicles!' she shouts, tapping at the board in an agitated manner. 'Bloody vehicles, vehicles, vehicles! Even the initial investigation focussed on vehicles—assuming it was a *car* that hit Iona. As though *all* vehicles are cars. What if it wasn't a car; what if it was a motorbike?' She turns to Dinkel. 'In the report on the vehicles that were checked in 1989, is there a single mention of a motorbike?'

He shakes his head. 'No, ma'am.'

A momentary hush falls over the room.

Prisha turns to Frank.

'Me and Zac searched Hampton's classic car garage after his abduction.'

'What about it?'

'All the cars were parked in neat rows. Polished, gleaming, pristine. Every tool in place. But at the back of the garage was a tiny shed, the sort of thing you'd keep gardening equipment in. Inside, a broken down, old motorbike. It was out of place. Why keep a decrepit, knackered bike?' She spins to Zac. 'Remember?'

'Aye, I do. A late-80s Honda GB500. Bit of a boy racer's bike in the day. It had been involved in some sort of acci...'

He tails off as the pieces fall into place.

Prisha finishes the sentence for him.

'Accident. A broken headlight. Bumps and scratches, and what looked like dried blood on the fuel tank.'

Frank drags a hand across his face. 'Christ! And Lord Hampton lost a foot in a motorbike accident. Never specified the exact date. Kept the amputated foot in a jar of formaldehyde as a reminder of his reckless ways.'

'Maybe he kept the bike for the same reason?' Zac suggests.

'Or possibly he stored it out of sight during the investigation and never got round to disposing of it,' Prisha adds.

Frank takes command. 'Right, I want another search warrant for Hampton's gaff and then, Zac, Prisha, get over there and seize that bike for forensics. And while you're near Ashenby, call in to see Lilac and Morrigan Penhallow. Present them with the Crucifix Knot and see if they know who makes them.'

Zac nods. 'Okay, boss. I also want another chat with the landlord, Edwin Featherstone.'

'What for?'

'I want confirmation about the white Citroen; see if he can verify Eileen Selkirk's claim that the car belonged to Hartley.'

'Good idea. Dinkel?'

'Sir?'

'Another job for you. Find out the exact date of Hampton's accident. Search all the public hospital admission records for June 4th, 1989, and see if his name crops up.'

Zac cuts in. 'Hang on, Frank. Hampton would have used one of the top surgeons in the land, which means a private hospital. He wouldn't have gone to the NHS.'

'True. But when he was initially peeled off the road, it would have been a taxpayer-funded ambulance that transported him to a public hospital, probably York. From there, then yes, he may have been transferred to a private hospital. There's always a trail, Zac, always a trail.'

He grins at his team.

'Okay, gang, what are you waiting for? Let's get to work!'

30

The great oak doors of Ravensbane Castle tower above them, sun-warmed and pitted with age. Prisha is standing alongside Zac on the wide stone terrace, the midday heat pressing gently against her skin. Behind them, the estate stretches out in picture-perfect symmetry—sweeping lawns, a shimmering lake, a peacock dragging its feathers like royalty. In the middle distance, a handful of men work in silence, hedge laying, weaving young saplings into a dense barrier. Members of the Wicca commune, like apparitions from another century. No women. No chatter. Just a quiet, methodical efficiency. Only one man glances over—Oak, unmistakable by his sheer size.

Zac rings the bell again, distant chimes ringing out. He turns and watches as the white forensic transit van comes to a gentle halt on the driveway, scrunching pebbles underneath.

'Lady Hampton's going to drop her shit when we serve her with this,' he says, waggling the search warrant in front of Prisha.

Prisha is distracted as she studies the Wicca men hard at work.

'It's an odd setup, don't you think?'

Zac follows her gaze. 'Not sure about odd. Unconventional, yes.'

'No, I don't mean the lifestyle. The way the men do all the manual work. Their only purpose, toil, and procreation. It's like they're enslaved. And don't make any cheap jokes about sex.'

The door creaks open.

'Yes, can help you?' the maid, Magdalena, asks, ripples of concern sweeping across her face.

Zac offers her a warm smile. 'Are Lord and Lady Hampton at home?'

'Lord Hampton—yes. But Lady Hampton give me strict instructions he not disturbed. He unwell. In bed.'

'And Lady Hampton?'

'No. She go to market in village, then to York for her, how you say—pampering? Manicure, pedicure, massage. She no back until late afternoon.'

Zac frowns and hands her a copy of the warrant.

'We have a search warrant for Lord Hampton's garage.'

She takes the papers in total confusion. 'What this?'

'We—the *police*—need-to-search-shed,' he explains, talking louder, enunciating each word as if it might help.

'Oh, okay. You know way?'

'Yes, we'll let you know when we're finished.'

'Okay. I clean house. Sometime not hear bell.'
'Understood. Thanks.'

Prisha and Zac wait outside the garage as three white-suited forensics officers enter.

'That little storage shed right at the back,' Prisha says, pointing.

They nod and silently begin their mission.

Spinning around, Prisha takes in the stunning views of the verdant hills at the back of the castle. Sunlight flashes from a row of greenhouses in the distance.

'Fancy a walk?'

'The warrant is for the garage only.'

She grins. 'I know. It's a walk, that's all. Nothing to do with police business.'

He pulls a doubtful face. 'Aye, I believe you. Thousands wouldn't.'

They amble along a gravel path that dips steeply, leading them down below the stone terrace above. Following its curve, they pass clipped hedges, small fruit trees, and a crumbling folly where a cherub raises a trumpet to the sky. At the end, they push open a wooden gate and step into the space behind the glasshouses, where the air is still and the scent of damp earth and a pungent, herbal smell hangs like warm fog.

They're struck by the scale. Three tall glasshouses, each at least sixty feet long, stretch east to west across the rear of the grounds. Inside, a dense swathe of greenery thrives in the filtered light, with fat red tomatoes hanging pendulous from tangled stems like ornaments.

'Shit the bed,' Zac whispers as they creep along. 'You could feed a small town with this lot.'

'It's not a hobby, is it? This is business.'

They push open a door and walk inside, immediately hit by the sticky heat, coddled in stringent aromas.

Zac saunters off left as Prisha heads right, ducking and weaving past overhanging leaves and stems.

She glides along past tomatoes, sweet peppers, chillies, cucumbers, aubergines, runner beans, onions, garlic, and a dozen cold frames containing salad greens, lettuce, rocket, baby spinach.

Rounding a corner, she's confronted by a myriad of herbs: basil, sage, parsley, mint, oregano, thyme, and lemongrass.

It's warm and unbelievably peaceful, the soothing trickle of water the only sound. It's almost as if she can hear the plants gently growing.

Leaving through the opposite door, she takes a deep breath in the refreshingly cooler air before entering the next greenhouse. It's a similar layout. But the foliage is denser, the vegetables at a later stage, obviously the first sowing of the season, she thinks. Removing her lightweight jacket, the sweat slides down her back, her blouse already sticking to her. At one point, she feels like she's an explorer in a dense tropical rainforest, the vegetations is so thick. She emerges on the opposite side and pauses to catch her breath.

In the corner are a set of plants she doesn't recognise. Edging forward, she studies them. There's a sign half blotted out by leaves that she gingerly brushes aside.

APOTHECARY BEDS
Caution: Do not eat. Wear gloves when handling.

Each plant is grouped with its kin, a wooden name marker stabbed into the soil beside it. Prisha pulls on a pair of latex gloves and moves methodically from one to the next.

Yarrow. Comfrey. Feverfew. Mugwort. Henbane. Poppy. Skullcap. Mandrake. Hemlock. Foxglove.

She takes out her phone and takes a few quiet photos, before her gaze catches on a plant set slightly apart, like a banished neighbour.

Monkshood.

It stands tall and composed, its deep violet petals curled into a monk's cowl, exuding a faint, woody bitterness—a warning of its potency.

'Aconite,' she murmurs, and fires off two quick shots.

She pauses.

A soft creak behind her—wood flexing, maybe glass expanding. There's not a breath of air, so it's not the wind.

She turns sharply. Rows of foliage and stems stand motionless under the greenhouse haze. Nothing moves.

'Zac?' she calls.

Her voice feels small in the moist air.

Silence.

She swallows as a shadow flickers through the foliage a few beds away.

There and gone.

The fine hairs on her arms lift.

'Hello?' Her tone hardens. 'Who's there?'

No reply. Just the soft ticking of water dripping onto soil and the faint buzz of fat bumblebees.

She takes a slow step back, heart beating faster, every leafy rustle amplified.

Looking at her phone to call Zac, she notices there's no signal.

The hothouses are in a deep hollow behind the house, the dense foliage probably also inhibiting the signal.

'Damn it.' Slipping the phone away, she peels off the latex gloves and stuffs them into her pocket and turns to leave. She pushes aside a thick tomato plant—and is abruptly halted.

'Ah!'

She looks up into the face of Oak.

'Have you got permission to be in here?' the deep, bass timbre voice growls.

'Yes, Lord Hampton said it was all right to have a wander around,' she replies, frugal with the truth.

His suspicions dissolves.

'Hmm...'

He's uncomfortably close. Prisha retreats a little.

'You're that copper,' he says. 'Saw you at the funeral last week.'

'Yes, that's right. And by the size of you, I'm assuming you're Oak?'

'Aye. That be me.'

Nervous, vulnerable, a single female alone, she points indiscriminately.

'Some place you have here. Very impressive.'

He doesn't look. Simply reaches out and plucks a ripe tomato from a plant, wipes it down his checked shirt then slowly sinks his teeth into the flesh.

A drizzle of juice meanders through his beard in a tiny rivulet.

Swipes it away with his hairy forearm.

'Sweet,' he whispers, as his eyes drift to her breasts.

He offers the tomato to her.

'Bite?'

A nervous smile. 'Thanks, but I won't. I'm sure it's delicious.'

He sticks the whole fruit into his mouth, chews, then pulls another from a stem. His left thumb massages the red skin slowly, provocatively, around and around.

'Pomme d'amour,' he murmurs, inching closer. 'Learnt that. Took me ages.'

'Sorry?'

'Miss Violet says that's what the French call them—pommes d'amour. Love apple. They're an aphro...

aphro... aphro...' he stutters and twitches, struggling with the word.

'Aphrodisiac?'

A large grin. 'Yeah, that's the word. Good for sex.'

Prisha cringes. 'Really. That's interesting.' Another step back. 'Ahem... I was just admiring your apothecary beds. Enough poison there to wipe out an army.'

Oak glances over her shoulder at the plot and frowns.

'Miss Violet says everything is a poison if you have too much of it. They're herbal medicines. Nothing they can't cure, if mixed in the right hands. Hope you didn't touch anything. Even the smallest amount of sap can be deadly... *if it enters the body.*'

'No. I saw the warning.'

'Prisha!'

She breathes a sigh of relief at the sound of Zac's voice.

'Over here!' she yells back. 'You certainly must have a green thumb; this place is thriving.'

He bites into the tomato. 'Nature's gift. Good soil, clean water, natural fertiliser, no chemicals. It's not hard to do.'

'And the apothecary patch—I suppose you've got to be cautious?'

His face hardens. 'That's women's work. Bad luck for men to go anywhere near the plants. Not allowed. Miss Violet says so. Only those with the knowledge are allowed to reap and sow.'

'And who has *this* knowledge—Miss Violet by any chance?'

He nods, grinning inanely.

'Aye, that's right. Just Miss Violet, Lady Hampton, and... the Wicker Girl.'

31

Tuesday 1st July 1:05 pm

The car glides along the deserted country lanes before coming to a stop at a T-junction. Zac gives a cursory glance both ways, then pulls out.

His phone lets out a loud ping.

He turns to Prisha.

'Check that, will you?'

Prisha picks it up. 'Your battery's at ten per cent,' she says, reaching for the charger and plugging it in.

'That little bugger—Sammy,' he grumbles.

Prisha grins. 'What's he done now?'

'I had my phone on charge last night, and he said he needed to plug his in. I told him to swap it back when he was done. Clearly, he didn't. Doesn't matter how many chargers and leads I buy—the kids always bloody lose them. And the wife's just as bad.'

He glances across at her and smiles.

She catches it. 'What?'

'You look different today.'

'In what way?'

Another admiring glance.

'Not sure. I think it's your hair.'

'I always wear it in a ponytail.'

'Yeah, but it's... different.'

'It's a high ponytail today. That's the only change.'

'Hmm. Well, it suits you. Makes you look—impish.'

'Impish?'

'Yeah, you know—sporty, a bit wild.'

She laughs, repeats the words, and feels the heat rise in her cheeks.

'Sporty. Right.'

'And that yellow hair tie, scrunchie thing—it's a nice contrast against your jet black hair.'

'Thanks.' She clears her throat, more flustered than she'd like. 'Anyway—when we get to the village, I'll hop out near the post office and call in to see Lilac Penhallow and, hopefully, Morrigan. See if we can get to the bottom of who makes the Crucifix Knots.'

'The person who makes them isn't necessarily the one who left them at the crime scenes.'

She throws him a look. 'I'm aware of that. Once you've finished at the pub with Edwin Featherstone, I'll meet you on the village green. It's market day, so we can grab something to eat and drink.'

'Sounds like a plan. And remember—be tactful when questioning Lilac and Morrigan. Neither of them has done anything wrong.'

'As far as we know. Anyway, you know me—tact and diplomacy.'

'Yeah. That's what I'm afraid of.' He takes one last look at her. 'Yeah, I really like your hair like that.'

The brass bell above the door gives a delicate tinkle as Prisha steps inside the post office. Two older women are deep in animated conversation with the postmistress, Lilac Penhallow, their voices bubbling with gossip and laughter.

The moment they see Prisha, all three fall silent.

Lilac offers the faintest nod to her companions. Without a word, the women gather their bags and shuffle out, heads low.

Lilac's voice is warm, bright.

'Inspector. What can I do for you?'

'I've got a few questions, if you don't mind.'

She smiles. 'Of course. Though if it's about the terrible deaths recently, I've already spoken to your uniformed colleagues. I've nothing more to offer, I'm afraid.'

'It's not that. It's about Morrigan.'

The smile falters—just a flicker.

'Morrigan? I hope she's not in any trouble?'

'No... I don't believe so.'

Lilac arches an eyebrow. 'You don't *believe* so?'

'I'd like to speak with her.'

'About what, exactly?'

Prisha reaches into her pocket and produces the evidence bag containing the Crucifix Knot.

She places it on the counter.

'Did she make this?'

Lilac studies the knot in silence, her expression unreadable.

A shrug. 'She makes all sorts of things. I lose track.'

'She gave a very similar one to my sergeant six weeks ago. It depicted a girl with long flowing hair in the centre, apparently, the Wicker Girl. Then she told my sergeant *she* was the Wicker Girl.'

Lilac lets out a low, brittle laugh.

'She's always had a vivid imagination. Even as a child.'

Prisha doesn't blink.

'She's not a child though, is she? She's thirty-six years old.'

Lilac begins shuffling envelopes into a neat pile. Her voice cools.

'You're just like the rest—quick to judge. So what's your point?'

Prisha taps the bag. 'This is a Crucifix Knot. A very specific symbol. One that's turned up at multiple crime scenes.'

'I'm aware of what it is, inspector.'

Prisha's patience wears thin.

'Where's Morrigan—I need to speak with her?'

'She's not here.'

'When will she be back?'

'Hard to say.'

'You don't know?'

Lilac looks up. Her smile is gone.

'I didn't say that.'

Prisha steps forward.

'Miss Penhallow, I'm investigating a series of suspicious deaths. Where is Morrigan?'

Lilac looks away.

'She's in Scotland. Visiting my sister. Morrigan's aunt.'

'And the address?'

Lilac offers a tight smile.

'I'm not at liberty to share that.'

'Why not?'

Lilac's face hardens. 'Because *I* choose not to. Morrigan has done nothing wrong.'

'Are you sure?'

'Positive. It's not in her nature.'

Prisha's eyes tighten, but she realises she's getting nowhere.

'Everyone's capable of bad deeds, Miss Penhallow.'

Lilac leans in slightly, her voice quiet but hard as stone.

'Not Morrigan.'

Her words are as final as an inscription chiselled into a granite gravestone.

Lilac turns and starts sorting mail into private boxes.

Prisha, jaw tight, snatches up the evidence bag and stalks out.

The bell tinkles behind her.

32

Market day on the village green, and the place hums with chaotic festivity—a riot of colour, clatter, and the mingled scents of street food and warm grass. Stalls bustle with movement, voices overlap in a constant churn of chatter and bartering, as children dart between legs with sticky fingers and wild laughter. Somewhere, a dog howls. Laughter rises; someone shouts across the crowd. The place feels alive; noisy, sun-drenched, in an atmosphere of freedom.

Prisha drifts between the stalls, weaving past tables cluttered with knick-knacks, bric-à-brac, leather belts, woven bracelets, watercolour prints, and rainbow-bright calico bags. One stall draws a small crowd. It's stacked with gleaming fruit and vegetables, arranged with obsessive precision. Heritage carrots, beets, and plump tomatoes sit in neatly tiered crates. Behind them, elevated on a wooden stand, are rows of vintage-style blue glass bottles—one-litre, capped with ceramic swing tops and rubber stoppers. Each is labelled in crisp, minimalist white:

RAVENSBANE SPRING WATER

Nature's Design. Unaltered.

A chalkboard propped nearby lists the price: £3.50 per bottle.

The two women behind the stall work briskly, scooping produce into paper bags while pitching the spring water like seasoned Cockney barrow boys.

Tucked just behind the water is another cluster of bottles—clear glass, filled with golden mead that catches the light.

RAVENSBANE WILDFLOWER MEAD
The taste of forgotten summers.

These are sealed with corks, capped with deep burgundy wax and stamped with a raven emblem. Priced at £16 each, they seem to be selling equally well.

Prisha glances at the sign above the stall.

Natures Natural Bounty

Being a stickler for correct grammar, the lack of an apostrophe grates with her.

She eyes the two women behind the stall—faces vaguely familiar, but it's the uniform that gives them away: white cheesecloth shirts under denim dungarees. Wicca, no doubt.

She points up at the sign.

'You're missing a possessive apostrophe. It's the natural bounty *belonging* to nature, so you need an apostrophe between the E and the S. The way it reads now implies plural, meaning there's more than one nature, which doesn't make sense.'

The two youngish women give her a synchronised *couldn't-give-a-shit* pout. From behind the stall, someone rises slowly, holding a crate of plump tomatoes.

'Ah, Inspector Kumar. A grammar Nazi as well—just when I thought you couldn't get any more charming.'

Prisha's expression flattens.

'Violet Fox. Funny seeing you here.'

'Not really. We attend all the local markets. Can I tempt you? The tomatoes are particularly sweet this year.'

'No thanks. I hope you're not selling any of your *medicinal* plants here? Wouldn't want to poison anyone.'

Violet's eyes narrow, just briefly, before she smirks.

'No. That would be reckless. Only fresh, chemical-free fruit and veg.'

Prisha hesitates, her eyes resting on the mead. She considers asking Violet if she has a liquor licence, then decides against it.

Let's not get petty, she thinks.

'Right, I'll leave you to it.'

She throws her a cool glance and moves on, watched intently by Violet, who whispers something to one of the women, then promptly melts away into the crowd.

A few stalls down, Prisha wanders into the food and drink area, stomach suddenly rumbling. She grabs a spinach and feta spanakopita, and a chicory-vanilla coffee.

'Oh crap,' she murmurs as she spots Lady Hampton trying on a silk scarf at a nearby stand. For a moment, she thinks about informing her of the warrant, but decides against it. The last thing she wants is to be berated in public. She takes a quick look around and sees an empty bench on the edge of the green, and makes a beeline for it, head down.

A short, doughy woman in a grubby white apron, with flaming cheeks and a shock of hair like she's just stuck her finger in a socket, barges past, knocking Prisha sideways.

She nearly spills her drink.

Before she can say anything, the woman has already stormed off—clearly on a mission.

'That's okay, I'm fine, thanks,' Prisha calls after her. 'Some people,' she mutters, settling onto the bench.

Relaxing, she lets the sounds, sights, and smells wash over her as she slowly munches and ruminates on the case.

This one's testing her. Usually, she has a good idea of who the killer is—it's just a matter of gathering the evidence and proving it.

But not this time.

There are two investigations running side by side: the hit-and-run of Iona Jacobs, and the murders of Malachi Abbott and Amos Baker. Plus the unresolved death of Reverend Hartley, and the *apparent* abduction of Lord Hampton.

It's a lot to hold in her head. She's certain the cases are connected, but she's not sure Frank and Zac share her conviction.

Too many suspects. Too many tangled leads. Some of it could be critical—some of it just white noise.

It's like trying to solve a thousand-piece jigsaw puzzle without the aid of the picture on the box.

Then there's this place—the village, and the Wicca commune. Not exactly evasive, but certainly not forthcoming.

It's like there's an invisible bond—or maybe a noose—that draws them together.

Too frightened to speak up, or simply too close-knit to let outsiders in?

She can't quite tell.

Finishing the spanakopita, she washes it down with the chicory coffee, smacking her lips together, tongue flicking against the roof of her mouth.

Another mystery—does she actually like this coffee, or has she just been emotionally manipulated by the marketing words, chicory-vanilla?

Her reflection is cut short as angry voices swell nearby, and a small crowd gathers around one of the stalls.

She has no intention of intervening—until the expletives start to fly.

'Oh, really,' she groans, spinning around in the off-chance there's a uniformed officer on the beat.

Fat chance, she thinks.

With a sigh, she sets her drink down and marches reluctantly into the fray, warrant card in hand.

'Detective Inspector Kumar. North Yorkshire Police. Stand back, please.'

The crowd parts like a confused haircut.

It's the little pocket battleship of a woman, bawling at the two women on the Wicca stall.

'You're out of *fucking* order! You're putting me out of business, selling your bloody shite here. And don't think I don't know what you've been saying—spreading lies, telling people my produce is covered in chemicals!'

The women on the stall look shell-shocked. Every time they try to placate her, she arcs up again.

Prisha taps her on the shoulder.

'Madam!' she says sharply. 'Please curb your language. There are young children around.'

The woman wheels around, eyes like saucers, and clocks the warrant card.

'These freeloading bastards are ruining my business!' she roars, pointing furiously. 'I've got rent, rates, electricity, VAT, taxes to pay. These buggers don't pay a single penny in tax. They want to live outside society when it suits them but still use the facilities that taxpayers fund!'

'Here, here! You tell 'em, love,' a male voice calls from the crowd.

Prisha grits her teeth.

'Madam, please calm down, or I'll have to arrest you for disturbing the peace—and that'll be a ball-ache for me and an expensive waste of time for you.'

The woman is now at full boil.

'What are you going to do about them?' she shrieks, jabbing a finger at the stallholders.

'This isn't a police matter,' Prisha replies.

'Then what are you doing here, love?' the unhelpful male voice from the crowd calls out.

Prisha ignores him.

'You need to take it up with the local council. If they own the Green, it's their jurisdiction. Put your case forward—rationally—and I'm sure they'll deal with it properly.'

'Ha! Shows what you know. The Green's owned by the Ashenby Village Co-operative. And they're *all* in cahoots—part of this bloody cult. It's not right. And you should arrest them for libel—spreading malicious rumours about me!'

'It's slander, not libel,' Prisha corrects. 'And again—that's a civil matter.'

'We haven't said a word about her, officer,' one of the Wicca women says meekly.

'Ooh! You lying cow!' the woman roars. 'Not five minutes ago, a woman came into my shop and said you were telling anyone who'd listen that my fruit and veg is covered in pesticides!'

'That's not true.'

'And don't think I don't know what you lot get up to in those woods with your filthy Pagan ways and disgusting, unnatural orgies!'

The dry voice from the crowd again. 'What's wrong, love—scared you're missing out?'

A ripple of laughter. The woman wheels around.

'Who said that?'

No one answers.

The crowd is now fully invested. If someone had half a brain, they'd be flogging popcorn and ice cream.

On the edge of combustion, the woman grabs a large tomato and hurls it at the women behind the stall.

They duck just in time. It splats harmlessly against the side of a white minivan behind the marquee.

That's enough.

Prisha grabs the woman's arm and twists it up behind her back.

'Right. Either you calm down, or I arrest you. Last warning. What's it going to be?'

'That's police brutality!' The annoying voice again.

Prisha locks eyes on the agitator—a wiry man with a sunken chest and a pot belly that could take out a toddler at shin-height.

'Oi, motormouth. Button it, or you'll be spending the night in a cell!'

He slinks off, muttering about a police state and freedom of speech.

Slowly, the woman simmers down. The crowd, disappointed the show's over, drifts away.

With the spot-fire doused, Prisha returns to the bench to finish her tepid coffee. She takes two gulps before her eyes spot the small, folded sheet of paper placed under the cup.

She opens it, eyebrows lifting at the handwriting—neat, deliberate, almost like calligraphy.

Meet me alone at Gallows Meadow in twenty minutes to talk.

There's a shortcut at the back of the church that will lead you there.

Morrigan

Pulling out her phone, she checks the time—1:20 pm, then taps Zac's image.

It rings.

And rings.

Her mind drifts back to the car journey over.

'I bet the idiot left it on charge in the car,' she mutters—just before voicemail kicks in.

Beep.

'Hi, Zac, it's me. Just a quick update. Didn't get anywhere with Lilac Penhallow. She said Morrigan is in Scotland visiting an aunt, which is odd, as a moment ago someone left a cryptic note under my coffee cup. Apparently, it's from Morrigan. She wants to meet me at Gallows Meadow in twenty minutes—to talk, alone. The meadow's part of Amos Baker's land—the field that grows maize. Opposite Ravensbane Woods on the outskirts of Ashenby. Make your way there when you get this message—but be discreet. Park up nearby and walk. Don't want to scare her off. See you soon.'

Slipping her phone away, she scans the crowd for Morrigan. Being short, she's hard to spot at the best of times. But she's also a slippery little bugger, like the Scarlet Pimpernel in wellies.

Takes one last gulp of coffee.

She grimaces at the bitter aftertaste, pours the remainder onto the grass, then sets off for the church.

33

The farm gate squeals as Prisha closes it behind her.

Feeling unusually tired, she stares at the field.

Maize grows in dense, shoulder-high rows, leaves rustling, tips beginning to tassel. The earth between each row is dry and cracked. A faint, sweet smell lingers. It's a living wall—dense, whispering, seemingly impenetrable.

Maize for stock feed in winter. Nutritious, easy to grow and store, long shelf life. Cattle thrive on it in the colder months.

A vehicle access track leads into the field, maybe eight feet wide, and circumnavigates the boundary. The sun beats down, illuminating the natural colours: green, yellow, ochre.

To her left, another field, resplendent with lush grass, swaying in time with the warm eddies of high summer. Hills melt away into the horizon.

To her right, a glorious, ancient oak stands in all its gnarled splendour. Below the canopy, hay bales stacked on an old cart.

Bees buzz. Insects hum.

It's like a scene from a John Constable oil painting—the English countryside from a bygone era.

She imagines pulling out a picnic blanket and hamper. Pouring a crisp, cold glass of white wine. A small cheese platter. Nestling down for a lazy summer afternoon—maybe a snooze, alone.

It's perfect.

Almost.

Apart from the sight fifty yards ahead.

A scarecrow. Tied to a cross.

A scaffold of ancient wood—vertical and horizontal timbers joined high, a cruciform gallows, at least twelve feet tall.

The effigy strapped to it stares directly at her, almost lifelike.

It's dressed in old blue dungarees, a checked shirt, Wellington boots, and the obligatory straw hat—Grandpa Walton.

Creepy enough.

But the face is the worst.

A plastic mask of a child. Freckled. Laughing eyes.

She yawns. Blinks.

Remembers why she's here—to meet Morrigan.

Walks forward, calling:

'Morrigan! It's Inspector Kumar. You said you wanted to talk.'

Silence.

'I'm alone, Morrigan!'

Shakes her head, feeling woozy.

'Must be the heat. And that coffee obviously didn't have any caffeine in it,' she mutters, chasing half-formed thoughts around her foggy brain.

A few more steps towards the cross.

A slow creaking sound.

Peers at the scarecrow. The twine securing it to the crossbeam is taut.

The field darkens.

She looks up.

A large, dark cloud rolls in front of the sun.

And yet...

The other fields are still bathed in brilliant light.

A rustle through the maize.

Movement.

Fleeting.

Licks her lips—but there's no moisture.

Hot. *Unbearably* hot.

A bird call. One she knows all too well.

A raven's caw.

She turns. There it is. Sitting on the fence wire.

Its head cocks to one side, watching her. Inquisitive.

Another joins it.

And another.

The trio inspect the inspector.

Tries to swallow—but can't.

Remembers her recurring nightmares.

Three ravens.

The wolf's claw around her neck tingles.

The necklace the clairvoyant gave her at the fair, the night she was with Adam.

Adam.

Why did he take something beautiful and innocent and poison it?

Creaking again.

The twine snaps.

The scarecrow sags. Drops, slumping against the upright.

Her heartbeat spikes.

Breaths come fast.

Vision blurs.

The heat's burning her up.

She's choking.

Claustrophobic.

Trapped.

She pulls the yellow hair tie from her head, shakes her ponytail loose.

Jet black hair.

The hair Zac admires so much.

'Okay, Morrigan! Very funny. Game over. Did DS Stoker put you up to this? Is it a joke? Stop messing about. I'm not in the mood.'

The three ravens take flight, wings slicing the air, heading towards the sun.

She scratches at the burning sensation around her neck.

A whisper. Or was it the wind through the maize leaves?

She pulls out her phone—but isn't sure why.

Just stares at the blur.

It slips from her hand.

Kneels to pick it up—

—and sees it.

A hand.

Not straw.

Flesh.

Grey. Rigid.

Protruding from the scarecrow's sleeve.

'No...'

She reaches for the mask—plastic, childlike, freckled.

Yanks it off.

The face beneath is unmistakable.

Human.

Familiar.

Cold, dead eyes stare back at her.

The scream dies in her throat.

She slumps backwards.

The world spins.

Her last thought is of chicory-vanilla coffee.

Followed by darkness.

34

A short, rising whoop from the police siren pierces the heavy silence. The patrol car, lights flashing, completes its second slow circuit of the maize field. It vanishes over the brow of the dirt track, swallowed by the landscape once more.

Frank stands in the double teapot position—hands on hips—watching, thinking, his face set like granite. He scans the maize field from behind the gate. To his left, a hill rises, with a discernible track cutting through meadows. Peeking out at the top is the steeple of St Mary's Church, maybe a mile away.

Dead ahead looms the cross—twelve feet high, dark, and foreboding, leaning slightly with age or intent.

To the right, in the distance, a giant oak punctures the sky, its thick canopy spilling shade over a dozen square hay bales stacked neatly beneath its drooping limbs. Behind them, an old-fashioned hay cart.

His eyes finally settle on Zac.

'If she was hiding, she'd have shown herself by now,' he mutters—then erupts. *'Sweet merciful shite!* What the bloody hell were you playing at, Zac? Letting her go on some secret rendezvous alone. *Bloody amateur hour!*'

Zac—rarely, if ever, one to show fear—is white as a sheet.

'I'm sorry, Frank. As I explained, I was at the pub questioning Featherstone when she rang. My phone was charging in the car. As soon as I heard the message, I hightailed it down here.'

'Let me listen to her message again,' he demands as Zac hits the voicemail button, then hands him the phone.

Zac rubs his face, agitated. 'The message was left at 1:20 pm. By the time I left the pub it was 1:45. She'd have already been here. I arrived about 1:55 and there was no sign of her. I drove around the track a couple of times whilst trying to ring her, but her phone was dead. I even spent ten minutes tramping through the bloody maize. But this paddock must be five acres in size, and that maize is like a jungle.'

Frank hands the phone back and casts a glance over his shoulder at Dinkel, who is keeping out of the firing line.

'What's the latest, constable?'

'A search team of twenty, along with sniffer dogs, is setting off in forty minutes from York, sir.'

'*Forty bloody minutes!*' he roars. 'Get back on the line and tell them to set off now, otherwise I'll have someone's bloody arse in a carrier bag by the end of the day. What else?'

'Ahem, the drone team are on their way. High-def cameras and body heat sensors attached.'

'Good. And the telco?'

'Superintendent Banks issued a Gold Command, fast-track authorisation on Prisha's phone. They said they should have something within the hour.' He checks his watch. 'Which is in a few minutes, sir. But...' He trails off.

'But what?'

A nervous shuffle. 'Well, we're not in an urban area where cell towers are typically three to four hundred metres apart. It's North Yorkshire, sir. Rural. The towers could be miles apart.'

Frank nods, acknowledging the gravity of the situation.

'Meaning, the information will be next to useless.'

'Quite possibly,' Dinkel quietly concurs.

He returns fire on Zac. 'Show me the hair tie again.'

Zac pulls the yellow scrunchie from his pocket and hands it to him.

Frank tenderly rubs it between his finger and thumb then hands it back.

'And you're certain she was wearing that?'

'Positive. One hundred per cent. I even commented on it earlier. I found it near the cross.'

'So what does it mean—she left it here as a clue? Got into a fight, a struggle, and it was pulled loose, or what?'

'I don't think it was a fight, boss. There're two or three strands of hair caught in it, but if it was a fight and was yanked clear, a lot more hair would be attached.'

'And what about Morrigan? Prisha said on the voicemail Lilac told her Morrigan was in Scotland. If that's true, then who wrote the bloody note to Prisha?'

Zac shrugs, feeling guilty and useless. 'I don't know, boss.'

Frank ponders for a moment, eyes still scanning the maize field, and the cross.

'If it is true,' he murmurs.

'Boss?'

'If Morrigan's in Scotland, then she didn't write that note. But if she *did* write the note, then Lilac Penhallow was bloody lying,' he snaps. 'Ever since this case began, we've encountered nothing but stonewalling and bloody lies. And to be quite honest, I've had enough of it.'

He turns again and growls at Dinkel.

'Are you onto York yet, constable?'

Dinkel has the mobile to his ear. 'Yes, sir. Ringing now.'

'Good. And Dinkel, lay the bloody law down to them. Make them aware, *in no uncertain terms*, I want that search squad on the road right now. And tell them to have a cavalry escort, a patrol car, all guns blazing and bugger the speed limit. Time is of the essence. Understood?'

'Yes, sir.'

Dinkel swallows hard as his call is answered.

'DC Dinkel here again. In regard to the missing police officer and your search team, I'd ask that you expedite the matter forthwith... please, if you could.'

A pause.

Then a frown.

'What I mean is, set off now. None of this forty minutes nonsense, my good man.'

As Dinkel remonstrates rather politely on the phone, Frank and Zac share a resigned smile, a brief pressure relief.

Frank shakes his head in weary despair.

'What are we going to do with that lad, Zac? Christ knows we've all tried to toughen him up.'

'Not sure, boss. The last option is to drop him off with the SAS boys for six months, see if they can put some lead in his pencil. But I wouldn't put my house on it.'

'You know what my rank is, sergeant,' Dinkel continues. 'I'm a detective constable. Although I'm not sure what relev...' Wincing, he pulls the phone away from his ear. 'No, sergeant, I wasn't being impertinent.'

Frank's had enough and strides forward, snatching the phone from Dinkel.

'Who am I speaking to?' he bellows down the line. 'Ah, Sergeant Mellows. DCI Finnegan here. What? How am I going? Let me paint a picture for you, sergeant. My day has gone from bad to worse and has now turned into *a fucking shitshow!* One of my most senior officers has mysteriously disappeared off-grid whilst investigating a series of brutal murders. How do you think my *fucking day is going?* Now listen up, and listen good, Mellows. You get that search team on the road—NOW! And don't spare the horses. I want your guys on the ground in less than an hour. Otherwise, in the next couple of days I'll be paying a little visit to York, and when I get there, I'll be kicking arses and banging heads together! And there'll be a certain sergeant, *mentioning no names*, who will be filling in forms for a *very* early retirement *without* a pension. Now, do I make myself clear? Good. Then we're both on the same page. Thank you. Have a pleasant day and give my regards to your missus.'

He thrusts the phone back into Dinkel's hand.

'They're on their way.'

Dinkel beams, holding the mobile a few feet in front of him like a trophy.

'And let that be a lesson to you—sergeant!' he declares. Then quickly adds, 'No disrespect, sir.'

He hangs up in a hurry.

'I fear the worst, Zac,' Frank murmurs as he takes a handkerchief from his pocket and dabs sweat from his brow. 'I care about that girl likes she's one of my own.'

'I know you do, Frank. We all do. I'm really sorry. I blame myself.'

Frank pats him on the shoulder. 'No, son, don't blame yourself. I was just venting earlier. Prisha's headstrong and impulsive. She should have known better than to agree to a meeting in the middle of nowhere, alone.'

'That's what I don't get, boss. If someone was out to harm her, she'd have seen it coming out here in the open. Not only can she give as good as she gets, but she's also fast on her toes. There's not many who'd be able to catch her if she took off.'

'You don't run if someone's pointing a gun at you.'

'No, I guess not.'

'Right, we can't hang around here like limp dicks at a wedding. I want you to head back to Ashenby and speak with Lilac Penhallow. Find out *exactly* where Morrigan is. And if she is in Bonnie Scotland, then liaise with Police Scotland to caution her and bring her in for questioning to the nearest border station. Then drive up to collect her.'

'And if she refuses to come voluntarily?'

'Obtain a warrant for her arrest.'

Zac turns and heads to his car.

'Oh—and Zac.'

He stops, and glances back. 'Yes?'

'Gloves off, yes. This is a bare-knuckle fight now. Understood?'

He smiles. 'I hear you, Frank.'

Frank gazes at the sky, the sun beating down, the shirt clinging to his back.

'What a bleedin' summer. It's either all or nothing.'

Dinkel's phone rings.

'DC Dinkel, speaking. What? Are you certain? When? Right, this matter is of the utmost urgency. You must keep me informed of any further developments. Bye.'

'What is it?' Franks demands as Zac's car speeds off.

'The telco, sir. Prisha's phone's been off—or out of range—for over an hour. It just reconnected to the network. They got a ping from a cell tower two minutes ago. But the next nearest mast is over five miles away, so the triangulation covers a wide area.'

'Where's the tower?'

'A place called Grinton. About ten miles from here.'

'I know the place. But that information's not a lot of use, is it, constable? She could be anywhere within a five-mile radius.'

Dinkel's eyes suddenly widen.

'Wait!' he blurts, fumbling for his phone. 'Last year, during the Happy Camp murders—'

'What about them?'

'During the investigation, me, Prisha, and Zac all got Life360.'

Frank grimaces. 'What's that—some kind of private health insurance?'

'No, sir. It's an app—GPS location sharing. We used it during ops so we could see where each other was, as a backup. If Prisha didn't disable it, or hasn't removed me from her circle, I should be able to see where her phone is.'

He's already tapping at his screen, fingers trembling.

Frank casts a glance across the field as another short, sharp whoop from the patrol car breaks the silence. He strides over to Dinkel.

'Calm down, lad. You're shaking like a shitting dog in a thunderstorm.'

'Come on, come on,' Dinkel urges, holding the phone aloft and slowly turning in a circle to get a better signal.

'YES!' he shouts. 'I've got her location. Wait—wait—let me zoom in.'

He pinches the screen, squinting.

'Well?' Frank asks as the patrol car pulls up beside the gate.

'Got it! Her phone's at a place called Grimscar Quarry.'

Frank's heart sinks.

'Hell's bells,' he murmurs. 'That's the quarry where Lord Hampton's car was found burnt out after his abduction. That doesn't bode well.'

He motions sharply to PC Jackson in the car.

'Jacko! We need to get to Grimscar Quarry—*quick* as. Dinkel, call Prisha's phone. It's a long shot, I know, but worth a try.'

The car lurches forward. Frank races towards it, yanks at the passenger door.

'It's ringing, sir.'

Frank hesitates, one foot on the ground, one inside the vehicle.

Dinkel's nose scrunches up.

'What is it, lad?'

'It's music, sir. A song.'

'What song?'

'I don't know it.'

'Put it on speaker, lad.'

Frank is overcome with nausea, recognising the song instantly as it reaches the chorus.

'Sweet Jesus. It's the Hollies—*All I Need is the Air that I Breathe.*'

35

Her eyes flicker open.

Or do they?

Black. Total. Absolute.

A half-yawn, stifled.

What woke me?

Can't remember now.

Thick air clings.

Stale, musty, flat.

No breeze, no sound.

Did I shut the window?

Thought I left it open.

I usually double-check.

Third-storey flat.

Dormer bedroom above.

A cat-burglar wouldn't even try.

There—

A siren blast.

Short, sharp, urgent.

Police outside, below.

Probably pulled someone over.

Hope it's that biker.

A voice—

Gritted, raised, raw.

Frank?

No, surely not?

Could be anyone.

Sounds carry strangely at night.

Silence again.

Heavy as water.

Comforting. Close. Complete.

Another yawn.

Eyes flutter.

Floating... yet pinned.

36

High above the Grimscar Quarry, a buzzard glides the thermals—watchful, patient. Its forked tail flicks like a scythe in the wind. It calls: a cutting, tremulous skreigh slices the air. A warning to the living... or a lament for the dead?

Frank and PC Jackson walk to the edge of the quarry and peer down.

'Bloody hell, Jacko, I've got déjà vu. How long ago since we were last here searching for Lord Hampton?'

PC Jackson removes his cap and runs a hand through his hair.

'About six, seven weeks back, Frank. Do you want me to go down and start searching?'

'Aye. I'll call Sergeant Mellows and tell him to send half the search team up here.'

PC Jackson slips on a pair of latex gloves and gazes at the steep, precarious track that leads down to the quarry floor.

'Hang on, Jacko, wait a moment,' Frank instructs as he pulls his phone out and taps at Prisha's smiling face. 'I'll try her phone first.'

As Frank's phone connects, the faintest of melodies can be heard.

'That's definitely Prisha's ringtone.'

Both men tilt their heads and take another step towards the edge.

The music ends.

"You've called DI Kumar. Please leave a message."

Jackson drops to his knees, lies flat, and shimmies along on his stomach until his head is peering over the edge.

'Try it again, boss.'

Frank jabs at the screen.

The simple jingle repeats.

'I can't see it. But there's a ledge about fifteen feet down covered in a tuft of grass. I think it's there.'

'Certain?'

'Not really. Try it one more time.'

Frank waits a few seconds before repeating.

Again, the faint but unmistakable sound of Prisha's phone.

'Yep, it's definitely coming from the ledge.'

Frank gingerly inches forward and peeks down.

'That's a hell of a sheer drop. At least a hundred feet.'

Jackson jumps to his feet.

'I have a rope in the boot of the car.'

Frank stares at him.

'And which one of us daft buggers is going over the edge?'

Jackson grins and casts an eye over Frank's large, stout physique.

'I fancy my chances a lot better if the rope is around me, with you holding it, than the other way round.'

Frank glances around. 'No anchor points and you won't get the car up here. Okay, nothing for it. Get the rope.'

As Jackson fetches the rope, Frank takes in the scene.

The limestone quarry is situated on the edge of moorland—desolate, remote upland pasture. Rugged and exposed to the elements, it's not ideal land for man nor beast to inhabit.

Jackson hauls the coil of rope from the boot of the car and jogs back.

Frank plants his feet wide and holds his arms out.

'I hope you were in the Boy Scouts and passed your ropes test, Jacko.'

He laughs. 'Can't say I was, Frank. But I was on the school football team.'

'Oh, great. We'll have a kick about after this, then, shall we?'

Jackson loops the rope twice around Frank's torso, just under the arms, then ties it off with a figure-eight follow-through, checking the tension.

'Right,' Jacko says, unwinding the slack. He forms a rescue seat harness from the rope—one loop under the thighs, one around the waist, tied off at the front with a double fisherman's knot. Crude but safe enough.

'Ready?' Frank asks, testing his stance. Feet firm, knees slightly bent, bodyweight low and braced.

Jackson slips on his gloves, takes a breath, then nods.

Frank leans back slightly, counterbalancing as Jackson begins his descent—half scramble, half controlled slide.

Dust and shale slough away beneath his boots. The rope tugs taut with every jolt.

'Steady!' Frank calls, adjusting for the shifting weight. His fingers tighten around the rope.

'About five feet to go!' Jackson shouts from below, breathless. 'I think I can see it—give me a little more slack!'

Frank places one steady foot in front of the other and edges forward.

'Bit more. Okay, I'm on the ledge. Keep the tension on the rope. Right—got it.'

Jackson slips the phone into his back pocket.

'Okay, start walking me back up.'

'Easier said than bloody done,' Frank grumbles, sweat beading on his brow, a large dark patch forming under the armpits of his blue shirt.

'This would be a lovely place for a picnic,' Jackson calls up, voice tight with nerves.

'Daft bugger,' Frank chuckles.

He methodically stalks backwards, the dead weight on the other end starting to take its toll.

'Nearly there. Another couple of feet!' Jackson cries.

Frank's left foot hits loose gravel.

'Shit!'

He loses his footing and lands hard on his backside.

The rope jerks violently.

Jackson yells out as he drops five feet in an instant.

His body swings free, then slams against the quarry wall.

He's now dangling in midair.

'Hold on!' Frank bellows, pain flaring through his spine as he plants his feet, leans back, and becomes a human anchor.

Jackson's arms flail, boots scraping at rugged limestone, searching for grip.

Nothing.

'You all right, Jacko?'

'To be honest, Frank, I've had better days!'

The rope trembles with every kick and sway.

Frank clamps his jaw, muscles screaming, legs splayed wide, every inch of him braced like a human grappling hook.

Jackson steadies himself, takes a breath, then swings. Fingers scrape rock.

Tries again.

Third try—he lands it and regains a tentative foothold on the rock face.

'Okay. I think I'm good. Start pulling.'

Frank rises slowly.

He roars, summons everything he has, leans back with a grunt that tears from his chest.

Step by painful step, he retreats.

'One more heave and we're there, Frank!'

Frank bellows like a bull, the sound ricocheting off the quarry walls like a jet breaking the sound barrier.

Jackson scrambles over the edge, and rolls onto solid ground, chest heaving.

Frank collapses onto the rough surface, both men silent save for their breath.

A moment of solitude passes before Jackson squats and rubs the dirt and dust from his clothes.

'Beats sitting at your desk replying to emails, eh, boss?' he says with a grin

Frank lets out a pained laugh.

'I'll get back to you on that one.'

Regaining his composure, Jackson hands the phone to Frank as he lifts himself up.

Frank presses the side button and is surprised to see the home screen flash up.

'Huh, well there you go. She doesn't use a screen lock.'

Swiping down, he sees the long list of missed calls from Zac, Dinkel, and himself.

Then another notification.

An unanswered text message from an unknown number.

He taps it open.

Ha, ha! Guess what, Chief Inspector Finnegan, she's not here. But damned fine effort on retrieving her phone.

Be quick now. The Hollies are getting to the end of the song.

Tick Tock.

Frank gazes at the puzzled expression on Jackson's face, then at the silent landscape that sneaks up on him.

'We've been set up, Jacko, and someone's been watching us... maybe still is,' he adds spinning in a slow three-sixty arc.

37

Releases a deep sigh.

Police car's gone.

Quiet again. No voices.

The bed's hard. Unyielding.

Really must buy a decent mattress.

Rolls onto her side.

Thud.

Shoulder hits something solid.

Bedside drawers?

Rolls onto her back.

Stretches legs. Waggles toes.

They feel trapped.

Too tight. Too hot. Dead still.

Better get up. Need a drink.

Lifts to sit.

Crack.

Her head smacks something above.

Hard. Unforgiving.

Heartbeat stutters.

Lifts a hand.

Touches wood.

Coarse woodgrain.

Dry. Uneven.

Faint scent of hay.

Throat tightens.

Breath catching, gasping.

Shallow. Shallow. Shallow.

Claws at the sides.

More wood.

Walls—close. Solid.

No, no, no.

Please, God, no.

Terrifying realisation.

Underground.

Buried alive.

And running out of air.

In a coffin.

38

Zac has wasted thirty precious minutes sitting across the road from the post office. A sign on the door reads: **BACK SOON**.

He'd knocked on the rear door too—no answer.

They're either out or hiding inside.

He glances at the village green. Stallholders are beginning to dismantle their marquees, packing goods into the backs of vans and cars. A few members of the public still loiter, without much intent.

He refocuses on the post office door.

Movement.

A disembodied arm flips the sign, followed by the click of a bolt sliding back.

He's in luck.

Opening the door, he steps inside and shuts it firmly behind him. Flips the sign to **CLOSED**, drops the latch, and yanks the roller blind down.

Lilac Penhallow scowls.

'Sergeant Stoker, what do you think you're doing? It's market day—one of my busiest times.'

'Yeah, looks like it.' He steps towards the counter, his shoes squeaking on the old linoleum.

'Where is she?' His voice is slow, calm, but with steel beneath it.

Lilac licks her lips. 'Who?'

'Don't play games, Miss Penhallow.' His tone rises slightly. 'Morrigan—where is she?'

'Didn't you speak to your inspector? I told her earlier—Morrigan's staying with her aunt in Scotland.'

'Address?'

'I'm not at liberty to divulge that.'

His palm slams hard onto the counter, sending a jar of pens clattering to the floor.

Lilac flinches and steps back, hands clasped tightly at her waist.

'Inspector Kumar disappeared just over an hour ago. She received a note from Morrigan, asking to meet her at Gallows Meadow. Now where is she!' he roars.

'That's nonsense. Morrigan didn't leave a note. She's not even here.' Her voice is trembling, but she stands her ground.

Morrigan appears in the doorway to the living quarters.

Silent steps. A faint, admiring smile as she looks up at Zac.

'Hello, Zac,' she says, her Scottish brogue soft, entrancing.

'You can wipe that smirk off your face for a start,' he snarls.

It fades slowly.

'I didn't leave a note. I haven't seen her today.'

'Are you telling the truth?'

'I told you before, in the churchyard—it's a sin to lie.'

Zac runs a hand through his hair, frustration showing.

He can't figure these people out. No emotion. Like automatons.

Prisha was right—it's the village of the damned.

'Do you understand how serious this is?' he snaps. 'A police inspector has disappeared under suspicious circumstances. She said the note was from you. Found under her coffee cup on the village green. Around 1:20 pm.'

'I told you—I haven't been out.'

'No—you said you hadn't seen the inspector today.'

'Same thing. Are you in love with her?'

He shakes his head in confusion. 'What?'

'You heard.'

'What the hell has that got to do with anything? And what business is it of yours?'

A whisper of a smile. 'I have my answer.'

Lilac frowns at her granddaughter. 'Morrigan. Enough.'

A contrite wince. 'Sorry, gran.'

Zac hears Frank's words in his head: *Gloves off*.

But how? He's staring into the face of a sweet old woman who lost her daughter and has carried the grief all these years.

And Morrigan—thirty-six years old, yes—but with a disarming, childlike face that somehow makes her harder to confront.

He tries again.

Mellower. Almost pleading.

'Morrigan, Miss Penhallow… Lilac, please, if you know anything, if you can help—I'm begging you. I couldn't live with the guilt if anything happened to her.'

Lilac's eyes grow cold. 'Yes. Guilt is a burden. It says hello in the morning, and waves goodbye at night. Except it's not a goodbye. It sneaks into your dreams. Never leaves.'

Zac is getting nowhere, and time is slipping away.

He moves to the door, lifts the blind, unlatches the lock.

Lilac Penhallow falters. 'Sergeant, wait.'

He pauses. 'What?'

'If you bring something that belongs to the inspector, Morrigan might be able to help.'

'What sort of thing?'

'Clothing. Jewellery. Something worn close to the skin.'

He hesitates—then steps back to the counter and pulls out the yellow scrunchie.

'This is hers. Found it at Gallows Meadow. Will it do?'

Lilac studies it. 'Hmm. A few strands of hair. Yes… this should work.'

'Work for what, exactly?'

'Morrigan has the Second Sight. She can see things. It's stronger if she touches the person—but items like this can work—sometimes.'

'Second sight?'

'Visions.'

If Prisha were here, she'd scoff—her mind locked tight against anything beyond reason.

But Frank and Zac have both experienced things that defy logic.

Lilac holds the scrunchie out.

Morrigan pouts, then snatches it, scowling.

'Very well. But I'm doing this for Zac. Not for *her*.'

She rubs it between her fingers. Closes her eyes.

Hums a low, sorrowful tune.

Breaks into song—soft, strange words, foreign to Zac.

He shivers. The temperature hasn't changed.

Her arms lock. Body goes rigid.

Collapses to the floor.

'What's happening?' Zac asks, stepping forward. 'Is she all right?'

'She's with the inspector now,' Lilac whispers.

'What does that mean?'

'Shush.'

Morrigan lies still. Perfectly still.

Her breath quickens—ragged, panicked.

Hands twitch. Push out. Press against invisible barriers.

'No... no... no...' she moans.

Zac's skin crawls.

'What's going on?' he growls.

'I'm trapped,' Morrigan gasps. 'Can't move. Black. A box. There's no air. Hot. Thirsty. And something else...'

Her voice breaks.

'Something terrible is in here with me!'

Her body convulses—brief, frenzied thrashes—before she falls still. Breathing slows. Sleepy. Silent.

Eyes snap open.

Lilac helps her to her feet.

'Where is she?' Zac demands.

Morrigan gazes at him, pale and shaken.

'She's buried.'

His heart stops.

'Is she alive?'

'Yes. But not for long.'

'Where?'

No hesitation.

'Gallows Meadow.'

39

Panic is a merciless predator.

Cannot be reasoned with.

Nor ignored.

It scoffs at logic.

Ignores your pleas.

Heartless. Rapacious.

Someone once told her...

Don't fight it. Let it in.

Accept the fear.

It *will* stalk you.

A tiger on the prowl.

Hunting. Searching for weakness.

Let it.

Let it do its worst.

Then it will leave.

Thinks of nothing.

If that's even possible.

Heartbeat slows.

Calm breaths.

How long can I last?

How much air?

Claustrophobia lies in wait.

Waiting for panic.

Panic circles—hungry still.

Cramped. Compressed. Constricted.

Enclosed. Entombed.

Sealed.

So uncomfortable.

Lumpy.

Back hurts.

Reaches underneath.

Something there.

Touches soft fabric.

Clears her mind.

For three seconds.

Exactly.

Feels again.

Fingers trace something.

A seam?

Touches.

Squeezes.

Realises.

A hand.

Human.

Panic feasts

Now—she screams!

40

Dinkel is sipping from a bottle of water, his car parked in the shade, when he notices Zac's vehicle tearing down the narrow country lane. It comes to a screeching halt, kicking up a flurry of dust.

Dinkel steps out as Zac climbs from his car, accompanied by a young girl.

He's puzzled—who is she, and why has Zac brought her here?

He masks his confusion as the girl strides towards the gate, Zac just behind.

'Hello, young lady,' Dinkel says, grinning. 'And what brings you here? Hope you're not wagging off school?' he adds with a chuckle.

She halts. Her piercing jade eyes lock onto his.

Dinkel's grin falters. He leans forward as if to pat her on the head, but when her eyes widen slightly, he thinks better of it.

'Ahem... yes, well.'

Zac joins them. 'Morrigan, this is Detective Constable Dinkel. Dinkel, this is Morrigan Penhallow.'

Dinkel instantly realises his mistake. He knows the name only too well, but he's never met her or ever seen a photo.

'Ah. I see. Didn't realise. My apologies, madam... er, lady... woman.'

'Shut up, Dinkel,' Zac mutters.

'Yep. Will do.'

Morrigan turns and walks into the field without a word as Zac follows.

'Is he always an idiot?' she asks, deadpan.

Zac rubs the back of his neck. 'Only on weekdays. Apparently, he takes Saturday and Sunday off.'

'Huh.'

She surveys the field, eyes roving slowly from the maize to the wooden cross, then back to Zac.

'So, where is she?' he asks.

Morrigan tilts her head. 'How would I know? I was in the coffin with her. It was dark.'

Zac frowns as a creeping doubt takes hold.

Has he been played? Is this all some elaborate game because she's got a crush on him?

'You said she was here,' he says, a note of frustration slipping in.

'She is,' Morrigan replies calmly, gazing into the distance.

Her eyes track the line of trees, then drift south to the spire of St Mary's church, hazy in the heat. She turns slowly in a half-circle, scanning the field, until her eyes settle on the old oak tree, two hundred yards away.

She lifts an arm and points.

'There.'

Zac looks. 'I thought you said you didn't know where she was? Don't tell me—you've had another vision?'

Her gaze returns to him—cool, unreadable.

'No. I used common sense and knowledge of my surroundings. I thought you were supposed to be the detective.'

'And what does that mean?'

'You're not very good at your job.'

'Thanks.'

'My pleasure. Now… what do you see under the oak tree?'

Zac squints. 'A dozen or so hay bales.'

'Exactly. Why would Farmer Baker leave hay in a field growing maize for winter fodder? He'd never graze cattle here. So why the hay? And Baker was meticulous. Always stored his bales in a barn—dry, protected, safe from vermin. And no farmer with any sense would stack hay under an oak tree.'

'Why not?'

'Because acorns are toxic to cattle. If they got mixed into the hay, it could kill the beasts.'

Zac's scepticism fades fast.

'She won't be buried too deep,' Morrigan adds.

Zac studies her. 'How do you know?'

'You try digging under an oak tree. You'll hit a root every few inches.'

Zac hesitates just a moment longer, then turns and breaks into a jog.

'Dinkel!' he shouts. 'Get the car! The oak tree!'

His jog becomes a sprint. Morrigan follows behind, swift and silent.

Zac reaches the tree and immediately starts dragging hay bales away. Dinkel skids to a stop in the car, leaps out and joins in.

Within a minute, the stack is cast aside.

All three stare at the disturbed patch of earth beneath.

Zac and Dinkel drop to their knees and claw at the dry, friable soil. Morrigan remains motionless a few feet back, her expression blank.

The earth yields quickly, followed by the unmistakable shape of a flat wooden lid.

'Dinkel, tyre lever—boot of the car.'

'Wilco.'

Zac raps his knuckles on the lid. 'Prisha? Can you hear me?'

A faint voice answers from within. 'Get me out.'

Dinkel reappears with the lever and hands it over.

'I'm lifting the lid now, Prisha,' Zac bellows, jamming the metal into the non-existent gap between lid and frame.

It barely makes purchase. He stands, kicks the heel of his boot against it once. Twice. The lever bites deeper.

Back on his knees, he grips the bar with both hands and heaves. His muscles tremble with effort.

Still, Morrigan watches on without a flicker of emotion.

Zac grits his teeth and strains. 'Arrrghh!'

The wood groans. Screws squeal loose from the frame.

Dinkel jumps in to help, grabbing a corner. 'Ready?'

'Pull!'

With a crack, the lid breaks free. Dinkel falls backwards as the panel crashes on top of him.

Morrigan doesn't flinch.

A splutter rises from within the coffin. Gasping. Choking.

'It's all right, Prisha. You're safe,' Zac shouts.

'Get me out!' Her voice is frantic. She can't move, her limbs numb from confinement.

'Okay, okay. Just breathe.'

Zac reaches down, grips her hand, and hauls her upright into his arms.

She sobs, coughing, clinging to him.

Morrigan watches on.

Dinkel scrambles up, brushing off soil and splinters. He peers down into the box, then glances at Morrigan—who finally steps closer.

Prisha tries to speak, but her words collapse in muffled gasps.

Zac pulls her into his chest, protective, cradling.

All four peer into the coffin, silent.

There, at the bottom, is the lifeless body of Birch.

41

The fluorescent strip lighting flickers overhead, adding to the sterile environment of the interview room.

Morrigan is sitting bolt upright on a hard plastic chair. Her arms hang down, rigid. Fingers grip the underside of the seat as though she's scared of falling off.

Opposite are Frank and Zac, weary from the day's travails. Frank smiles at Morrigan in a fatherly way.

'Do you understand why you're here, Morrigan?'

'Yes. I'm not stupid. You haven't arrested me. You asked me to attend, and I came voluntarily. I'm free to leave at any time. You've read the caution, informed me of my rights, and you're recording the interview.'

Frank nods. 'Good.'

'When did you reopen the case into the murder of my mother?'

The question takes Frank by surprise. He shuffles uncomfortably in his seat and taps the table with a finger.

'About seven weeks ago.'

'Then why did you only tell gran about it last week?'

'To be honest, it seemed like a lost cause. I thought if we ever found something solid—a new lead—then we'd inform you.' Frank coughs, embarrassed. 'Yes, well, moving on.'

'I have another question.'

'Very well.'

'Why my mother's case, and why after such a long time?'

Frank takes a deep breath. 'Your mother's case spoke to me. I felt something.'

'She was reaching out for your help.'

'Well, I never said that.'

'No. I did. She must see something in you.'

Frank frowns and fidgets, aware of the inference, but not at ease with it.

'And you didn't inform me or gran because you didn't want to give us false hope?'

'Yes. After all these years of carrying the burden of grief, of not having answers, I can imagine what it would be like to be offered a sliver of hope and then have it snatched away again.'

Morrigan stares at him, assessing, studying.

'Yes, you can imagine, can't you?' she murmurs softly.

She leans forward and reaches out, placing a hand on top of his.

He stares at it. Feels the heat.

'It's happened to you, hasn't it? You lost someone in a tragedy. I can feel it. They were close. A niece, perhaps? No, someone even closer—a young girl. Your daughter.'

Frank frowns and pulls his hand away as Zac interjects firmly.

'Morrigan! Just stop. You're bang out of order!'

Her head swivels between the two men.

'You two are close, aren't you? Not just colleagues. Something deeper, way deeper. Like father and son.' She leans back into her rigid position. 'Sorry. Go on.'

Both men stiffen and avert their eyes. Showing true emotion is not in their DNA. In fact, it's downright embarrassing, but Morrigan doesn't appear to have any filters.

Frank reaches into his pocket and tosses the Wicker Girl medallion she gave to Zac as a keepsake.

It skitters across the table and lands in front of her.

Without moving her head, her eyes drift down for a second.

Shoots a glance at Zac, then back to Frank.

'You gave this to Sergeant Stoker a while back.'

'Yes.'

'It's exquisitely made. Did you make it?'

'Yes. Zac knows that. I told him.'

'And the motif in the middle—a young girl with long flowing hair which flares out into the circle—that's the Wicker Girl?'

'Yes.'

'And you're the Wicker Girl?'

'That's right.'

'And what exactly is the Wicker Girl?'

'It was a name I picked up when I was very young. I was good at embroidery, sewing, and making things from wicker and rattan.'

'What sort of things?'

'Everything. Baskets, hats, fruit bowls. Then, as I became more adept, more intricate and finer things. Necklaces, medallions, bracelets. They started calling me the Wicker Girl, and the name stuck. Better than the alternatives.'

'Alternatives?'

'Freak, weirdo, misfit, abortion—to name but a few.'

Frank shifts uncomfortably. He pulls something else from his pocket. This time it's in an evidence bag. He places it down carefully in front of her.

'Look at them both. Lot of similarities, aren't there? The same shape, the same fine expertise, a similar style. Did you also make this?'

With a candour that surprises both men, she replies, 'Yes. It's a Crucifix Knot.'

Neither Zac nor Frank can help but expel a loud rush of air and push back slightly in their chairs, the legs squealing against the floor.

Frank folds his arms. 'Two recent murders: Malachi Abbott and Amos Baker—the Crucifix Knot was found in the car of Malachi, and in the tractor cab of Amos Baker.'

'Yes. I put them there.'

They're both stunned.

Is this going to be an open and shut confession?
'Why?'
'As a warning.'
'A warning? As in you were warning them to stop doing something, or to back off—a kind of threat?'
'No. A warning in the truest sense.'
'Which is?'
'Their lives were in imminent danger, and I wanted to make them aware of that, so they could take measures to save themselves.'

Zac clears his throat and leans forward.

'Morrigan, Malachi's murder six weeks ago is common knowledge. But the death of Amos Baker, well, everyone thinks it was a farming accident. A faulty slasher and tractor. We, the police, know different. It was murder. Someone lowered the slasher down on top of him. Now, until a moment ago, there were only four people who knew that, and they all work in this station. DCI Finnegan was very precise with his words—he said Malachi and Amos were murdered. How could you possibly know Amos was murdered when it's not common knowledge?'

She blinks.

'Because of the vision.'
'Vision of what?'
'Of his death.'

Becoming frustrated, he pushes back in his seat.

'Stop playing bloody games, Morrigan. It's been a long day, and I want to go home to my family and enjoy a nice relaxing meal, then put my feet up in front of the telly.'

'There are no games, Zac.'

Losing patience, he slaps his hands down hard on the table.

'Then start talking.'

She doesn't flinch one iota. Still the same passive stare.

'Okay. You only had to ask. No need to get nasty. Although I'm used to that.'

He relents. 'Sorry, I apologise.'

'Accepted. Malachi was universally disliked by everyone in the village, apart from me. Which is odd, because he despised me. Called me a freak. But I saw something different in him. Yes, he was a hopeless alcoholic, but there was something inside him that was broken. A darkness in the pit of his stomach. I believe that's what turned him to drink. I felt sorry for him... in a way. About a week before his death, I was running some errands for my gran. I came out of the butcher's shop as Malachi staggered in, reeking of booze as usual. We bumped into one another. He said, to get out of the bloody way, you little freak. That's when I saw it.'

'Saw what?' Frank asks.

'The vision. He was in his Land Rover going down a steep hill, frantically pumping the brakes. He crashed through a wall, cracked his head, and the car careered down a field and entered the water. He was unconscious. I felt the water rising as he breathed… until it reached his nostrils. I wanted to help save him despite how he was with me. On May Day, I saw his car parked outside the pub. I placed the Crucifix Knot on his passenger seat hoping he'd be extra vigilant.'

Frank and Zac share a brief glance.

'And Amos Baker?'

'Farmer Baker was a nice man. Could be grouchy, but underneath, good. Looked after his cattle and sheep. Caring. Tends the land. He occasionally came into the post office to collect parcels or to buy the local paper. The day before his death, he came in and collected a parcel. As I was handing it to him, our hands touched. And that's when I saw what was about to happen with the slasher. Again, I went and placed the Crucifix Knot in his cab the night before as a warning—a good warning—to take care.'

Neither man is convinced.

Zac takes up the mantle.

'Okay, what do you know about the death of Reverend Hartley?'

'Murder.'

Zac is shocked but doesn't show it.

'How do you know that, Morrigan?'

'I was walking through the graveyard the day before his death. We got speaking. He was a nice man, but again, he had something inside.'

'Inside?'

'Yes. A thorn, scratching away. We were chatting about the abundance of bluebells in the grounds. When we parted, he patted me on the shoulder. That's when I saw him swinging from the rope. But he didn't put it around his own neck. Someone else did.'

'Who?'

'I don't know. I don't see the lead-up to the deaths. Only the death as it's unfolding.'

'Why didn't you leave a Crucifix Knot as a warning for Reverend Hartley?'

'I did.'

'No, you didn't. One was never found.'

A pause. 'Well, I don't know what happened to it.'

Zac sighs as Frank takes over.

'On the day Malachi was murdered, Lord Hampton was abducted in the early hours, outside his home—castle. He was placed in a disguised mineshaft.'

'Yes. Maggie's Tomb. I know it well.'

The men share a glance. 'We think he was the first intended victim of this killing spree. Did you get any visions about him?'

'No. But I only have the visions when I touch someone or hold a personal item belonging to them. I haven't seen Lord Hampton for a while. Although he did used to come into the post office sometimes. Another nice man. Unlike his wife.'

'Lady Hampton?'

'Yes.'

'And why don't you like her?'

'She's another one who's swallowed a thorn. It wriggles inside her. She's calls me a freak. Thinks I can't hear her, but I can.'

'And what can you tell us about Birch, the young man found dead in the coffin?'

'He belonged to the Wicca.'

'Yes, we know. Anything else?'

A nonchalant shrug. 'How did he die?'

'We won't know until after the post-mortem. When was the last time you saw him?'

'During Litha.'

'Litha?'

'Yes, the summer solstice. We held a gathering on Solmere Tor to honour the sun at the height of its power and celebrate light, fertility, and abundance.'

'And what happened at this gathering?'

'We lit a fire. There was food, wine, and mead. We performed a sacrifice—of an old, lame ram. We watched the sun rise, paid homage and then all went home.'

'Anything else?'

'No.'

Frank takes a quick glance at the clock on the wall.

'Okay. Thanks for your time, Morrigan. We may need to speak with you again. I can arrange for a patrol car to drop you at home. Just wait in reception.'

'That won't be necessary, Mr Finnegan. I have a cousin in Whitby, and I've already texted her to ask if I can stay the night. I'll catch the bus back to Ashenby tomorrow.'

'Are you sure?'

'Yes.'

They escort her out into the reception.

'Oh, by the way, Morrigan,' Frank begins. 'Do you drive?'

'No.'

'What about your gran?'

'She still has her licence, but she stopped driving five years ago. Her eyesight. She felt she was becoming a hazard to other road users.'

'Must be hard getting about?'

A nonchalant shrug. 'Not really. Gran has a lot of friends who drive. And the public transport is quite good if you know the timetables. Anything else, Mr Finnegan?'

'No. That will do for now.'

Before leaving, she turns and throws her arms around Zac, squeezing him tightly.

Perplexed, his hands hover in the air for a moment before coming to rest on her back.

He's six-three—she's four-eight. Her head barely passes his belly button.

'Thanks, Zac,' she mumbles into his midriff.

Abruptly, she pulls away and marches like an automaton out of the door, head held high.

Frank stares at Zac.

'Not getting too close, are we, sergeant?'

'No,' he replies, wistful, reflective.

'Then what's the matter?'

'I don't know, Frank. If she's genuine, then I feel desperately sorry for her. The names people call her. Look at her, poor wee mite. It can't be easy. She's either the most honest, truthful person I've ever met or...'

'... she's a lunatic fantasist with a penchant for killing?'

'Aye.'

42

Dinkel places the cup of tea on Prisha's desk and takes a seat.

'Thanks,' she says, completely washed out. 'How long have Zac and Frank been with her?'

'Oh, twenty minutes, perhaps.'

'They'll probably charge her then interview her tomorrow. Let her stew in the cells overnight.'

'Yes, probably. What did the doctor say?'

'I'm fine. They took blood tests and sent them to toxicology to see exactly what was in my coffee. They measured my oxygen levels—all normal, and heart rate and blood pressure are all good.'

'What was it like being in the coffin?'

Sipping the tea, she peers above the rim at him.

'Take a punt.'

'Not very nice?'

A weary chuckle. 'Erm, yes, you could say that. And when I realised I was lying on top of a body, well, that was the icing on the cake.'

Dinkel grimaces. 'Not sure I could have survived that. I don't like confined spaces. I blame my brother. He locked me in the wardrobe when we were kids.'

'How long for?'

'Eight hours. My parents had gone to London for the day.'

The gentle conversation is interrupted as Frank and Zac burst through the door, chatting intently. They stop in their tracks when they spy Prisha before rushing over to her.

'Hellfire, Prisha, what are you doing back here? Have they let you go?'

'Yes. And everything's fine before you ask. I just popped in to see what the latest developments are. I take it you've charged her?'

Zac and Frank back off a little.

Prisha places the cup down. 'Well?'

Zac is certainly not going to answer the question, so it's left to Frank.

'Actually, we've let her go.'

Prisha stares, mouth wide open. 'You are kidding me?'

'Ahem, no. We have no evidence of wrongdoing yet.'

'Apart from being able to locate my impromptu grave!' she yells.

'Now steady on, lass. Don't go getting all aerated.'

'How did she know I was there? At the very least, she's up for conspiracy to attempted murder.'

'You know how she found you. Zac gave her your hair tie, and she had a... ahem... a vision.'

She leaps from her chair. 'Bollocks!'

Frank holds his hands in the air defensively. 'On the face of it, yes, I share your scepticism. But until we have hard evidence, our hands are tied.'

Zac finally plucks up the courage to enter the ring.

'Actually, Prisha, putting the vision to one side for a moment, locating the coffin was more down to clever thinking on her part. The hay bales, you see. Maybe it's something one of us should have picked up on,' he says, glancing at Frank and Dinkel. 'She knew they didn't belong in that field for numerous reasons. Incongruous. She'd make a bloody good copper,' he says with a chuckle, trying to lighten the mood, which fails miserably.

Prisha glares at him. 'She's got *you* wrapped around her little finger,' she sneers. 'Has since day one.'

'Maybe she's cast a spell on him,' Dinkel adds, also trying to be humorous, which equally falls flat.

Prisha shakes her head in contempt. 'Morrigan left me the note to meet her at Gallows Meadow. It was *she* who spiked my coffee. What about the note? We can get a handwriting expert in. There'll be DNA and fingerprints on it.'

'The note hasn't been located.'

'It was in my jacket. It must have fallen out in the coffin.'

Frank and Zac glance at one another.

'It's not there, Prisha,' Zac murmurs. 'Whoever put you in the coffin obviously retrieved the note.'

'Neither Morrigan nor Lilac Penhallow drive,' Frank adds.

'What's that got to do with anything?'

'Your phone was located at Grimscar Quarry a few miles away, about the same time as Zac was at the post office questioning Morrigan and Lilac. Someone was watching at the quarry. They sent a text message. It couldn't have been Morrigan.'

'She obviously has an accomplice. There's no way she'd have been able to get Birch and me into that coffin alone. You're looking for two people as a minimum. And Morrigan is one of them. She orchestrated this whole thing.'

Zac slides into a chair. 'So why did she save you?'

'What?'

'If she concocted this elaborate plot to kill you, then why would she save you?'

'To make herself appear innocent. To divert attention away from her and the other murders.'

'But she hasn't made herself look innocent, has she?' He emits a resigned sigh. 'Look, Prisha, maybe she is involved, but if she is, then we need proof. And at the moment, all we have is circumstantial evidence—she happened to know where you were buried. That's all.'

'That's all,' she snorts dismissively. 'Where is she now?'

'Staying with a cousin in town,' Frank states. 'I explained we might want to speak with her again.'

'Too bloody right we do,' she snaps, grabbing her backpack and heading towards the door. 'We'll bring her in again tomorrow. This time, *I'll* interview her. She's obviously got a way of manipulating men without them realising. Well, she won't play that game with me.' She turns and glares at them all. 'I can't believe you've been duped by her playacting. We're the police. We deal in evidence, facts, forensics, witness statements—not bloody clairvoyants, and people who claim to have second sight. It's all completely irrational. *You're* irrational.'

Frank walks towards her. 'No, Prisha, it's you who's being irrational.'

'Yeah, of course it is. And how do you work that one out?'

'What you believe is irrelevant. What any of us truly believe is of no consequence. If Morrigan has this gift, or curse, of seeing people's fate, we'll never know for sure. But all that matters is whether *she* believes it.'

She yanks at the door. 'I'm going home. I need a large glass of wine. You lot are bonkers.'

The door slams shut so hard the windows rattle, sending a fine sprinkling of dust into the air.

Frank stares at the door. 'She's got a hell of a temper on her,' he reflects. 'Right, I'm ready for my tea and bed. What a bloody day!' His phone buzzes. He looks at the message. 'Christ, that's all I need. Meera wants me to pick up some Parmesan from the supermarket.'

43

The supermarket is a cathedral of the mundane—humming strip lights, scuffed floors, and piped-in cover songs nobody asked for. The aisles teem with life's great unwashed: the good, the bad, and the ugly—mostly the ugly. Harried mothers bargain with sugar-crazed brats. Elderly couples wage slow motion trolley wars, some with Zimmer frames for backup. And aimless deadbeats hover by the spirits aisle with the furtive air of a shoplifting rehearsal. Nothing to see here, officer... honest. People stop abruptly, slap-bang in the middle of walkways as if posing for a portrait, or spend entire geological epochs inspecting jars of pesto. Some just stop altogether—mid-aisle, mid-thought, mid-universe—to hold loud conversations with people they probably live next door to, while traffic backs up behind them like a motorway pile-up. It's not shopping. It's an endurance test.

Doctor Bennett Whipple is so far out of his depth he'd need sonar and a wetsuit just to find the cornflakes.

'Confounded place,' he grumbles, pushing the trolley with a wobbly wheel. He peers at the shopping list his wife handed him, and groans at the length of it. At least thirty items. He's been in the store for ten minutes, and the only thing in the trolley is a pack of toilet roll. Even that, he's not entirely sure about as his wife didn't specify the brand. He picked the cheapest.

'If Beelzebub ran a branch of retail, it would look very much like this.'

Glancing down the aisle, he groans even louder as he spots DCI Finnegan heading towards him with a genial smile.

'Sweet merciful Jeremiah.'

'Ah, Bennett.'

'Chief Inspector Finnegan,' he replies in his deep sonorous boom.

'How are you going?'

'Going, inspector? I'm not going anywhere. I have become stalled in a quagmire of urban excrement.'

'You need to watch where you're walking.'

'I was speaking metaphorically.'

'You're the last person I'd have expected to see in a supermarket.'

'Indeed. The procurement of comestibles, accoutrements, and appurtenances is the sole domain of Mrs Whipple. Alas, she's incapacitated.'

'Oh, sorry to hear that. What's the matter with her?'

Whipple sighs and stares at the endless jars of mayonnaise.

'Mrs Whipple has unfortunately succumbed to a partial inversion injury of the lateral ligamentous complex in her right tarsus, rendering her temporarily incapacitated in terms of ambulation.'

After three years, Frank is *nearly* fluent in Whipplese—a complex stew of medical Latin, archaic nonsense, and post-mortem gibberish.

'A sprained ankle?'

'Indubitably. Consequently, I have been dispatched to this Satan's den of iniquity to purchase various items required for the sustainment of life,' he grumbles, now staring at a child picking their nose.

Frank glances at the trolley. 'You haven't made much progress, Bennett. A packet of kitchen towel is all you have.'

Whipple frowns.

'Kitchen towel? You are mistaken, inspector. That is ablutionary tissue substrate. I find the dry wipe a most lamentable state of affairs. I did engage a workman with regard to the possibility of installing a bidet. Alas, our ablutionary domicile is too small.'

A pause as he recollects.

'I once visited Japan, inspector.'

'You don't say.'

'Indeed I do. A far more civilised society.'

Frank winces. 'You should have spoken to my grandfather. He worked on the bridge over the River Kwai. And I don't mean the film.'

Whipple raises an eyebrow, impressed.

'Ah—a structural engineer. A most noble profession.'

'Nay, Bennett. He worked on the production line at McVitie's biscuit factory in Carlisle. Got drafted at the start of the war. Captured during the fall of Singapore. My grandmother said when he came home, he was as thin as a stick of spaghetti. If he turned sideways, you couldn't see him. Mind you, to give him his dues he never held a grudge.'

Frank ruminates on his last comment for a moment.

'Although... he wouldn't have anything made in Japan or Germany in the house. For my sixteenth birthday, I asked him for a Sony Walkman. Ended up with a Pye stereo system instead. Not the most portable of things. Size of a small car. He couldn't look at a bowl of rice. Daft bugger wouldn't even entertain a hamburger—thought they were made in Hamburg.'

Both men fall silent. They have a knack of discombobulating one another.

Frank eventually breaches the impasse.

'Actually, Bennett, I'm glad I bumped into you. I'm working on a peculiar case at the moment, and I wondered if I could pick your brains?'

There's a growl like distant thunder. 'Hmm... if you insist. I find our interlocutions banal at the best of times, but anything to divert my mind from this cesspit of crass commercialism would be a blessed relief. Of course, the exchanging of information would be smoother if there were some reciprocal benefit.'

'Such as?'

Whipple waggles the shopping list at Frank.

'This damnable inventory of comestible tedium.'

'Ah, you want help finding the items.'

'Indeed.'

'Sounds like a fair swap. What's first on your list?'

'Butter.'

'Right, follow me. Butter is kept in the outside aisle along with milk, cheese, yogurt. Let's walk and talk.'

As they set off, Whipple keeps veering violently to the left.

'You alright there, Bennett?'

'I am the unfortunate owner of a perambulating menace, its rogue wheel conducting a symphony of squeaks and judders, intent on dragging me sideways through every aisle of purgatory.'

Frank chuckles. 'The old wonky wheel, eh? Anyway, this case. There's a person of interest—a woman, thirty-six, but to look at her you'd swear she was a pre-pubescent girl of about twelve. Apparently, it's something to do with an underdeveloped pituitary gland that didn't release the growth hormone when it should've.'

'Ah yes, classic isolated growth hormone deficiency, likely congenital hypopituitarism. The anterior pituitary, that most capricious of glands, fails to dispatch its hormonal emissaries, leaving the body suspended in an arrested developmental state. Physically juvenile, though chronologically adult. A curious case of time's passage being acknowledged by the calendar but not the flesh.'

'Yes, right,' Frank says, mentally unscrambling meaning. 'Anyway, I wondered what sort of effect that could have on a person. Not just the physical but also the emotional and psychological aspects.'

'From a psychological and social perspective, the implications are profound. Such a condition would undoubtedly influence interactions and psyche. They would be underestimated, possibly infantilised by society at large, which could foster adaptive behaviours.'

'Adaptive behaviours?' Frank repeats, desperately trying to keep up.

'Their perceived youthfulness could be utilised as a tool for manipulation or subterfuge. Moreover, the psychological burden of such a condition cannot be overstated. It would have indelibly shaped their identity and modus operandi.'

Frank scratches his head. 'Right. You're saying someone like this could use their looks to get away with stuff. Makes sense. Right, here's the butter. What brand?'

Whipple is bamboozled as he scans the list.

'My wife hasn't specified.'

Frank picks up a tub of Lurpak and tosses it into the trolley with abandon.

'That's my choice of heart disease. Next?'

'Porridge oats.'

'We need to head to the cereal aisle. So, back to the case. What else?'

'Their medical history would have been one of perpetual scrutiny, subjected to innumerable examinations and tests. This ceaseless invasion of their privacy could drive them to... unconventional actions.'

'Such as?'

'Consider, for instance, the possibility of utilising their youthful visage to evade suspicion or garner sympathy,' Whipple elaborates. 'It is a strategic advantage, one that could be employed with remarkable efficacy in nefarious endeavours. And yet, we must not overlook the tragic dimension of their existence. The social isolation, the incessant patronisation—such factors would inexorably shape their personality, perhaps driving them to acts of desperation—hypothetically of course.'

Frank rubs thoughtfully at his chin, absorbing the information. 'Anything else I need to know?'

Whipple shakes his head, the tension in his shoulders easing. He stares glassy-eyed into space.

'That is the crux of it, Detective Chief Inspector. But do remember, appearances can be profoundly deceiving. In such a case, the deception is not merely skin-deep, but woven into the very fabric of their being. I would imagine the most profound aspect of this unfortunate condition would be—loneliness and isolation. Take for example...'

As Whipple drones on, Frank receives another text from Meera telling him she's serving up spaghetti bolognese in five minutes. He slips the phone away and dashes down the aisle, block of cheese in hand.

Whipple continues rambling on for a few minutes as dubious shoppers give him a wide berth. Belatedly, he realises he's been talking to himself.

44

Wednesday 2nd July 9:10 am

The interview room is airless, stuffy. Both women stare at one another across the table. Another warm day.

Prisha's reviewed the interview Morrigan gave to Frank and Zac the previous evening and has a list of questions for the so-called *Wicker Girl*.

'Yesterday, you told DCI Finnegan the death of Reverend Hartley was murder.'

'Yes.'

'And you know this because of a vision you had?'

'Yes.'

Prisha taps the Crucifix Knot in the sealed bag on the table.

'You said these knots are a sort of warning for a potential victim.'

'That's right.'

'A question for you—instead of skulking about placing the Crucifix Knot in people's vehicles, where they may or may not have been seen, let alone understood, why didn't you just tell them in person? Why didn't you tell Malachi,

Amos Baker, and Reverend Hartley you'd had a vision their lives were in peril?'

'I used to a long time ago, but not anymore.'

'Why?'

'Inspector, remember about six weeks ago when you chased me down the high street and accosted me?'

Prisha leans back and sighs. 'I didn't accost you. I touched you on the shoulder to get your attention and ask you something. But yes—I remember.'

'I had a vision. You were in Gallows Meadow approaching the scarecrow on the cross. Three ravens were watching. They scared you. You have a thing about ravens. I could tell you weren't feeling good. Disorientated, woozy, then you collapsed, fainted.'

Prisha's not falling for it. All the information is obvious, apart from the ravens, which only re-enforces her belief that Morrigan was in that field yesterday, watching, scheming. But she's good at diverting questions.

'Let's keep on track. Why did you stop verbally warning people?'

'I was trying to explain. That day on the high street, if I'd told you your life was in danger in Gallows Meadow and not to go there alone, would you have believed me?'

'No, I wouldn't because there's no such thing as second sight, or visions. It's make-believe. A way for you to manipulate people and make yourself look mysterious and profound. Maybe a compensatory factor for your condition, your height. I know it can't be easy, everyone automatically assuming you're a child. I imagine people are dismissive of you. Having these visions is a way for you to gain attention, maybe even reverence.' She holds her hands up in the air and waggles them in mock fashion. 'Ooh, the mysterious Wicker Girl.'

She instantly regrets her words. They were needlessly cruel.

'And that's why I stopped telling people. And you're wrong. There was no reverence, only mockery at first, a bit like what you just portrayed, followed by fear and suspicion. The Wicker Girl—keep away from the little freak.'

Prisha places her arms on the table and leans forward.

'No Crucifix Knot was found in St Mary's, yet you said you placed one there to warn Reverend Hartley.'

'I did.'

'Where?'

'In the belfry. I put it there the night before. I intended to place it on his desk in the office, but it was locked. I knew they'd been working on replacing the rope on the bell, and Norm and Old Tom, the workmen, are messy, and Reverend Hartley was a stickler for cleanliness. He'd have gone up there to clean.'

She taps the plastic bag again. 'Forensics went over St Mary's, Morrigan. They're experts. They can detect a strand of hair, a fingerprint, a fibre, a molecule of sweat. There's no way they'd have missed something the size of this.'

Morrigan shrugs. 'Then I'm not sure what happened to it.'

Nothing. Not a flicker of emotion or doubt. None of the usual telltale signs—shuffling, body language, averting the eyes. She's good is this one. A change of tack. Let's see how she reacts.

'Tell me about the Wicca?'

'What do you want to know?'

Damn her poker-face!

'Are you part of their clan, their cult?'

'They're not a cult. Simply a group of like-minded people who respect nature and live by the old ways.'

'That wasn't the question.'

'No, I'm not a Wiccan. I'm a Pagan.'

'What's the difference?'

'Wicca is just one thread in a much older weave,' Morrigan says, eyes wide. 'They light fires on solstice, bless the fields, chant in a circle. It's grounding—ceremonial. But Paganism? That's the soil beneath your feet. The old bones and blackthorn. It doesn't need robes or rites. It's in the wind when it changes. In the way birds flee before a death. It's natural, universal. Older than names. Older than God. I suppose it's like Christianity,' she says softly. 'You can be a Christian, but which path? Church of England, Catholic, Baptist, Lutheran... they all sit under the same sky. Paganism's the same. Wicca's just one branch.'

'And do you take part in their ceremonies?'

'Yes, I'm anointed as their spiritual guide.'

Prisha's gaze sharpens.

'Because of your visions?'

'That's part of it. But not all. They say I walk a path back to the old ways. That I remember things most have forgotten.'

'And some of these ceremonies involve ritual sacrifice?'

'Yes. But only of sick or injured animals that would be slaughtered, anyway. We're not cruel.'

'A sort of offering to the gods?'

'To the spirits and ancestors.'

'And this is a Wicca tradition?'

'No, Pagan.'

Prisha has dealt with some clever suspects in her time, and always, eventually, she starts to break down their outer wall. But not this time. Morrigan's apparent honesty is disarming.

'You said the last time you saw the young man, Birch, was on the summer solstice?'

'Yes.'

'Were you friends?'

'No.'

'Why not?'

'I don't have many friends, for the reasons I explained before.'

'But surely, if you were his spiritual guide?'

'So? If you were a Catholic, would you hang out with the Pope?'

Prisha chuckles. 'Big noting yourself, aren't you—comparing yourself to the Pope?'

'It was an analogy. Not a comparison. I wasn't flattering myself.'

'Back to Birch; when was the last time you saw him before the solstice?'

'At the May Day Parade in the village.'

Prisha hesitates.

'The same day Malachi was killed?'

'Yes.'

'The same day you placed the Crucifix Knot in his car?'

'Yes.'

'Outside the pub?'

'Yes.'

'Where and when, *exactly*, did you see Birch?'

'I placed the warning on Malachi's passenger seat. I then headed up the main street to join in the parade. I passed Birch.'

'Did you speak?'

'No, he crossed over. Gave me a wide berth.'

'But he was heading down the street, away from the parade?'

'Yes.'

'Towards the pub?'

'In that direction, yes.'

Prisha rises.

'Right, time for a short break. Is there anything I can get you—a glass of water, tea, coffee?' she asks, heading for the door.

'Could I have a glass of milk, please?' Her voice is soft, uncertain, carrying the tremor of someone asking for permission rather than a favour.

The request halts Prisha, mid-step.

She turns. Morrigan's eyes are on her—wide, unblinking, almost luminous in the harsh light.

For an instant, she doesn't look like a woman in a murder inquiry, but a small girl asking for comfort in the only way she knows how.

'Milk... right. I'll ask the sergeant to bring you a glass.'

Outside, Prisha leans against the wall, deep in thought.

That look. For a moment, she seemed like a lost child. Frightened, even.

Stop it, Prisha.

It's part of her act—draw you in, tug at your sympathy.

Pull yourself together.

I'm not sure if she's the killer or not, but either way, she's up to her armpits in this.

45

The duty sergeant collects the empty glass and leaves the room.

'How much longer, inspector?' Morrigan asks, concerned.

'Not long,' Prisha replies, scribbling a note in a folder.

'It's just that my gran has a heart condition. She's on medication, but sometimes she forgets to take her tablets.'

Prisha glances up from her notes. Again, the flicker of emotion pulls at her.

'I'll try to be quick.' She closes the folder and clears her throat. 'You said you don't have many friends?'

'That's right.'

'But some?'

'Yes.'

'Who?'

'Some from the Wicca.'

'Like whom?'

'Violet, some of the other women.'

'Tell me about Violet.'

'She's funny, educated. She believes in me. Thinks I have a destiny. We're very close.'

'Like sisters?'

Morrigan tilts her head, considering. 'Yes, I suppose. An older sister, perhaps. A mentor. Although she can be very strict.'

'With you?'

'Sometimes, but mostly with the men. They're scared of her.'

'Why?'

'In case they're banished.'

'You mean asked to leave the commune?'

'Yes.'

'And do you have any friends amongst the men?'

'Just Oak. He's probably my best friend. He calls me—My Lady.'

Prisha is surprised. 'Ah, Oak. Yes, I've met him. A giant of a man.'

'You should be in my shoes looking at him,' she says with a faint smile.

Prisha chuckles. 'Yes, I can imagine he'd be quite intimidating.'

A shake of the head. 'No. He's a gentle giant. I feel sorry for him.'

'Why?'

'He's not allowed to seed with the women.'

Prisha pulls her head back. 'Seed? You mean have sex?'

'Yes.'

'Why?'

'He's simple-minded.'

'He has an intellectual disability?'

'Yes. The mind and outlook of a child. Violet says if he fathered a child, then the likelihood is it would be simple as well. She wants strong stock. He's innocent; that's why I like him.'

Not that innocent, Prisha thinks, recalling his overtly sexual nature in the glasshouse.

'And why does he call you—My Lady?'

'He says that one day I'll live in a big castle and have servants. He's joking of course. But I play along with him. We're both different. Outsiders. We see that in each other.'

'And what about the villagers—any friends amongst them?'

'The sisters.'

'The Ashcroft sisters, Lunara and Prudence?'

'Yes.'

'So, since the Wicca arrived three years ago and were allowed to stay on Lord Hampton's estate, you've gained a handful of new friends?'

'Yes.'

'That must have been nice for you. Someone to chat with, kindred spirits. Not judging, not being cruel. A bit different from most of the villagers.'

'To live among people and still be made to feel alone—just because of how you came into the world—that's the quietest kind of cruelty. Humans are no different from sheep, cattle, horses. We crave to be part of the herd. It's the natural way.'

'I'd imagine the manner in which you've been treated would have created a sense of injustice in you?'

No reply.

'It would hurt. Sting. Simply because you're different. It's unfair.'

'Prejudice is always unfair. That's why it's called prejudice.'

'That sort of thing could eat away at you. Resentment, embarrassment, shame at who you are. Could manifest in other ways too. Hatred, revenge, maybe?'

'No. Just sadness.'

You clever little madam.

'You've never harboured any ill will towards anyone?'

'No.'

'That's not true though, is it, Morrigan—what about me?'

For the first time, Morrigan averts her eyes and stares at the white breeze-block wall.

Aha—Gotcha!

'From the very first time we met, you were unpleasant towards me. And for no reason. You even kicked me in the shin, for God's sake. I had that bruise for over a week. And another thing, if it's true you had a vision of me in Gallows

Meadow, my life in danger, then how come you didn't warn me like you did the others?'

Utter silence.

Prisha waits... and waits.

She's pressed her buttons, but now Morrigan's pulled the shutter down.

'I'd like to go home now,' she asks meekly.

Prisha picks up her folder and rises.

'Okay, that will do for today. I'll be in touch if we need to speak with you again. Shall I arrange for a patrol car to drop you home?'

A shake of the head.

'Right, well, thanks for your time.' She reaches for the door.

'He's in love with you.'

Prisha freezes, her mind racing.

How the hell did she know about Adam? I've never mentioned him to her. Bloody Zac! He must have said something. He's like Edward the Confessor when he's around her.

She wheels around.

'Who's in love with me?'

'Zac.'

The reply stuns her.

'That's why I've been unpleasant towards you. Jealousy. I resent you. It was wrong. I apologise. And I didn't warn you because I knew he'd save you at Gallows Meadow. He'll always be there to save you—until the one day he's not.'

'Zac—DS Stoker?'

'Yes.'

Footsteps echo off the concrete steps as she slowly trudges up the stairwell, deeply troubled.

When Prisha first entered the interview room, she was composed, but underneath, angry as hell. She was intent on finding the truth. It's one of her strengths—her interviewing technique. She's learnt how to build slowly and then catch people out. She really believed she'd be able to crack Morrigan Penhallow.

Now, less than an hour later, she has more questions than when she began.

Like Frank and Zac the night before, she's deeply torn. Even though she didn't show it, Morrigan's tale has affected her deeply. The fact she looks like a child only adds to her disquiet.

Then again, was it all an act, a performance so convincing it could sway the minds of three seasoned police officers?

Maybe.

But what if she's telling the truth?

And then, to confuse the situation further, all the stuff about Zac. That's a whole heap of trouble brewing—if true.

And what did she mean by—he'll always be there to save you until the one day he's not?

Has she already foreseen Prisha's death?

Or did she mean Zac wasn't there because something had happened to him?

Morbid thoughts are interrupted as her phone rings. She pulls it from her pocket and stares at the caller—Professor Marcus Eldridge.

'Hello, Marcus.'

'Ah, Prisha. Just a quick call—I've been digging into the topic we discussed last week.'

'The Crucifix Knot?'

'Yes. My research suggests the symbol predates Christianity by at least a thousand years. Of course, it wasn't called the Crucifix Knot back then. In Old Gaelic it was known as Lámh-Sgàth, which translates, more or less, to "Hand of Shield." It was given to those about to face danger, or venturing into hostile territories.'

'A bit like people giving St Christopher medals to travellers today?'

'Exactly. And as you know, when a new religion takes hold, it often appropriates the symbols of the old, reshaping them to fit its own narrative. During the witch trials of the seventeenth century, the Lámh-Sgàth was reinterpreted—anglicised into what we now call the Crucifix Knot, but with a meaning turned completely on its head.'

'So from protection to... doom?'

'Exactly. I hope that sheds some light?'

'It does... I think.'

'I enjoyed our last chat. We must do it again sometime. Anyway, must dash. Best of luck with the investigation. Goodbye.'

'Bye.'

She hangs up and ponders. His theory correlates with Morrigan's explanation.

It's not what she wanted to hear.

46

As she enters the incident room, Frank, Zac and Dinkel are gathered around the whiteboard, quietly debating the case.

Frank glances over. 'Eh up, Prisha. How'd you go?'

She traipses over, absorbed in conflicting thoughts.

'She's heading home.'

The three men glance at one another.

'I see. No breakthroughs as such?'

'Only one.'

'Oh, aye?'

'The day of Malachi's death, after she placed the Crucifix Knot in his car, she passed Birch walking towards the pub as she headed towards the top of the village.'

'Hmm... interesting.'

'And another thing.'

'What?'

'I spoke with Birch six weeks ago, on my second or third visit to the commune. He was fixing a battery bank connected to the solar panels. Seemed like a nice lad. Idealistic. Maybe a little impressionable. Apparently enjoying life now he was out of the rat race.'

'And?'

'I asked what he did as a profession before he joined the commune. He said he was an auto electrician.'

'An auto electrician,' Zac repeats. 'Meaning he probably trained as a vehicle mechanic first, then moved into auto electrics.'

Frank rubs his neck. 'He'd have known exactly where the brake lines were on a car, and how to operate a tractor.'

'Exactly,' Zac concurs. 'And now he's dead. Anyone get the feeling this killer is tidying up loose ends?'

Prisha takes a seat. 'Any news on Hampton's motorbike, or cause of death for Birch?'

Zac shakes his head. 'No. I spoke with Terry Claymore from vehicle forensics, and he said he should have something for us this morning. And Whipple is performing the autopsy on Birch today. Won't have anything official but he'll let us know, off the record.'

Frank harrumphs. 'Talking of Whipple, I bumped into him last night at the supermarket.'

'Condolences,' Zac says.

'I told him about Morrigan and her condition in generic terms, no names. He provided some fascinating insights into the emotional and psychological impacts it could have on a person, having the appearance of a youngster.'

'Such as?'

'According to Whipple, that sort of thing would mess with your life. People would treat you like a child—talk down to you, underestimate you, poke and prod you in hospital. The constant scrutiny and isolation could shape how you behave.

'She might've learnt to use her appearance to her advantage; slip under the radar, gain sympathy, mislead people. But he also said...she could be very lonely. A square peg in a round hole. Someone who's been treated like a sideshow freak her whole life and doesn't know how to trust anyone or how to fit into society.'

Zac sighs. 'Either she's playing us, or she's on the level.'

'Aye, something like that.'

'None the wiser then.'

'No. Right, Prisha,' Frank begins, 'me and the boys were just having a recap on the investigations. Zac, do the honours.'

'Before I begin, I spoke with Featherstone, the landlord, yesterday. Asked him if he could remember what type of car Hartley drove.

Frank frowns. 'I hope you didn't prompt him?'

'Of course not. Unfortunately, he couldn't remember. Which means we only have Eileen Selkirk's word that Hartley drove a Citroen. But I did pick up another little morsel. He asked how the cold case was going. I fobbed him off with the usual vague nonsense about a complex case with various lines of enquiry. As I was leaving, he said it was nice that *people* were taking an interest in Iona after all these years. It showed she hadn't been forgotten.'

'People?' Frank queries.

'Yes. I asked him who, apart from the police, had shown an interest.'

Frank bites his lip. 'Don't tell me—Violet Fox?'

'Yep.'

'What's her bloody game?' He muses for a moment. 'Righto, let's have that recap.'

'Righto. We have a lot of riddles to unravel, so let's focus. Our theory is that the recent deaths of three of the Four Amigos, Malachi, Hartley, and Amos Baker, and the attempted murder of Hampton are related to the hit-and-run on Iona Jacobs back in 1989.

'We have no hard evidence, but we're guessing at least one of the four had something to do with her death—accidental or intentional—we don't know yet. Hampton is probably top of the list at the moment, and that's why we recovered his battered old motorbike. If it has Iona's DNA on it, then we have the bastard.

'And Dinkel checked the postcards Iona sent to her mother. Iona started working at the pub, mid-March 1989—meaning—she was still employed at Ravensbane Castle when she conceived. Let's assume one of the four was the father of the child. Three of the four wouldn't have been particularly enthused by that idea.

'For Reverend Hartley, getting a parishioner up the spout out of wedlock would not have been a good look. And considering the rumours that he and Iona were in a hush-hush relationship at the time, he is our prime candidate for being the father.

'Lord Hampton was married four weeks *after* the hit-and-run. Meaning wedding preparations would have been well under way when Iona became pregnant. If news broke he was the father, that wouldn't have just been embarrassing for him—it would have been a scandal. Local lord fathers an illegitimate child to village barmaid while engaged to Lady Whoever. If the tabloids had got hold of it, they'd have had a field day.'

Zac taps the board as an image of Baker pops up.

'And Amos Baker? His first child, Martin, was born in December 1989, *meaning* his wife was pregnant at the time of Iona's hit-and-run. A young local farmer, well respected in the area. Less likely than Hampton or Hartley, but still possible he didn't want an illegitimate child to another woman running around the village.'

Frank strokes his chin. 'So the least likely culprit is Malachi. Never married, and we're not aware of any relationships he was in at the time.'

'True. But can't rule him out. So, how does all this relate to the recent killings? If there is a link, then it appears someone has formed the same theory as us and is exacting retribution for Iona's death. Which brings me on to—who?

'The most obvious answer is mother and daughter—Lilac and Morrigan Penhallow. And yet, as contradictory as it sounds, they're also the least likely. Lilac isn't in the best of health, and she's in her late sixties. And Morrigan, well, can you see her snipping brake lines, starting a tractor and lowering a slasher, or manhandling Hartley and placing a rope around his neck, or abducting Lord Hampton for that matter?'

Frank grimaces. 'Aye, it seems unlikely, but as discussed, they could have accomplices.'

'True.'

'So who else is on the radar?'

'Well...'

'Go on.'

'Lady Hampton, possibly?'

Frank throws his hands in the air, exasperated.

'Nay lad! You're sailing the ship way off course. As unlikely as the idea is that Lilac and Morrigan are behind the murders, the thought of Lady Abigail Hampton cutting brake lines, starting a bloody tractor, and climbing a bell tower is preposterous.'

Zac holds his hands up. 'Hear me out, Frank.'

'Okay, carry on,' he says, puffing his cheeks out, then expelling a loud gush of air.

'What if it's all been a ruse—i.e. the link between Iona's death and the current murders? What if the real brains behind the recent killings used that as a red herring, knowing we'd eventually join the dots and point the finger at those with a grudge to bear—Morrigan and Lilac Penhallow?'

'Okay, I'm listening. What's Lady Hampton's motive?'

'If Lord Hampton hadn't escaped from the mineshaft, who stood to benefit the most from his death? Answer—Lady Hampton. Would you say she's a happy woman?'

Frank considers the question for a moment.

'No. I've met people with weeping haemorrhoids who have a happier disposition.'

'Exactly. She's what, fifteen-twenty years younger than her husband? No kids. That estate would be worth tens of millions, if not hundreds of millions with all the land.'

'It would mean she's working in cahoots with someone.'

Zac nods in agreement. 'Aye, or possibly more than one. Maybe someone from the Wicca.'

Frank slumps into a chair.

'Okay. Any more suspects?'

'Violet Fox?' he proffers hopefully.

'Motive?'

'She's into girl power, you know, women running things. Maybe she's figured out who's behind Iona's death and is paying out her own justice. It's weak, I know, but possible.'

Frank isn't impressed. 'Any more?'

'Only one—Lord Hampton. What if his illness is faked? Let's say he had something to do with Iona's death and the other Three Amigos knew of it. He killed them off in case they talked.'

'After thirty-six bloody years? Why now?'

Zac shrugs. 'Just throwing out suggestions, boss. Of course, it could be someone who's not flown onto our radar yet.'

Frank explodes. 'Give me bloody strength! It could be Morrigan with an accomplice, or Lilac with an accomplice, or both together. Or possibly Lady Hampton and the Wicca folk. Or Violet Fox on a feminist retaliation rampage. And then again, it may be Lord Hampton knocking off his former mates in case they talk. Or possibly someone we haven't even come across, a lone rider, a maverick—we've more suspects than the cast of West Side Story!'

Zac falters, then regains his composure. 'Or maybe it's a misstep,' he says quietly, shooting a glance at Prisha.

Prisha doesn't miss the inference. 'What does that mean?'

'Well, we did discuss it—running two cases side by side. One present day, the other from 1989. What if there is no connection between them?'

Prisha uncoils slowly. Rising to her feet, she slams her hands down on the table, making Dinkel spill his hot chocolate.

'Fiddlesticks,' he mumbles.

'Of course there's a connection,' she yells. 'Three murders in exactly the same manner as the witch trials. It's a copycat. A lord who *could* have died, and a gamekeeper, a parish priest, and a local farmer who *did* die. Do I need to spell it out for you?'

Zac takes a step back. 'I'm not saying that, Prisha. Yes—a connection to the witch trials but not necessarily to Iona's death.'

'Bullshit! It's connected.'

Frank rises like a father breaking up a fight between siblings.

'Oi, oi, oi! I'm the only one who's allowed to shout in here. Do I make myself clear?'

Zac nods as Prisha drops to her seat.

Dinkel dabs a tissue over his stained shirt.

Frank sighs, rubs a hand through his hair, frustrated, then calms. He glances down at Dinkel.

'Have you got anything for us, lad? How'd you go with locating the people who gave the original witness statements?'

Dinkel grins. 'Bit of a breakthrough, sir.'

'Let's hear it then.'

47

Dinkel picks up his folder. 'Firstly, remember the white paint flakes from the accident scene?'

'Aye. The samples have gone AWOL, and the report was so badly scanned it was indecipherable,' Frank grumbles.

'Exactly. Yesterday afternoon I contacted the RMU. That's the record management unit, sir.'

'I know what it is, Dinkel. I didn't come down in the last bloody shower.'

Dinkel frowns, unsure what he means. 'Yes, well... the actual samples of the paint are still missing, but the lab report made at the time was still there, on paper and intact. And I have a copy,' he explains, pulling out three stapled sheets.

'Good work.'

'Right—so, paint flakes recovered from the scene were analysed and compared against all known vehicle manufacturers at the time. No match found. Chemical analysis shows it's consistent with a generic aerosol-based paint, commonly used for superficial repairs.'

Zac scratches his beard. 'So the paint was from a DIY job—someone's gone over the damage with a rattle can from Halfords. Cheap touch-up stuff you'd use to hide a scrape, not respray an entire car?'

'Precisely, which brings me to my next breakthrough. Locating people who gave witness statements. I prioritised three people of interest.

'Firstly, Carl Lawrence, nineteen at the time. If you recall, he drove a red Mini Cooper and witnessed Iona cycling down Ashenby Lane at around 2:45 pm, matching Reverend Hartley's account. Carl joined the army aged twenty-one and was unfortunately killed by a landmine in Bosnia in 1994.'

'Poor bugger,' Frank mutters.

'Next,' Dinkel continues. 'Remember the two friends who saw Iona outside The Crown on the day of the hit-and-run?'

'Yes,' Zac says. 'Howard Price and Mark Hardaker. Both aged eighteen. And one of them drove a battered white Ford Fiesta.'

'Correct. The Fiesta belonged to Howard Price. Again, sad news—Price was killed in a parachute accident in Greece in 1997.'

'Hellfire,' Frank groans. 'What happened?'

'Parachute failed to deploy. Landed in a pig farm. By the time emergency services located Price, there wasn't much left of him. I never thought a pig would eat human flesh,' he adds, wincing.

'Pigs will eat anything, Dinkel, especially human flesh and bone. In fact, that tactic has been used many times to dispose of bodies. The only things left behind are teeth and hair. That's why the brighter criminals remove the teeth, and shave the body before cutting it up and feeding it to the pigs.'

Dinkel swallows hard. 'Yes, well moving on. That leaves the friend of Price—Mark Hardaker, and here we're in luck. He owns four holiday cottages in Sandsend.'

'Good work, lad. I suggest you make contact and arrange an interview.'

'Already done, sir. I have a meeting with him at 10 am this morning.'

Frank checks his watch. 'You better get a skedaddle on, then.'

'Yes, sir. On my way now.'

Dinkel hurriedly collects his things and departs as Zac becomes distracted with his emails.

Frank rises and stretches, noticing how quiet Prisha has become.

'How are you feeling?'

'Fine.'

'Hmm...' He's not convinced. 'Now, due to the traumatic events of yesterday, *our* team hasn't had a chance to interview the Wicca lot yet. Uniform got statements from them regarding Birch yesterday, and they're all singing from the same hymn book. Zac and I went through the statements earlier, but I want you two to head out there and dig deeper.'

'Yes, Frank.'

'Donkey bollocks!' Zac cries.

'What?' Frank asks.

'Got the interim report from vehicle forensics on Hampton's motorbike.'

'Not good news, I take it?'

Zac turns and looks at them both. 'No. They took samples from the frame and under the mudguards. It is blood, but not human blood. An animal of some description.'

'Bloody hell!' Frank cries. 'There goes our main lead—down the toilet pan. Back to square one. Right, while you're out there chasing up the Wicca folk, call in to see Lord Hampton and tell him the news.'

Prisha groans. 'Can't we just ring him?'

She already knows the answer.

'No, you can't. That's not how my team operates. You do it face to face, with humility and grace. Taking his motorbike for analysis was tantamount to accusing him. He deserves an apology. Swallow your pride, Prisha, and suck it up.'

'Yes, boss.'

'Oh, and one last thing to brighten your day. Superintendent Banks has directed that I, *along with my team*, attend a community meeting at Ashenby Village Hall tonight at 1800 hours. It's part of a reassurance initiative. Given the current speculation, she wants us to provide a clear account of the facts, dispel rumours, and take questions from residents.

'I've already deployed a couple of uniforms to the village with leaflets—door knocking, letting people know about the meeting.'

'Wouldn't it have been quicker to post it on social media?'

'And invite every rubbernecker, conspiracy theorist, and morbidly curious numpty in North Yorkshire? No—keep it low-key and local. Now then, are you two still here?'

48

Dinkel parks up in the idyllic seaside town of Sandsend and kills the engine as he clocks the sandstone cottage with its squat front and prim white bench in the front garden. The roof tiles are uneven, weatherworn. A double chimney leans askew, like a tired drunk. To the left, a whitewashed flank of wall presses close, giving the place a slightly pinched feel, like it's been squashed in by time and neighbours.

He makes his way up the narrow path, past a lone potted shrub and low garden wall. He knocks once, eyeing the polished door with its tiny square window—and waits.

He's learning fast—already savvy enough to know this is probably a waste of time.

If Mark Hardaker, or his friend, the deceased Howard Price, were involved in the hit-and-run, then Hardaker's certainly not going to divulge any fresh information after thirty-six years. But most likely, Hardaker will only have a fleeting memory of the event and provide no new insights.

The door creaks open to reveal a man—late fifties, stocky build, with the sturdy calm of a man who's spent more time outdoors than in. He wears a pale polo shirt, collar slightly wilted, and thick-framed glasses that give him a studious air despite the deep tan across his forearms. His face is round, ruddy, with that faint, habitual squint of someone unused to visitors—or perhaps suspicious of them.

'Mr Hardaker?' Dinkel quizzes, brandishing his warrant card.

'Ah, Constable Dinkel. I've been expecting you. Please come in. I'm just making a brew. We'll sit out in the back garden. Bit of a sun trap. Make your way through, lad, and grab a pew.'

The accent's pure North Yorkshire—earthy, warm, and, in Dinkel's mind, treacherously prone to obtuse proverbs. He braces himself, praying he's not in for another bout of Frank-style riddles. Prisha has a bibliography of them somewhere. He makes a mental note to borrow it.

The garden is a courtyard hemmed in by centuries-old limestone walls, their surfaces mottled and flaking with sea salt and time. A glossy black rattan table and chairs dominate the patio, gleaming in the morning light, while a set of bi-fold doors open into a modernised kitchen-diner—incongruously sleek against the weathered charm of the courtyard.

Mark Hardaker places the tray down on the table and pours the tea.

'Milk and sugar if you take it,' he says, quickly filling the cups and then relaxing into a chair.

'Thanks, sir.'

Taking a satisfying sip, Hardaker studies the young officer.

'So, you've reopened the case into Iona Jacobs?'

'That's right.'

'And what do you want to know?'

'I've gone over your original statement from 1989 and wanted to ask you a few questions about the case.'

He chuckles. 'Hell, lad. Fire away, but it's a lifetime ago.'

'Specifically about the last time you saw Iona.'

He pushes out air, vibrating his lips.

'Well, I do remember the last time I saw her as clear as day. The only thing that is clear, mind.'

Dinkel readies his notebook and pen.

'It was a Sunday, and me and my best mate, Howard Price, came out of The Crown in Ashenby. We'd not long turned eighteen, and drinking was a bit of a novelty for us. We spent all our spare time and cash at the pub. Anyway, it was a beautiful summer's day. Must have been a bit after two, as the pubs called last orders at two in them days. Howard had recently bought a knackered old Ford Fiesta. A real rust bucket. We saunter over and jump into the car and turn the radio on. As we reversed, we saw Iona coming out of the pub. She worked there as a barmaid and helped in the kitchen.' He pauses, reflective, and smiles. 'Oh my, she was a stunner, all right. A real beauty. Wasn't caked in makeup, false eyelashes, and Botox filler like young lasses today. Au naturel.'

He doesn't quite nail the French accent.

'And she had a beautiful Scottish brogue. Sweet, gentle, melodic. It was a pleasure to listen to her speak. And as sharp as a tack, mind—you know, witty, on the ball, quick as. No flies on her. She had this sort of—aura about her. Can't rightly explain it.'

Dinkel smiles at the fond memories. 'Fair to say you were smitten with her.'

'Oh, aye. She was older than us, maybe twenty-one, twenty-two. But me and Howard didn't half reet fancy her. Of course, she was out of our league by a country mile. Wouldn't have given us the time of day. Anyway, she had this old-fashioned bike she used to go everywhere on, one with a basket on front. She climbed on her bike and pulled her sunglasses down as we drove past. There was a song on the radio, a hit at the time—*She Drives Me Crazy*—by The Fine Young Cannibals. I cranked it up full blast, and Howard tooted his horn. She gave us this pout, all regal and posh, like. As if to say—*Yeah, dream on, boys.* Then we took off.'

He sighs and stares blankly at the back wall.

'Little did we know it would be the last time we set eyes on her.'

'And do you remember the police investigation and the mood around the village?'

'Aye, CID turned up a couple of days after. I recall being questioned, mainly about Howard and his car. They went over his Fiesta with a fine-toothed comb. But we had alibis, you see. We'd gone back to Howard's gaff after we'd left the pub, and his dad was home. We stayed there until the pub reopened at seven—except it didn't open. They'd heard the news about Iona by then and closed in respect. It was all around the village. Sad day.'

'And what about rumours?'

'Well, that's why they paid special attention to Howard's Fiesta. Someone had blabbed and said me and him, and another lad called Carl Lawrence were speed freaks, whizzing around the countryside.'

'And were you?'

'Not particularly. No more than any young lads with their first set of wheels.'

Dinkel checks his notes. 'You said the Fiesta was a rust bucket?'

'Aye, held together with fibreglass and spray paint.'

'Were you working at the time?'

'Yes—apprentice mechanic at the local garage.'

Dinkel's ears prick up. 'And what did Howard do for work?'

'He had a job at the local ironmonger's shop. It was a real working village back in those days. Post Office, baker, butcher, grocer, greengrocer, newsagent, even had a blacksmiths. It was vibrant. All village folk. None of your weekend warriors or second-homers. A reet good buzz.'

'So, if you worked as an apprentice mechanic, did you ever work on Howard's car?'

'Aye. We both did. Always patching it up with fibreglass, followed by a lick of rustproof. Let that dry, then a spray of paint. It was passable. In fact, we got so good at it, we did other folks' cars as well. Earned a bit of beer money. And we enjoyed it. I miss those days. Young, carefree, single. Special times.'

'Do you recall the names of other people's cars you worked on?'

A sharp intake of breath. 'Now you're bloody asking,' he says, looking to the heavens. 'I think we did the landlord's car—Colin Featherstone. And we did Howard's dad's car. And a few others, but I can't remember now.' His face darkens. 'Of course, I moved away when the garage shut down. I guess we lived in the village towards the end of its glory days, though no one knew it at the time. I'm not sure how long after, but Howard died in a bloody parachute accident. Of all the ways to go.'

'Yes, I read about it.'

'Poor bugger was eaten by pigs where he landed. I just hope to God he was dead when he hit the ground.'

'I'm sure he would have been. Mr Hardaker, you've been very helpful. Before I go—is there anything else you can tell me? About Iona, the events of that day, or anyone she might've been seeing?'

He shuffles uncomfortably. 'Well, it was only a rumour, like, but some said she'd been having a fling with the local vicar.'

'Reverend Hartley?'

'Aye, that's the fella. Not your typical vicar. He was tall, rakishly handsome. Jet black hair in a side parting. Looked more like a Hollywood film star than a member of the clergy. Mid to late twenties, I'd say. Not a bad lad. Not that I went to church, apart from weddings and funerals, but you'd see him around the village and at all the local events. Outgoing, charming, funny. Also liked a few pints at the pub. Always said hello and stopped for a chat. Of course, it soon filtered out that Iona was in the family way. People whispered, but I'm not sure if any of it was true or not. Apparently the bairn survived. Lived in Scotland with her gran, by all accounts.' He chuckles. 'I'm sure you know this already.'

Dinkel smiles, slips his pen away, then finishes his tea. He rises and shakes hands.

'Thanks once again for your time, Mr Hardaker.'

'No problem, lad. I hope I've been of some assistance, but I doubt it. I hope you find out the true story. Would bring peace of mind to her surviving family if they knew the truth. As I said, she were a special lass, that one. God broke the mould when she was born. What a bloody waste. I'll escort you out,' he says, stacking the tray.

'No need. Enjoy the rest of your day.'

Dinkel saunters inside and lets himself out of the front door, hesitating for a moment on the path as he wonders if he should have been more incisive.

'Oh, constable, that reminds me—talking of Reverend Hartley.'

Dinkel spins around. 'Yes?'

'Just remembered. Me and Howard worked on his car. It was also full of bloody rust. Perennial problem back in those days. He drove an old Citroën 2CV—you know, the weird-looking French car? Patched it up and spray-painted a couple of side panels.'

49

Zac rings the bell at Ravensbane Castle as Prisha, withdrawn and silent, hangs at his side.

He glances at her.

'Want me to do the talking?'

'Please, if you don't mind. I feel so bloody foolish. I was convinced Hampton's motorbike would have Iona's DNA on it.'

'Aye, well, as Frank says—don't die wondering.'

'That's the second time I've been wrong about him. He'll think I have a vendetta.'

The door swings open, and they're confronted by a frazzled-looking Magdalena.

Zac reaches for his warrant card but is abruptly stopped as the maid ushers them inside.

'Come, come,' she says, agitated as she closes the door then picks up a tray from a sideboard.

It contains a bowl of soup, an empty glass, and a bottle of water.

Zac is puzzled. 'Ahem, we're here to see...'

'Yes, yes,' she says, hurriedly setting off down the hallway at a rate of knots. 'Follow me. Lord Hampton is still on sickbed. This place is nightmare.' She hangs a right down another long corridor, heading towards an opulent set of stairs. 'Lady Hampton—she sack cook. Not good enough, she say. Now, guess who does cooking? Me and Lady Hampton. Not in my job description. And does she pay me more? Ha! Of course not. That woman has—how you say—something stuck up her backside, yes?'

Prisha and Zac exchange glances.

'Someone's not a happy bunny,' Zac whispers.

'Can't say I blame her.'

Turning abruptly, Magdalena climbs the stairs as she launches into Polish.

Unfamiliar with the language, the officers have no idea what she's saying, but there are certain words, accentuated, that they assume are expletives.

'I look for other job,' she continues, hitting the landing and taking a sharp left. 'Not fair. Magdalena this, Magdalena that. Come. Go. Come. Go away. She, how you say... *fucking bitch?* I had enough.'

She stops outside a door on another long corridor adorned with ancient pictures, coats of arms, and old military memorabilia.

Zac taps on the door.

'Come in, Magdalena.' The clipped, unmistakable tones of Lady Hampton.

He turns the handle and pushes it open. Magdalena nods appreciatively as she steps inside.

'Ah, Magdalena. Have you brought the soup?' Lady Hampton asks, her back to the door.

She's perched on the side of the bed, gently wiping Lord Hampton's face with a damp cloth.

'Yes, madam.'

Zac coughs, and Lady Hampton spins around.

'For the love of God! What is it this time? First, you accuse my husband of being involved in the death of Malachi Abbott. Then you release him. Then you confiscate his old motorbike without so much as an explanation. And now you're back again. Can't you see he's ill?'

Prisha and Zac glance at Lord Hampton.

He's propped up on the bed, two pillows behind him, but he looks shrunken, as if the mattress is swallowing him whole. His skin is sallow and stretched too tightly over bone. His chest rises and falls in shallow, uneven bursts. Sunken eyes flutter open, unfocused.

'Apologies, Lady Hampton,' Zac says. 'We'll be brief.'

She turns back to her husband.

'Noah, I've made you some chicken soup. Please try to eat.'

Magdalena sets the tray down on a side table. Lord Hampton stares at the officers.

'I can't eat. I've told you.'

'Just try a little.'

'No, it'll only come back up.'

She gently mops his brow again, then pours a fresh glass of water.

'You must drink something, at least. Keep hydrated.'

'No—damn you!' he snaps, knocking the glass away. It bounces on the carpet, spilling the contents.

Zac steps forward, picks up the glass, and places it back on the table.

Lady Hampton rises, visibly shaken.

'And damn you too, Noah,' she murmurs. 'You're your own worst enemy.'

She throws a flustered glance at the officers and sways slightly.

Prisha steps in, steadying her by the arm.

'Are you all right, Lady Hampton? You look a little pale.'

'I'm fine. Just tired—and a little overheated. It's this damn weather. I think I'll take a nap.'

She moves to the door, Magdalena trailing after her.

'Magdalena, check on Lord Hampton every hour. And please—try to get some fluids into him.'

'Yes, madame.'

'It's ma'am, not madame. How many times must I tell you?' Her rebuke is feeble now, half-hearted. She drifts out of the room.

'Yes, ma'am.'

Magdalena pulls a face behind her back, sticking out her tongue. As she closes the door, she winks at Zac.

'What do you two want this time?' Lord Hampton mutters. 'Can you not leave a man to die in peace?'

'Just a courtesy call,' Zac replies. 'We've got an update on your motorbike. It should be back with you in the next couple of days.'

'What the hell did you want with it in the first place? I haven't ridden that thing in thirty-odd years. It's the one I crashed—the one that cost me my foot.'

'I see. We seized it in connection with a cold case we recently reopened.'

'A cold case?'

'Yes. The hit-and-run that killed Iona Jacobs in 1989. We believe she was once employed here.'

His eyes widen. 'Iona.' He says the name as if her ghost has just stepped into the room.

'There were bloodstains on the bike and we thought—'

'You thought I was the one who knocked her down.'

'It was a theory,' Zac says, wincing and glancing awkwardly at Prisha. 'But it's been ruled out. Forensics confirmed it's animal blood. So—you're in the clear.'

'Oh, wonderful. I feel so much better now,' he snaps, voice thick with sarcasm.

Zac nods. 'Well, we just wanted to let you know and offer our apologies. We'll see ourselves out.'

Lord Hampton shifts in bed, propping himself up with effort.

'Wait. While you're here, you may as well make yourselves useful.'

He motions weakly towards an old wooden dressing table.

'Top drawer. Below my underpants. There's a folder. Bring it here—and grab a pen.'

Prisha hesitates, frowning, then obliges. With a curl of the nose, she slides open the drawer, shifts a few neatly folded pairs of underwear aside, and pulls out the folder. She retrieves a pen from her jacket as she nears the bed.

'Glasses,' he says, pointing at the bedside table.

She hands them to him.

The officers exchange a glance—*what now?*

Hampton fumbles the spectacles on and flips open the folder, revealing a sheaf of papers.

'It's my new will,' he announces. 'I need two witnesses. You'll do.'

'Your will?' Prisha echoes.

He seems temporarily invigorated.

'Yes. Had it drawn up a while back. Once I sign it, and you both witness it, it supersedes the old one.'

'Why the change?' Zac asks, stepping closer.

'Because when I go, I don't want her to see a penny of it.'

'Lady Hampton?'

'Of course. Who else?'

Prisha frowns. 'She's your wife. She's legally entitled.'

He chuckles bitterly. 'Oh yes—*entitled* is the word, all right.'

'What's brought this on?'

He takes off his glasses and fixes them both with a steady gaze.

'About a year ago, I came into possession of some rather startling information. Changed everything.'

'What kind of information?' Prisha asks.

'There's a young woman from the village. Has a... condition. Her name is Morrigan Penhallow.'

He pauses.

'She's my daughter.'

50

The room is silent, save for the rustle of paper as Lord Hampton flips through the pages, turning them towards the *Sign Here* tabs that jut from the sheets like yellow flags.

Prisha and Zac are stunned.

They'd entertained the idea that one of the Four Amigos might've been Iona's lover and Morrigan's father. But their prime suspect was Hartley, not Lord Hampton.

'Morrigan's your daughter?' Zac says at last.

'That's what I said.'

'How do you know?'

He looks up, meeting their gaze.

'Professor Fox. From the commune. She was researching the history of the area and came across the story of Iona Jacobs. Dug a little deeper and realised that Iona's daughter is living right here in the village. Less than five miles from this very room.'

'But how did she know *you* were the father?'

'An educated guess that I confirmed.'

'Does Morrigan know?'

'No. And she won't. Not until I'm gone.'

Prisha leans in slightly. 'And Violet Fox told you this directly?'

'Yes, I'm not a fool, inspector. I did my own detective work too. Went on the Ancestry.com site. It's all there. Irrefutable. Of course, the father is listed as unknown, but I can assure you, *I* am the father. I had sex with Iona. Just the once. She confirmed I was the father.'

Prisha folds her arms. 'You do realise Lady Hampton will contest the will?'

'She hasn't got a leg to stand on. When I married Abigail, I insisted on a prenup. Wasn't sure about her then, still not sure about her now. She's a lot younger than I am. Thought she might be a gold digger—I needed to protect what was mine.'

'And is she a gold digger?'

He considers for a moment. 'Not exactly. She has expensive tastes, but she's not reckless. That said, she assumes I know nothing about the many affairs she's had over the years.' He scoffs. 'Well, she's wrong. Cheating, deceiving... she doesn't deserve a penny. Everything will go to Morrigan. I'm just glad I found out in time.'

Zac exchanges a glance with Prisha. 'And you're absolutely certain Morrigan doesn't know?'

'One hundred per cent. Violet promised she'd never breathe a word. She's an honourable woman. And under her leadership, the Wicca have done wonders with my land. They've been a godsend.'

He scribbles on the page. 'Sign here, please.'

Both officers reluctantly sign and date the document.

Hampton slides a large white envelope out of the folder, slips the will inside, and seals it.

He hands it to Prisha.

'Pass this on to Magdalena. Ask her to drop it off at the post office today. She'll need to purchase a stamp. I'll reimburse her.'

She takes the envelope and studies the name and address.

Langford, Pike & Brewster – Estate & Legacy Advisers
Greyfriars Chambers, Minster Gate, York

They turn to leave.

'Oh, and take that damn soup with you. The smell's making me queasy,' he barks, slumping back into the pillows, suddenly spent.

'I wouldn't be surprised if she's trying to kill me,' he murmurs as his eyes flicker shut.

They pull the door closed behind them.

Magdalena has her back to them as they enter. She's up to her elbows in soap suds, scrubbing a large pan in the sink.

She turns as Zac places the tray with the untouched soup on the table.

Prisha lifts the envelope and waves it in the air.

'Lord Hampton asked if you could take this to the post office in the village today. You'll need to buy a stamp. He'll pay you back.'

Magdalena tuts and shakes her head.

'And now I am errand girl.' She sighs. 'Ah well. It will get me out of this place.'

Prisha steps forward.

'Magdalena, do you know Morrigan Penhallow?'

She looks surprised.

'Yes. Everyone know Morrigan. She work at post office with grandmother. She has...' Hesitating as she searches for the words, she pinches the skin on her forearm. 'She have something missing. A gene, no?'

It's not quite accurate, but close enough.

'Yes, something like that. Have you ever seen Morrigan inside this house?'

She shakes her head.

'No. Never. I see her in village. At Wicca camp, sometimes, when I go walk. She look like girl, but she woman. Sometimes she worried, scared. I feel sorry for her.'

Zac grimaces. 'Have you ever heard Lord or Lady Hampton speak about her?'

Magdalena pulls the plug, turns on the tap, and rinses the pan while she thinks.

'Only once. In study, I overhear Lady Hampton say something nasty. Call Morrigan little freak. She unkind woman. Not nice. Very demanding.'

Prisha's gaze shifts to a stack of empty glass bottles, upside down, in an old-fashioned milk crate on the counter. She walks over and picks one up, recognising the distinctive shape and blue colour. The same as the ones she saw at the Wicca market stall—except those had a label on the front which read: **Ravensbane Spring Water.**

'Where did these bottles come from, Magdalena?'

Magdalena sets the pan on the draining board and glances over.

'From commune. Is spring water. They bring crate every Wednesday. Is supposed to be cure.' She giggles and twirls a finger at her temple. 'They crazy—but harmless. They bless seven bottles, especially for Lord Hampton. Say it will make him better.'

'Have you ever drunk the water?'

She pulls a face. 'Once. Gave me pain in stomach. I stick to tap. Is clean. Spring water... I not so sure. They say is pur... pur...'

'Purified?' Prisha suggests.

'Yes! Purified. But maybe not.'

'And does Lady Hampton drink the water?'

Magdalena tilts her head, thinking.

'I not sure.'

Zac studies the bottles and notices that seven of the dozen bottles have a raven embossed on their old-fashioned stoppers.

'What's with the raven?' he asks, lifting one for her to see.

'I already say. Those bottles are blessed. Especially for Lord Hampton. Crazy people.'

Prisha pulls out her phone and snaps a couple of photos.

'Who brings the bottles to the house?'

Magdalena dries her hands on a tea towel.

'Usually Oak. Sometime Violet.'

'Never anyone else?'

'No.' She hesitates, eyes narrowing slightly, suspicion creeping in. 'Why you ask?'

'No reason. Right, we'll leave you to it. Enjoy the rest of your day.'

'Ha! I wish.'

Zac pulls his card out and hands it to her.

'If Lord Hampton deteriorates, could you ring me to let me know?'

She takes the card and gives Zac the once-over.

'Of course, Sergeant Stoker,' she says with an alluring smile and a provocative flutter of the eyelashes.

'Oh, give me a break,' Prisha mutters under her breath.

51

Zac rolls the sleeves up on his shirt and undoes another button as he and Prisha follow the familiar trail to the commune.

The haze makes the sun appear closer and larger than normal. The air is heavy and still, like a warm, wet towel. Not a breath of wind. The usual countryside chorus of animals is absent. Even sheep on distant hills have taken a vow of silence.

'What do you make of all that?' Zac asks in a hushed tone as if the trees are listening.

'Hampton's will?'

'Yeah.'

'Bizarre. I'm not sure we should have agreed to be witnesses. I'm wondering now if he's mentally stable.'

'Physically he's a wreck but mentally, I'd say he's still switched on. Do you believe him about his wife cheating on him?'

'No reason to doubt him, but still, it's a massive turnaround.'

'What is?'

She stops and pulls a small water bottle from her jacket and takes a swig.

'To ruthlessly strike from your will the woman you've shared your life with for twenty years, and leave everything to a daughter you barely know. It smacks of spite.'

'Or guilt.'

'Guilt?'

'If he killed Iona, then leaving everything to Morrigan could be some kind of penance.'

'Zac, we've already been down that route with the motorbike. We've no way of proving his guilt. We can't just keep going after him because we think he *might* be involved. Unless we gather new evidence, we need to back off, especially considering his condition.'

They carry on in silence as the Wicca encampment comes into view.

As usual, a small fire burns in the central clearing between the wooden lodges. Gathered around the smouldering embers are the members of the commune, in a circle, holding hands. Low chants emanate, occasionally accompanied by the dull thud of a drum, and the clank of a bell.

Prisha shakes her head. 'This lot are seriously into it, aren't they?'

'Aye, true believers.'

'How do you take a group of thirty people, from all walks of life, and get them to believe in a doctrine?'

'Not sure. Mind control?'

Prisha chuckles. 'Yeah, subtle mind control. Repetition, symbolism, and a set of rules that must be obeyed. Consequences if you flout the laws.'

'Not much different from our way of life then.'

'I guess not.'

As they near the edge of the camp, Zac nudges her. 'How do we play this?'

'I'll question the women, one by one. You take the men. I want to know the last time anyone saw Birch alive. What his mood was like in the preceding weeks and days, and if they've heard any rumours or seen anything suspicious. Let's try to coax something out of one of them.'

'I wish Whipple would hurry up with that bloody autopsy,' Zac mutters. 'Would help to know what actually killed him.'

As they step into the clearing, the chanting stops. The commune turns to face them as one.

Silent. Still. Eyes like pools of calm water.

Violet Fox breaks from the circle and walks towards them—slow, composed, theatrical in her grief.

'You're interrupting, inspector,' she says coolly. 'We're holding vigil for Birch, guiding his spirit beyond the veil. In Summerland he'll rest until the Wheel turns and his soul returns anew. It's a private ceremony of his kin.'

'That's as may be,' Prisha retorts, unimpressed. 'You can continue your vigil once Sergeant Stoker and I have finished speaking with you all.'

'Have you no respect? Would you halt a funeral service at a church to question the mourners?'

'To hold a funeral, you need a body. And considering Birch is lying on a cold slab in the mortuary awaiting a post-mortem, then my murder investigation takes precedence.'

'We gave statements yesterday. Nothing's changed.'

Prisha's expression doesn't flinch.

'Perhaps the officers yesterday weren't asking the right questions.'

Violet's nostrils flare slightly as she reluctantly nods at the mourners.

'We'll be using two of the lodges,' Prisha continues. 'I'll interview the women. Sergeant Stoker—the men. Form an orderly queue outside. We'll call you in one at a time. And I'll start with you—Ms Fox.'

The women lock eyes. For a moment, the heat of the day seems to crackle between them.

Neither looks away.

Inside the lodge, it's dim and cool.

Violet Fox sits straight-backed in a plain wooden chair, hands folded in her lap, expression unreadable.

Prisha doesn't waste time on pleasantries.

'Tell me about Birch. When was the last time you saw him?'

Violet doesn't blink. 'Two days ago. Around dusk. He was gathering hawthorn from the boundary hedgerow.'

'Was he alone?'

'As far as I know.'

'Did you notice anything unusual about his behaviour recently? Anything out of character?'

A pause. A slight tilt of the head.

'He'd been distracted. Quiet. Not himself. He'd fallen behind on his duties.'

'What duties?'

'Birch was responsible for grouse management—an early start each day, checking grit trays, inspecting nesting sites, and walking the heather to monitor brood numbers. It's a very important income stream for Lord Hampton come the grouse shooting season. Lately... Birch was slipping.'

'Why?'

Violet shrugs.

'I assumed his thoughts were elsewhere. He'd been spending time alone, wandering off without saying where. I counselled him. Told him to refocus.'

'And if he didn't?'

'We have systems.' Her voice remains soft, even. 'Consequences. A few days of silence. No participation in ritual. Food rationing. No voice in the circle. It's not punishment in the way you think—it's reflection. A reset.'

'Was he under this... reset yesterday?'

Violet smirks. 'Nice try, inspector. I told you—I hadn't seen him for two days.'

'Any arguments? Disputes with others in the commune?'

A slow shake of the head.

'We don't have arguments. Everything is discussed within the circle of elders. Then resolved.'

'So he was wayward. Neglecting his duties. But hadn't yet been punished?'

'A reflective reset, inspector. Not punished. And no, I'd spoken to him quietly, and planned to leave it a few days to see if he reset voluntarily.'

'Anyone from outside the community hanging around lately?'

'No.'

'I know you all come into the village regularly—did Birch have enemies in Ashenby?'

'If he did, no one here knew. But I doubt it. He was a regular at the pub.'

'And that's allowed?'

Her eyes narrow. 'We don't impose rules. Our members come and go as they choose—so long as they contribute.'

'So where did he get the money?'

'Each member receives a monthly allowance. Fifty pounds. They're free to spend it how they like, provided it's not on drugs or cigarettes.'

'And who hands out the money?'

'I do.'

Prisha leans forward slightly. 'So you're in charge of the money. You decide when someone needs "reflection". You have quiet words when they fall short. For someone in a group with no leaders, you're doing a fine job of acting like one.'

Violet leans back slightly, letting the silence hang. She knows how to wait.

Prisha stands. 'That's all for now. You can go.'

She rises without hesitation and moves towards the door. Her hand is on the latch when Prisha speaks again.

'One last thing. The spring water.'

Violet pauses. Just for a second. Then turns.

'What about it?'

'Where does it come from? The source, I mean.'

'It comes from the lake. Drains through natural sandy beds before we tap into it not far from here. We bottle it directly from the catchment well.'

'And it's safe? You've had it tested?'

'Regularly. We have an arrangement with a private lab in York—same lab that tests for microbials and heavy metals in commercial spring facilities. We keep the reports. You're welcome to see them.'

Not a flicker. Not a single nerve out of place.

Prisha nods once. 'Maybe later.'

Violet inclines her head and steps outside, the door closing softly behind her.

Prisha doesn't move. She watches the empty chair for a long moment.

Strands of drying herbs hang in loose bundles from the rafters, stirring faintly in the sluggish heat. Oak sits hunched on a low bench, his broad frame swallowing the space. His beard is wild, his fingernails thick with soil, his knees splayed wide. He stares down at his hands as Zac takes the seat opposite.

'Oak,' Zac begins evenly. 'I want to ask you about Birch. When was the last time you saw him?'

Oak blinks, slowly lifting his gaze, his eyes pale, filmy.

'I saw him near the elder tree... or maybe by the beehives. He liked the bees. Said they quieted his mind.'

His voice is slow, deep as if there's a slight intermission between what he sees in his head and articulating it into words.

'And when was that?'

A shrug.

'Could've been two days ago. Or before. It rained that morning. The smell of wet soil... I remember that.'

Zac frowns. 'Oak, it hasn't rained for over a week.'

Oak's brow creases. 'Oh. Then maybe I dreamt it. Sometimes my days... get mixed up.'

Zac studies him.

No guile. No attempt to dodge. Just fog.

'Had Birch been acting strange lately?'

Oak nods. 'He said the trees were unsettled. The wind was full of whispers, but no one heard. He didn't smile so much anymore. I told him to talk to the soil. The soil listens.'

Zac keeps his expression steady. 'So, he was not himself. Any idea why?'

Oak picks absently at a dried leaf stuck to his sleeve.

'Miss Violet said he needed to restore balance. That he was out of rhythm. But Birch wasn't bad. Just... sad.'

'Who said he was bad?'

'No one.'

Zac sighs. 'Okay, then why was he sad?'

'Dunno.'

'Was he being punished?'

Oak's eyes flick up, uncertain. 'Not punished. Just quieted. So he could hear the earth again.'

Zac leans back slightly.

'Did you see him yesterday?'

Oak hesitates. 'I saw... something. Might've been a shadow. I don't like the dark, sergeant. The dark takes things.'

'Do you know Gallows Meadow?'

Oak nods without lifting his head.

'Were you there yesterday afternoon?'

'Gallows Meadow is cursed. Bad things happened there. Witches. Hangings.'

'You remember Malachi Abbott—he was Lord Hampton's gatekeeper before your group took over the estate.'

His eyes narrow. 'He *was* a bad man. Miss Violet said drink turned him mean. Fogs the brain. Dulls the spirit.'

'Did you know Amos Baker?'

'Knew of him. Never spoke.'

'What about Reverend Hartley?'

Oak smiles faintly. 'He told me jokes. Made me laugh sometimes.'

Zac studies him in silence. He can't tell if Oak's hiding something—or if the world just doesn't arrange itself properly inside his head.

By the time they leave the commune, it's gone 3 pm. The heat hasn't broken, but the light has shifted—less gold now, more grey at the edges, a darkening.

Prisha and Zac walk the path in silence for a while, the crackle of dry grass underfoot.

'Every single one of them said the same thing,' Zac mutters eventually. 'I thought I might have got somewhere with Oak.

He has the mental age of a six-year-old child. He was either telling the truth or had been extensively coached.'

Prisha nods. 'Same here. Not one contradiction. Not one slip. Like they were all reading from the same script.'

'You think Violet told them what to say?'

'I think Violet *always* tells them what to say *and* think.'

Zac kicks a stone, sending it skittering into the undergrowth.

'That punishment she mentioned, the reset—silence, exclusion, and food rationing—it's not just some spiritual detox, is it?'

'No, it's control and coercion dressed up in folklore and incense.'

52

Ashenby village green lies dormant, wrapped in afternoon stillness. The church bell hasn't rung all day. The only sounds are the slow rustle of leaves and the soft crackle of paper bags as Prisha and Zac work their way through a very late lunch.

They sit on a wooden bench near the war memorial, bottled water at their feet, half-eaten ham salad rolls in hand.

'What did you make of Lord Hampton's parting comment this morning?' Zac mutters, wiping mayonnaise from his thumb.

Prisha screws up her face, chewing slowly, eyes scanning the green.

'What parting comment?'

'He said—I wouldn't be surprised if she was trying to poison me. Was he referring to Lady Hampton or Magdalena?'

'Oh, that. I think he was referring to his wife. It was said with a certain irreverence. I wouldn't take it seriously.'

'Wouldn't eat the soup though, would he? Looked bloody tasty too.'

Prisha gazes upward, thoughtful.

'And Abigail Hampton's sacked the cook. She now shares cooking duties with Magdalena. Why would she do that?'

'What if she'd come across his unsigned will and decided to poison the old bugger before he enacted it?'

She grimaces. 'Every time we've visited, Lady Hampton's been very defensive of her husband—protective, caring, in her own cold way. Mopping his brow, trying to get fluids into him. Is that the behaviour of a woman trying to bump him off?'

'Could be an act for our benefit.'

Taking a gulp of water, she sighs. 'I keep coming back to the knots. We know Morrigan made them. She admitted to leaving one in Malachi's car. Another in Amos Baker's tractor cab. And one in the bell tower for Hartley, which has never been found.'

'You think she's lying?'

'That's the thing. Why lie about one and not the others? It doesn't make sense. Unless...' Prisha trails off.

'Unless someone removed it?'

'Exactly.'

'So, what happened to it?'

'Not sure,' she replies, turning it over in her head.

A long silence settles between them. Somewhere in the hedge, a blackbird lets out a startled trill.

'Unless…'

She turns to Zac with that unmistakable look—the one that says—Eureka!

'Go on,' he says.

'After Hartley's funeral, we were standing outside as the mourners drifted past.'

'Aye.'

'The church cleaner, Peggy Thornton, spoke to us. Reflected on Hartley. But it was her brother I noticed—stocky bloke, nervous energy. He looked at her—prompted her with a glance, like he wanted her to say something. She didn't. Changed the subject.'

'And?'

'As they left, the brother said—you know where we live, inspector. I remember thinking it was a strange thing to say. After all, we'd already taken a statement from Peggy at the church when she found Hartley. It was the way he said it—like it was an invitation.'

'You think Peggy has more to tell us? She didn't want to say it at the funeral with all the villagers about?'

'Possibly.'

A faint rumble follows—so low it could be distant thunder or a heavy lorry careering along country lanes.

'It builds quietly,' Prisha says softly. 'You barely notice it until it's right on top of you.'

Zac glances at the sky. 'You talking about the weather?'

Prisha finishes the last bite of her roll and brushes crumbs from her lap.

'No, I'm talking about this case.'

She stands, tosses her bottle into a bin, and checks the time.

'Come on. Let's go see Peggy Thornton. Maybe this time she'll be more forthright in the privacy of her home.'

The bungalow is a modest, pebble-dashed affair tucked behind a neatly trimmed privet hedge, its front garden bright with geraniums and a gnome or two watching from the borders.

Inside, the place is spotless but dated—patterned carpet, net curtains, a ticking wall clock, and the faint scent of lavender polish. Prisha and Zac politely decline the obligatory offer of tea as they settle onto a floral two-seater. They face Peggy Thornton, who perches on the edge of her armchair, hands clasped tightly in her lap, fingers fidgeting like they're trying to wring the truth out of one another.

Her taciturn brother is seated near the window in a high-backed chair, arms folded, watching with tight-lipped scrutiny—scrutiny of whom though, Prisha isn't quite sure.

She keeps her tone light.

'We just wanted to check in, Peggy. See how you're bearing up after what happened at the church.'

Peggy nods quickly, eyes flicking to her brother and back again.

'Oh, I'm... I'm all right. Bit shaken still, I suppose. But thank you for coming.'

'Quiet day?' Zac asks, trying to ease the tension.

'Yes. Been pottering in the garden, mostly. Keeps my mind off things.'

Prisha offers a faint smile. 'There's going to be a meeting in the village hall tonight. Six o'clock. Just a chance to answer questions, settle some nerves.'

Peggy's fingers work overtime in her lap, twisting and untwisting.

'Yes, we got a leaflet through the letterbox. I'm not sure if I'll go.'

'You should,' Prisha says gently. 'It might help.'

Her brother shifts in his seat, exhaling sharply through his nose.

'Peggy,' he says, voice taut, 'if you don't tell them, then I bloody will.'

She doesn't respond. Just sits, frozen, hands locked tight in her lap, eyes fixed on the carpet. Her brother stands and walks over to a walnut bureau tucked into the corner of the room. He pulls down the lid with a click, then carefully lifts something from a compartment.

He hands it to Prisha without a word.

A Crucifix Knot, exactly the same as the others.

'She found this,' the brother says, voice low. 'On the floor of the bell tower. On the day of—well. You know what. I told her to hand it over to the police.'

Peggy makes a strangled sound in her throat, then bursts into a flood of words.

'I didn't know what to do. I—I was scared. Terrified. I'd just found poor Mr Hartley up there and then I saw that thing lying on the stone. I recognised it. From his book, *The Three Crones*. He wrote about those knots. Called them signs or omens. Said they meant death was near.'

She wipes her eyes with a trembling hand.

'I picked it up and put it in my pocket without thinking. Then I forgot about it. It must have been the shock. I remembered that night. Woke up in a cold sweat. I didn't know what to do. I thought I'd be in trouble, or that you'd suspect me. In the end, I decided to do nothing.'

Prisha's expression hardens. The missing Crucifix Knot has already burned through enough of her mental bandwidth.

'You do realise, Peggy, that you removed evidence from a crime scene? That knot could be a vital clue. It's a serious matter—tampering with evidence or obstructing a police investigation can carry a custodial sentence if convicted.'

Peggy begins to cry, softly at first, then with growing sobs.

'I didn't mean—I wasn't trying to—oh Lord, I didn't know what to do!'

Her brother leans forward and places an arm around her shoulders.

'All right now, Peg. It's all right.'

Prisha opens her mouth to speak again, but Zac steps in as he throws her daggers.

'Don't go upsetting yourself, Peggy,' he says gently. 'Probably nothing will come of it. We'll note it in our report, but I doubt there's any serious damage done.'

Peggy hiccups out a watery laugh. 'Oh, thank heavens. I've not slept a wink wondering when you'd come knocking on the door to take me away.'

'No one's taking you anywhere,' her brother says, patting the back of her hand. 'Now stop worrying.'

Prisha and Zac stand.

'Thank you,' Prisha says, voice softer now. 'The knot may still prove important.'

'And better late than never, eh?' Zac says with a cheery smile and wink.

Peggy nods, tearful but thankful. Her brother sees them to the door.

'Sorry about that, officers. I have been on at her to come forward, but she was worried sick about the consequences.'

Zac nods. 'We all stuff up occasionally.'

The brother leans forward, closing the door slightly. 'Can I assume you'll take no further action, Sergeant Stoker?' he whispers.

Zac nods. 'Yes. It was a silly mistake but done without malice. And anyway, we have enough on our plate. That's the end of the matter. Make sure Peggy knows that, so she can sleep soundly. Thanks, Mr Thornton.'

Zac strides down the path but stops by the garden gate and scowls at Prisha.

'What was all that about?' he snaps.

'What?'

'You know damn well. You really laid into her. She's a little old lady. A seventy-something church cleaner, not a hardened criminal on Britain's most wanted list.'

Prisha exhales sharply, jaw clenched. 'She removed evidence.'

'She was scared witless. Put it in her pocket. Forgot. It was innocent.'

She remains silent for a moment, stony-faced, before eventually softening.

'All right. Maybe I overdid it,' she murmurs, contrite. 'I'm a little stressed.'

'You think?'

She glances back at the house. A curtain flutters behind the window.

'I'm sorry.'

'Not me you should be apologising to.'

He doesn't wait for her reply. Simply turns and marches on ahead.

53

The village of Ashenby is deathly quiet on the oppressively hot, humid summer evening.

Empty streets. Bitumen glistening with stickiness. Shops display **Closed** signs. The village green lies lifeless, save for two ducks gliding languidly across the pond. The pub is temporarily shut, with a handwritten notice taped to the door: **OPEN AT 7 PM**.

Insects are the only creatures with purpose—though even they seem sluggish in their endeavours.

The sun yawns as it begins a slow descent towards the earth, casting golden rays over fields, hills, and woods.

It should be an uplifting sight, yet it feels like a sad reflection, a melancholy ballad singing of better times long ago.

And on the horizon... dark clouds mass, like shadowy assassins awaiting instructions.

A distant rumble barrels overhead.

Tempers are fraught.

Nerves frayed.

Logic scrambled.

The invisible villagers are silently willing the distant thunderstorm to reach them.

To break the pressure.

Offer relief.

Everyone needs to cool down—in more ways than one.

Backstage inside the village hall, however, there is movement—of sorts.

Frank and Zac are sitting around a table in the kitchen, sipping on a brew, as Dinkel merrily whistles a nerve-grating tune while he pulls open the fridge door and rifles inside.

Frank checks his watch. 'Ten to six and the hall's still empty, Zac.'

'Still time,' he responds. 'No one will fancy turning up early to sit in that oven sweating their cods off.'

'Aye. I suppose. By the way, forgot to mention—Dinkel obtained a little nugget of intel this morning when he interviewed Mark Hardaker. Apparently, Hardaker was the go-to man for fixing up rusty old motors around the village back in the day. One of his customers was Reverend Hartley. Spray-painted a couple of panels on his Citroen.'

'Really? It confirms what Mrs Selkirk said. But why didn't the police check the car at the time?'

'It could have been hidden. If the investigation team didn't know it existed, then they wouldn't have known to ask about it. And possibly it wasn't registered to him, but to the parish.'

Zac reflects. 'Circumstantial though. And the car will be long gone.'

'Aye, I'm aware of that. But still good work by Dinkel.'

Zac shoots a glance across the room as Dinkel drops a carton of milk onto the floor, sending a cascade of white liquid everywhere.

'Aye, good work. Shame he's an uncoordinated fuckwit, though.'

'Don't panic! It's under control. I'll get a mop and bucket.'

Frank barely reacts.

'I think the pieces are starting to slip together, Zac. Hampton confessing that Morrigan Penhallow is his daughter—sorts out one riddle.'

'Not the riddle we need to solve though, boss. Doesn't get us any closer to who knocked Iona off her bike or who's behind the murders.'

Frank pulls his phone out and swipes. 'That reminds me—Whipple was in touch. Birch died of a broken neck.'

'A broken neck,' Zac murmurs. 'That is a surprise.'

'I'll read you Whipple's preliminary summary. *Cervical vertebral fracture at the atlantoaxial joint, resulting in catastrophic spinal cord transection. Instantaneous disruption of autonomic control, respiratory arrest, and cardiac asystole. Death would have been immediate. Painless, but decisive.'*

'I always find Whipple's summaries somewhat lacking in detail,' Zac adds drily.

They share surprise as the tinkling notes of a piano ring out from the hall, carrying a tuneful melody.

'What the hell?' Frank mutters. 'Is that what I think it is—Gershwin's *Summertime*?'

Zac cocks his head. 'Sounds like it.'

Prisha enters. 'People are starting to drift in,' she says as the open door momentarily amplifies the music.

'Who the hell's that on piano?' Frank asks.

'The schoolmistress, Prudence Ashcroft.'

'What's she think this is—*Britain's Got Talent?*'

'What was I supposed to say?' Prisha replies, filling a glass with water from the tap and taking a thirsty gulp.

Frank rises with intent. 'Right, come on. Let's get this over and done with. Dinkel, when you've finished mopping the floor, go and stand at the back of the room.'

'Yes, sir.' He hesitates. 'Do you mean this room or the main hall?'

'Strewth,' Frank whispers. 'The main bloody hall, lad.'

'Yes, of course. May I ask what for, sir?'

'Because I bloody said so, that's why. This is a serious meeting, and I don't want you turning it into a vaudevillian slapstick routine by falling off the stage.'

Prisha and Zac follow him up a little flight of stairs to the stage, still invisible behind heavy curtains. He taps the microphone, and a dull thud bounces around the hall as muted chatter abounds.

Prisha parts the curtains and takes a peep at the crowd.

'Not a bad turnout. Filling up quickly.'

As *Summertime* comes to an end, another song immediately follows it.

'I don't bloody believe it,' Frank gasps in disbelief.

'Isn't that the theme...' Zac begins.

'Yes, the scary organ music from *Phantom of the Opera*. Prudence Ashcroft missed her vocation. She should be on a cruise ship entertaining wealthy retirees, not running a school. Okay—lights, makeup, action, or whatever they say in Hollywood. Let's get this show on the road.'

Prisha presses a button, and the curtains slowly glide back as she and Zac take a seat at the side of the podium.

The chatter subsides as people hurriedly sit in chairs, the manic pianist still in full swing.

Frank clears his throat and stares across the hall at the piano player.

'Ahem. Thank you for attending the audition, Liberace. Don't call us—we'll call you.'

The music stops, and the room falls silent as all attention fixes on Frank. He's about to launch into his opening monologue but hesitates. He's certainly not one to be overcome by stage fright, but the way a hundred pairs of eyes bore into him with absolutely no expression unnerves him. No creased brows, nervous tics, anxious whispers—nothing but complete and utter cold appraisal, almost reptilian.

Most people are seated, but a large cohort is standing at the back near the entrance—all of them from the Wicca commune. Front and centre is Violet Fox, arms folded, lips pursed.

'Thank you all for coming,' he begins, his voice bouncing back at him from the mounted speakers. 'I'm sure you all have better places to be; at home with your feet up watching the telly, or down the pub enjoying a quiet drink, or taking a stroll on a lovely summer's evening—so I won't beat about the bush. My team and I are here to give you the facts as we know them, and at the end we'll try to answer your questions.'

A few arms fold, but otherwise, no response.

'Ashenby is a quiet village. Until recently, crime here's been almost non-existent. I understand the shock, the fear, the confusion you're all experiencing.'

He clears his throat and gives the crowd the once-over.

'Malachi Abbott's death is a murder investigation. Amos Baker's death is a murder investigation. Reverend Hartley's death is being treated as highly suspicious. And the untimely death of Kelvin Potter, also known as Birch from the Wicca community, is a murder investigation.'

A sudden outbreak of whispers and murmurings abounds as chair legs squeak across the floor. The temperature, already unbearably hot, rises a notch.

'Now, we are making headway in our investigations. My team and I are working tirelessly day and night to get to the bottom of this. What I can say is we don't believe the murders are random. This isn't some crackpot killing on a whim. The deaths have been carefully orchestrated, and there is a connection. I appreciate that's cold comfort to most of you, but I can assure you all...'

He hesitates as he realises he's talked himself into a blind alley.

Bloody hell, Frank, you can assure them all of what? That they're safe? That this killer won't come after one of them?

'I can assure you all, we will catch this killer, and sooner than you might think. Right, questions,' he says, nodding at Prisha and Zac, who rise and stand at the side of him.

He notices the Wicca group all slowly file out en masse.

'Yes, the gentleman at the front,' Frank says, pointing at an elderly man.

'You said there's a connection, but what? As far as those present are concerned, these murders are random. No one feels safe. Everyone's wondering who'll be next.'

'I can't divulge what links the murders, as that information is sensitive and could impact on apprehending the killer. Yes, the young lady near the back?'

'You said the death of Reverend Hartley is highly suspicious. Everyone in this room knows there's no way Reverend Hartley would have taken his own life, especially not inside the church. It's unthinkable.'

'Yes, I know my terminology may seem confusing, but from a forensics point of view there's a difference between being one hundred per cent certain of murder and being ninety-nine per cent certain of murder. Reverend Hartley's death falls into the latter.'

'So, you do believe Reverend Hartley was murdered?'

'Possibly, but proving it unequivocally is difficult. Yes, the lady at the front.'

'I'm a man, actually.'

'Oh, I do apologise, sir. It is rather gloomy in here, and I haven't got my glasses on.'

'You've referred to *a* killer. Singular. Are you certain this lunatic is working alone?'

Frank turns to Prisha and neatly handballs the question to her.

'DI Kumar, if you'd care to address the gentleman's question.'

She glares at him and takes a step closer to the microphone.

'The murders share characteristics that suggest a single perpetrator. However, we can't rule out the possibility of an accomplice—someone assisting behind the scenes, even if they haven't committed the acts themselves.'

The landlord, Edwin Featherstone, stands.

'Inspector, this is no good for business. Folk are scared to leave the house after dark. How long before you lot catch this bastard?'

A ripple of applause and cheers breaks out.

Prisha turns to Zac. 'I'll let DS Stoker answer that.'

'Bitch,' he whispers. 'Edwin, I can assure you we're working round the clock...'

He's cut off by a sharp voice from the crowd.

'Weasel words! Answer the bloody question!'

The mood shifts. Faces harden. Postures bristle.

Edwin doubles down.

'He's right. We don't want reassurances—we want this maniac off the streets before he strikes again.'

Zac holds up his hands. 'As I said—'

'The killer could be right here in this very room! Are you getting anywhere or just fumbling around in the bloody dark?'

Frank's phone vibrates in his pocket. He slinks off behind the curtain to answer it as the meeting teeters on the edge of chaos.

He checks the caller—Doctor Julian Brant, the Hamptons' private physician. He hits the answer button.

'Doctor Brant, how can I help?'

'DCI Finnegan—I hope this isn't a bad time. Just finished surgery and checked my emails.'

'Go on.'

'The toxicology report came in—Lord Hampton's blood sample. It shows traces of aconite. Not lethal, but enough to cause a slow deterioration and eventual death. Aconite is...'

'I know what aconite is, Doctor.'

'I've tried calling Lord and Lady Hampton but have had no response. Frankly, I'm rather concerned about Lord Hampton's welfare. I intend to drive out to Ravensbane Castle and see if I can convince him to go into hospital. I'm not sure if this is an accidental poisoning or deliberate, but either way he needs care and supervision.'

'I couldn't agree more.'

'I'll set off now, but I'm in York and the traffic will be bad, so I won't get there for at least another hour.'

'Okay, I'll meet you at the castle. Thanks for letting me know.'

He returns to the front of the stage and whispers in Prisha's ear as Zac is bombarded with increasingly aggressive questioning.

'Prisha, the results are in from Hampton's blood test. Aconite poisoning. I want you and Zac back at the castle now. The doctor should be there in about an hour. I'll join you after I've finished with this baying mob. Come on, look lively.'

Prisha tugs at Zac's arm and leads him backstage as Frank tries to appease the crowd.

'Ladies and gentlemen, please!' he bellows. 'One question at a time. This *is* England, after all. Let's show some decorum and respect for one another.' He eyeballs the crowd in a stern, fatherly manner. 'Good. That's better. Right, the gent in the white polo shirt near the piano. Yes, you, sir. Your question?'

'Where have your two officers gone? Has there been another murder?'

Pandemonium.

54

As Zac opens the passenger door, he sniffs the air.

'Smell that?' he says.

Prisha jumps in, starts the engine, then lowers the windows.

'What?'

'Rain in the air.'

'I can only smell woodsmoke. Some idiot is having a fire on a day like today.'

'I hope that storm hits soon. This weather's oppressive,' he notes, slipping into the seat and fastening his seatbelt. 'Christ, I'm glad to get out of there alive. I thought they were about to lynch me.'

Prisha hits the accelerator hard and takes off up the village main street, before indicating right at St Mary's Church and turning onto Ashenby Lane.

'Did you notice the Wicca lot standing at the back?' she asks.

'Aye. Moody-looking bunch. Buggered off as soon as Frank finished his opening spiel.'

'Didn't spot Oak or Morrigan, though.'

'No.' He grimaces at the speedometer. 'Steady on, Prisha. Don't want another fatality along this road.'

She eases off as Zac's phone rings.

He doesn't recognise the number.

'Hello, DS Stoker? Oh, Magdalena... wait, I'm going to put you on speaker. Yes, yes, slow down a bit. You're not making sense.'

He taps the speaker button.

'Now what's the matter? Is it Lord Hampton?'

Magdalena is clearly panicked. 'No, yes. What I mean is, Lord Hampton he still sick, but it's Lady Hampton.'

'What about her?'

'She now very sick.'

'What do you mean by sick?'

'She in pain. Holding her stomach. Her mouth numb. I think she die.'

'She's dead?'

'No. I mean, she may die.'

'What has she eaten today?'

'Nothing. Maybe toast this morning. But she drink full bottle of spring water. Oak delivered new crate today. I take one to her as she very thirsty. When I check thirty minutes ago, water all gone. Now she holds stomach. Crying. She hot. Very, very hot.'

'Okay, Magdalena. Have you called an ambulance?'

'Yes, I call. But they say busy. Maybe one hour or more. I think she die before then. Should I give her tap water and salt, make her vomit?'

'No!' Prisha cries. 'That's the worst thing you can do. You could try giving her a glass of milk or Gaviscon—or something similar—but it won't make much difference. It might offer short-term relief from the stomach pain.' She turns to Zac and whispers, 'If she's ingested aconite, it'll already be in her bloodstream. It acts fast.'

'What is this... Gaviscon?' Magdalena asks.

'It's an antacid. Like Mylanta. Check the medicine cupboard. See if you've got anything thick and chalky.'

'Okay, I check.'

Zac rubs a hand through his hair. 'We'll be there in about ten minutes, Magdalena. You're doing well. Make sure the gates are open at the front.'

'Okay. Gates, yes. Bye.'

Zac puts his phone away as Prisha increases the speed to dangerous levels.

'Looks like someone is escalating events very quickly,' he says.

'Hmm... that rules out Lady Hampton as a suspect. Hardly likely to poison herself, is she?'

'No. And as one suspect drops from the list, another comes to the fore—Oak.'

'Possibly, but he's not got the brains to think of such a devious plan carried out over time. But I know who does.'

'Morrigan?'

'Yes. Oak's her best friend. She's played us all, Zac. She had you and Frank fooled, and even I began to believe her. And you heard what Whipple said to Frank—she's used her appearance to her advantage. Gained sympathy and appeared innocent all the while she's scheming and plotting.'

'What about the murders?'

'Who's the most likely to want revenge for Iona's death?'

'Her daughter, Morrigan. You think she got Oak to do the dirty work?'

'It's looking that way.'

'I can't believe it,' he murmurs. 'But it makes sense. If Morrigan found out about Hampton's will, then she's decided not to hang about.'

Prisha slaps her forehead. 'Of course, the will. Magdalena dropped it at the post office today. It was addressed to a fancy solicitor in York.'

'I wonder if Magdalena posted it or just left it behind the counter?'

'Yeah. Easy to peel it open and take a look inside.'

'And then enact the final part of her plan. Get Lady Hampton out of the way quick, then Lord Hampton next and bingo—she's the proud owner of Ravensbane Estate.'

'My Lady,' Prisha murmurs.

'What?'

'When I interviewed her, she said Oak calls her *My Lady*.'

'Why?'
'Oak believes Morrigan will own a castle one day.'
'He might be right.'

55

Zac strides across the dark bedroom, rips back the curtains, and pushes the window open.

'Let's get some bloody air in here. It's stifling.'

Prisha kneels at Lady Hampton's side as Magdalena watches on, a look of horror in her eyes.

Abigail Hampton is curled in a ball on the floor at the side of the bed, her skin ashen, forehead dripping with sweat. Lips tinged blue, hands tremble, torso occasionally twitches. Her eyes are scrunched closed in agony.

Prisha presses two fingers to her wrist. The pulse is erratic—fluttering beneath the skin like a moth trapped in a jar. Too slow one moment, then skipping ahead the next.

'It's not good,' she whispers, looking up at Zac. 'Come on, let's lift her onto the bed. At least make her comfortable.'

Zac grabs her under the arms as Prisha lifts her feet. They gently lower her down as she groans.

'Lady Hampton, it's Inspector Kumar. An ambulance is on the way, so hang in there, right?'

A groan of acknowledgement.

She turns to Magdalena. 'Try to offer her comfort. Keep wiping a cold flannel over her face. If she's thirsty, icy cold milk, okay?'

'Yes, yes. I understand.'

Prisha picks up the empty spring water bottle and studies it. A raven is embossed on the stopper.

'Did Oak say anything when he dropped the water off?'

'He said that special bottle and been blessed. I tell him Lady Hampton now not feeling well. He said water cure her.'

'And when was the last time you checked on Lord Hampton?'

'Maybe one hour ago.'

'Okay. Come on, Zac. Let's see how he is. Oh, Magdalena, did you post Lord Hampton's letter?'

'Yes. This afternoon. I get lift into village with Violet.'

'And who was serving at the post office?'

'Morrigan. Woman we talk about this morning.'

'And did you post the letter in the postbox outside?'

'No. I pay stamp. Morrigan say she fix it up and put in mailbag.'

As they enter the bedroom, they fear the worst.

Lord Hampton is still propped up on the pillows, his chin resting on his chest, eyes closed, the pallor of a corpse.

'Shit, I think we may be too late,' Zac says as they creep over to his bedside.

'Lord Hampton?' Prisha says quietly, reaching out to take his wrist.

His eyes pop open.

'Bugger. Am I still here? I was hoping I was dead,' he croaks, clearly disappointed with the state of affairs. His eyelids flutter, confused. 'What are you two still doing here? Have you moved in?'

The officers breathe a sigh of relief.

'Lord Hampton, we've had a message from Doctor Brent. He took a blood sample and sent it for tests. The results came back today. You're suffering from aconite poisoning.'

'Aconite poisoning?'

'Yes. It's obtained from monkshood.'

He takes a moment to digest the news before becoming agitated.

'I bloody knew it. I said she was trying to kill me.'

'Lady Hampton?'

'Yes.'

'No, she's not. She's extremely unwell. An ambulance is on the way now. We believe she may have been poisoned too.'

'But why? How?'

'We're not certain yet. But we think it may have been in the spring water you've been drinking.'

'How long have I got left?'

Prisha swallows. 'I... I don't know. You may not even die if the ambulance reaches you in time.'

'You're humouring me, inspector. I knew I was dying, and no one believed me. I'll not go to hospital. I'll meet my maker here at Ravensbane.'

'How are you feeling?' Zac asks, taking his pulse, which is dangerously weak.

'How do you bloody think? I'll not fight it. It's my time, and that's all there is to it.' He gazes wistfully across the room. 'It's funny. I was just dreaming about her.'

'Who?'

'Iona. A sweet girl. She didn't deserve what happened to her. I mean, it was an accident, but how we treated her afterwards was reprehensible.'

Zac and Prisha exchange looks

Prisha sits on the bed. 'What do you mean it was an accident? Was it you who knocked her off the bike?'

He shakes his head, chest wheezing. 'No. But it may as well have been. All my bloody fault.'

'Do you want to tell us the whole story, get it off your conscience, just in case?'

'Just in case I peg it, you mean?'

'It may bring you some comfort. And also for your daughter, Morrigan, and Iona's mother, Lilac. It would bring some peace of mind for them too.'

He takes a huge sigh. Prisha fears it could be his final death rattle, but it's merely a weary expulsion of air.

'Very well. It's been a burden long enough, and I don't want to carry it into the next life. I'll tell the truth, so help me God.'

Prisha and Zac both know a voluntary confession is gold dust—if the rules are followed.

Prisha shifts slightly. 'Do you mind if I record the audio on my phone?'

Hampton snorts. 'Don't give a damn.'

'I'll also need to read you the formal police caution.'

'Get on with it, inspector,' he grizzles.

With the caution read, she places her phone down on the bed in front of him.

'Okay, in your own time.'

Hampton motions to Zac. 'Sergeant, do you mind lifting me up a little and puffing up my pillows?'

'Of course not.'

Zac performs the duties with care and ease.

'How's that?'

'Perfect. Thank you, sergeant.'

He glances down at the phone.

'I'll start on the day of the hit-and-run. Sunday 4th June 1989—a warm sunny day, much like the weather we've been having recently.'

56

1989 Sunday 4th June 2:45 pm

'Pull!' the voice echoes out.

A circular clay disc spins through the air before hovering on the horizon, as if in slow motion.

Amos Baker, both barrels loaded, squeezes the trigger.

The clay pigeon explodes into a hundred pieces. He only needed one shot.

Snapping open the shotgun, he lowers his earmuffs, and turns to Noah Hampton.

'I think that tenner you wagered is heading my way,' he says with a toothy grin.

Noah offers him a disdainful look.

'Not over yet, Amos.' He snaps the barrels shut. 'Pull!'

The disc shimmies into the sky. Hampton fires off two quick shots, but the clay projectile drops unscathed to the ground some distance away.

Amos holds his palm out as Noah places the shotgun down and pulls a tenner from his wallet.

Normally gracious in defeat, Amos detects his friend's truculence.

'What's wrong, mate? You don't seem yourself today.'

Noah grabs two cans of lager from a picnic hamper and hands one to Amos.

'Let's just say I have a lot on my mind,' he replies, cracking the beer open, and taking a large slurp.

Amos peels the ring-pull but hesitates. 'Come on, out with it. Is it the upcoming wedding? Cold-feet? Second-thoughts?'

Noah sighs and slumps into a camp chair. 'Yes and no,' he replies cryptically. 'I've fucked up, Amos—big time.'

Amos chuckles and takes a swallow of beer. 'We all fuck up. It's called being human,' he says, with a cheery tone, taking a seat beside his old friend.

Noah sighs and shakes his head. 'No. This is different. I've really pissed on my own strawberries this time.'

Amos frowns.

He's known Noah Hampton since he was a boy. They may have taken different trajectories in life, he a young farmer, Noah the Lord of the Manor in-waiting, but the bond between them has always been strong, unbreakable.

He tries again. 'A problem shared is a problem halved.'

Noah places the can down and rests his arms on his knees.

'Hmm... but rarely solved. Very well. But no one must ever know of this. It goes in the vault, right?'

'You have my word.'

'It's Iona.'

'Iona Jacobs, the girl Hartley has the hots for?'

Noah nods. 'Yes.'

'What about her?'

'She's pregnant.'

Amos grimaces. 'Wait, hang on. Who's the father—Hartley?'

A sheepish glance. 'No. I am. She told me last week.'

Amos emits a long, slow whistle then takes a gulp of beer. 'Okay. I think you'd better start from the beginning.'

'A few months back, when she was working here as a maid, I was alone for the week. My parents had buggered off to some rich relative in Monte Carlo.'

'Yes, I remember. We had a cards night.'

'That's right. Well, a few nights later I was at a loose end. I decided to open a bottle of white wine at the end of the day. I wasn't even aware Iona was still in the house. Then I spotted her as she was about to knock off for the day. I asked if she'd care to join me for a glass. She agreed. We chatted on the terrace. Had a few laughs. Another bottle was opened, and well, one thing led to another.'

Amos rubs his face. 'That's poor form, Noah. You know how fond Hartley is of her. How could you do that to your friend, *our* friend?'

'There was nothing official between them. I know he's sweet on her, but all's fair in love and war. Anyway, it was an accident.'

'Sticking your dick into another woman is not an accident. And you're due to be married in six weeks. Have you no morals?'

Noah Hampton riles. 'I don't feel great about it. In fact, I feel like a right shit.'

'And so you should.'

'I don't need a lecture, Amos. I just needed to tell someone.'

Amos softens. 'Sorry. So, what's the state of play now?'

'It's a bloody mess, to be honest. If this gets out, there'll be no wedding.' He glances at the castle in the distance. 'And if my old man finds out, he'll do his nut. You know what a short fuse he has.'

Amos laughs, but not in a mean way. 'Have you never heard the expression—never shit on your own doorstep?'

'Thanks for that.' He hesitates. 'And that's not the worst of it.'

'Go on.'

'She accused me of... well, you know...'

'Please don't say rape?'

'She wasn't that forthright, but she implied it. Said I deliberately got her drunk and took advantage of her. Which is not bloody true, by the way. I admit, we were both drunk. But she was up for it just as much as I was. She said she intended to get rid of it—the baby. Naturally, I offered my assistance in finding a suitable, discreet doctor to perform the necessary task. And obviously, I'd pay for everything.'

'Obviously.'

He taps at the lager can. 'Then two days ago she called around. I thought she'd come to make arrangements. Instead, she said she was having second thoughts.'

'About the abortion?'

'Yes. Was beginning to feel differently. Of course, that would be an absolute disaster for me. I can't have an illegitimate child. There could be legal ramifications in the future.'

'Such as?'

'Legal rights to the estate, not to mention the rumours and innuendo that would undoubtedly surface. She could hold this over me for years, extorting money.'

Amos shakes his head. 'No, not Iona. I don't know her well, but she's not like that.'

'Then why else would she be reconsidering the abortion?'

'Idiot! Because she has a baby inside her. It's called motherly instinct, and you can't fight that. It's a powerful force. Believe me. Since my missus fell pregnant, she's become a different woman. The only thing that matters is the welfare of our child. I feel the same way, but with Polly it's like... well, like an obsession.'

Hampton touches his friend's hand. 'What am I to do, Amos?'

Amos takes a moment to consider the predicament.

'I think you need to sit down with her and say you'll offer her your support in whatever she decides to do. And you'll provide financial help, but *only* if she agrees to keep quiet about you being the father. Look at it from her point of view—it may be nearly 1990, but views on unmarried mothers haven't changed much. She won't want to draw attention to herself. Anyway, she's from Scotland; maybe she'll move back there to be closer to her family.'

'You think?'

'It's an option.'

Noah Hampton taps his lips. 'And what about Hartley? It would kill him if he ever found out about this.'

Amos pauses as he twirls the lager can around in his hand.

'Then you don't tell him, and I'm pretty sure Iona won't. Sometimes the truth is best hidden. Believe me, Noah, this will all blow over. Yes, it's a misstep, a pretty big one, but you're not the first, nor the last to get a girl pregnant.'

Noah smiles and reaches over and pats Amos on the thigh.

'Cheers, mate. I feel a lot better.' Abruptly, he stands. 'Come, let's get the barbecue fired up. I have some nice porterhouse steaks to cook. But first, to the shed. I want to show you the latest car I've bought.'

Amos groans. 'You've more money than sense. Another clapped-out so-called classic?'

Noah laughs. 'Yes. But this time it *is* a classic. A 1964 Aston Martin DB5. The Bond car. Got it for a song.' He grimaces. 'It will take me the best part of a year to fix up, but it'll be worth it in the end.'

57

1989 Sunday 4th June 2:55 pm

Reverend Hartley's anger rises like volcanic unrest. Building slowly, seething beneath the surface. He drains the silver-plated chalice of sacramental wine, then picks up the bottle to refill the cup, but it's empty. Twisting the corkscrew, he pulls the cork from a fresh bottle, and tops up the chalice. He stares out from behind the altar.

'Damn him, and damn her!' he yells, his voice reverberating off the cold walls. 'That bastard Hampton. He knew my feelings about her. Some friend he turned out to be!'

Another slug of wine.

'He really does believe he's some feudal lord,' he mutters. Then, with a bitter laugh, he adds in Latin, 'Jus primae noctis. The right of the first night. The law that gave a lord the right to take a bride's virginity before her wedding night.'

For a moment, his anger abates, replaced by burgeoning grief. Something pure lost forever. What hurts most is not knowing the truth.

Did Iona willingly give herself to Hampton, like a cheap hussy, or did Hampton force himself upon her?

If it's the latter, he can live with that, just about. If the former, then may they both rot in hell for eternity.

Swigging the contents of the chalice down in one, he staggers down the altar steps, cursing.

'I'll get the truth out of one of them,' he growls as he rolls the sleeves down on his white shirt and buttons up his waistcoat.

He fumbles the keys into the ignition of his white Citroen, and shakes his head violently, trying to block the dizzying effects of the alcohol. He looks at his watch—twenty-five minutes since Iona departed on her bicycle. She set off on the scenic route to the pub, so should nearly be back by now.

He stalls the car twice before finally setting off at a sedate speed through the village high street.

It's a soporific Sunday afternoon. Most people will have finished their Sunday lunch and be snoozing in an armchair in their living rooms, or in a deck chair in the garden enjoying the warmth of the sun.

He slows nearing the pub. She always leaves her bike propped up at the side of the main door, but it's not there.

'She can't be far away.'

He fumbles the radio on and almost weeps as *Eternal Flame* by The Bangles drifts from the tinny speakers. The very same song that played when Iona helped out at a church event six months ago. They washed and dried dishes together alone in the kitchen. That's when he first felt something for her. When he knew she was the *one*.

He wipes a tear from his cheek. Sniffles, feeling sorry for himself.

At the end of the village, he follows the road around to the left. A signpost reads—**Ravensbane Castle - 4 Miles**.

Another stab of betrayal.

'You bastard, Hampton. You're going to pay for this, whatever the truth is.'

With the narrow lane empty and the village safely behind him, he squeezes down on the accelerator, the puny engine of the Citroen whining as if in pain.

Sunlight flashes through the tangle of leaves like a nightclub strobe-light.

With the windows down and music cranked up, his neatly styled hair flurries in the wind.

Spots the T-junction sign, but still no sight of Iona.

A horrible notion materialises. The very idea makes him want to vomit.

What if she was heading to the castle to see him? A tryst? Another afternoon of unbridled passion. Afterwards they'll lie together, arm in arm, and laugh about poor old Hartley, such an innocent fool.

The Citroen swings violently left, almost on two wheels.

The circular route back to the village.

If she's not along this stretch of road, then there's only one place she can be—with him! And if that's the case, I'll confront them. Have it out with both of the buggers!

His vision is blurry, unaccustomed to so much wine so quickly.

Sweet summer scents drift through the air, accompanied by the bucolic sounds of the countryside.

All are lost on Reverend Nicholas Hartley.

I trusted her with my heart, and she pawned it for thrills, like a cheap trinket.

As he rounds a tight bend, a sliver of something catches his eye.

He slams the brakes hard.

Too hard.

The wheels lock.

Rubber squeals.

Fate is sealed.

58

1989 Sunday 4th June 3:02 pm

Malachi Abbott breaks off from re-papering the kitchen-dining room in his tiny cottage. He places a glass under the tap and waits for the tepid water to turn colder.

Taking a thirsty gulp, he peers out of the window at his neighbour, Mrs Selkirk. She's busy in the garden, cutting sprigs of lavender and placing them on a sheet of newspaper. A few rose blooms join them.

Malachi chuckles to himself. 'Best time of the year.' He opens the door and steps out into the yard. 'How yer going, Eileen?'

She looks up. 'Oh, fair to middling, Malachi. Beautiful run of weather we're having.'

'Aye. But make the most of it. A cold front is on its way. Should hit early evening. Then it's going to be cool and blustery for the rest of the week.'

'Typical. By the way, did you hear about…'

Malachi becomes distracted by a distant whining engine as Eileen Selkirk witters on about some village gossip.

Rapidly changing gears catch on the breeze.

He tilts his head.

Frowns.

Being a gamekeeper, he's in tune not only with the sound of nature, but with unnatural sounds. And someone's driving like a maniac. Been happening too often of late. He blames those young lads from the pub. Only just got their licences. He's spotted them more than once, flinging their cars around the country lanes as if they're at Brands Hatch. Reckless young fools.

A squeal of brakes.

A dull thunk.

Not good.

He rushes into the house and grabs his car keys as Mrs Selkirk, bent double plucking weeds, carries on wittering, oblivious to her surroundings.

Malachi jumps into his Land Rover and fires the engine, swerving out of the small yard onto the road.

Mrs Selkirk rises, rubbing her aching back.

'Rude bugger,' she mutters.

Less than a mile up the road, he rounds a notoriously tight bend and squeezes the brakes, spotting the white Citroen parked askew across the road, driver's door wide open.

'Christ almighty,' he whispers.

His friend, Nicholas Hartley, is on his knees at the side of the road. It appears he's praying, head bowed, palms together.

Cautiously, Malachi exits the vehicle and approaches.

It's then that he notices the bike at the side of the car.

'Nicholas.'

No response.

'*Nicholas?*'

Hartley gazes up, tear-stained cheeks. 'What have I done?' he murmurs.

Malachi edges towards the ditch at the side of the road and the protruding leg, with red toenails. Peers into the culvert. Sees the gash to the head, the facial features of someone who is sound asleep... forever. Wild strawberries are strewn across warm bitumen.

'Oh, sweet mercy. Is that...'

'Yes, Iona.'

In anger, he turns to Hartley. 'What the hell happened, Nicholas?'

'I... I wanted to speak with her. Have it out. To know the truth. I rounded the bend. All I saw was a blur, a flash, and then a sound. I hit her. It was horrible. She flew through the air like a rag doll.'

'You were speeding. I bloody heard you at my place.'

Malachi rubs a hand through his hair, then grabs Hartley under the armpits and yanks him to his feet.

'Listen, Nicholas, it was an accident, right? You came around the bend and were dazzled by the sunlight. Didn't even see her. Do you follow?'

Hartley staggers forward and vomits onto the grassy verge.

Malachi sees the red slurry and winces at the fruity smell, mixed with the acrid stench of sick.

'Have you been drinking?' he bellows as things turn from bad to worse.

Hartley sucks in deep. 'A little altar wine.'

'How much is a little?'

'A bottle. Maybe two.'

Malachi drops his head into his hands. 'Oh, help me God. I can't believe this is happening. You could do fourteen years for this, you bloody, stupid fool!'

Hartley rubs his shirt sleeve across his mouth.

'What am I to do? I'll be finished. You've got to help me.'

For a moment, Malachi is aghast at his words. Then weakens.

He's always had a soft spot for the Reverend since he arrived in the village. They're friends. Same outlook. Same sense of humour.

Panicked, he weighs up the options.

Sometimes in life, a split-second decision can have enormous ramifications that ripple down the decades.

59

1989 Sunday 4th June 3:17 pm

The shed door rattles along the rollers and clanks shut as Noah Hampton slips the padlock into place.

'Well, what do you think?' he asks.

Amos pulls the cigarette from his lips and exhales a grey plume. He smiles.

'You've got your work cut out, but the chassis and interior are still in good nick. The engine? That's another story.'

'We all need a hobby.'

'Only if you've got as much time and money as you do. Talking of money—have you thought any more about my offer on Gallows Meadow?'

Hampton chuckles. 'I rang my land agent. Your offer of three thousand pounds is about a third of what it's worth.'

Amos flicks the cigarette onto the ground and grinds it in with his heel.

'Nine grand? You're having a bloody laugh. I can't afford that. I've just invested in a new tractor. Things are tight, and with Polly expecting, they'll get even tighter.'

'Gallows Meadow's the finest land for miles around—soil so rich you could plant a broom handle and it'd sprout leaves.'

'Don't oversell it, Noah. It's good land right enough, but it's not the Garden of Eden.'

Hampton pats Amos on his shoulder. 'I didn't say I'd sell for nine. You're my best friend—I'm sure we could come to an arrangement that suits us both.'

Their discussion is cut short by the whine of a tinny engine tearing through the countryside. They turn as a car hurtles up the driveway, past the castle, leaving a trailing twist of dust devils in its wake.

Amos frowns. 'That's Hartley's car. And by the looks of him, he's in a rush. Were you expecting him?'

Noah swallows hard. 'No. He's got Evensong at six. He's off-grid on Sundays, as you know.'

The car slews to a stop just yards away, the handbrake ratcheting hard.

Malachi Abbott leaps from the driver's side, leaving the door open, engine running.

'Malachi?' Noah says, bemused but sporting a welcoming smile. 'What's happening, my friend?'

Malachi rushes over, red in the face. 'Not good, Noah. In fact, a right balls-up.'

Noah and Amos exchange worried glances as Reverend Hartley staggers from the passenger seat.

'What's the problem?' Noah asks.

Malachi paces, agitated. 'Christ, I don't know if I've done the right thing or not. I had to make a decision.'

Noah places a hand on his shoulder. 'Calm down, old chap. What's happened?'

'It's him,' Malachi replies, nodding at Hartley, who's gulping air, swaying like a sapling in the wind.

'What about him?'

'He's been in an accident.'

Amos steps forward. 'What sort of accident? He looks all right to me—apart from the dent in the wing of his car.'

'He's hit someone. A cyclist. On Ashenby Lane.'

'Who?' Noah asks.

'Iona Jacobs. She's dead in a ditch. And... he's pissed as a fart. Been at the altar wine.'

Amos is aghast. 'But he barely drinks.'

'Aye, well, he's had a bloody gutful today. Christ knows why.'

Noah's stomach lurches. 'Wait—you're saying Hartley knocked Iona off her bike, and she's dead?'

'Yes,' Malachi replies, as Hartley vomits into a hydrangea.

'Have you reported it to the police?'

Malachi rubs his face. 'That's what I'm trying to say. If it were an unfortunate accident, yes, I'd have called them. But Hartley's hammered. That's a maximum of fourteen years.'

Amos shuffles back. 'So instead of calling an ambulance and the police, you brought him here?'

'That's right.'

'You bloody dickhead!' he yells. 'And you've left Iona alone in a ditch?'

'She's a bloody goner, I'm telling you. I know when something's dead or not—man or beast.'

'Did you check her pulse?'

'No! She's bloody dead—okay!' Malachi bellows.

Hartley staggers towards them, leering.

'Ah, Noah, good friend—or should I address you as the future Lord Hampton? And how are you this fine afternoon?'

'Christ, Hartley, do you realise what you've done?'

Hartley wags a finger. 'Ah, ah, Noah. One mustn't take the Lord's name in vain. Blasphemy's a grave offence against God.'

'Unlike killing a woman?'

Hartley's grin fades as the full enormity of his actions registers. He breathes deep.

'Your fault, Hampton. All your f... fault.'

'What the hell are you rambling about?'

'Oh, don't play the innocent. Anyway—this is from Iona, and me.'

'What is?'

Noah doesn't see the punch coming. It slams into his face, knocking him down. Hartley launches himself onto him, pummelling with clenched fists.

Amos and Malachi yank Hartley to his feet, as Noah wipes a drizzle of blood from his nose.

Hartley wobbles, swaying. 'You bastard! You had to ruin it all, didn't you? Like you haven't got enough—the land, the castle, the money, the title. You had to take what was mine. Couldn't keep your hands off.'

Noah's worst fears have come home to roost. 'Ah, I see. She told you, then?' he says, rising unsteadily.

'Not in so many words. But I filled in the blanks—and you've just confirmed them. If we never speak again from this day on, answer me this: did you rape her, or did she willingly have sex with you?'

'It was consensual.'

Hartley begins to weep.

Noah, despite the bloodied nose, feels a stab of sympathy.

'Wait, Nicholas—it's not straightforward. We were both drunk. If we'd been sober, it would never have happened. It was a one-off. I swear on my father's life.'

Hartley sneers. 'And you think that makes it all right?'

Amos steps between them. 'Can you two shut the fuck up! Who cares how or why it happened? It's done.' He turns to Malachi. 'When did the accident happen?'

'Less than fifteen minutes ago. I heard the bang from my front door.'

Amos rakes a hand through his hair.

'Right—listen up. Hartley's ploughed into Iona while pissed. Malachi reckons she's dead, but nobody's called it in. And you,' he jabs a finger at Malachi, 'you bloody desert the scene and bring him here. If we don't get on the phone right now, we're all in it up to our necks. And we don't even know if she is dead.'

'I'm telling you, she's dead,' Malachi growls.

'You're not a doctor. And what about her unborn child?'

Malachi frowns. 'What?'

Hartley sways, pointing at Noah. 'She was pregnant—with that monster's child.'

Noah walks away, staring out over the Dales, thinking. He slowly turns to face them.

'Everyone needs to take a minute and calm down. I have an idea.'

60

1989 Sunday 4th June 3:26 pm

The four of them stand in a circle, silent, watching each other.

Noah Hampton, the natural leader, is the first to speak.

'Malachi, where's your vehicle?'

'There's an access gate into the woods about twenty yards from where the accident happened. Near the tight bend on Ashenby Lane.'

'Yes, I know the spot.'

'I parked it there behind a bush then got Hartley into his car and drove him here.'

'And the bicycle?'

'In the back of my car.'

Amos shakes his head. 'This is madness. We need to call the authorities now, before we all end up in the shit.'

Noah, now calm, stares at him. 'Unfortunately, Amos, we are already in the shit—together.'

Amos backs off. 'No, wait, hang on. This has nothing to do with me.'

'You said it yourself, earlier, we're all accessories after the fact. If we all want to get out of this mess, then we must stick together, not just now, but forever. This is a secret that can never be told to a single soul. Everyone in the village knows that bend is hazardous, and we get a lot of day-trippers whizzing around the countryside, especially on sunny days. No one will be any the wiser. Are we all on the same page?'

Malachi and Hartley reluctantly and sheepishly nod in agreement.

But not Amos Baker.

He shakes his head and walks away.

'I'll have no part of it. It's wrong.'

Noah quickly follows and steps in front of him.

'We need you, Amos. All for one and one for all, yes? United we stand—divided we fall.'

Amos is adamant. 'No. You don't rule the roost on this one, Noah. People need to be held accountable for their actions.'

He continues to walk off.

Noah calls after him. 'Amos—Gallows Meadow...'

Amos stops and glances behind. 'What about it?'

'I think we can come to an arrangement. As you say, it would be excellent for growing maize for winter cattle feed.'

'Why the fuck would you bring that up at a time like this?'

Noah advances. Places an arm around his shoulder.

'Tomorrow's Monday. What say I ring my land agent and organise for that five-acre plot to be transferred into your name?'

'What? How much?'

'Nothing. Free. Gratis. A thank you for being a... *friend.*'

Amos snarls. 'A payoff for my silence?'

'Your words, not mine. I always intended to sell it to you at a knockdown price one day. I was just stringing you along for a while.'

'Playing your power games?'

'You know I get bored easily. What do you say? Iona's dead. There's nothing anyone can do about it. She cannot be brought back. Hartley's a good man who made an error of judgement. Do you want to see him in prison?'

Amos is no mug. 'And of course, with Iona out of the way, and assuming her unborn child is dead, it would solve your little problem, wouldn't it?'

Hampton offers a weak smile. 'That's what I've always liked about you, Amos. You're sharp. There need be no losers here.'

'Apart from Iona.'

'She's already gone. So, what's it to be? I'll give you a minute to think about it.'

He saunters back to the other two.

Reverend Nicholas Hartley is fast sobering up.

'Nicholas, you have two options. You hand yourself in, confess all and spend at least ten years in prison, and be defrocked. Or you play the game. You're with friends, and we're here to protect you. The choice is yours, and I suggest you look to more earthly solutions than divine intervention.'

Hartley cannot even raise his eyes to look at him.

'We'll do it your way,' he sniffles, barely audible.

'Sorry. Didn't quite catch that?'

'We'll do it your way,' he cries, louder.

'Good. If you ever breathe a word of this to anyone, it will be you in the dock, not us. Understood?'

He nods as his empty stomach retches.

Lastly, Noah turns to his good friend *and* employee, Malachi.

'Malachi, I pay you well. We hang out together. You enjoy your work, and let's face it, I'm not sure who else would employ you. Gamekeepers are a dying breed. If you want our relationship and your *employment* to continue, then follow my instructions to the letter. And... you take the events of today to the grave with you. Are you on board?'

Malachi suddenly sees their real relationship in black and white. He nods and says for the first time, 'Yes, boss.'

The deal is done.

61

Present Day

Lord Hampton breathes heavily from the effort of lifting his head from the pillow. He gestures weakly towards the table.

'Water,' he croaks.

Zac picks up the bottle and sets it on the dresser.

'Not this. We'll need it as evidence. I'll get you some tap water.'

Hampton motions towards the bathroom. 'There's a clean glass in there.'

As Zac disappears, Prisha studies Hampton. He may be an old man on his deathbed, but quite frankly, she wants to smash his face in. She forces her anger down, composing herself.

'What happened once you'd all agreed on the cover-up?'

'We parked Hartley's Citroen in my garage. I dropped Malachi off at his car, hidden in the woods. He took the bike from the boot and laid it out on the road exactly as he remembered, then went home and called the police and ambulance. Meanwhile, I dropped Hartley at the vicarage. He made a quick call, and I left.'

'Who did he call?'

'The verger. Told him he was unwell—stomach upset—and that Evensong was cancelled.'

'And Amos?'

Hampton shrugs. 'Back to his farm and pregnant wife, I assume.'

'And did you follow through on your promise about the land?'

'Yes. The very next day I set the wheels in motion.'

'And Hartley's Citroen?'

'Parked it in my shed. I patched it up the next day—good as new. It stayed there until the police investigation petered out. My account of Hartley's and Malachi's actions is second-hand—I wasn't there. We reconvened in the shed the next day to go over things. That's when I got their full story. What we did was wrong, inspector, I know. But Malachi was convinced she was already dead. When we found out she was alive on life support, it was a mix of relief and fear. Had she seen Hartley? Or did it happen so fast she didn't see the vehicle?'

Prisha's stomach turns. 'So even when you found out she was alive, you were still thinking about your own necks?'

'Yes, I'm ashamed to say we were. That's when we began to drift apart. The joy of friendship was tainted. Eventually, we'd cross the street to avoid each other. Over the years, Malachi lost himself in the bottle. Amos became embittered and withdrawn. Hartley was a broken man. And me? I buried myself in other things. If it's any consolation, we all suffered too.'

Prisha's nails bite into her palm.

'Not as much as Iona's mother. Have you any idea what it feels like to lose a child?'

'You're right to be angry, but I can't undo the past.'

Zac returns and puts the glass to Hampton's lips. He takes a feeble sip, then slumps back.

The distant sounds of engines and sirens carry through the open window as Zac glances out.

'Hell, it's getting dark out there.'

Prisha picks up her phone. 'Lord Hampton, does your wife know about any of this?'

'No. It all happened long before she came on the scene.'

'What about your first wife?'

'No. The fewer who knew, the better. There was nothing we could have done to save Iona.'

Prisha bristles. 'You perverted the course of justice. There were at least thirty to forty minutes between the accident and Malachi calling it in. Those minutes could have been crucial.'

'She was brain dead, inspector. You must have read the medical report. The moment Hartley hit her, her fate was sealed.'

'And what about her unborn child—your unborn child? You couldn't possibly have known its fate.'

He turns away.

Prisha's voice hardens. 'But of course, that's what you were hoping for, wasn't it? With Iona and the child gone, you were free of any future hassle.'

'I think about my actions constantly. I was wrong. The situation was heated—febrile. We all acted with what we thought were the best intentions at the time.'

'Best intentions for yourselves. Not Iona nor her baby.'

Hampton coughs. 'There's nothing more to add. I did what I did, and I've lived with the consequences.'

'But you haven't, have you? You've had thirty-six years without being held accountable.'

'The burden has been its own jailer. Are you going to charge me or not?'

Zac gives Prisha a small shake of the head.

She rises from the bed. 'We will. But not yet. We have your confession.'

Hampton tries to chuckle, but it breaks into a wheezy cough.

'I'll be long dead before I'm brought to trial.'

'Maybe. Maybe not. But justice must be seen to be done. No one is above the law—not even a privileged lord.'

62

Frank slams the car door shut and scurries up the castle steps with Dinkel close behind. They almost bump into Prisha and Zac as they emerge from the entrance.

'What's the state of play?' Frank asks, looking decidedly hot and bothered.

'Hampton's fading fast, boss,' Zac says. 'But we have a confession. It was Reverend Hartley who knocked Iona off her bike. Drunk to the gills. Lord Hampton was the instigator of the cover-up, protecting his good friend and also solving a problem of his own.'

'Iona being pregnant with his child?'

'Yes. With his impending marriage, it was a convenient confluence of events for him if mother and baby passed away.'

'Bastard! And the others?'

'All in on it. Malachi, Amos Baker, Hartley. All kept quiet and hoped it would go away. Which it did.'

'Until now,' Frank reflects thoughtfully. 'Okay, good work.'

Prisha steps forward. 'Lady Hampton's in a bad way, Frank. We believe she's been poisoned with aconite as well. We think the Ravensbane spring water has been selectively spiked. Not sure if she'll make it. Magdalena's with her now.'

As the sirens rise louder, they all cast a glance down the long sweeping driveway.

'And any further developments regarding the murders?'

Prisha nods. 'We've got a pretty good idea. Morrigan and Oak in cahoots with one another. She's the brains; he's the brawn. Everything points to her. She has the motive for the murders—revenge for her mother's death. And she has a motive for the poisoning—to inherit Ravensbane Estate. Not sure how Birch fits in unless he found out what they were up to.'

'Blood and sand,' he replies, dabbing a handkerchief at his neck. 'I'd never have picked it. She's a canny bugger, that one. And dangerous.'

'Not for much longer. Me and Zac are heading down to the commune now. Oak was noticeable by his absence at the meeting tonight.'

'And Morrigan too,' Zac adds.

Frank nods. 'Okay. But remember, he's a big unit. Watch yourself.'

Zac smiles. 'I think we can manage him, Frank. Anyway, he's supposed to be a gentle giant. I think he'll come quietly.'

63

The sun has retired early. From the northeast, rumbling bass notes cartwheel across a bruised sky, the occasional magnesium-white flash of sheet lightning turning a spotlight on the Dales.

A hush has smothered all life.

To the south, Ravensbane Wood. Never the most inviting of places, it now appears darker, more sinister, as if harbouring demons deep in its underbelly.

Gravel crunches beneath their feet as Prisha and Zac hurry their way down the steep track towards the Wicca camp.

'Christ, it's eerie down here,' Zac mutters. 'Like something out of a horror film.'

Prisha nods, scanning the treeline. The air is heavy, electric, charged with the approaching storm. A faint smell of woodsmoke drifts on the still air, mixed with the sweet scent of hay and impending rain.

'There,' she says, pointing ahead. 'The commune. Can't see any activity.'

The collection of wooden cabins sits in the hollow like a forgotten village. Subdued yellow light glows from a few windows, and a small fire burns in the central clearing, its flames barely visible in the gloom. The place feels abandoned, quiet.

Almost too quiet.

A movement catches Prisha's eye—something black scuttling through the trees at the edge of the camp. Short, hunched, fast, moving with purpose.

'Did you see that?' she whispers.

'What?'

'Something black. It's nearing the lodges. It's the same thing I saw in the woods the very first time we came here.'

They quicken their pace as another flash of lightning illuminates the scene for a split-second, casting stark shadows across the wooden buildings.

As they approach the lodges, a sound stops them cold.

Sobbing.

Raw, heartbroken weeping that dissects the silence like a scalpel.

Zac reaches the door first, pushes it open, the hinges creaking in protest.

Inside, a single lamp offers a morbid, creamy glow.

Morrigan is kneeling on the wooden floor, her black robe pooled around her like spilt ink. She cradles Oak's massive head in her lap, tears streaming down her face.

Oak lies sprawled out, his enormous frame wracked with spasms. His hands clutch his stomach, knuckles white with pain. Sweat drips from his forehead. An empty mead bottle lies on its side nearby, honey-coloured dregs staining the floorboards.

'Oh, God,' Prisha breathes, stepping forward. 'Morrigan, don't tell me you've poisoned him as well?'

She looks up, green eyes wide with terror and grief.

'What? Of course I haven't. I found him like this a moment ago. He's in so much pain.'

'Where's the rest of the commune?' she demands.

'At the stones,' Morrigan whispers, not taking her eyes off Oak. 'The Three Crones, in the woods. Violet's holding a purification ceremony to banish the evil that's entered the camp.'

'Why aren't you with them?'

Her voice cracks. 'I was until I noticed Oak was missing. I came looking for him. He never misses the ceremonies. I could feel his pain. I knew something was wrong with him.'

Thunder crashes overhead. The windows rattle in their frames.

'What's the matter, Oak? Speak to me.'

Zac picks up the empty mead bottle and sniffs it.

'What?' Prisha asks.

'It has a strange smell.'

'Poison?'

'Possibly.' He pulls his phone out and curses. 'Damn, no bloody signal down here. I'll nip out and see if I can reach Dinkel. Tell him we need another ambulance.'

As Zac exits, Prisha kneels down. 'Oak, who gave you the mead?'

'Miss Violet.'

Morrigan shakes her head. 'That can't be true, Oak. You're only allowed to drink it on special occasions. Violet would never allow it.'

'It's true,' he groans as another stab of pain racks his body. 'Miss Violet said it was a gift for all my hard work.'

'What hard work?' Prisha asks with a creeping sense of unease.

He clutches at his stomach and weeps.

'I didn't want to do it. He was my friend, but she said I had to—to save My Lady.'

'Do what?' Morrigan sniffles.

'Birch. She said I had to kill him and put him in the coffin with the copper.' He looks up at Prisha. 'Sorry, miss. Didn't want to put you in there but I had to.'

'Who told you to kill Birch?' Prisha demands.

'Miss Violet.'

'Why?'

'Said he was a bad seed, and bad seeds produce bad fruit. She said he killed Malachi, Reverend Hartley, and Farmer Baker. He was evil, and evil must be purged. An eye for an eye. She said if I didn't do it, then My Lady would never get her castle.'

The confession hits Prisha like a physical blow as it all falls into place.

I've got it all wrong. Morrigan's not behind the murders—Violet is.

Zac re-enters. 'I managed to get onto Dinkel. Another ambulance is on its way.'

Prisha gazes at him, stunned, pale.

'What is it, Prisha?'

'We were wrong. It's not Morrigan. Birch was the killer all along, manipulated by Violet into committing murder,' she murmurs. 'And when he became a liability, she ordered Oak to kill him. And now it looks like she's tried to eliminate Oak.'

Morrigan strokes the back of Oak's hand as his laboured breathing gets worse.

He takes a deep breath. 'I wanted to tell you, but I wasn't allowed. She said I'd be banished if I ever breathed a word. I had to keep the secret.'

'The secret about Birch?' Morrigan snuffles.

Painfully, he shakes his head. 'No. The secret about you.'

'What secret?'

'That you're the rightful heir. Lord Hampton is your father. Miss Violet said he was dying and that everything would go to Lady Hampton and she'd kick us all off the land.

I'd have nowhere to live, and I'd never see you again. She said the castle rightfully belongs to you.'

Morrigan gazes open-mouthed at him.

'She's lied to you, Oak. Lord Hampton is not my father.' She looks to Prisha and Zac for reassurance but is met with embarrassed eyes.

Zac offers her a pitiful smile.

'It's true, Morrigan. Lord Hampton told us this morning. We witnessed his will. Your mother worked at the castle back in 1989. You are Lord Hampton's daughter.'

Her face turns white, mouth opening, and closing without sound.

Oak lets out a ghastly groan as white saliva forms around his lips, dripping into his beard. His massive body convulses, back arching with pain.

'Do something!' Morrigan yells. 'He's dying.'

Zac stares at her, emotion pulling at his heart.

'There's nothing we can do, Morrigan,' he whispers. 'If it is poison, then it's already in his bloodstream. All we can hope is that he hangs on until the ambulance arrives.'

'No. I don't believe you. Water! I'll get water. Flush it out.'

She jumps to her feet and clatters around in the kitchen.

Prisha takes Oak's wrist, feeling for a pulse. It's rapid and thready.

His gaze rolls towards Prisha.

'Birch was my friend,' he weeps.

'How did you kill him, Oak?'

His eyes scrunch up. 'I broke his neck. She said it was the quickest way. That he wouldn't feel a thing. Made me tie him to the cross in Gallows Meadow. She took your phone and drove to the quarry and ordered me to put Birch and you in the coffin.'

'When did you dig the hole for the coffin?'

'A week ago. I didn't know what it was for.'

She looks up at Zac. 'She's had this planned for a while.'

Morrigan returns with a glass of water and drops to his side.

'Lift your head up, Oak. You need to drink this. Flush the poison out.'

Cradling his head, she lifts the glass to his mouth.

A crack of thunder explodes directly overhead, followed by silence, as Oak reaches out and strokes Morrigan's cheek.

His body relaxes, arm drops to his side, eyes wide.

'No, Oak!' Morrigan screams. 'Don't go, don't leave me!'

Zac leans over and removes the glass from her hand.

'He's gone, Morrigan,' he murmurs.

She sobs in pitying gasps, rocking back and forth on her knees.

Rain falls—slow, heavy, splatting on the tin roof.

It's merely a prelude before the sky relinquishes its cargo and a fusillade of water explodes above them.

The noise is deafening.

Zac and Prisha melt into the background and watch on.

After a few quiet minutes, Morrigan places her fingertips on Oak's eyelids and closes them. Kisses him on the forehead. Says a few words in an ancient tongue, the tears subsiding.

'He'd never have survived in prison,' she whimpers. 'Like putting a grizzly bear in a cage. It would have killed him. His spirit will rest in Summerland until it's time for him to renew.'

Zac looks at Prisha. 'What now?'

She drags her gaze away from the heartbreaking scene.

'What now? I'll tell you what now,' she hisses, anger flaring. 'We go and arrest that conniving, manipulative *bitch—Violet Fox!*'

64

Morrigan leads the way through the woods, fleet-footed, vanishing like mist between the trees. Prisha and Zac stumble after her, soaked to the bone as the storm intensifies—rain slicing down in slanted sheets, wind roaring louder with every step.

Without Morrigan, they'd have no hope of finding the stones.

They tear along narrow trails, dodging rocks, ducking under branches, fighting to keep her in sight. Just when the path looks clear, she veers left or right, dragging them deeper into the woods.

Prisha loses sight of her for a second and halts—Zac barrels into her back, torch beam bouncing.

He tries to stifle a laugh. Fails.

'What's so bloody funny?' she snaps.

'Your face. Your mascara's run, your lipstick's smeared, and your hair... looks like something's nesting in it.'

'Thanks,' she mutters, wiping her forearm across her face. 'Morrigan! Where are you?'

'Over here!'

'Left,' Zac says, as they jog on.

Morrigan is a blur ahead, her black robe billowing. Half-seen, half-imagined.

'Christ, she's like a bloody hobbit,' Prisha mutters, shoving a branch aside.

It whips back and smacks Zac in the face.

'Ouch! Thanks for that!'

'Sorry.'

They slosh into a hollow, water rising above their ankles, thick with mud that clings and sucks. Up the other side, Morrigan scuttles under a broken bough.

Prisha follows—and screams.

Zac lunges forward. 'What is it?'

She flails at her face. 'Spider's web!'

'Softy,' he grins. 'Keep moving.'

They plunge deeper. The trees thicken. Boughs sway, leaves and twigs rain down. The wind screams through the canopy like a living, snarling creature.

The sharp sting of woodsmoke swirls through the undergrowth.

Up ahead—orange firelight, flickering in a battle against the rain.

They slow, fall into step. Zac taps Morrigan's shoulder, draws his telescopic baton out and flicks it open.

'You stay back.'

'No.'

'Yes, you will,' he says, steely voiced.

She throws him a defiant pout, but nods.

Prisha and Zac advance through the shadows, approaching the clearing.

A circle of hooded figures. Holding hands. Chanting. Eyes closed. Heads down.

At the centre—Violet.

Her robe crimson. Hood up. Arms raised.

She grips a curved ceremonial blade in both hands, chanting low and rhythmic, her followers echoing in a dead-eyed monotone.

'Hang back a little,' Prisha whispers to Zac. 'Just in case they turn violent.'

Zac scans the eleven men standing on one side of the circle. Young, broad-shouldered, solid. If this turns ugly, he and Prisha are in deep trouble.

She edges forward, Zac a step behind, as Violet continues her soliloquy, her hair whipping wildly in the wind.

'The veil has thinned, and through it, something foul has crept amongst us. It walks in shadow and feeds on fear. We've all felt it—the sickness in the air, the turning of the animals, the nightmares that do not fade with waking. This place, once sacred, now trembles beneath the weight of its presence. It must be driven out. By fire and by ash, by root and by bone, we cleanse what has been defiled.

'But hear this also. One of our own broke the First Law—the law of nature. He took life where it was not his to take. Three innocents slain by his hand before taking his own life. For this, Birch is no longer with us. He has been banished beyond the circle, beyond memory. His name is not to be spoken again. Let silence swallow it, as the earth swallows the unworthy.

'Let this night be our reckoning. Let this fire burn away all shadows. And let no tongue betray what passes beneath this sky, for the sacred sacrament binds us all. Break it, and you walk alone; nameless, without kin, cast into the dark.'

Prisha takes a breath, uncertain how to play it.

She decides on amused scepticism, and claps slowly.

'Bravo, bravo! Any chance of an encore? You could be on stage. You're a dead ringer for Lady Macbeth.' She glances around the ring. 'Mind you, I suppose you are on stage.'

Violet's eyes snap open. Low murmurs ripple through the acolytes.

'What are you doing here?' she hisses. 'This is sacred ground. Only initiates are allowed.'

'You're under arrest, Violet.'

'On what charge?'

'Hell, I'm not even sure where to begin. Conspiracy to commit murder, soliciting murder, accessory to murder, attempted murder, kidnapping, false imprisonment... and let's not forget administering a noxious substance with intent.'

Violet doesn't flinch. Her voice is calm, almost serene.

'You walk onto sacred land, speak of man-made laws, and think they hold sway here?' She steps forward, the firelight catching the blade in her hand. 'You're outnumbered, inspector. Two of you. Thirty of us.'

She tilts her head, almost pitying.

'You want to arrest me? Then do it. But ask yourself this—will you make it out of these woods alive?'

Prisha glances around as the circle tightens.

'Listen, everyone!' she calls out, pointing at Violet. 'It's true, Birch killed three men, but Violet orchestrated it, controlled him. And he didn't take his own life. He had to die to protect *her*. Killed by Oak, on Violet's orders. Now Oak is dead, poisoned by her.'

'She's lying!' Violet shouts. 'Don't listen to her. Birch took his own life. And Oak has been punished before for drinking too much. He'll be unconscious somewhere. I'll deal with him in the morning. This inspector—she carries a darkness. She despises who we are. She doesn't understand our ways.'

She turns to the men and nods.

'Take them. Tie them up.'

Zac brandishes his baton. 'Stand back!' he yells.

A woman steps into the centre, lowering her hood.

Prudence Ashcroft, the school principal. She gives Prisha a dismissive glance.

'The inspector is a sceptic. She's always looked down on us—a peaceful, law-abiding fellowship. Don't listen to her lies.'

Violet smiles, the smug, satisfied smile of someone who knows the crowd is hers.

She's cocky now.

'You've overplayed your hand, Inspector Kumar. A serious error of judgement. You should've stayed away from things you don't understand. Obey the natural law.'

Prisha briefly considers flashing her warrant card, threatening mass arrests, but it would only highlight their impotence. They're outnumbered. No hiding the fact.

A couple of the men bend to pick up nearby fallen branches, short and thick, perfect as clubs.

'I'm warning you!' Zac shouts.

'Wait!'

A figure slips through the crowd.

Slight, pale, ethereal.

Morrigan.

She steps into the firelight like a ghost.

'The inspector isn't lying. Oak is dead. Poisoned by a bottle of mead, Miss Violet gave him. Violet was behind all of it. Oak told me. And Oak didn't know how to lie.'

A ripple of unease spreads through the gathering.

Violet lets out a brittle laugh. 'Morrigan, what are you saying? She's corrupted your mind with lies.'

'No, you're the corrupt one.'

Prisha turns slowly, facing the group. Her voice carries.

'Violet's master plan was to kill off Lord and Lady Hampton, and Morrigan would be the sole heir of

Ravensbane Estate. And then I'm guessing, after a period of time, she'd have coerced Morrigan into signing a will leaving everything to the Wicca commune, with Violet as guardian of course. And here's a stab in the dark—then she'd slowly poison Morrigan. Am I on the money, Violet?'

She doesn't reply.

Lunara Ashcroft stares at Violet. 'Is this true?'

A false laugh. 'Don't be ridiculous. It's pure fantasy.'

'No, it's not,' Morrigan says, steady now. 'You've manipulated everyone. Me, Birch, Oak—all for your own gain. Greed and avarice... don't you know they're mortal sins?'

The men waver, still clutching their makeshift clubs. Their eyes flick from Violet to Morrigan, to Prisha, back again. The chant is gone now—only uneasy breathing remains.

Violet lowers her tone, measured, coaxing.

'You know me. You've walked this path with me. Do not let outsiders poison your minds. You've seen the change, felt the power in the circle. Do you think that was trickery? Do you think I'd lead you into ruin?'

Lunara stares at her, torn. 'Why didn't you tell us Morrgan was Lord Hampton's daughter?'

Someone else mutters: 'Oak wouldn't have lied. He didn't know how.'

The ripple grows, uncertain, brittle. Some step back, others stand frozen, still gripping branches that suddenly feel heavy in their hands.

Violet's composure cracks. Her voice hardens, a hiss.

'You think you can walk away? The circle isn't something you leave behind. It's with you for life.'

Her words hang, but the spell is gone. The men drop their branches with a dull thud. Another turns and melts into the treeline. One by one, they melt into the dark wood, leaving only Violet, Prisha, Zac, and Morrigan in the firelight.

Prisha inches forward, Zac close by her side.

'It's over, Violet. Drop the knife. Hands behind your back.'

Violet spins the blade, grips the handle, and raises it high—the tip angled down toward her chest, face twisted in righteous anger.

'You don't win this game, inspector. I'm in charge, not you. I control my own destiny.'

'Put the knife down!' Zac bellows.

She hesitates, arms trembling slightly.

A final glance at Morrigan, who remains still, expressionless.

A pitiful whisper. 'I did it all for you, Morrigan.'

'Liar. You did it for yourself.'

Zac lunges, but too late.

With a calm serenity, Violet drives the blade into her chest.

Lightning forks through the canopy above, thunder rolling over the Dales. The rain eases.

65

Sunday 6th July 11:45 am

The car turns right onto Ashenby Lane and rolls past St Mary's Church.

Zac adjusts the rear-view mirror and shoots a glance at Lilac and Morrigan in the back seats, then smiles at Prisha.

'Lord and Lady Hampton are on the mend,' he says. 'Early days, but they're both out of intensive care.'

'What will happen to Lord Hampton?' Morrigan asks.

'He's been charged with perverting the course of justice.'

'Will he go to prison?'

'Possibly. He's made a full confession about covering up your mother's death. He's extremely remorseful, has no prior convictions, and he's sixty-seven. The judge will take all that into account.'

Prisha turns in her seat to face them.

'Miss Penhallow, what would you like to see happen?'

Lilac stares out across the sunlit fields and sighs.

'All these years of pain, of not knowing. I prayed for justice. I wanted the person responsible to rot in prison forever. But revenge... it's not a good emotion. It eats away at you. Now I know the truth. Reverend Hartley knocked Iona off her bike. He was drunk. If he'd stopped, maybe he couldn't have saved her, but at least we'd have known the truth.

'As for Hampton and the others covering it up—the boys' club—I don't know. Three of them are dead now, and Hampton's recovering in hospital. And to find out he's Morrigan's father... I'm not sure what I want anymore.'

'What would mother want?' Morrigan asks quietly.

Lilac smiles at her granddaughter. 'Iona wasn't one for grudges. She was bubbly, carefree, and lived life to the full. I dare say she's somewhere, watching all this unfold. I think she'd want you and me to move on and stop looking back. I won't say I'm at peace now, but a weight's been lifted from my heart. Whatever the judge decides, I'll live with it. Let justice prevail—then let it go. What about you, sweetheart?'

She affectionately rubs Morrigan's shoulder.

Morrigan shrugs. 'There's been too much bad feeling. Too much death. I forgive Lord Hampton for what he did... but I won't forget.'

Zac catches her eye in the mirror. 'Actually, Morrigan, Lord Hampton asked if you'd like to visit him in hospital?'

She pouts, considering. 'Maybe. I suppose he is my father. But not just yet. Maybe in a few days.'

Zac flicks the indicator and pulls over.

Everyone steps out as he opens the boot and takes out the wreath and hands it to Lilac, who accepts it with a wistful reverence, sniffling.

It's made from twenty-two white Yorkshire roses arranged in a perfect circle. Feathery fern fronds and moss pack the spaces between the blooms. A tartan ribbon in muted sea blue and heather purple is threaded through the lower edge, with a white card clipped in place reading:*Her spirit will always shine in the hearts of those who remember.*

'It's beautiful, Zac.'

'The roses signify Yorkshire. The ferns and tartan ribbon, Iona's Scottish heritage.'

'It's a very kind thought.'

He smiles. 'I'd like to take the credit, but it was DCI Finnegan's idea.'

She looks over her shoulder at the ditch. 'I've walked this road a thousand times wondering exactly where it happened. Are you certain this is where she...' Her words dry up.

'Yes, we're certain. We have photographs of the scene. This is definitely the spot.'

She walks to the roadside and gently places the flowers next to the ditch—the very place where Iona's body was found by Malachi Abbott all those years ago.

Morrigan walks up behind and touches her on the arm.

'I'll let you have a moment, gran.'

'Thanks, love.'

She returns to Zac and Prisha, who stand a respectful distance back, and stares up at Prisha, impassive.

'Did you know ravens were once white?'

Prisha shifts her weight. 'Erm, no.'

'In Greek mythology, Apollo sent a white raven to spy on his lover, Coronis. The raven brought back bad news that Coronis had been unfaithful. In anger, Apollo scorched its feathers black. Punished it... for telling the truth.'

She tilts her head, voice dipping.

'Since then, the raven carries sorrow on its wings. A messenger of endings.'

'Right, well there you go. You learn something new every day,' Prisha says with false bonhomie.

Morrigan's gaze lingers, then drifts, as if listening to something far away.

'Beware the raven, inspector. Especially the one that walks in human skin.'

Her attention shifts to Zac, body language changing. She appears a little shy, hands clasped in front of her, twisting from side to side.

'Zac?' she asks, her tone completely different from a moment ago.

'Yes?'

'Can we see each other?'

He frowns. 'Morrigan, you know I'm a married man.'

She giggles, embarrassed, and looks away. 'Not like that—silly. I meant as friends. Occasionally.'

Zac chuckles. 'Ah, right. Yeah, I don't see why not. Next time you're in Whitby, give me a call. I'll introduce you to my wife and the boys. Maybe we can grab fish and chips and go for a walk along the beach. Sit on a picnic blanket and watch the world roll by.'

A giant beam spreads across her face. 'I'd like that.'

She glances back at her grandmother, who pulls a handkerchief from her pocket, dabs her eyes, then blows her nose.

'Listen,' Zac says, 'are you sure I can't drive you and your gran back to the village? It's no bother.'

'No, thanks. We're good. It's a beautiful day. We'll take the shortcut through Gallows Meadow.'

He nods. 'Fair enough.'

Prisha and Zac step back into the car as grandmother and granddaughter set off hand in hand down the leafy lane—Lilac shuffling gently, Morrigan with her distinct, mechanical stride.

Zac starts the engine and pulls away.

'That was nice,' Prisha says.

'What was?'

'You two. Being friends. Did you mean it?'

'Aye, of course I did. I took a shine to her the first time I met her.'

'And she definitely took a shine to you.'

He laughs. 'I cannae help it. I have this raw animal magnetism. Women flock to me like moths to a flame. Some days I have to bat them away with a shitty stick.'

She slaps his arm and grins. 'Big head.'

66

Sunday 6th July 11:47 am

Cigarette smoke curls from the ashtray as Frank re-reads his diary entry.

High above, seagulls mew, their calls drifting into the open shed. A gentle breeze carries in from the sea, rustling the leaves of the vegetable patch. He takes a slow drag, exhales, then lifts the tumbler and sips his whisky.

He picks up the fountain pen and hovers it over the paper, gathering his thoughts for the final lines.

"We may never know the full truth, but I think we're as close as we'll ever get to it. Birch killed Malachi Abbott, Reverend Hartley, and Amos Baker. It fits with what we know. Then Birch was killed by Oak.

But the real Machiavellian brains behind it all was Violet Fox. A woman who craved control, and got her way even in death. In charge to the last.

We have Oak's deathbed confession, and that's good enough for me. A simple, honest man with no reason to lie. He admitted to killing Birch, so why lie about the others?

I believe Prisha's theory is right. With the Hamptons out of the way and the new will leaving the estate to Morrigan Penhallow, Violet's plan was nearly complete. She'd have manipulated Morrigan into making a will, with herself as trustee.

Given time, I believe Morrigan would have started showing the same symptoms as the Hamptons. A slow, creeping death by aconite poisoning.

And with Morrigan's passing, Violet's scheme would have run its full course.

I visited the Hamptons the other day. They're not out of the woods yet, but they're on the mend. I feel for Lady Hampton most of all. Not the warmest soul, but she was innocent in all of this.

Lord Hampton is a shadow of himself. But he repeated his confession under caution with his solicitor present. He's remorseful. I think he genuinely wants to make amends. Whether the judge allows him that chance or not, we'll see.

Brutal, needless deaths. Dark deeds in the night. They leave a bitter taste.

But one mother finally knows the truth, and maybe—just maybe—that will count for something. Whether the wound heals or not is a different matter, but I doubt it.

And let's not forget Iona Jacobs. Twenty-two, full of life, and taken far too soon. Even in a coma, her spirit shone through, long enough to bring her child into this harsh world. A testament to her inner strength.

And what of her child—Morrigan?

It could all have been so very different if she hadn't gone to search for her friend, Oak.

If my officers had found Oak dying, would he have confessed without the presence of Morrigan?

Maybe not.

And if he didn't confess, then all fingers would still have pointed at Morrigan, who would have been blamed for his death as well.

But fate intervened as it so often does in life, for better or for worse.

A sad tale.

No winners. Just survivors.

These are dangerous games people play.

Cast a pebble into a pond, and it creates ripples.

And finally...

When Lord Hampton stood at the altar, giving his eulogy at Reverend Hartley's funeral, he ended with this line:

Remember Not Our Sins

A quote from scripture.

A plea as you near death, asking God to forget your earthly misdemeanours and only take into account the good deeds you did on earth.

Maybe God does forgive.

But in my experience—man *never* does.

DCI Frank Finnegan, signing off."

He takes one last drag and stubs out the cigarette. Drops the journal into his satchel.

Rising, he finishes the whisky, then closes the bureau as the latch on the allotment gate clicks.

'Yoo hoo! Frank, it's me.'

He checks his watch. 'That woman runs like clockwork,' he murmurs. 'I'll be right with you, Meera, love.'

Grabbing his jacket and satchel, he steps outside, as his gaze falls onto the faded photograph hanging on the far wall of the shed. A sharp pain stabs his heart. He steps back inside and strokes the glass.

'Bye, Rosy. See you soon.'

He clicks the padlock shut behind him and turns to find Meera admiring the vegetable patch.

'My, my, your Brussels sprouts are looking magnificent, Frank. I'd like to sink my teeth into them,' she says.

'Haven't heard you say that in a while, love. I'm sure it can be arranged.'

She throws him a disdainful glance as he slips his arm through hers. They set off down the path together.

'How was church?'

'Wonderful, as always. I feel like a new woman.'

'Aye, me too. Any suggestions?'

She shakes her head. 'In one of those moods, are we?'

'What hymns did they sing?'

'A few of your favourites. The Lord is My Shepherd, and How Great Thou Art.'

'How Great Thou Art—that was my mother's favourite. Always think of her when I hear it. God rest her soul.'

'Maybe if you came to church once in a while, you could sing them yourself instead of always asking me about them.'

He pulls open the gate.

'Dinner on?'

'You ask me that every flaming week. Yes, the dinner's on.'

'Smashing. What's on the menu?'

'Cottage pie, greens, and roast tomatoes.'

'Lovely,' he says, rubbing his hands in anticipation. 'Tell you what, after dinner, how about a walk along the prom? Stop by the arcade, lose a few quid on the slots, grab an ice cream and a couple of doughnuts. Then maybe find a quiet pub for a pint. There's a new place open on Church Street called The Meeting Place.'

Meera laughs. 'You certainly know how to show a girl a good time.'

'And when we get home, we can make passionate love on the stairs,' he adds, clicking the car fob.

The lights flash.

Meera's eyebrows arch as she pulls open the door. 'On the stairs? You're nearly sixty-one, Frank, not twenty-one. And with your dicky knee? That's an accident waiting to happen. I'd like to see you explain that to the paramedics as they wheel you out of the front door.'

'Ah well,' he says, slipping into the driver's seat. 'Can't blame a man for trying.'

He glances out to sea.

A raven-dark bank of clouds swells on the horizon, brooding over the sea.

'I think we're in for a change, Meera. There's a storm brewing. Looks like a bad 'un as well.'

Little does he know... how prophetic his words will become.

Author Notes

When I began writing Crucifix Knot, I knew I wanted to pull the threads of **Wicker Girl** tighter, while twisting them into something darker, stranger, and more unsettling. Ashenby, with its shadows and secrets, had more to give, as did Ravensbane Wood. The village still had blood in the soil, and as a crime writer you can't resist going back to a place that refuses to heal.

This book grew out of two overlapping fascinations: folklore and history—although maybe they are one and the same. I've long been drawn to the way old superstitions linger beneath the surface of modern life. Scratch away the veneer of progress, and you'll find ancient fears—knots tied for protection, charms against the evil eye, whispered curses passed from one generation to the next. The Crucifix Knot was inspired by the Pagan Celtic knot: intertwining threads with no beginning or end, representing an endless connection, or eternity.

Of course, **Wicker Girl** was inspired by that folklore cult classic The Wicker Man, starring Edward Woodward,

Christopher Lee, and Britt Ekland. I remember watching it (unbeknownst to my parents) when I was a boy with my brother. There was no bloodthirsty gore, no slasher elements, no clichéd "scary" moments. It was far more unsettling—*the unknown*. Peculiar behaviours, the sideways glances, the odd rituals—and, yes, a few naked women, which is always a bonus when you're a young lad.

And the twist at the end was perfect. If you've never seen it, I highly recommend.

I tried to capture that same unease in *Wicker Girl* and *Crucifix Knot*, most notably with Morrigan Penhallow, a woman with the body and face of a young girl. The condition Morrigan suffers from wasn't invented—it was based on a real-life account of a woman in the USA, who has her own reality show and, at first glance, looks like a child.

I have to admit, Morrigan unsettled even me. At first she was intended as the villain, the arch manipulator. But as the story unfolded, she grew on me, and I began to feel sympathy for her. Towards the end, I even liked and respected her for the stoic determination she showed, and her refusal to harbour anger towards a society that had mostly shunned her.

And then there are the backstories—Prisha's relationships, Frank and Meera's everlasting heartbreak. I know some readers dislike backstory. They want the investigation and nothing else. Well... no excuses. That's the way I write, and always will. Backstory makes characters real, relatable, human. Without it, all you have are one-dimensional crime-fighters.

So thank you for walking with me through the rain-soaked woods of Ravensbane Estate (based on Swinton Estate) and the unsettling streets of Ashenby (based on Masham in North Yorkshire). I hope you enjoyed both books as much as I enjoyed writing them.

For me, great crime fiction is a mirror of society—showing the evil some inflict, and the good others do in stopping it, sometimes at great personal cost. But I suppose that's not really fiction at all—that's reality.

Lastly, if you've made it this far, here's the good news. The next book in the series returns you to the familiar shorelines of Whitby.

A divisive character returns—whether to help or *hinder* the investigation remains to be seen. The usual faces will be there, and some new ones, as we traverse the hidden yards and narrow, cobbled alleyways of Whitby, and occasionally take to the high seas in pursuit of justice.

It will be wild, unsettling, intriguing—and *definitely*, entertaining.

Whale Cemetery is on pre-order now, out 27th December 2025.

Thank you for your time.

All the best,

Ely North

Keep In Touch

Thank you for reading. I hope you enjoyed the latest book in the DCI Finnegan series. Your continued support is immensely important to me. If you're eager for the next gripping instalment then, 'Whale Cemetery', the twelfth book in the series, is on pre-order.

Whale Cemetery – published December 27 2025

Your thoughts and feedback are incredibly important. If you enjoyed the book, please consider leaving a **review** on **Amazon** or **Goodreads**, or a review/recommendation on **Facebook**.

Such reviews are not only deeply appreciated, but they also help fellow crime fiction enthusiasts discover and enjoy the DCI Finnegan series. For a quick gesture of support, you can also leave a rating directly on your Kindle. Or even better, why not tell someone you know about the book? Word of mouth is still the best recommendation.

I thank you for giving me your time.

All the best,
Ely North – August 2025

Ely North Newsletter

If you're not a fan of pre-orders, then why not sign up to my entertaining newsletter where I write about all things crime—fact and fiction. It's packed with news, reviews, and my top ten Unsolved Mysteries, as well as new releases, and any discounts or promotions I'm running. I also have fascinating insights into my writing process and the publishing world. I'll also send you a free copy of the prequel novella – **Aquaphobia – Body In The River.** Here's the link.

Sign up to Ely North's Newsletter

Also By Ely North

DCI Finnegan Series

Book 1: Black Nab

Book 2: Jawbone Walk

Book 3: Vertigo Alley

Book 4: Whitby Toll

Book 5: House Arrest

Book 6: Gothic Fog

Book 7: Happy Camp

Book 8: Harbour Secrets

Book 9: Murder Mystery

Book 10: Wicker Girl

Book 11: Crucifix Knot

Book 12: Whale Cemetery

Prequel: Aqua Phobia (available free by joining Ely North Newsletter)

All books are available on Amazon in ebook, paperback, and some in audio. Paperbacks can be ordered from all good bookshops, distributed by IngramSpark.

Printed in Dunstable, United Kingdom